CRUEL DEVIOUS HEIR

DUET TWO

HEIRS OF ALL HALLOWS'

CAITLYN DARE

Copyright © 2024 by Caitlyn Dare

All rights reserved.

No part of this book may be reproduced in any form or by any electronic or mechanical means, including information storage and retrieval systems, without written permission from the author, except for the use of brief quotations in a book review.

Editing and proofreading by Sisters Get Lit(erary) Author Services

Cover by Sammi Bee Designs

CRUEL DEVIOUS HEIR: PART ONE

1

TALLY

Nervous energy thrums through as I wait backstage in the hall.

"Hey, you good?" Sebastian Howard asks me.

I nod, gnawing the end of my thumb.

"You don't look—"

"I'm fine," I snap, instantly feeling guilty. "Look, I'm sorry. This is a big deal. It's—"

"Yeah, I know." He gives me a strange look.

"Tallulah, Sebastian." Mr. Porter approaches, smoothing down his All Hallows' silver and green tie. "Are you both ready?"

"We are, sir," I answer.

"And you're absolutely sure you want to do this?"

"We are."

"Good, well, let's get this show on the road." He doesn't look very pleased about it, but as Head Girl and Boy, it's mine and Sebastian's job to launch a campaign that will elevate student voices and improve well-being. Even if the headteacher doesn't like it.

Even if this year's campaign is set to make waves.

I've always had a strong moral compass. It hasn't made life

at All Hallows' particularly easy for me, but when your father is Thomas Darlington, a beacon for integrity and social justice, people tend to be wary of you.

It's never really bothered me before. I like flying the flag of fairness and equality. It's why I became Head Girl, after all. But it's the final year of sixth form, and suddenly, I'm doubting myself. Doubting all the sacrifices I've made in the name of doing the right thing.

This is the right thing, though; I silently reassure myself. I've always believed in using your platform to fight injustice and speak on issues that are important. And now's my chance.

Mr. Porter ushers us onto the stage while the student body files into the grand hall. It's one of my favourite buildings on campus with its vaulted ceilings and original stained-glass windows.

I stand awkwardly next to Sebastian, clutching my presentation notes in my hand. Of course, he volunteered me to do most of the talking, since it was my idea. Public speaking has never really bothered me before, but today is different.

Forcing myself to take a deep breath, I scan the crowd, instantly regretting it when Olivia spots me and gives me a little thumbs up.

A strange sensation snakes down my spine. My friendship with Olivia Beckworth is... complicated. She's Oakley Beckworth's twin sister. And he's an Heir. He and his three best friends—Reese Whitfield-Brown, Elliot Eaton, and Theo Ashworth—rule the halls of All Hallows' with an iron fist and their special brand of debauchery. It's how it's always been in Saints Cross. The elite families and their evil spawn take what they want, when they want, with little consequence.

It makes me sick. It's always made me sick.

Which is why I've always done my utmost to avoid them.

But then, at the start of second year, I struck up an unlikely friendship with Olivia. Like me, she seemed to despise the patriarchal system ingrained in our town's history.

Until she went and fell for an Heir, that is. Now, she's deeply in love with Reese, and I'm trying really hard to not let it come between our new friendship. But it's not easy.

Not when being around Olivia ultimately means being around them.

Around *him*.

I hear them before I see them. The All Hallows' Saints, led by none other than the Heirs.

Elliot leads them into the hall, barely acknowledging anyone as a low rumble of murmurs and even a couple of cheers goes around the room. The teachers start demanding order, but it does little to dampen the excitement their arrival stirs.

Please.

I fight the urge to groan.

They're rugby players, not royalty. Yet, because of the names they bear, the legacies bestowed on them, they're placed on pedestals and worshipped like gods.

"Darlington," Seb grits out, and my eyes nap to his.

"What?"

"I said your name like three times."

"Oh, sorry. What's up?"

"We're almost ready." He motions to the lectern and a wave of nausea rolls through me.

Breathe, Tally, just breathe.

I've been over this presentation so many times, I could probably recite it in my sleep. But when Mr. Porter approaches the lectern, my heart begins to crash violently in my chest.

"Okay, okay, settle down." He waits until silence falls over the room. "This morning, I want to welcome our Head Boy and Girl onto the stage to present to you this year's student campaign. As you're all aware, every year, we encourage our student voice team to come up with an idea for improving student life here at All Hallows'. Tallulah Darlington and

Sebastian Howard are going to introduce you all to this year's campaigns. Let's give them a warm round of applause."

Mr. Porter leads the room in a half-hearted applause. I'm used to my fellow students' apathy, though.

"Hello," I say into the mic, letting Seb adjust it a little. He gives me a reassuring nod, despite his initial reservations about this campaign.

"This year, Seb, myself, and the rest of the student council have chosen something tangible. Something that will make a real difference to the students of All Hallows'. Therefore, we're proposing a new home for the student welfare committee and the excellent work they do for the students of All Hallows' around supporting and improving mental health and well-being.

"We're all aware of the difficulties facing the committee in recent years. Mental health and well-being has never been more important for young people. They need safe spaces to meet and talk and get advice. Safe spaces to be themselves. And right now, they do not have the space, resources, or budget to provide this."

I take a little sip of water from the table beside the lectern, letting my eyes run over the sea of faces all watching, listening, daydreaming about wherever they would rather be than here, listening to me and my pie-in-the-sky ideas.

But I don't let it deter me.

"We all know that the school prides itself on the success of the rugby and hockey teams." A raucous cheer goes up around the room and I silently fume.

This is exactly the problem. People don't care about facilities for student welfare; they care about new equipment for the athletic department. Because a successful athletic department means more investment. Better facilities. More publicity.

"The education board pumps money into athletic teams. But what about the students who need extra support with

CRUEL DEVIOUS HEIR: PART ONE

other things? Counselling? Access to extra tutoring? Help with access issues?"

Mr. Porter shifts uncomfortably in the wings, no doubt unappreciative of my assessment of the school's priorities. But everyone knows the truth. Certain things matter more at All Hallows'.

"Now, we could petition the board for extra funding for a new student welfare facility. Or we could redistribute the resources the school already has to ensure a better commitment to supporting the welfare and well-being of students at All Hallows'."

I glance up at Seb and notice his stalwart expression. His eyes seem to say, 'You don't have to do this.' But the thing is, I do.

I have to do it—for more reasons than one.

Which is why I take a deep breath and stare out at my classmates. I find the Heirs in the crowd, letting my eyes run over each of them. Elliot. Reese. Theo... and Oakley. He shoots me a cheeky smile. One that might have made my stomach flutter a couple of weeks ago.

Not anymore.

Before I lose face, I clear my throat.

"Therefore, for this year's student voice campaign, we are proposing that The Chapel be decommissioned as the Heirs' private on-site residence and be reimagined into a brand new student welfare facility that the entire student population at All Hallows' can access."

As my words land, and their implication with them, Oakley's smile falls, replaced with confusion and anger. His brows pull tight as he levels me with a look that makes me wither. But I stand tall, letting Mr. Porter take over to usher the room into silence once more.

Because Oakley isn't the only one reacting.

A ripple of surprise, shock, and disbelief goes around the room, and Seb mutters under his breath, "Here we fucking go."

"Shut up," I hiss, and he slides his eyes to mine, giving a little shake of his head.

"What did you really expect, Tally? You just declared open war on the Heirs."

"I..."

"I hope you have a good insurance policy," a shiver goes down my spine at his warning as he continues, "because you're going to be public enemy number one now."

"Tally, wait up." Olivia jogs after me as I hurry down the hall before the rest of the student body empties out.

I don't know what I was expecting after I delivered my presentation, but it wasn't for the room to fall into complete chaos. Mr. Porter struggled to regain control, but, at that point, I slipped out, needing to catch my breath—and lie low until the dust settled.

"Tally." She grabs my arm and I whirl around, pasting on a weak smile.

"Oh, hi," I say to Olivia.

"What the fuck was that?"

I wince at her harsh words. "I..."

"So that's why you've been avoiding me all week? Because you knew you were going to pull that bullshit." Her brow lifts, accusation glittering in her eyes. "I thought we were friends. I thought—"

"We are. I mean, we were..."

"Were?" She pales. "Jesus, what the hell is wrong with you? I know you've never liked the Heirs, what they stand for. But do you have any idea how awkward you just made things for me? I stood up for you. I vouched for you." Disbelief coats her words, and I feel a stab of regret.

But I can't tell her the truth. She won't understand.

"What's really going on?" Her eyes narrow. "You've

always been a thorn in their side, but you've never openly declared war on them before. And you promised me—"

"It's time," I say, lifting my chin in defiance. "They're out of control, and the student welfare—"

"So befriending me? Befriending Abigail? What was that? A way to get close? To infiltrate the enemy? Because I don't buy it."

"It doesn't matter. I'm committed to this campaign. I already have permission to take the petition live. If I collect enough signatures, Mr. Porter will present it to the school board and they'll have to consider the request."

"Unbelievable."

"We can still be friends," I blurt, my conviction wavering. Because I like Olivia. I like having a friend.

"Seriously? And how do you propose that's going to work? I mean, Jesus, Tally. You didn't even give me a heads-up. I'm with Reese. I *love* Reese. Not to mention Oakley is my brother."

"So you're choosing them, then?" My heart sinks, but I shouldn't be surprised.

Of course she's choosing them.

"It's not like you chose me, either."

"It's only the Chapel, Liv. I'm sure they can live without it."

Bitter laughter spills off her lips as she pins me with a look of sheer disappointment. "You're more stupid than I thought if you truly believe that."

2

OAKLEY

Chaos ensues around me as Tally flees the stage, closely followed by her partner in crime, Sebastian Howard.

"Is she having a fucking laugh?" Theo barks, utter disbelief covering his face.

"She's fucking brave, that's for sure," Elliot mutters, looking as unfazed by this latest development as usual.

There's a twisted part of me that's weirdly excited for the day something happens that actually rattles his cool exterior and hard expression. But apparently, our on-campus home being threatened by Miss Prim and Proper Tallulah Darlington isn't it.

I mean, I get it. No one in their right mind will actually sign her stupid fucking petition.

Eighty percent of this sixth form lives for our Chapel parties. There's no way they'd let those go in favour of turning the place into the student welfare committee's new home.

Hell, it is student welfare now. We help kids let go and forget about their worries almost every fucking weekend. What more could the wealthy students of All Hallows' want than free booze and the best drugs to be found in this town?

And the other twenty percent who are made up of the geeks, the terrified, and the goody two-shoes like Tallulah and Sebastian can kiss our royal arses.

Jealousy is a cruel, cruel beast. But it's a really fucking low blow to try and bring us down just because they don't fit into the social norms at All Hallows'. It really isn't our fault they have sticks shoved so far up their arses there's no chance of pulling them out.

"She hasn't got a leg to stand on. Did you see Porter's face? I think even he was scared for her safety after that," Reese laughs before a small hand smacks him upside the head. A hand belonging to none other than my twin sister.

"Oh, come on, babe. You're not actually going to stand up for her after that brazen hit on us?" he asks, looking back over his shoulder at his girlfriend.

A shudder rips down my spine as I think about her being that to him.

Reese, my lifelong best friend, and my fucking twin sister.

Together.

Fucking.

Ugh. Even now it makes my stomach knot uncomfortably.

I know what a dog Reese is. I have literally witnessed his antics with my own eyes over the years, so to have him claiming to treat my sister right and to be in love with her... well, it takes some fucking believing.

"N-no, I just—"

"She's declared war," I spit, cutting Olivia off before she really gets started. "I fucking told you that becoming friends with her, letting her into our inner circle was a bad idea. But no one ever listens to me," I add bitterly, shooting a glare at Reese.

One rule. There was one rule.

Do not touch my fucking sister.

"She told me she wouldn't," Olivia argues, hurt filling her eyes.

"Well, she just fucking did. And don't even think about warning us not to retaliate."

"You can't," she gasps.

"We can," Theo argues.

"She went after us publicly. Questioned our authority, our position, our importance in All Hallows'. Do you really expect us to roll over like good little puppy dogs?"

Something in the corner of the room catches my sister's eye before she swallows the argument on the tip of her tongue.

"You know how much I fucking hate this patriarchal bullshit system that puts you all above everyone else," she spits.

Reese turns to her, wraps his arm around her waist and tugs her closer despite the row of chairs between them. I roll my eyes, my fists curling at my sides as he stares down into her eyes.

"Come on now, sweet cheeks. I thought you liked me above you."

"Whitfield," I bark, aware that he's only pulling this shit to mess with my head.

"It's true though, isn't it, babe? You love it when I—"

"I'm done with this," my sister says, thankfully cutting whatever was about to fall from Reese's lips that would probably have scarred me for life. She walks away now her row is empty, but she turns back at the last minute. "If you hurt her, I will hurt you," she warns.

Theo throws his head back and laughs at her threat, totally unfazed. Elliot remains stone-faced while Reese's lips curl up in a smirk.

"Anytime, babe. You know that."

But she ignores his offer and locks her eyes on me.

"I'm serious. I might disagree with her actions, or more so, the way she's gone about it. But she doesn't deserve your wrath for her attempt to make this school better. Leave her alone."

CRUEL DEVIOUS HEIR: PART ONE

Her eyes narrow in warning, but my sister's anger isn't something that overly scares me. What can she really do? Share naked photos of me as a kid? Spill some of my secrets? None of that will touch me. A high proportion of the school population has seen me naked, and not just as a kid. And embarrassing secrets? Ha. My life is an open book, baby. Share away. I don't have anything hidden in my closet that will scare the girls off, and honestly, that's all that's really important here.

Nothing she can do will ruin my rep. Tallulah either, for that matter. All she's doing is bringing a whole heap of pain and suffering to her doorstep, and I'm more than happy to be the one to deliver it.

I think I'll quite enjoy watching her fall from her stupid pedestal.

Tallulah fucking Darlington isn't the special little princess her perfect, law-abiding, prosecution lawyer daddy thinks she is.

And I have every intention of proving it.

The prospect of us losing our on-campus residence is all everyone talks about all day. I even hear teachers discussing it as they walk down the hallway after lunch.

Tally isn't stupid; she has to know what kind of waves this campaign would make. The question is, why? Why would she even attempt to go up against us like this?

She knows how much power we have, and ultimately even as Head Girl, how little she has.

I know both her and her father love the challenge of fighting for what is right and all that. But going into a battle that you're going to lose before you've even begun seems like a waste of good energy to me.

"Am I boring you, Mr. Beckworth?" Mrs. Hart snaps when

I pack all my stuff up ten minutes early and stand from my desk.

"Sorry, I've got somewhere I need to be," I announce, much to the amusement of the rest of the class, if their sniggers are anything to go by.

This shit is pretty normal for us, though.

"Somewhere more important than understanding how to succeed with this year's psychology coursework?"

"I've got it under control, Mrs. H. Don't you worry about me." I wink at her as I march toward the door.

Just as I expected, a bright blush hits her cheeks, and with one knee-weakening smile in her direction, I pull the door open and disappear.

I've got thirty minutes until training starts, and I've got a little rat to catch in the meantime.

After taking a piss, I hide myself in an alcove just a little down the hallway from Tally's last class of the day. Part of me expected her to run after the amount of backlash she's received for her announcement this morning, but it seems she's let all the abuse roll off her back.

Apparently, she's stronger than I gave her credit for.

Although, after everything she did when shit hit the fan with Olivia and Reese recently, she had started to prove that she's not just some goody two-shoes pushover. She's actually got a backbone, and fuck if that doesn't make her even more intriguing.

The bell rips through the ancient hallways of the Orwell Building the sixth form is situated in, and excitement tingles deep in my stomach.

We agreed after the assembly this morning that we'd give our little traitor some time to fester. She has to know we're coming for her. There is no way on this earth she's stupid enough to think we'd just let it go. But we also thought it would be fun to keep her waiting, looking over her shoulder for our strike.

Well, Prim, it's about to hit you.

And I was the one who was lucky enough to land this job.

I rub my hands together as students begin to spill into the hallways, their excited chatter for the end of the day filling my ears. After a second or two, they begin to file past me, completely oblivious to the fact I'm hiding here. It's one of the benefits of going to school in such an old building; there are hiding spots all over the place to do all kinds of wicked things in.

My eyes remain locked on the crowd before me, searching out her blonde hair, and the second I spot her, I strike like a viper. A small shriek rips from her lips as I wrap my fingers around her upper arm and yank her from the flow of students on a quest to leave this place for the day.

If anyone sees me tug her into the darkness with my other hand covering her mouth to stop her from screaming, they don't try to stop me.

I drag her back against me, pinning my arm around her waist to stop her from running. Her arms thrash and her legs kick fiercely. And honestly, I'm impressed by her strength. Obviously, it's nowhere near enough to fight me off, but it seems she's stronger than she looks.

Leaning forward, I risk getting closer and the chance of a broken nose by whispering in her ear, "Keep fighting and rubbing your arse against my dick like that, Prim, and we're going to end up having even more fun than I was initially planning."

She stills in an instant, a violent shiver rippling down her spine.

Tally mumbles something against my hand, but it's impossible to make out the words, although I can probably hazard a guess.

"What was that, Prim? I couldn't quite hear you."

She screams, a blood-curdling sound that vibrates through

her whole body. But I don't release her to allow anyone else to hear her.

"We're going to go for a little walk," I explain, pushing from the wall and leading her deeper into the darkness.

I, like most of the All Hallows' students, had no idea there was a doorway down here until I was hooking up with some Heir chaser one day and we accidentally fell through it. The guys and I went back later to discover what hidden treasures might be behind it, and what we found is perfect for our little traitor.

I pause when we get to the old wooden door. "Scream and this isn't going to end well for you, Tallulah," I warn before releasing her face.

I wait for a beat to see if she's going to comply, and when she does, I reach for the handle, give it a solid test, and then kick the heavy door open. The thing creaks eerily, and Tally trembles in my hold.

Good. You should be terrified, sweetheart.

"W-where are we going?" she whispers, having little choice but to move forward into the darkness.

"Somewhere quiet so we can talk."

A whimper spills from her, but other than that show of fear, she doesn't do any of the things I was expecting.

I wanted her to cry, to beg for me to let her go, to promise to drop this campaign. Apparently, her hidden strength isn't just physical.

She will, though. Eventually, I'll break little Tallulah Darlington, and I'll have her sobbing at my feet and begging for forgiveness.

Together, we sink deeper beneath the main building, the darkness getting thicker and the air around us cooling, but still, even as the stairs end and the vast space of the basement spans out before us—if we could see it, of course—she still refuses to give in to me.

Silly, silly girl.
She has no idea who she's gone to war with.

3

TALLY

"What the hell are you doing?" I snap at Oakley as he shoves me into a cold, murky space. "What is this place?"

"Like I said, somewhere quiet we can talk."

"I have nothing to say to you." I lift my chin in defiance, a crackle going through the air.

I can't believe he manhandled me down here.

"Well, I have plenty to say to you." He stalks toward me, and I stumble back, only stopping when the backs of my thighs hit an old desk.

"Oakley." Blood roars in my ears. He's too close, too everything as he glowers at me, anger and frustration swirling in his blue eyes. "What?" I hiss when he doesn't say anything.

"What was that bullshit this morning? The Chapel? Really, Prim? Are you seriously that fucking dumb?"

"Hey, you can't talk to me like that." I steel myself.

Who the hell does he think he is?

He might be an Heir, but he's just another student at All Hallows'.

"I'll do a hell of a lot more than just talk to you, Tallulah." He says my name like a challenge as he lays his hands flat on the table on either side of my hips, caging me in. "You totally screwed us over. Right when we—"

"When we what?" My chest squeezes, but I refuse to let him see the effect he has on me. "We're not friends, Oakley. You made that perfectly clear."

His brows furrow. "The fuck are you talking about? We let you into our circle. You're Liv's friend. She vouched for you, and you go and pull this bullshit." Anger ripples across his expression. "I want to know why. Was it all fake? Get close to my sister so you could get close to us and fuck us over? Is that it?"

"What? No," I shriek. "I like Liv. We're..." The word 'friends' dies on my lips, and Oakley sneers.

"You can't even say it, can you? I knew we shouldn't have let you get close. You're a Darlington. So fucking righteous, just like your father."

"You don't know anything about me," I spit, frustration tearing up my spine.

"Oh, I think I know plenty." His smirk turns feral, heat blazing in his eyes as he leans in, running his nose along my jaw.

I can't breathe.

My lungs won't work right, my brain short-circuiting at how close he is. How good he smells. Like freshly washed linen and something a little citrusy.

A whimper crawls up my throat, but I trap it behind pursed lips. I won't play this game with him.

Not again.

Not when he—

"Tell me, Prim. If I touched you right"—his hand slips down to the hem of my pleated skirt, dipping underneath, fingers brushing my thighs, and I tremble—"here, what would I find, huh?"

"Oak," I choke out, air caught in my throat.

He wouldn't dare.

He wouldn't—

But his fingers walk higher.

"Don't." My voice cracks.

"Ask nicely." He chuckles, inching his fingers higher still until he's right there, toying with my knickers and the embarrassingly obvious damp spot there.

"Hmm, just as I thought. Wet for me. So that begs the question... why the fuck are you coming after the Heirs when it's so obvious you want to get on your knees and—"

Oakley's pained grunt fills the air as he staggers away from me. "What the fuck was that?" he grunts, clutching his crotch, his eyes watering as he gawks at me like he's never been kneed in the balls before.

"That was your sign to stay the hell away from me."

"You... you... *fuck*," he hisses. "That fucking hurt."

"Aww, is your little fella hurt? Maybe you'll remember that before you put your hands on me again."

"Little?" He sneers. "There's nothing little about my dick, Prim."

I roll my eyes, huffing, and he smirks.

"You loved it, and you know it."

My eyes narrow, hating that he's right. But it doesn't matter. He's burned any bridge that might have existed between us. The fact he hasn't even mentioned what happened tells me everything I need to know about Oakley Beckworth.

For a second, I'd thought he was different. I'd thought he might actually have a heart under all that arrogance and bravado.

How wrong I was.

Which is exactly why I talked Sebastian into backing my idea for the campaign. It's time somebody brought the Heirs down a peg or two. And I have zero problem being the girl to do it.

"Go screw yourself, Oakley." I step around him, moving toward the door, irritation rolling through me in violent waves.

"I'd rather screw you," he calls after me, but I ignore him. "Drop the campaign, Tally," he adds, and I stop just short of the door.

"Or what?" I throw over my shoulder.

His eyes flash as if he can't believe I even have to ask. "Or else you'll put a target on your back, Prim. And trust me when I say you won't like what happens then."

"Is that a threat?"

I'm not stupid; of course it's a threat. But I want to see what he'll say. I want to give him one last chance to prove he isn't as bad as people think he is.

But as his lips twist with amusement, I know it was a fool's hope.

"No." Oakley's smirk grows if this is all just one big game, and he lands two little words which seal our fate. "It's a promise."

"Ah, sweetheart, just the girl I was looking for." Dad breezes into the kitchen and gives me a warm smile.

I came home straight after classes today. Usually, I stick around to do some homework or meet with the student council, but I couldn't move around the Orwell Building without everyone pointing and staring. It had gotten so bad in class that the teacher had to intervene and demand we work in silence for the rest of the lesson.

Not my finest moment, but Sebastian was right—I've declared open war on the Heirs, and now I have to suffer the consequences.

But my issues with Oakley aside, it's the right thing to do. It's the twenty-first century, for God's sake. The Heirs don't need a private residence on campus. Not when everyone knows it's only used as a glorified gentleman's club.

Everyone's heard the stories, but nobody cares. The Heirs are some of the wealthiest families in the county. Their parents all make big enough donations to the school to keep their sons from ever making Saints Cross headlines.

Sold to the general public as tradition, it's nothing more than a patriarchal system built on misogyny and elitism, and it reeks of corruption. But Mr. Porter and the school board are too scared to go up against the likes of Johnathon Eaton and Christian Beckworth.

Luckily for me, my father isn't. He's been waiting for just the right reason to try and loosen their iron grip on our town.

"Tally, sweetheart, are you with me?"

"Uh, sorry, Dad." I blink at him. "I must have zoned out."

"I hope you're not working too hard. How did the assembly go?"

"As well as to be expected. The school is in uproar that we dared to suggest something as scandalous as going after the Chapel." I roll my eyes.

"Well, Mr. Porter and the school board need to move with the times, sweetheart. Your suggestions will benefit the entire student body."

"They won't give it up without a fight," I say, feeling a ripple of defeat going through me.

"Nobody said it would be easy. But if you get enough student signatures for your petition, Mr. Porter will have to consider your proposal."

"God, I'd love to see that. Can you imagine?"

There are other students like me who want to see the Heirs' reign crumble. But signing the petition means going up against them, and I don't know how many will have the backbone for that. I'm hoping that the fact the petition can be signed digitally will help. No one will have to own up to it unless they want to.

"It sure would rock their world." My father nods right as his phone starts blaring. He checks the screen and frowns. "I need to take this."

"Of course."

He leaves the kitchen and heads for his office. Dad is away a lot for work, but when he's not, he's usually holed up in his office, working on his next big case.

I've always admired his work ethic, his commitment and dedication to justice. But it's been a lonely life, growing up, trying to compete with his casework and Mum's charity work.

I grab a snack and head up to my room, already dreading the pile of coursework I have to get through. But if I want to secure a place at Saints Cross University, I can't drop the ball now.

My bedroom is like a living museum, every award and certificate I've ever received framed and hung on the wall opposite my bed. It was Dad's idea right from when I was little and received my first spelling certificate. Over the years, I've added more academic awards than I can count. But I don't feel the same sense of pride looking at them as I used to.

Most girls have a bedroom wall decorated in band posters and photographs of their friends and all their adventures. I've never had that.

Mum and Dad like to remind me there'll be time to spread my wings and experience life when I go off to university. And I've always believed it.

Until recently.

Until I got close to Olivia and Abigail and realised that having friends didn't have to be a distraction.

But then I watched Olivia fall in love with Reese, and I started to want more.

And look where that got me.

A fresh wave of anger swells inside me, but I shove it down. I can't lose focus here. I've seen how brutal and cruel the Heirs can be to anyone they deem an enemy. And now that person is me.

I expected backlash. I expected my announcement at the assembly would paint a target on my back. What I didn't expect was Oakley to drag me down to that basement to try to terrorise me into backing down.

He really is one of the most infuriating boys I've ever met. But the way he'd touched me...

No.

I am not going there.

Ever. Again.

Oakley Beckworth is the devil, and I know better than to play his games.

4

OAKLEY

I'm walking funny as I push the door to the locker room open so hard it slams back against the wall with a loud crash. Every set of eyes inside turns on me, but none are more interested, okay, amused, by my sudden limp than my three best friends.

"What the fuck happened to you?" Theo asks as I move closer, the ache in my balls ever-present.

"Fuck off," I grunt, shoving my hand inside my boxers to check for damage. Everything seemed to still be in place before I left the basement, but the fear of her busting one of my nuts is real.

"I thought you were going to have a gentle word with her," Elliot says quietly so the rest of the team can't hear.

"I did. She got a little—"

"Feisty?" Reese offers with a smirk. "I told you that Olivia said—"

"Oh, Olivia said," Theo teases.

"Fuck off. You want inside information on the little traitor, then you need to listen to her."

"She kneed me in the nuts," I confess. "She's wilder than she looks."

"Just your type then," Elliot offers.

"That stuck-up bitch? I don't fucking think so."

"Aw, but she touched your balls and everything," Reese quips, struggling to disguise his amusement.

Fucker.

"You know, any of you could have gone and tried to talk some sense into her," I sulk.

"I already said I'm not getting in the middle of this shit."

"Only because you want to continue getting laid. Ow," Theo complains when I punch him in the arm with my free hand.

"My fucking sister," I remind him.

"And you're going to have to get used to it," Reese says with a shit-eating grin spreading across his face. "Because I'm not planning on letting her go anytime soon."

"Or fucking ever. You're stuck with her now, unless you want to face the consequences for hurting her," I warn, finally tugging my hand from my boxers and cracking my knuckles.

Reese shakes his head and I turn my back on him, opening my locker and pulling my training kit out.

"So, what happened other than good little Tally having her first encounter with your cock?"

"That was not any kind of encounter," I mutter, dragging my shirt over my head and unbuttoning my trousers. "But I think it's safe to say that she's not dropping this bullshit."

"You need to try harder," Theo teases.

"Fuck off. I like my balls as they are, thank you very much."

"Well, Reese is out. Theo's got shit going on with Millie," Elliot explains, making my eyes narrow at Theo in question, but he just shakes his head, not wanting to get into it. "And I've got more important shit going on than to play games with Tally fucking Darlington. She's all yours, Beckworth."

"Lucky fucking me," I scoff, shoving my feet into a pair of shorts.

"She'll break," Elliot agrees, looking a little too excited by the prospect, seeing as he doesn't want to be the one to make it happen.

"We don't need to break her," Reese points out. "She just needs to understand that she can't mess with us."

"Fucking hell, Reese," I hiss.

"Don't tell us, Olivia said that," Theo taunts.

Reese's lips purse in frustration. "Whatever, fuckers. I'm out."

Before I've even had a chance to shove my feet into my boots, Reese takes off, but his steps soon falter when Elliot's voice rings through the locker room.

"Who rules this school?" he bellows.

"The Heirs rule," comes back from the rest of the team, the volume of their chant vibrating around the walls.

One glance at the victorious smile on Theo's face, and I can't help my own twitching at my lips.

Tally Darlington can try to knock us from our thrones with her irritating moral compass, but it's going to take a hell of a lot more than one bullshit campaign to get rid of us.

We hold more power than she could ever dream of.

And she's about to learn just how influential that can be.

Seeing as Olivia point-blank refused to hang out at the Chapel tonight after the day's revelations, it's just the three of us kicking back with beers and an Xbox championship later that night.

Our socials are going wild with gossip and everyone's plans to ruin Tally's campaign before it's even started. She naïvely posted a link earlier to her online petition that everyone is blasting her for.

Well, everyone but us. As per Elliot's instruction, none of us have engaged.

It's not necessary. The rest of the school is doing it for us. Plus, Tally should be more than aware that we're far more dangerous than anything we could type on social media.

We never hide behind a screen when we have punishments to hand out.

We turn up and deliver whatever pain is necessary in person. And we fucking love every single second of it.

Elliot and Theo are both lost in their online battle against some seriously skilled zombies when a loud knock sounds out on the front door.

"Who the fuck is that?" Theo barks.

"Hang on, let me just grab my special glasses that allow me to see through two-foot-thick ancient walls," I quip, unable to miss the fact that neither of them takes their eyes off the screen. "I'll get it then, shall I?" I mutter when whoever it is knocks again.

When neither of them responds, I push from the sofa to find out who's bold enough to come and interrupt our peaceful night.

Unless we're having a party, no one really comes out here. They're not brave enough. Who knows what kind of mood the Heir who answers the door will be in.

Abandoning my empty bottle on the kitchen counter, I continue toward the front door and pull it open. "Evening," I say politely when I discover the person on our doorstep.

He shuffles forward to shelter from the rain that's lashing behind him.

"I guess you should come in," I say, taking a large step back.

"Who is it?" Elliot calls, although when I step back into the room, I can't help noticing that the motherfucker hasn't moved from his seat or taken his eyes off the TV.

"Mr. Porter," I announce as the man himself stares around the Chapel like it's some kind of museum.

A disapproving grunt spills from Elliot, and Theo's

CRUEL DEVIOUS HEIR: PART ONE

attention is finally stolen from the game in favour of our headteacher.

We discussed going to talk to him earlier, but Elliot was convinced it would appear weak if anyone saw the four of us stalking toward Porter's office.

Instead, he insisted we hold our heads high and just allow this shit with Tally to play out. Plus, he's right; she's made enough waves today alone to have Porter watching very closely.

Although, why he allowed her to get up on that stage this morning and announce her intentions like she did makes me wonder what his thought process was behind the whole thing. Surely, he doesn't agree with her?

But even if he does, the school board—mostly made up of the elite of this town—would never allow him to push through the idea.

The whole thing is just a bullshit attempt to bring us down. And. It. Won't. Work.

"Evening, lads. How's it going?" he asks in a weird voice, as if he's suddenly trying to be one of us.

The sound of the game finally pauses, and Elliot turns his full attention on Porter. "Evening, sir. What can we help you with?"

He glances somewhat nervously at the three of us. "I just want you to know that while I allowed Tallulah to get up and announce her campaign this morning, I have no intentions of pushing it forward."

Elliot stands, moving closer. "Is that right, sir?" he asks, staring him dead in the eyes.

"It is. You know I'm behind you and the traditions this school upholds. I just wanted to come by to make sure you weren't feeling threatened."

"Threatened?" Elliot sneers. "By Tallulah Darlington? It's like you don't know us at all, sir."

"W-well, I just wanted you to..." he trails off, looking

totally unsure of himself. "This place is looking incredible. Much more homely than how your brother styled it, Elliot."

Silence ripples around the room as Porter struggles to maintain the power in this situation.

"We're glad you appreciate it. Now, is there anything else you wanted, sir? I'm sure you're a very busy man," Elliot taunts.

"Y-yes. This was just a fleeting visit to reassure you."

"Well, consider us assured. Now, as you were." Elliot steps around Porter and pulls the front door open.

"Oh, um... sure. Yes. Well, enjoy your night, lads. And long live the Heirs." He pumps his fist, looking like a right fucking pussy.

Elliot's face remains as cold and emotionless as ever, but Theo can't contain his amusement and snorts a laugh.

"We're glad to have your support, sir. But I don't think Tally's thoughtless plan is going to gather steam."

"I believe you're right. Goodnight."

The second Elliot closes the door, he finally cracks, or at least as much as he ever does, and throws his head back on a laugh.

"Is he actually for real? Tell me he didn't really think we were over here shaking in our boots over this bullshit."

"Fucks knows what he's thinking. But something tells me that he's the one who's scared. He knows that we'd go after him just as much as anyone else if he was behind the plans. And his life wouldn't be worth living if our fathers were to find out."

Theo pulls fresh beers from the fridge and the three of us crash back onto the sofa.

"So what next, then?" I ask.

"Isn't it obvious?" Elliot growls. "We need to remind the rest of the school why we're in charge and that they don't want this building to be used for anything other than it currently is."

"We need to throw a party," Theo says, following Elliot's statement for once.

"We do," Elliot agrees.

"And guess who isn't going to be invited?"

"She won't care. She's only ever attended once," I point out, a hazy memory of her here last weekend filling my mind.

"No, but something tells me that she'll be pissed when every other member of the school sides with us and ostracises her for this."

"And how do you suggest we do that?"

"I don't suggest we do anything other than call in a favour or two."

"From?" Theo asks, making Elliot roll his eyes.

"The chasers. You've heard them today; there's been nothing falling from their lips but plans to take down Tally."

I think back to some of the things I've heard throughout the day.

"And they'll do anything if the promise of getting a taste of our cocks is so much as mentioned."

Theo rubs his hands together, his eyes lighting up with excitement. "I'm in, especially if it comes hand in hand with a few blowies."

"Of course, you would be."

"They'll be brutal," I say. "Those girls are bitches."

"And? Tally's not stupid. She knew she was starting a war."

"Against us," I argue, unsure of why I'm pushing this. She deserves it.

She deserves everything coming her way.

"The chasers are just an extension of us. Plus, they have more access to her. And more than that, they'll make sure Tallulah Darlington forever regrets the day she stood up there and tried to take us on."

Dark, twisted intent shines in Elliot's eyes, and for a moment, I can't help but see a bit of Scott in him. And that's something I have no interest in seeing regularly. Every other day of the week, Elliot would hate to be compared to his formidable older brother, but when our world is threatened, I have a sense that he'll stoop to whatever means necessary to stay on top.

"Tomorrow, we talk to the girls, and we call a party for everyone bar Tally. Let the retaliation begin."

5

TALLY

"Watch it, bitch," someone hisses as the group of girls fan out around me, shoulder bumping and glaring at me as they continue down the hall.

I gawk after them, rubbing my arm. One of them got me pretty good.

It's only eleven a.m., and I've already been called rat, bitch, traitor, and had numerous paper projectiles thrown at me in class.

Fun times.

I knew the response to my campaign would receive pushback, but maybe I underestimated just how much sway the Heirs hold in the school.

So far, my petition has a handful of signatures. A far cry from the number I'll need for Mr. Porter to take my idea to the school board. It's frustrating as hell that people would rather let the Heirs keep their beloved den of debauchery than turn the Chapel into a space for all students to use and benefit from.

"Seb," I call, spotting him at the end of the hall. He glances around and finally notices me, his brows furrowing a little. "Hey, how are things?"

"Uh, fine. Why?"

"So you haven't been wading through a sea of threats and insults all morning? Lucky you." I smile but know it doesn't reach my eyes.

"What did you expect, Tally?" He shrugs, hitching his bag up his shoulder. "I told you it was a bad idea."

"Yeah, but it's the right one. We agreed that the Chapel—"

"Yeah, I know. I know." His voice gets lower as a group of students rush past. "Just... try and lay low for a bit until it blows over. People will lose interest eventually."

"What? I don't want them to lose interest, Seb. We need to actively be encouraging people to sign the petition. In fact, I was thinking—"

He checks his watch and murmurs, "Shit, I need to go. We can talk about this later."

Seb barges past me and takes off down the hall.

"Dissension in the ranks?" a soft voice says, and I turn to find none other than Misty Dalton smirking at me.

"Excuse me?"

She steps toward me, her tartan skirt swishing around her thighs. Misty is one of them—an Heir chaser. And everyone knows her Heir of choice is Oakley.

Including me.

"Sebastian didn't seem too keen on sticking around to chat. Could it be that you've even alienated your own team?"

"Whatever, Misty." I go to move past her, but she grabs my arm.

My gaze drops to where her perfectly manicured nails wrap around my blazer. "Get your hand off me," I warn.

"Look, a little bit of advice, girl to girl... think long and hard about whether it's worth it."

"What—"

"You know exactly what I'm talking about, Tallulah." She smiles, but it's full of bite. "No one goes up against the Heirs and lives to tell the tale."

"How do you do it?" I ask, and she frowns.

"Do what?"

"Spend your life chasing after a boy who will never commit to you?"

"I don't know what you're talking about."

"No? Everyone knows you want Oakley. I suspect you've even had him a few times." I suppress a shudder at that nugget of well-documented information. "But you'll never keep him."

"Fuck you, bitch." She yanks her hand away. "I was trying to do a nice thing by warning you, but do you know what? You deserve everything coming your way and more. See you around, rat." She slams her shoulder into mine and saunters off down the hall.

I let out a thin breath, a trickle of awareness going through me. Doubling back around, I come face to face with Oakley at the end of the hall, watching me.

"Making friends, I see." He smirks, sending my heart into a tailspin.

Oakley might be one of the most infuriating, cocky, arrogant guys I've ever met. But he's also one of the most gorgeous. Intense blue eyes framed by dark lashes, soft full lips that are usually crooked into a playful smirk, and a body honed by years of physical training.

I mean, I get it—the obsession with him and the other Heirs. Rich, popular, and easy on the eyes, and if the rumours are to be believed, more than familiar with the intimate workings of the female body. But none of those things make them good people.

My father always taught me respect should be earned, not given freely. Those rules have never applied where the Heirs are concerned. Their surnames alone demand the kind of blind worship thanks to years and years of tradition and history.

I narrow my eyes at Oakley, fighting the urge to call him out.

But I don't.

He doesn't deserve the truth, not when he clearly thinks this is all one big game.

"You should watch your back, Prim," he drawls. The Heir chasers can be brutal when they sense a traitor in their midst."

"I'm nothing like them," I whisper, more to myself than him.

"No, you're not." He pushes off the wall and takes a step forward. Hands jammed causally in his pockets, Oakley lets his eyes drop down my body and slowly work their way back up.

I silently remind myself that he's nothing more than the kind of boy who spews pretty lies, so long as it gets him what he wants.

It's on the tip of my tongue to ask him what he's doing but before I can get the words out, Oakley gives a little shake of his head, spins on his heel, and takes off down the hall.

Leaving me standing there, gawking after him.

The day only goes from bad to worse. The stares and whispers follow me as I move from class to class. The Heir chasers are particularly vicious with their taunts and catcalls.

Frigid whore is just jealous she'll never catch the eye of an Heir, is my favourite so far.

If only they knew.

But for the most part, I haven't engaged, refusing to stoop to their level. Until a commotion in the corridor garners my attention.

A half-naked rugby player dressed in little more than a royal cape and plastic crown charges through the crowd, ringing a bell.

"Hear ye, oh hear ye." He stops right opposite my locker and pulls open a scroll. "By royal decree, the Heirs demand the presence of the entire sixth form Friday night at the Chapel to celebrate their long and prosperous reign. Long live the Heirs."

"Long live the Heirs, long live the Heirs," the majority of students begin to chant, howling with laughter at the ridiculous display of pomp and ceremony.

I barely resist the urge to vomit, instead, choosing to carry out the menial task of grabbing some things from my locker. But when I'm done and turn around, the boy is still there.

"Can I help you?" I demand, aware we're pulling an audience.

He pulls out a smaller scroll and unfurls it, clearing his throat. "Tallulah Celia Darlington, you are hereby cast out of All Hallows' social ladder." His voice rises above the hushed whispers and rumbles of amusement. "Anyone caught fraternising, colluding, or supporting you will also be cast out."

Before I can process what's happening, a couple of girls rush up to me and grab my arms.

"W-what the heck?" I choke out, disbelief and rage coursing through me as they hold me still while he pulls out a permanent marker and approaches me.

"Don't you dare," I hiss, trying to break free. But Misty's friends Tasha and Lauren are freakishly strong, and I'm powerless as he grabs my jaw and brings the tip of the marker to my forehead, drawing something.

"What are—"

"There. Behold, the outcast." He grabs my shoulders and whips me around in a circle as everyone laughs and mocks me.

This is low, even for the likes of Tasha, Lauren, and some lowly All Saints minion.

"Mr. Middleton," a voice calls from the other end of the hall, and everyone starts dispersing. "Do we have a problem?"

"No problem here, sir."

"Didn't think so. Miss Darlington?" His eyes home in on whatever he drew on my forehead, but he doesn't mention it.

Unbelievable.

The level of power and control the Heirs hold over this place is really quite sickening.

Refusing to lose face in front of my peers, I hitch my bag up my shoulder, hold my head high, and walk calmly toward the bathroom.

As soon as I'm safely inside, I hurry to the mirrors and gasp at the ugly O with a diagonal cross drawn through the middle. Grabbing some blue paper towels, I run them under the tap and start scrubbing. But the ink doesn't shift. It doesn't even smudge.

"Ugh," I slam my hand down on the counter in frustration. I can't go to my next class like this. There's being defiant in the face of school bullies and being plain stupid.

Pulling off my bag, I rummage inside to find my small make-up bag and retrieve the stick of concealer. It isn't a fail-safe plan, but at least it'll get me by until I can go home and have a proper wash.

When I'm satisfied with the results, I pack up my things and take a deep breath. I made my choice; there's no going back now. But I'm under no illusion it won't get worse before it gets any better.

Before I can leave, the door swings open and I brace myself for a verbal assault. But it's Abigail Bancroft.

"Tally, are you okay? I saw what Josh did. It was not cool."

"I've had better days." I grimace. "Is it still really noticeable?"

"Not really. But here." She approaches slowly, reaching for me. "May I?"

"Sure."

Abi plucks and pulls my hair, manipulating it into a slightly off-centre parting, leaving a thicker strand down my left-hand side.

"There, it's barely noticeable now."

"Thank you." I smooth my hair down.

"I've had a lot of practise at hiding things I don't want people to see."

"I'm sure they'll get bored soon, when the next scandal breaks."

"I think it's admirable, taking on the Heirs. Although, are you sure it's the right move?"

"It's time." I nod, refusing to reveal anything else. "I suppose you'll be going with Liv to the party?"

"I don't know. It feels weird now you're not hanging out with us. I'll probably stay at home. Or we could go to Dessert Island?"

"That would be... no, we shouldn't. You heard what they said. Anyone caught with me will suffer the same fate. And I don't want to make life any more difficult for you."

"Sometimes, I really hate this place." A flash of anger lights up Abi's emerald-green eyes. But it quickly melts away.

"If you change your mind... about Dessert Island, I mean. You know where to find me."

"Thanks, Abi. I appreciate it."

I did, more than she would ever know.

But I had no plans to put her in the firing line. She already had it hard enough.

6

OAKLEY

"Ready for a nice meal with the 'rents?" Reese asks with a smirk playing on his lips as we pull our clothes on after practice.

"Nice meal? You have attended all the ones we've attempted to have since you came back, right? There is nothing fucking nice about them," I mutter, thinking of all the cringe-worthy 'family' moments we've had to endure recently.

If Reese and I aren't going at it after his disappearance this summer, then he and Liv are making come-fuck-me eyes at each other across the table and putting me off food for life. And if we're really, really, lucky, Dad and Fiona will start talking about work and bore the shit out of us in punishment for misbehaving.

It's annoying as fuck. I have every intention of following Dad into the firm, and I want to learn everything I can. But the bullshit they come up with to talk about over dinner is just that. Bullshit.

I'm over it. All of it.

Today has been... hard work, and I'm more than ready for it to be over.

Yeah, okay, Elliot's dumb-arse idea to dress Middleton up

as a prick and send him into the masses with our party invite was funny as fuck. That dick has been fucking up all over the place, both in school and on the pitch. It's fucking embarrassing that he's meant to be one of the Heirs to take over from us next year when we embark on the next chapter of our lives as Scions at Saints Cross University.

A shudder rips down my spine at the thought of being at the bottom of the food chain where the elite leaders of the future are concerned.

We're going to be ripped straight out of our leadership here at All Hallows' and thrown back into a life as Scott Eaton's little minions.

It's almost enough to make me want to go elsewhere. Not that Dad would allow it.

We're going to get our year as Heirs, and then we're expected to become Scions, and be tested all over again. Apparently, being a Scion is where the fun really starts. Right now, I call bullshit. Even if Scott Eaton isn't top dog yet, he'll still be above us, and that is all he needs to ensure our life is going to hell.

"It'll be fun. My favourite hobby right now is watching you and your old man squirm while I eye-fuck your sister."

Reese barely reacts when I slap him around the back of the head. In fact, all he does is smile at me like a fucking psycho.

"You know I'm going to spend the whole time planning on how fast I can get her away from the table to eat—"

"Finish that sentence and you won't be able to digest your food, let alone eat anything ever again."

His chuckle fills the air around me as I throw my bag over my shoulder and head out. I don't get very far away from the motherfucker.

"You driving or me?" he asks, jogging up to my side.

"Depends on whether you're planning on staying the night, because I don't want to be stuck anywhere where you're—"

"Fucking your sister?"

"I fucking hate you, you know that, Whitfield?" I hiss.

"No, you don't. I'm your bestie, remember?"

"Were my bestie," I point out, the memory of a summer without him slamming into me and turning my irritation with him up a notch. "That was before you fucked off and started banging Liv."

"Is that it? Do I need to get you off, too? Will that make it better and force you to finally forgive me?"

"Don't even think about coming anywhere near me."

"Just in the bedroom next door?"

"You getting in my fucking car or not?" I spit when we get to the car park.

"As much as I'd love to tell you all about how good your sister is in bed all the way home, I think not. I want my cock still firmly attached to my body so she can choke—"

Crack.

"Motherfucker," Reese grunts as he stumbles back from the hit. "Fuck, man. I was only yanking your chain," he barks, lifting his hand to mop up the small trickle of blood that runs from his split lip.

"No, you fucking weren't," I bark, ripping my driver's door open, starting the engine and flooring it away from the motherfucker.

He's happy, I get it. But fuck. He needs to learn when to shut his mouth.

My hands wring the wheel as irritation surges through me like a storm. I've been in a weird-arse mood all fucking day, and I haven't been able to shake it. Even letting Misty blow me around the back of the locker rooms during fourth period didn't help.

Just like yesterday, all anyone could talk about was Tally and her bullshit campaign.

The second we stepped into the sixth form common room

this morning, it was immediately clear that no one had forgotten about it overnight.

And unsurprisingly, Tally was nowhere to be seen.

For a while, I wondered if she'd figured out her mistake and was keeping her head down. But then, as I was walking toward my first class of the day, I saw her making her way toward me with her head held high as if she wasn't currently fighting a losing battle against the entire fucking school.

Credit where credit's due. The girl has some fucking balls.

Shame she's also fucking stupid.

She's got a target so huge on her back that by the end of the day, rumour had it that even her partner in crime, Sebastian Howard, had switched sides.

Smart guy.

But no amount of grief from the Heir chasers was enough to topple Tally. It will, though. At some point, they'll hit a sore spot that she's trying to hide, and she will fall from her pedestal.

The party won't do much. It's not like she's going to feel like she's missing out, seeing as she's only ever shown her face to one, and that was because my sister practically dragged her to it. The point of it is to show her just how much support we have compared to the measly few signatures on her online petition.

When I looked earlier, I almost pissed my pants laughing.

She really should give up.

I'm still on edge when I pull up beside my sister's car outside the house and make my way in. The scent of homemade lasagne hits my nose the second I step into the hallway, and my stomach growls loudly. But that's not the most surprising thing. It's the speed at which my sister flies at me with her fists curled and a fierce expression on her face.

"Liv, what the fuck?" I bark when she comes at me with her less-than-impressive punches.

Damn, I need to give this girl some training if she wants to start beating people's arses.

I block most of her punches, but I allow her to take her frustrations out on me for a few minutes before I overpower her, grab her wrists, and pin her back against the hallway wall. "Enough," I bark as she glares up at me, her chest heaving with exertion while I've barely broken a sweat.

I thought all that yoga shit was meant to be good for her.

"What the fuck, Liv?"

"You need to call off your bloodhounds, Oak," she seethes through gritted teeth.

"What? Those bitches aren't my responsibility."

"I don't give a fuck. They listen to you."

"So?" I ask, risking releasing her and taking a step back.

"Did we not attend the same school today? Did you see and hear what they were doing to her?"

A laugh of disbelief spills from my lips. "She's gone up against almost the entire school, Liv. We had nothing to do with what went down today."

Sure, we had the intention of setting the chasers on her, but it turned out it wasn't necessary.

"But she's gunning for you. And you can stop this."

The front door opens behind me, but I don't stop to look back, and nor does Liv.

"What Tallulah fucking Darlington does is none of my fucking business, Liv. You should be gunning for her along with all those bitches. She lied to you too, remember?"

"She doesn't deserve this, Oak."

"What the fuck are you doing?" Reese growls, wrapping his hand around my shoulder and dragging me away from my sister, forcing me to release her, as if I'm about to what... hit her? Fucking hell.

"None of your business," I spit, shooting him a cutting look.

"It is when you're touching my girl."

"Fucking hell," I groan, throwing my hands up in defeat. "Then you fucking tell her that we had nothing to do with any of that bullshit that went down today."

"Can't," he says with a smirk. "I wasn't in your 'Tally retaliation' meeting last night. I've no idea what you idiots decided on."

"We didn't have a fucking meeting." Okay, so kind of a lie, but whatever. "We just called a party as a public show of power. That's it."

"So you didn't send the chasers after her?"

"Why the fuck would we do that? We can fight our own battles, Liv. Especially against a jumped up, opinionated, self-righteous goody two-shoes like Tally."

"Jeez, don't hold back," Reese mutters, but I don't take my attention from Liv as she glares at me.

"What *are* you planning, Oakley?"

"Nothing," I lie.

It's something that's become a bit of a habit that I really don't like over the past few weeks, but it is what it is. I have no intention of letting my sister know that while the Heir chasers are doing their thing, I'm going to ensure Tally realises her mistake in coming after us. I'm just going to be a little less... public. Less... obvious.

Tally thinks she's so much better than everyone else at All Hallows'. Something she's inherited from her prick of a father. Taking her down a peg or two has been a long time coming. We've battled for years, but almost always in the classroom.

She's made things personal with this little vendetta, so I only feel like it would be fair to do the same.

Little Miss Perfect can't actually be perfect all the time. There is no way. And I am determined to find something that will prove to her where she really stands among us. And it certainly isn't at the fucking top, trying to pull the strings and run the school how she sees fit.

"Why are you bleeding?" Liv asks, finally moving her attention to her boyfriend.

Puke.

"Oakley hit me," he replies with a shit-eating grin.

"What?" she shrieks.

"Kids, stop arguing, dinner is almost ready," Fiona calls, interrupting my comeback.

"He deserved it. Just like Tally does. You don't like it? Go and be on her side," I threaten before marching toward my bedroom to take a few minutes before I'm forced to endure this fucking family meal.

The second my door closes behind me, I pull my phone from my pocket and fall back into my bed, tapping Tally's name into Instagram. Her smiling, innocent face fills my screen, and I stare at it for a few seconds too long.

It's not fair that she's so fucking hot.

Reaching out, I rearrange myself in my sweats as I think about how it felt having her at my mercy down in that basement.

Fuck, she bent to my will so quickly, so easily.

It makes a smile curl up at my lips as I scroll through her feed.

She's going to be so fucking easy to break.

All I need is a little time, and I'll have her exactly where she belongs.

Before I do something stupid like start jerking off over the traitor, I switch to the images that she's been tagged in.

"Fucking hell," I breathe.

Those chasers didn't waste any time.

7

OAKLEY

"Bro, let's fucking go. The party is starting without us," Theo shouts, his fist pounding on my bedroom door.

Tipping a little pill onto the top of my dresser, I throw it back, washing it down with a shot of vodka.

"Hell fucking no it's not," I boom back as he twists my door handle, inviting himself in like I was expecting him to do the second he knocked.

Knocking is more warning than any of us usually get. Fucker walks in on us doing all sorts of fucked-up things.

"Coach will have your balls when he finds out you're still popping those," he says, a frown marring his brow as he watches me pocket the baggie before reaching for my phone.

"What he doesn't know won't hurt him. Plus, it'll all be worn off by Monday."

"What the fuck are you two still doing up here?" Elliot barks, coming to a stop in my doorway.

"Could say the same about you, oh fearless one," Theo teases.

Elliot's teeth grind as a tic starts up in his temple. "Just get your arses downstairs. There's fuck all point to this party if we're hiding away like little pussies."

"The only one who should be hiding is Tally," Theo confirms.

My stomach knots at what the chasers have planned for her.

There's a part of me that wants to warn her of what's coming her way. But then I remember her standing up on that stage, her eyes locked with mine as she laid out her intentions.

Yeah, actually. Fuck it. Fuck her and her self-righteous bullshit.

This is our school, our fucking Chapel, and she can fuck off if she thinks she has the power to take us down.

"Let's go," I bark, the tingle of the pill I took already starting to have an effect. "I'm ready to party with the masses."

"Look out All Hallows', there is no taking down the Heirs," Theo booms, his voice rising well above the pounding music that's coming from downstairs.

"That's more like it," Elliot scoffs, gesturing for me to follow Theo out of my room "Where the fuck is Reese?"

Almost as if he'd planned it, Reese's door swings open, revealing him standing there in a dark green Henley and a pair of jeans. "You rang, master," he quips.

"Where the fuck have you been?"

"Banging my—"

"Shut the fuck up, Whitfield," I growl. I'm in no mood to listen to his bullshit.

A grin twitches at his lips before he pushes his door wider, revealing my sister still straightening up her clothes.

"Oh, hey, brother. How's it going?" she asks, forcing a lightness into her tone that I know she doesn't feel.

"Surprised you're even here, Liv."

"What the fuck is that supposed to mean?" Reese barks.

"I thought you were Team Tally?"

"Fuck you, Oak," she sneers. Shoving her feet into her shoes, she storms over.

Her make-up is a mess. The sight of it makes my

stomach twist up painfully, because I know that if I were to look over at my best friend, he'd be wearing it around his mouth, too.

She shoves me hard in the chest, and I'm so lost in the horror of my previous thoughts that I stumble back like an idiot.

"I'm not on a team, Oakley," she hisses. "I might be your sister and Reese's girlfriend"—a violent shudder rips down my spine at that confession—"but Tally is my friend. It doesn't matter if I agree with her or you arseholes; I am not taking sides. All I do know is that she's trying to make this school a better place, and she doesn't deserve the bullshit that's being thrown her way."

She narrows her eyes at me, I assume waiting for me to agree.

But while she might be happy hanging out on the fence with the people she cares about on either side—although, admittedly, she should have more loyalties to us over her new friend—I am firmly on this side.

I might agree that what the chasers are doing to Tally is harsh, but I am in no position to put a stop to any of it. Not unless I want to stand beside her in this campaign. And that is never going to fucking happen.

I haven't spent my eighteen years looking forward to the moment me and my boys got the key to this place to throw it all away so soon. It's all we've talked about for years. There is no fucking chance of me giving any of this up because of some pretty blonde whose moral compass is pointed way too fucking north.

"It's out of our hands," I say, pushing past her, ready to head down to get the party started.

"You own this fucking school," my sister screams after me. "You can stop this in a heartbeat if you want to."

Heavy footsteps follow me down the stairs, and I can't help but look back to see who's with me. Elliot is to my left,

Theo to my right, and surprisingly Reese takes up the rear, leaving my sister fuming on the top step.

I guess I should look on the bright side. That decision he just made has ensured he won't be getting laid tonight... again. Ugh.

As if they sense the change in the atmosphere as we descend, every set of eyes in our living quarters turns to look at us. Not a second later, someone kills the music, ensuring anyone who hadn't noticed our arrival is now fully aware of our presence.

A sense of power washes through me and I can't help my chest puffing out a little at the adoration in the eyes staring at us. Every motherfucker in this room either wants to be us, or wants to fuck us. It's a pretty fucking great life to live.

One of the rugby team rushes over with a tray of whisky for us. His cheeks are flushed, and he has a little sweat beading on his brow. Fucking pussy is going to need to get it together better than that if he wants to survive.

Simultaneously, the four of us reach for a glass and knock the amber liquid back.

"Fuck yes," Theo booms before Elliot stalks toward the lectern and waits for silence to fall.

Seeing him up there commanding the masses is a massive head fuck. It's so far removed from the little boy I remember playing Hot Wheels with not so long ago.

But all of us knew this time would come. His name, his legacy, means he takes the lead.

He might not be his vindictive older brother, or any of the arseholes who came before him, but leadership has run through Elliot's veins since the day he was born, and he takes on this role as easily as he commands control of the rugby pitch.

"All Hallows'," he starts, his deep voice rumbling through the ancient building that makes the hairs on my arms stand. "Are you ready to show this school who's really in charge?"

CRUEL DEVIOUS HEIR: PART ONE

A roar of agreement sounds out as the three of us move into position behind him.

"Louder. Let's hear what you really think. If you're loud enough, it'll get back to those who are against us."

"Long live the Heirs," one of the crowd starts, and no sooner has the first word rolled off his tongue than the chant filters through the rest of the students.

In only seconds, every single person who is standing before us is chanting, the words bouncing off the solid walls and echoing up to the vaulted ceiling.

"Let's party," Elliot barks a beat before someone turns the music back up and chaos ensues beneath us.

More drinks are delivered to us, and we throw each one back before moving to the next.

The Heir chasers descend, Misty making a beeline straight for me. One of her hands wraps around the back of my neck, while the other descends south until she's groping me through my jeans. "Fuck, you look hot tonight, Oak," she purrs.

"So do you, Mist," I reply, mostly because she's expecting it.

Sure, she's pretty enough to look at. And yeah, she can suck good dick, but that's about where her qualities end.

She's too desperate to ever be anything more than a quick hookup. Not that I'm looking for anything other than that, of course.

So while she's willing to get on her knees for me, I'll fill her head with what she wants to hear. Although, I won't lie to her. At no point will I make her any promises.

She bites on her bottom lip, looking up at me through her lashes. "I want to taste you, Oak."

My cock jerks under her hand, my semi quickly giving her the illusion I can't think of anything but her.

It's tempting. Really fucking tempting. No better way to kick a party off than whisky, E, and a blowie.

But just before I take her hand and lead her somewhere a

little more private, my sister appears in my eye line and my desire sinks. She doesn't just look pissed; she looks really fucking sad, and it cracks something inside me.

"Later, yeah?" I say, detaching myself from Misty and making my way toward Liv.

"Don't stop on my account," she sneers when I get to her.

"I don't give a shit about Misty, Liv."

Her eyes flash with something I don't like. "No, of course not. All you care about is your position and the amount of power you have."

"Have you been drinking?"

"No more so than you've been popping pills again." Her eyes narrow on me accusingly.

"Just having fun."

"So am I." She grins at me, but I barely see any of my twin sister in it. It's pure malice, and I'm pretty sure just a little bit of hate. It hurts.

But not as much as when she dismisses me in favour of my best friend. The second he's in touching distance, she throws herself around him, slamming her lips down on his and giving him little choice but to join in.

Reese's eyes find mine. There's some kind of apology within them, but I don't accept it.

I can't. He's fucking my sister.

Flipping him off behind Liv's back, I take off through the party, shoving away anyone who tries to get close to me. This is meant to be an epic night, but right now, I feel anything but epic.

I take the drinks that are offered to me until my head begins to spin.

Everyone around me is enjoying themselves. Bodies are grinding it up on the dance floor. Theo is... I'm pretty sure fingering some girl I've never seen before in the kitchen. Elliot is holding court with some of the rugby team. And Reese...

well, the less I think about where he and my sister are, the better. If they're in the basement...

Needing some fresh air, I stumble through the open front door. There are almost as many people out here as there are inside. Many of them have never been to a Chapel party before. It's obvious who hasn't. The stars in their eyes are a huge giveaway.

Ignoring them, I keep moving toward the dark tree line of the woods that hide the Chapel from the rest of the school campus.

"Oakley?" a shrill voice calls, making me wince.

"Go back to the party, Misty. I'm just taking a piss," I lie.

"Don't be long. I've got plans for you."

"Of course you have," I mutter to myself as I'm swallowed up by the shadows.

I instantly relax as I navigate through the trees like I've done a million times before. There's a cut-through to get back to Dad's place through these trees, and the four of us have escaped through it more times than I can count over the years.

Voices and music filter to me, but I pay it all little mind in my need for solitude. And just when I think I've found it, I spot a figure up ahead, cloaked in darkness.

Taking a step closer, I run my eyes down what is obviously a female body. Even in the shadows, her curves are more than obvious.

Suddenly, she moves almost as if she's been startled, and she begins to hurry away in the opposite direction.

Not willing to let my prey go, I take up the chase, but the second I step into a thick pile of leaves, it alerts her to my presence, and she turns around. My breath catches in my throat when her blue eyes lock on mine. And for the first time tonight, some real excitement floods through my veins.

I move closer, unable to stop myself as I force a dangerous sneer onto my lips. "Well, well, what do we have here?"

She sucks in a sharp breath, her chest heaving, her eyes wide in fear. "I... I'm just leaving."

Naïvely, she attempts to run. I'd have thought she knew me better than that by now. And instead of allowing her the escape she craves, my hand darts out and I wrap my fingers around her upper arm, hauling her close and shoving her roughly against a tree.

"I don't think so, Prim," I growl, getting right in her face. "You and me... are going to have a little talk."

8

TALLY

I beat the eggs harder, taking out every ounce of frustration I have on the cake batter.

"Sweetheart?" Dad comes into the kitchen. "What did those eggs ever do to you?" His lips twist with amusement, but it's lost on me. "Bad day at school?"

"You could say that," I murmur getting angry all over again. "Sebastian completely flaked out on me. The Heirs decided to throw a party and Sebastian is going. I can't believe it. So much for sticking together..."

"Ah, so that's what got you so worked up. This war with the Heirs. You know, Tallulah, if you can't handle—"

"I can handle it, Dad. I just need to bake my frustrations away. Hence the mess."

I glance around our kitchen, wincing at the state of the place. Eggshells and flour litter the counter, while dirty bowls and wooden spoons, dishes and pans are piled up in the sink.

I love baking. It usually helps me relax.

But I never claimed to be tidy.

I thought the week would get easier, that the Heir chasers' hate campaign would die down once they got over the initial shock. But things have only gotten worse. Yesterday after school, I found a dead rat on my windscreen. And this morning, I opened my locker, only to find a very big, very angry looking dildo and a bottle of K-Y jelly accompanied by a note telling me to go fuck myself.

I didn't need to see the smirk on Misty's face to know she and her friends were the culprits. But instead of rising to her games, I simply dumped them in the bin at the end of the hall and went about my day.

So what if I disappeared around the corner, hurried into the girls bathroom and cried for five minutes? They were tears of frustration, nothing else. But I wouldn't give them the satisfaction of seeing me break.

"Well, sweetheart. There's no shame in admitting defeat. You always knew the pushback from the Heirs would be difficult. I can speak to Mr. Porter if you—"

"No, Dad. No. I've got it under control."

Of course he doesn't think I can handle it. That's my dad for you. The first to support my ideas... and the first to tell me there is no shame in quitting.

I can't work him out. He believes in a fair, just world. Has instilled those morals in me my whole life. But sometimes, I wonder if he's disappointed that his only child is a girl. Because women can't possibly have the tenacity and backbone to succeed in this male-dominated world we live in.

It's why he sent me to ju-jitsu lessons from the age of ten.

"Where's Mum?" I ask, changing the subject.

"You know your mother, Tallulah. Off fixing the world one charity gala at a time."

I grimace, focusing my attention back on the cake batter, wondering if he realises how dismissive he is of her endeavours.

"So can I assume you won't be attending the party tonight?"

"Why on earth would I do that?" I don't tell him that I couldn't even if I wanted to.

"Maybe you need to think outside the box, sweetheart. If you want Mr. Porter and the other school board members to take your petition seriously, maybe you need some evidence to support your case."

"Evidence?" My brows furrow. Surely he isn't suggesting what I think he is?

Dad chuckles. "It's okay to bend the rules in the name of justice, sweetheart." With a wink, he walks out of the kitchen as if he hasn't just landed a bomb at my feet.

Evidence.

Everyone knows that parties at the Chapel are wild. But unless you've been to one, it's all just conjecture and rumour.

Maybe Dad's right. Maybe I need proof if I'm going to win people over.

And there's only one way I'm going to get it.

"Thanks for agreeing to do this," I say to Abigail, clipping my seat belt into place.

"Talk me through it again, what are you going to do?"

"I just need you to drive me to the back gates at school and wait, okay?"

"Yeah, I understood that part. But what are you going to do?"

"You don't need to worry about that." I give her a reassuring smile despite the nervous energy bouncing in my stomach.

This is probably a bad idea, but my dad is right. If I want to convince everyone that the Chapel would be better repurposed as a student welfare hub, then I need to open people's eyes to what really goes on there.

"I'm not sure this is a good idea, Tally. If they catch you—"

"No one will catch me. They'll be too busy snorting coke and downing shots to even realise I'm there."

"Fine, okay. Just don't say I didn't warn you when this all goes wrong."

I flash her a droll smile. "Come on. The sooner we get this over with, the sooner we can head to Dessert Island for cake."

"Did you invite Liv?"

"Of course I didn't. She's with Reese."

"She's still your friend."

"I don't want to put her in a difficult situation." My chest constricts. "I like Liv, I do, but I don't expect her to choose me over Reese."

"Does it have to be a choice?"

"Of course it does, we're at war, Abi."

"War, Jesus..." she murmurs under her breath, taking the road for All Hallows'.

"How's your dad?" I ask her, aware that Judge Bancroft is sick.

"He's okay, thanks."

"You know, if you ever need to talk..."

"Thanks."

The rest of the drive is silent, but I'm okay with it. I'm too highly strung from the events of the last few days. It's on the tip of my tongue to confide in Abi, but I decide against it. She has enough on her plate without me adding to it.

Besides, I can handle the Heir chasers.

"Okay, pull over near the wall up ahead."

"You're sure? It's quite a walk to the Chapel from here."

"I'll be fine. You've got your phone on you?" I ask, and she nods. "I'll text you when I'm heading back to you, okay?"

"Maybe I should come with you."

"No. Absolutely not. You're my getaway driver, nothing more." I tug the zip up on my plain black hoodie and slip the hood over my braided hair. Okay, I'm ready."

"Very stealthy." Abi fights a smile.

"That's the plan. Wish me luck."

"Good luck."

Shouldering the door, I climb out of her car and close it behind me. There's a chill in the air tonight, but it's nothing compared to the chill that goes through me as I slip through the gate and trudge up the path toward the Chapel.

I stick close to the tree line, blending with the shadows. No one is out here. It's Friday night, the teachers have better things to be doing with their time. The Orwell Building looms up ahead, a couple of lights on inside. But I don't let myself get distracted. Pulling out my phone, I check social media, doing a quick search of the Heirs hashtag. I'm hardly surprised at the numerous tags they're in, videos of the Saints rugby team doing ridiculous drinking dares. I spot Oakley in a couple of videos, grinning like a fool before he downs some disgusting looking concoction, wipes his mouth the back of his hand, and roars at the camera.

I roll my eyes. To think I ever found that attractive. Clearly, it was a moment of madness on my behalf. I let myself get sucked into their orbit and let my guard down.

Well, never again.

I'm determined to see this through. Determined to expose the Heirs for the arrogant, selfish, spoiled boys they are. I just need to collect enough evidence of their misdeeds.

The faint sound of music pulses in the air and the Chapel looms up ahead. Adrenaline courses through me as I clutch my phone, determined to see this through.

I just need to make sure that I don't get caught.

My heart crashes against my chest as I draw closer. A few people mill around outside the vaulted doors, drinking and laughing, and I'm pretty sure there's a couple getting it on against the wall.

Heat flashes inside me.

It's always been like this. The reigning Heirs have always been allowed to party out here as if they own the place. The Chapel is far enough away from the rest of the school buildings, cloistered on the edge of the trees, that it affords them some degree of privacy. But it's still school property.

A loud cheer filters out of a window, and I slip around the side of the building to get a better look. There aren't any windows I can access, but there is a back door that leads directly into the thicket surrounding the place.

I decide that's my best option. And sure enough, when I round the back of the building, a small group of people huddle outside, smoking and drinking.

I hover in the trees, watching. Listening. At least two of the guys are rugby players, and I recognise one of the girls from my English class.

"The Heirs sure know how to party," one of them says.

"I still can't believe this place. It's insane. I mean, I've heard the stories..."

I quickly open my camera app and start recording.

"It's a damn shame they don't let the team downstairs though," another boy says. "I'd like to play in the dungeon." He grabs the girl's rear aggressively, hoisting her into his side. Her giggles fill the air. "Would you like that, babe? Would you like me to take you downstairs, tie you up, and fuck you until you you're screaming my name?"

"Marcus," she scolds playfully. "The only way anyone goes down there is with an Heir. I heard Misty telling Tasha and Lauren that Oakley took her down there the other weekend."

I tense at her words.

"She's hoping he'll make it official soon, but everyone knows Oakley won't settle down."

"Reese did."

"Yeah, with an Heir's sister. He kept it in their circle," the girl says. "They don't trust anyone else. And now this shit with Tally Darlington... I'm surprised if they'll ever trust a girl again."

I stop recording and slip my phone in my pocket.

This was a bad idea. I'm not going to get any real evidence of what goes on at these parties without going inside. And no way can I do that.

I double back the way I came and take off into the trees, but the crunch of leaves behind me makes me pause. I glance back, sucking in a sharp breath when my eyes find Oakley, watching me.

His lips twist as he takes a step closer, the air thinning around us. "Well, well, what do we have here?" he drawls.

"I... I'm just leaving." I go to walk off, but his hand darts out, grabbing my arm.

"I don't think so, Prim." He pushes his face right into mine and I can't breathe. "You and me... we're going to have a little talk."

9

TALLY

The air crackles between us as Oakley's dark gaze flits between my eyes and my mouth.

"Let me go," I hiss, trying to break free from his hold. But his fingers curl tighter around my arm.

"Not going to happen, Prim. Not until you tell me what the fuck you're doing out here."

"I..." Crap. Panic claws up my throat as my body trembles. I can't tell him the truth; it'll only give him and the Heirs more ammunition to come after me.

"Well?" He sneers, getting right in my face, his eyes glittering with anger. But there's something else there, too. Something I don't want to acknowledge, even if my body is already responding, heat licking my stomach.

It's Oakley.

The boy I literally just heard those girls talking about. Him and Misty doing things I most definitely don't want to think about.

"Start talking, Prim or else—"

"Or what?" Irritation rolls through me. "What are you going to do about it, Oakley Beckworth? It's a free country. I'm allowed to be here. I—"

He presses the length of his body against mine, resting his hand on the tree above my head. "You really are something, Tallulah Darlington." My name rolls off his tongue almost seductively, but I won't fall under his spell.

Not again.

"And you really are an entitled—" I stop, forcing myself not to be drawn into his games. I don't like to swear.

"Go on, say it," he challenges. "Tell me what you really think of me."

I mash my lips together, trapping the many words I wish to call him but won't. Because there are other ways to express yourself besides resorting to vulgar language.

His mouth quirks. "You can't do it, can you? Daddy's prim little angel can't say it."

"Just let me go, Oakley. I'm sure you have better things to be doing than standing out here with me. Misty is probably—"

"Jealous, Prim?" His warm breath caresses my cheek. I try so hard to resist the urge to look at him, but I'm powerless as my eyes lift, our gazes colliding.

His pupils are blown wide, his expression smug and lazy.

There's barely a hair's breadth between us, and if I moved a fraction, we'd be kissing. But I don't want him to kiss me. I don't—

"Royal arsehole," he drawls. "Gorgeous, conceited wanker. Cocky, self-assured prick."

"Oakley..."

"Humour me. What are you thinking? Right now, this very second, what's going around in that pretty little head of yours?"

Pretty.

He called me pretty.

It's the wrong thing to be fixating on. So wrong. But he's so close, and it's dark and kind of eerie out here. And it reminds me of another night when he found me in the shadows.

I mentally scold myself. Now is not the time to remember.

It's the time to steel myself against Oakley Beckworth and his mind games.

"Sex god," he murmurs, letting his mouth ghost over my cheek. "Yeah, I bet that's the one. I bet you're thinking all kinds of dirty things about me, aren't you, Prim?"

"You are such a... an... idiot."

He throws his head back with laughter. "Idiot? Is that really the best you can do?"

"I'm leaving," I snap, shoving my chest into him, trying to get him to move.

But he grabs my hands, pinning them above my head. "What are you really doing here, Prim? Because something tells me you were spying. Maybe looking for evidence to support your cause?" His brow lifts, amusement playing on his lips.

God, he's infuriating.

"Or maybe you want to see what all the fuss is about? Maybe you're back to finish what we started the other day." One of his hands releases my wrist and glides down my body, mapping my curves.

"Oakley," I choke out, although it sounds more like a moan than a warning, because his touch feels too good.

"Wet for me again, Prim?"

"Don't you dare," I warn despite arching into his touch. Because there's something about him like this—possessive and dominant—that calls to my innocence.

And I realise as he shoves his hand between my thighs, rubbing me through my leggings, that I like it. I like that he teases me and pushes my buttons.

Maybe a little too much.

Because he's the enemy. I can't forget that.

"You're saying one thing, but your body is saying another." He withdraws his hand a little, and I whimper.

God, this boy.

He's under my skin, and I need to get him out.

I need to—

He presses the heel of his palm right up against me, grinding it in the best possible way.

"Oak," I breathe, pleasure saturating my veins.

"Yeah, baby?" he croons, leaning in to nuzzle my neck, flicking his tongue over my pulse point.

I don't know how things escalated so quickly, but I don't want to stop. It feels too good.

He feels too good.

Lifting his head to stare at me, he crooks a smile. "Shit, look at you, Prim. Letting the Heir get you off."

My cheeks flush, heat burning through me.

"Tell you what," he smirks. "Let me fuck you right here, right now. I'll make you come so fucking hard, you'll see stars. Feel me." Oakley grabs my hand and presses it against his impressive erection. "This is yours. For one night only, I'll fuck you so good, baby. I'll even take you to the dungeon, if that's what you want. But you have to drop this stupid fucking vendetta against us. We'll never—"

"W-what?" The lust haze I've found myself in evaporates, shame building inside of me.

What the hell am I doing?

I shove his hand away and inhale a shuddering breath. "You're offering to... to sleep with me to get me to drop the campaign?"

"Well, yeah." He hesitates, his eyes glazed. "You want it, we both know you do. You were practically riding my hand like a desperate whore."

Everything goes still inside me.

A whore.

He called me a whore.

"Get away from me." I shove harder, aware that I could easily take him down if I wanted to.

But everyone knows it isn't wise to reveal your hand straight away.

"What the fuck is your problem?" he bellows, righting himself.

"You. You are my problem. You think you can do and say whatever you want, and I'm sick of it. I'm sick of—"

"Watch it, Prim." His lip curls, eyes fixed right on mine. "This self-righteous act you've got going on will land you in all kinds of trouble when you finally get on your knees for me. And it's going to happen, baby. One day, you'll beg me to fuck you."

Anger runs hot in my veins as I stare him down, my entire body vibrating with anger. "I will *never* be that girl, Oakley."

Confusion flits over his expression for a second, but then his trademark lazy grin reappears. "We'll see. Now get the fuck out of here before someone else spots you."

I don't need telling twice. I shove past him and take off into the trees, practically running back to Abi's car.

The second she spots me, she leans over and flings open the door. "Oh my God," she says, "what happened?"

I throw myself inside and slam the door behind me, my heart racing a mile a minute. "Just drive."

"But—"

"Please, Abi."

I need to catch my breath—to figure out what the hell just happened.

Because although I hate him, despise Oakley Beckworth with every fibre of my being, I couldn't deny that part of me wanted him. That a fire ignited inside me at his dirty words and brazen touch.

That's a problem.

A really big problem.

Because it gave him power over me.

It gave him control.

And I don't like feeling out of control.

Ever.

CRUEL DEVIOUS HEIR: PART ONE

Abigail drives us to Dessert Island, one of my favourite places in town. They open late on the weekend, and we manage to snag a table before closing.

"So, ready to tell me what happened?" she asks as we tuck into our desserts. Classic Victoria sponge for Abigail and a rich decadent coffee and walnut cake for me.

"I shouldn't have gone," I reply, barely meeting her gaze.

"I could have told you that. You don't want to mess with the Heirs, Tally. I know they—"

"Someone has got to stand up to them, Abi. Their unchecked reign of All Hallows' has gone on long enough."

"I don't necessarily disagree. But is it worth it?"

"Is what..." I let out a heavy sigh. "I can handle the Heir chasers, Abi."

"They won't stop. Those girls can be brutal. And you know Misty Dalton is all too happy to step into Darcie's shoes after she was dethroned by them."

Darcie Porter, the headteacher's daughter, went up against Olivia and the Heirs a few weeks back and lost. It was a whole thing. A thing that ended with rather scandalous photos of her and one of her father's friends being strewn around the halls of All Hallows' sixth form.

"The damage is done." I shrug. "Even if I drop the campaign"—and I'm not—"the Heir chasers won't stop now."

"Why did you do it?" Abigail asks, surprising me. "I mean, I get it. The principle of it. But you had to know you'd be starting a war."

"Because sometimes you have to make a stand. The Heirs are..." I hesitate, the half-truths tasting awfully like a lie on my tongue.

I have always wanted to bring the Heirs' reign to an end, but I'd never really considered going up against them, not like this. Not until that night.

Abi's right. It's personal for me. Which is why I can't keep letting Oakley get close. He clouds my focus. My end goal.

"Are what?"

"Entitled, little rich boys who think All Hallows' is their playground. They need bringing down a peg or two."

"And you're going to be the one to do it?" she asks, wearing a thin, uncertain smile.

A sense of conviction washes over me as I nod. "I am."

So long as I stay clear of Oakley and his mind games, I'm going to see this campaign through and figure out a way to make sure there's only one winner at the end of it all.

Me.

10

OAKLEY

I stand there in the darkness, staring in the direction she vanished in. My chest heaves, my mouth waters, and my cock aches behind the confines of my trousers.

She was right there, like putty in my hands. Mouldable, pliable. And then she was gone.

Jesus, she smelled so fucking good. Her curves were addictive, begging me to continue exploring, to find more, to take everything that she clearly wanted.

But in true Prim fashion, she couldn't pull that stick out of her arse for long enough to let me carry her away from all this bullshit. To prove to her who is in charge and who holds all the power, because there would be no doubt who that would be when she was chanting my name as she came all over my fingers. No. Fuck my fingers. She'd be screaming with my cock so deep in her traitorous cunt that she'd forever remember I was there.

I stumble back as a thought hits me upside the head.

Is Little Miss Prim and Proper still a virgin?

A smile spreads across my face, growing ever wider as that thought grows roots in my head. It sure would make sense if she was. And the thought of being the first man inside her, the one who holds the power to ruin her for any other that followed... Yeah, that sparks something inside me.

Excitement shoots through my veins as I shove my hand beneath the waistband of my jeans and grip my dick. Even I'm embarrassed by the wetness that coats my hand. Feeling her pressed up against me tonight affected me just as much as it did down in that basement earlier in the week. But having her tiny hand wrap around my length as I forced her to feel just how hard I was was a whole other level of torture I'd never experienced before. And let me tell you, I experienced a whole fucking lot at the hands of Scott Eaton over the past couple of years.

"Motherfucker," I grunt as I rip my jeans open with my free hand and pull my aching dick from my boxers.

My head spins with the whisky and E I've had tonight, and it only makes the sensation of my own hand feel that much better.

I stumble back blindly in the darkness, almost tripping over a tree root before my back collides with a thick trunk. I continue working myself, not giving two shits that I'm out here alone in the dark like a fucking creep.

Like I give a fuck if anyone finds me. Hell, for all I care, they can get on their knees and help me do this properly.

I squeeze my eyes tight, refusing to accept the wave of disappointment that hits me as I think about someone other than her on her knees, worshipping me like the motherfucking royalty that I am.

It was exactly the same with Misty earlier. One look at her down there and I instantly lost some of my high. She might have been giving me all of her best moves—moves that can only come from someone who has spent a considerable amount of time on their knees with their lips wrapped around a dick. It's just one of the many reasons why I'm never going to keep her around for the long haul.

Needing something more than my imagination, I dig my

phone out of my pocket and open up Insta. I hit the search bar and should probably be concerned that the person I'm looking for was the last one I typed in, but at this moment, I don't give a fuck about anything other than getting off.

And for that, I need her.

I stare down at her blonde hair and into her innocent blue eyes. They tell me all I need to know about my suspicion earlier.

Tallulah Darlington is a virgin. And fuck if I don't want to take that safely guarded V card and tarnish it, just like I want to do with her reputation.

"Fuck, fuck," I grunt, jerking myself faster as I scroll through her feed.

It's nothing like the chasers' accounts. There are no half-naked photos, no pouting at the camera. They're just basic photographs documenting her arguably boring life. But fuck if they don't give me exactly what I need right now.

Tally is a closed book. The only thing all of us really know about her is her fucking holier-than-thou morals. But looking at her in the safety of her room, studying what is around her gives me that little bit more insight. Not that it tells me much.

Her room is tidy, her life calm and organised, exactly as I would have predicted. All it does is make me want to fuck it all up. Ruin her calm, her fucking zen as my sister would probably say.

I want every part of Tallulah Darlington's life turned upside down for her attempt to do the exact same thing to us.

I finally land on a photo of her on a school camping trip in year eleven, and the look of pure innocence and excitement in her eyes pushes me over the edge.

My roar spills into the darkness as my release slams into me, my cock jerking violently in my grip as I shoot my load over the rotting leaves. "Fuck," I gasp, panting for breath as I come down from my high.

Tipping my head back against the tree, I stare up at the

starlit sky I can just about make out through the leaves as my chest continues to heave.

I have no idea how long I remain like that, but the second I hear voices coming closer, I jump into action, tuck myself away, shove my hand through my hair and stalk out of the shadows to rejoin the party.

I get a few curious glances from the students partying outside of the Chapel as I pass, but no one dares to say anything to me as I return to my lair with my head held high.

"Where the fuck have you been?" Theo booms the second I turn toward the kitchen to get a drink. Why a member of the team didn't come running up to me to deliver one the second I entered fuck only knows.

Grabbing a fresh bottle of whisky, I twist the top and swallow a shot before turning toward him. "None of your fucking business," I grunt.

His eyes shoot up to my hair, his brows pinched in confusion. "What the fuck is that?"

Lifting my hand, I search for whatever he's talking about, assuming it's probably just a leaf or twig from the woods, but when my finger hits something cold and sticky, I wince.

A smirk covers Theo's lips.

"Pretty sure she was meant to swallow that, not rub it in your hair like a new brand of wax, mate."

I shrug, allowing him to believe it was a girl and I wasn't getting myself off like a loser in the cover of darkness.

"I wasn't complaining," I mutter, reaching for one of the tea towels and rubbing it across my head.

If I weren't high, the thought of what I'm currently doing alone would make me shudder in disgust, but seeing as the pills are fully taking effect right now, I don't bat an eyelid as I drop the towel to the counter and return to the party, more than ready to enjoy myself. Although, I can't deny that there's a part of me that wants to go out in search of another taste of Tally. There's no way she hasn't gone running home like a scared little kitten. I can almost picture her sitting beneath the sheets of her pretty pink bed, still trembling in fear.

The thought makes me grin like a psycho.

"Come on, we're taking the first years out to see what they're made of," Elliot says, marching over to us.

"Fuck yes. I'll put a grand on Middleton being the first to barf up his dinner."

"Fuck off, I'm not taking that wager," Theo barks. "It's a fucking sure thing. The cunt is a right pussy."

By the time we get outside, the rest of the year thirteen team members have already got the year twelves lined up in chairs that have obviously been stolen from a classroom.

In front of our blindfolded teammates are a series of buckets covered in towels, hiding the contents. But from experience, I can guess the kinds of things that could be hiding within.

The crowd inside the Chapel clearly noticed our exit, and they quickly followed us outside and gathered around with everyone who was hanging out here. A ripple of tension and apprehension goes through the air as Elliot, Theo, Reese and I walk up to the buckets.

The volume around us quietens, helped by someone killing the music, and it allows me to hear the whispers of the students behind me.

"What the hell are they going to do?"

"What's in those buckets?"

"I've heard rumours about this initiation task. It's brutal."

Smiling, I turn to Reese, amusement lighting up his eyes for what's about to come.

"All Hallows'," Elliot bellows, "sitting before us is the future of the Saints. But everyone who knows our team knows that we don't allow the weak to join. And in order to filter out those who don't belong, there are a series of tasks that have been handed down through the generations," he explains.

For most of the students here, it's unnecessary. Those who

regularly attend our parties know exactly the kind of shit that gets delivered to the new members of the team, and more so, the future Heirs. But tonight isn't just any party, because we have more than a handful of new faces who need to understand how our leadership works.

"The first person to lose his bottle or his stomach is going straight to the top of the weak list. A position that no member of the Saints wants to be in. Isn't that right, Middleton?" Elliot asks.

Middleton immediately starts nodding. He's been on the wrong end of our wrath since the school year started, and if he's not careful, his right to be Heir next year is going to be ripped away from him.

"Okay, shall we get the party started?"

A roar of encouragement and excitement rips through the air as Theo steps up to the first bucket and rips the towel away.

"Oh my God, is that—"

I look down, finding a whole host of bugs crawling about under a clear lid.

"What are they going to do with those?"

"Whitfield, would you like the pleasure?" Elliot asks.

Reese steps up, but movement to our right makes his progress falter, and when I follow his line of sight, I quickly discover why. My sister shakes her head, warning him against what she thinks are our stupid games before she starts backing away from the crowd.

We all know what she thinks about us, about the rules and rituals and traditions we live by. Her opinions aren't all that different to Tally's. I'm quietly terrified that she's not going to side with us in all this and instead, follow her new friend.

If Elliot sees what's going on, then he doesn't care, because he barks out Reese's name when he doesn't move quickly enough, giving him a split second to make a decision.

I should be relieved when he chooses us, his reign as Heir,

but my stomach knots as I watch my sister vanish into the darkness.

Everything feels like it's falling apart right now.

And it's all her fault.

Tallulah fucking Darlington is going to pay for trying to ruin what should be the best year of our lives.

11

TALLY

I stare at the screen in the darkness of my room, watching with morbid fascination as Oakley and Theo grin in the direction of the camera, egging on some first year to eat a handful of... maggots.

Bile washes in my stomach as I dry heave. They're crazy. Completely and utterly lawless. But the rest of All Hallows' student population laps it up, cheering and howling with laughter as some poor rugby player pukes all over himself.

Ugh. Gross.

I quickly scroll down to another video. I've been stalking a few Heir chaser accounts since I got home from Dessert Island. Most of them have their profiles set to public, which is hardly any surprise. They're all attention seekers. Vapid, vain airheads who care more about bagging themselves an Heir than acing their A Levels and getting a place at university.

My attention snags on another video, inside the Chapel this time. You wouldn't know unless you'd been in there. It just looks like a wild party, full of drunk teenagers all cutting loose and having fun. But I've seen the inside of the Heirs' sanctuary.

The girl filming shouts something to her friend, the two of

them laughing and giggling when the camera zooms in on another girl being manhandled by Theo. Again, to the untrained eye, you might not recognise him.

His hand is up her skirt, and his lips are on her neck as she writhes against him. Unfamiliar heat sweeps through me as I watch, unable to tear my eyes away. I wish I could say I don't understand the appeal, but another face fills my mind.

Oakley.

The memory of his hands on me, his strong body caging me against the tree... the way my body reacted to his touch.

I never imagined myself as the kind of girl spellbound by a pretty face and cocky charm. But there's no denying the effect Oakley has on me. Or more so, my traitorous body.

A restless ache spreads through me as I continue to watch the video. Watch Theo touch the faceless girl, her features concealed in the darkness. I press my thighs together, trying to make it subside. But it only grows, making my stomach flutter, my heart hammer in my chest.

My fingers slip absentmindedly down my stomach, and I suck in a breath as they dance at the edge of my pyjama shorts. I've never touched myself before... not like this. But there's a needy ache inside me, one that makes me wonder...

I push my fingers into my shorts and touch myself, moaning quietly as my body stirs to life. My eyes close as I imagine Oakley pinning me against the wall, kissing and touching me in the dark. Whispering dirty words in my ear.

It's so wrong. I shouldn't want him. He's everything I despise. Everything that's wrong with this world.

Arrogant. Conceited. Entitled.

He thinks he can take whatever he wants without consequence. And deep down, I know if I try to play his game, he'll ruin me.

Because he's experienced. He knows what he wants, what he likes, and he knows how to get it.

He's nothing more than a cruel, devious Heir, and I'm nothing more than the prim, proper girl he thinks I am.

But I can't stop touching myself, drowning in the new sensations coursing through me. My nerve endings are alive, my skin vibrating with lust as my fingers glide over my clit.

It feels so good. It feels—

His voice pierces the air and for a second, I forget I'm in my bedroom, in the dark, with my fingers between my legs. Panic swarms me and I blink through the lusty haze surrounding me, trying to figure out how he's here. Only to realise he's not here.

He's on the video.

"Fuck yeah, shake that delicious arse," he yells, and I clutch my phone, bringing the screen to my face, trying to make sense of what he's doing.

Like a bucket of ice-cold water, the desire I felt only seconds earlier washes away, replaced with a sinking feeling.

Misty slut-drops in front of Oakley, who's seated on a chair. No, some kind of wooden throne. He's got a ridiculous plastic crown atop of his head, his pupils blown and grin sloppy as he grabs at her body. Her hips and bum and boobs.

I quickly exit out of the video and bury my phone under my pillow.

She's the kind of girl he wants. The kind of girl who can walk in his world. Confident and sexy with all the knowledge of how to please a guy like Oakley Beckworth.

It shouldn't bother me.

I'm proud I've waited to give myself to the right person. Not that I ever anticipate meeting him at All Hallows'.

But sometimes I wonder...

Sometimes my mind drifts and I imagine what it must be like to own your sexuality like Misty and the other Heir chasers. To say screw it and kiss and hook up with whomever you want. Safely, of course.

A heavy sigh slips from my lips. I'll never be that girl, and it's something I've always prided myself on. Because sex—being intimate with someone—means something to me.

I want what my parents have.

At least, I think I do.

Everything is so confusing now, the lines of my perfectly constructed world blurry.

And it's all Oakley Beckworth's fault.

"Good morning, sweetheart. How was last night?" Mum smiles at me as I enter the kitchen and take a seat at the breakfast island.

"Last night?" Panic dashes through me.

"Dessert Island with Abigail? You said you two were—"

"Oh, yeah. It was great, Mum."

Her brows furrow as she studies me. "Is everything okay? You seem a little off."

"I'm fine. Just tired." I force a smile, trying my best to ignore the restless ache inside me.

After seeing Oakley and Misty on the video, I'd tried my hardest to go to sleep. To forget all about him and the feelings he invokes in me—my body—but I couldn't sleep. I felt needy. Unsatisfied. I also felt guilty.

Guilty that I'd touched myself to thoughts of him. The boy I'm supposed to hate.

The boy part of me *does* hate.

"I wouldn't say no to a strong coffee, though," I add, needing to focus on something other than him.

"Of course. I'm making breakfast too, if you're hungry. Your father was in the mood for dirty eggs."

"Sounds good. Are you home for the weekend?"

"Hopefully. Things at work are a little calmer this week. But you know how it is."

I do.

Her work for a national charity is her life. Same as Dad. It takes priority, always. I've gotten used to it over the years, admired their dedication to social justice. But it can be a lonely life.

I guess, in some ways, it's why I've always thrown myself into extra-curricular activities. To fill the void being an only child with busy parents brings.

"Your father told me you made waves with your campaign proposal. Good for you, sweetheart. Nothing in life worth fighting for comes easy. You've got to keep ruffling feathers. Knocking on doors. I remember when I was your age, I was part of the CND."

"CND?" I ask.

"The Campaign for Nuclear Disarmament. We camped outside of parliament for a week straight. The weather was so terrible, we all caught a raging cold." She smiles wistfully, sliding me a mug of coffee. "Those were good times. I'm proud of you for making a stand against the Heirs, Tallulah. Lord knows somebody's got to do it."

A flicker of disgust passes over her. "Just be careful, sweetheart. Boys with that kind of entitlement can be dangerous."

She doesn't need to tell me.

"I can handle the Heirs, Mum."

"Of course you can, baby. You're my daughter." She winks, chuckling to herself as she starts preparing Dad's dirty eggs. "You know, a little birdie told me Deacon has been asking about you again."

Ugh.

Deacon Warrick. Son of one of my parents' closest friends, he's everything you might expect the child of two NGO directors to be. A priggish, arrogant young man who wants to change the world and doesn't care who he walks over to get there.

CRUEL DEVIOUS HEIR: PART ONE

I've never liked him. And I certainly don't plan on ever dating him. But our parents have other ideas.

Ever since we were children, they've had this idealistic dream that the two of us would grow up and fall in love and take the world by storm.

I'd rather stick forks in my eyes than have to listen to Deacon's vision for the future.

"Tallulah, I said—"

"I heard you, Mum. I've told you before, I don't like Deacon like that."

I don't like him period.

"Would it really hurt to give him a chance? There's the charity gala coming up soon, and your father and I, and the Warricks, thought it might be nice if the two of you went—"

"Mum!"

"What, sweetheart?" Innocence glitters in her eyes. "You're eighteen, baby. You're always so focused on your studies and your responsibilities as Head Girl, and I know your father and I have always encouraged that, but part of me worries that sometimes, you're missing out on the good stuff."

"The good stuff?" I balk. "Please don't start regaling me with stories of you and Dad and your sizzling summer romance."

"It was rather sizzling."

"It's too early for this," I grumble.

"How about I make you a deal?" Mum came around and grabbed my hand. "Give Deacon a chance. One chance. And I'll buy you that limited edition pink La Creuset bakeware set you've been eyeing up."

"Mum, not fair."

"It's a dog-eat-dog world, baby. Sometimes you have to play a little dirty." She winks. "Just don't tell your father. You know what a stickler for the rules he is."

"I'm not going out with Deacon, Mum."

"We'll see." A smirk plays on her lips. "I've seen you

lusting after that set. And it would really up your baking game."

She doesn't play fair.

I have had my eye on that set for months. But I can't justify dipping into my allowance for it. Not when I'm supposed to be saving for university.

My parents are well off, but not the way some of the families are in Saints Cross, and I've always been taught the value of money. The importance of working hard and making a difference. Of leaving my mark on the world.

It's always been important to me. To make my parents proud. To carry on the family legacy of social justice and philanthropy. But ever since befriending Olivia and getting first-hand, up-close experience of the Heirs' world, something has changed.

Or maybe it hasn't changed at all.

Maybe it was always inside me. Buried deep beneath the surface.

Oakley Beckworth has ignited something in me, and I'm terrified everything I've worked hard for will go up in flames.

And there's nothing I can do to stop it.

12

OAKLEY

I rest my head back on the sofa, exhaling deeply from my nose, letting the smoke wrap around me like a warm blanket.

I shouldn't cave to it. I'm more than aware of that. Elliot will have my arse for it when he returns and smells the weed, but that will be child's play compared to what Coach will do if he ever found out about my dirty little habit.

But neither of those concerns are enough to stop me. Just like Friday night, the promise of oblivion, of stamping out my own bullshit internal thoughts, is just too good to ignore.

The Chapel is empty and eerily quiet.

Reese is off with Liv, hopefully treating her right and like the fucking epic person that she is. Elliot is playing golf with his father and brother as if he actually likes being in their presence, and Theo headed out a couple of hours ago to collect his sister so they could go and have a family breakfast.

I might not have left my room before he stormed out of the building, but just from his heavy footsteps alone, I knew he was like a bomb ready to blow. He always is where his father is concerned. Theo hates him with a passion. Never quite got to the bottom of why, though. Other than that he seems to be an even bigger narcissistic, controlling cunt than Johnathon Eaton. Which is something that beggars belief, to be quite honest, because that man is a prick with bells on.

I briefly think about my dad and the very hazy memories I have of Mum now, and I can't help but feel grateful. We might have had some really fucking hard times over the years, and things might be far from perfect, but I'm proud of where I've come from. I'm not sure Theo can say the same. Or Reese, after the bullshit he discovered over the summer.

Things could certainly be fucking worse. Still doesn't stop me from wanting to escape it all, though.

Lifting the joint to my lips, I take a hit, holding it in my lungs until it starts to burn. I barely react to the noise at the front door. It's too late to try and hide what I'm doing now, anyway.

Elliot will just have to suck it up.

But it's not Elliot who throws the door back against the ancient stone wall like it personally offended him and blows into the room like a tornado of rage.

"What the fuck happened?" I ask, watching Theo pacing back and forth in front of the kitchen.

He doesn't say anything, or even look up to acknowledge my presence.

"Theo," I bark. "What the fuck?"

He startles at my voice and his legs finally bring him to a stop before he looks up at me. "You're one to talk. Elliot will kill you when he finds out you've been smoking weed in here. Didn't you party hard enough Friday night?" he spits, barely keeping a lid on his anger.

Friday night. Ah, yes. The night I tried to drown myself in pills and alcohol to force *her* image out of my head.

It never worked.

No matter how hard we pushed the initiates, no matter how many girls tried it on, no matter how much whisky I downed. Her scent, her touch, the promise of her taste. It. Never. Left. Me.

Gritting my teeth, I force a smile on my face—one I hope he won't be able to see is fake in his current rage. "It was epic. Just keeping it going."

Lifting the joint once more, I take another hit in the hope it'll help me believe my own bullshit. "So, what's going on with you?" I ask, sensing that he's calmed down a little when he marches over and falls onto the sofa next to me and steals my high.

"Millie," he says, not surprising me in the slightest that it's his little sister that has tipped him over the edge.

"What did she do now? Befriend a boy?" I tease.

Theo is so protective of Millie. It makes me look like a teddy bear when it comes to keeping Liv safe.

"She just won't fucking listen to me. It's fucking infuriating."

"She's almost a teenager. They're not meant to listen to you. I'm pretty sure their sole purpose in life is to push every single button their big brother possesses," I mutter, briefly considering the things my sister might be doing with my best friend right now.

A violent shudder rips down my spine.

"She hasn't got a boyfriend, has she?" I ask, partly hoping his introverted sister has for my own amusement.

"I should fucking hope not. Every single boy in this school knows that I'll kill them with my bare hands if they so much as look at her let alone touch her. She's too young for that shit."

"You know it's inevitable, right? No matter how much you might smother her and threaten everyone else, she will meet a guy."

"She won't. She's going to be a nun," he states, making me snort a laugh.

"Does she know that?"

"She will." He shrugs. "I don't trust men, and she deserves to be treated right so—"

"You figure she'll be better off being celibate for life," I surmise.

I mean, I see his logic. I think I'd much prefer to pretend that Liv spends her days worshipping a higher power than worshipping my best friend.

"Why are you sitting here alone smoking, anyway? Don't you have something better to do?"

"Not really," I mutter, hating the feeling of loneliness that sweeps through me.

His concerned stare burns into the side of my face.

I knew weed was a fucking mistake. I should have gone for something stronger.

"You can talk to me, you know," he says. "I know I'm not Reese, but—"

I can't help but scoff. I haven't had any kind of bestie bonding with Reese since he decided his life would be better without us in it at the beginning of the summer and fucked off out of Saints Cross without looking back.

If it weren't for how fucking happy he seems to make my sister, I'd probably think that it would have all been better if he'd stayed lost.

"Fuck this shit," Theo barks. "I'm not sitting around here with you, feeling fucking sorry for ourselves. Grab your shit; let's go."

"Where?" I ask, pushing to my feet.

"You ask too many questions," he mutters as he marches to the front door.

I catch up to him and together we walk toward the school buildings that loom in the distance.

While my curiosity might burn red hot, I keep my questions locked down. Mostly, I'm just grateful for the company. The distraction from my own head.

It's not until we've walked almost all the way around the

Orwell Building and Theo diverts around the locker rooms to another sports facility that I start to follow his train of thought. And I fucking love it.

"You got a key?" I ask as we approach the door.

"Ha, you're funny."

Hopping over a row of nicely pruned bushes, he comes to a stop at the second window that looks out over the sports fields, tucks his fingers under the frame and pops it open.

"Fair enough."

"It's not alarmed, either," he explains as he throws his leg over the sill and climbs inside.

"How didn't I already know this?"

"Too busy freaking out about Liv getting railed by Reese?"

"You wanna start talking about sisters again, man? I'm pretty sure I saw Millie ogling the rugby team when she walked past the other day."

Crack.

"Motherfucker," I hiss, spitting out a wad of blood that immediately fills my mouth from the force behind his punch.

"Can't take the heat, get out of the motherfucking kitchen, Beckworth."

"Fuck you," I bark, righting myself and reaching behind my head to pull my white t-shirt off.

By the time I've dropped it at my feet, Theo has already long abandoned his and is standing in the middle of the ring, cracking his knuckles.

"Gloves?" I ask naïvely, glancing at the rows lined up on the wall.

"Pussy," Theo scoffs. "Just get your arse in here and try and figure a way to work through whatever shit is up in your head."

"You might regret that," I taunt, ducking under the ropes on the other side of the ring.

"Fucking doubt it. We all know I'm better than you."

Oakley Beckworth, always second best...

A roar that doesn't sound like me rips from my throat as I fly at him, my fists colliding with his ribs with such force he goes crashing back into the ropes.

"Fuck you, Ashworth," I bellow a beat before he comes back at me with fists flying, the promise of that dark oblivion I craved back in the Chapel glinting in his mischievous eyes.

"Fuuuck," Theo groans, his arms falling like dead weights at his sides when he finally admits defeat.

"How's that for being better than me, prick?" I scoff, barely able to catch my breath as I fall to my arse next to him.

Both our chests heave with exertion, our skin slick with sweat and blood from the brutal hits we exchanged. But fuck if I don't feel better than I have since...

You had Tally pressed up against that tree.

Fuck.

Dropping my head into my hands. I chastise myself for the fact I'm still no better off. I need all this campaign bullshit to blow over. Once everyone has forgotten about her, she can slink back into the shadows where she belongs and we can go back to hating each other because of nothing more than the surnames we were given at birth, and all will be right in my world once more.

"What?" Theo asks, making me realise that the laugh of disbelief wasn't just in my own head.

"Nothing. We should head back. I'm starving."

Noise over by the window we broke in through hits my ears, but unlike Theo, I don't bother looking and instead climb to my feet, ready to duck out of the ring.

"Oh yeah. So am I. And I think I just found the perfect meal."

I finally follow his line of sight, and I can't help but groan as my eyes land on our fan club, whose faces are pressed up against the glass, trying to get a good look at us.

Misty's gaze lifts from my body and excitement explodes within them when she realises I'm looking at her.

Big fucking mistake.

"Oh yeah, they're in the fucking mood," Theo says happily.

"When aren't they?" I scoff.

"Fucking hell, something must be seriously fucked with you if the thought of getting your dick sucked by Misty doesn't cheer you up."

"Nothing about Misty cheers me up," I confess. "She's a shameless whore."

"Well, if you don't want her, I'm sure I can entertain all four of them while you go back to your pity party for one."

He pushes the window open after stuffing his t-shirt into the pocket of his sweats so the girls have plenty to ogle.

"Enjoying the show, ladies?" he growls, his voice rougher than it was just a few seconds ago. "Which one of you is going to be lucky enough to patch me up after that brute made me bleed?'

They all fall over themselves as they offer their bodies up to him. Theo shoots a look back at me, silently asking me what the fuck is wrong again.

Shaking my head, I grab my shirt, but unlike him, I drag it on, covering myself up.

"What the fuck are you lot even doing here on a Sunday?" I ask once I've reluctantly climbed out of the building, allowing them to crowd me.

"Oh, you know," Misty says, her hands skimming up my chest. "Having fun, causing trouble."

"Well, my boy and I can certainly help you with that. Shall we?" Theo offers, taking off in the direction of the Chapel, making me want to turn and bolt in the opposite direction.

13

TALLY

A sense of dread sits heavy in my stomach as I climb out of my car Monday morning and head toward the imposing building. It's the reminder I don't need that I'm the underdog in my vendetta against the Heirs and everything they stand for.

But I have a game plan.

Since I can't rely on Sebastian to help me without worrying that he'll sabotage my efforts by running off and sharing my plans with the enemy, it's down to me.

I spent all day yesterday on the computer, designing some flyers to give out around school, outlining my plan in detail. I included a link to the petition on the back in hopes that some students will give my campaign a chance.

I'm not the only student here who wants to see an end to the Heirs' reign. I'm just the only one brave enough to actually stand my ground.

At least, I keep telling myself I'm brave. But I can't deny there's a part of me that knows that I'm in too deep now to stop even if I wanted to. It isn't only about knocking the Heirs off their pedestal.

It's personal.

It's about showing myself that I'm not just another sheep who bows down to their arrogance and threats.

Oakley's face pops into my mind, the memory of his body pressed up against mine. I grow all hot and needy inside, my cheeks flushing at the images.

With a small sigh of disapproval, I shake all thoughts of Oakley Beckworth out of my head and precariously balance the two big boxes of cupcakes on my arm while I grab the door. It's still quiet, the morning rush not here yet. But I wanted to get here early and set up my table.

Because the other part of my grand plan is to seduce students to the dark side—or side of social justice and moral conscience, as the case may be—with a selection of decadent cakes.

I was at it all day yesterday, baking up a storm while Mum and Dad watched on proudly. I've even added some little flags that have motivational phrases on.

Be kind.
It's good to talk.
Nothing is impossible.
You are not alone.
Laughter is good for the soul.

They're super cute and tasty. I know; I sampled each flavour.

I just hope they work. That people give my petition a chance. Because I'm going to need to find a way to drastically improve the number of signatures I have—currently standing at a measly twenty-four—if I have any hopes of the school board considering my proposal.

"Tally." Seb glances up from his desk in the student council office when I enter. "I didn't expect to see you here this early."

"I have things to do." Placing the boxes down on a table, I give him a small shrug. "What are you doing?"

"Just finishing up some coursework." He quickly closes out

of whatever program he was using and stands. "I'll get out of your hair."

He makes a beeline for the door, but I call after him. "Seb?"

"Yeah?"

"I know we're not friends, but I thought you had my back on this."

"Honestly, I should never have encouraged it." He rakes a hand through his messy, dark hair. "Nobody goes up against the Heirs and lives to tell the tale."

"But—"

"Look, Tally, just... be careful. I know we're not friends, but I've always respected you. And part of me is impressed by your determination to see this thing through. But you have to ask yourself, is it worth it? You've painted a target on your back. And—" His phone starts ringing and he digs it out of his pocket, glancing at the screen. "Sorry, I need to take this."

I nod, unsure of what else to say.

Seb disappears out of the room, and I stand there for a second, gawking after him, wondering what the hell just happened. We're supposed to be a team, determined to improve the lives for students at All Hallows'. But he's nothing more than a coward.

With a little sigh, I pull my bag onto the table and start sorting out the flyers into piles. Mr. Porter agreed to let me have a stall outside the pastoral support office. But I also plan to visit the cafeteria at lunch.

I work for the next thirty minutes, printing off some extra flyers and making a little sign for my cupcakes, all while trying to ignore the pit in my stomach. But it isn't until the corridor grows noisier and I pack up my things to go to set up my stall that I realise my bad feeling isn't about the Heirs or their minions and what they might do in retaliation.

It's about Oakley.

About seeing him again after Friday night.

The Heirs don't scare me—but he does.

Because I don't trust myself around him.

He's the first boy to get under my skin. To push my buttons. To make me want to experience things.

And that terrifies me.

"Tally." I look up to find Olivia smiling down at me. "These look great." She eyes up one of the 'be kind' cupcakes.

"Help yourself. That one's a red velvet with cream cheese frosting."

"Don't mind if I do." She snags the cupcake and gently eases away the wrapper, taking a small bite. "Mmm, so bloody good. You made all these?"

"I did."

"I'm surprised they haven't been snapped up yet."

"Oh, this is my second batch. The first went in morning break."

"That's great."

I wish I could say the same, but the truth is, the hockey team spotted my stall and descended on me like a flock of birds. When they were done, the cupcake stands were empty, but the flyer stack was untouched.

Maybe my idea to seduce the student body with sugar and frosting wasn't the master plan I'd hoped for.

"You're really going to see this thing through, huh?" Her expression turns sad, but I ignore the pang of guilt that knots my stomach.

"I am." I lift my chin in defiance. "No backing down now." My smile is so forced I know it must look wrong, but she doesn't call me out on it.

"Tally, I—"

"You don't need to say anything, Liv. I know what I signed up for. And I know you have to take their side."

"That's not... Look, I'm worried is all. I don't want you to get hurt. But if you keep up this vendetta, I won't be able to protect you."

"I'm not asking you to." I bristle.

"I know, but be careful, okay? The Heir chasers can be vicious."

She doesn't need to tell me that; I know all about Misty Dalton and her friends. Besides, it isn't fear at the mention of her name strikes up inside me. It's a different emotion entirely.

One I'll never admit out loud.

Jealousy.

The bell rings and students start rushing up and down the corridor.

"You should probably head to your next class," I suggest, needing this awkward conversation to be over.

"Yeah, okay. See you around, Tally," Liv says, and she almost sounds sad about it.

Feeling deflated, I write out a little card saying 'eat me' and leave it in front of the cupcakes with a stack of flyers before grabbing my things.

But when I turn the corner to head for the second-year lockers, I'm instantly on alert. Misty and a couple of her friends are blocking my locker, laughing about something. When they notice me, they all go eerily quiet.

"Excuse me," I say, arching a brow.

"Sorry, can we help you?" Misty twirls a strand of hair around her finger, staring at me like I'm the one in the way.

"I need to get to my locker."

"Oh, of course. My bad." She smiles sweetly, stepping aside.

Irritation rolls through me as I open my locker and—

"What the heck?"

Laughter fills the hall as I scrape the wet, sticky latex off my face. "Oh my God, is that—" Bile rushes up my throat as I peel the condom off my face and throw it on the floor, embarrassment burning through me like a wildfire.

"Why would you do that?" I cry.

"Because, Tallulah," she sneers, getting right up in my face, "you walk around All Hallows' looking down your nose at the rest of us with your holier-than-thou morals and little-miss-goody-two-shoes attitude when really, you're nothing but a Dirty. Little. Whore."

Her words rock me to my core.

"E-excuse me?" I stutter. "I am not."

"I know your secret, Tally." Her smile turns feral, victory glittering in her eyes. And for a second, panic floods me because she can't know about Oakley.

Can she?

No way he'd fess up to our stolen moments... not unless he put her up to this.

God, no.

He's cruel, but he's not vindictive.

Of course he is.

He's an Heir.

"Sebastian told us all about your dirty little secret. How you liked to get on your knees for him in the student council office and let him—"

"Seb?" I balk, rearing back. "You think me and Seb—"

"I don't think, bitch. I know. And unless you want the truth to come out, I suggest you drop the campaign and go crawl back into whatever self-righteous hole you came out of."

"He's lying."

"Oh, really? And who are people going to believe? Sebastian, an upstanding student with an impeccable academic record, or the girl stupid enough to take on the Heirs?"

"I..." My comeback dies on my lips, because she's right. No one will ever believe me over Sebastian. He has friends at All

Hallows'. People like him. And it would seem Misty has made sure to hook her claws into him.

"It's a lie," I finally choke out, aware that we've drawn a bigger audience. But so far, there's no sign of Olivia or the Heirs.

I'm not sure whether that's a good or bad thing.

"That's what they all say. Happy Monday," she smirks before walking off, her friends following.

I glance around, looking for someone to help me or intervene, but I'm met with nothing but silence.

Until a boy calls, "Better get tested; who knows where the fuck that's been." He motions to the condom splattered on the floor and explodes with laughter.

Shame washes over me as I dig a tissue out of my bag, scoop it up, and dump it in the nearest bin.

Then take off down the hall, wishing the ground would open up and swallow me whole.

14

OAKLEY

I stumble toward the locker room covered head to toe in mud with my chest heaving and my shoulders tense with frustration.

I'd hoped that a good session out with the team would have helped me blow off steam, but it's done fuck all.

The past two days.

Fuck.

"ARGH," I roar, slamming my palms down on the door, leaving muddy prints on the previously pristine paintwork.

As I crash inside, I find that the football team beat us back.

But while many might look up and acknowledge my presence, three dickheads farthest away from me are too distracted with their gossiping to notice.

"I heard it was in the music room."

"Oh fuck, I've always wanted to bang some girl on the piano."

"You're such a pussy."

"Pfft, you wouldn't be saying that if Tally let me do what she did Seb in there."

My teeth grind as they continue the gossip that's been filling the All Hallows' hallways all week.

It's bullshit. I'm sure of it.

I think.

But I can't deny that there is a little bit of doubt that I'm trying not to think about, because if Tally has been secretly sucking Seb off then...

No.

I slam those thoughts down. Nothing good can come of me wanting my cock to be the first one she tastes.

I don't realise that I'm frozen in place, glaring death at the pricks who continue to talk about her, until a hand lands on my shoulder, scaring the shit out of me.

"Something wrong, Beckworth?" Reese asks.

I shrug him off, having absolutely no desire to get into the reason I stopped right in the middle of the locker room.

With the arrival of him and Elliot and Theo, who are hot on his tail, the three wankstains finally stop their gossiping and look up.

"Let's move," Elliot demands, marching toward the showers so that we can be the first members of the team to get clean.

Reese doesn't say anything, but his curious stare burns into the side of my face as I attempt to wash the dried-on mud from my body.

The cuts and bruises Theo left me with Sunday are finally starting to fade, but the bruising around my ribs still smarts. Having practice every night this week hasn't helped. But fuck if I'm going to let it stand in my way of our next game. We're going all the way this year. Anything else is not an option.

It's not until we're done and the others descend on the showers, leaving us in peace now the football team have left, that Theo finally speaks.

"You don't really believe all that shit about Tally, do you?"

I still at his question but quickly recover before any of them notice.

"Nah, there's no way she's been blowing anyone. She's All

Hallows' biggest prude," Elliot says, making me feel a little better.

"I dunno," Reese chips in. "It's always the quiet ones that are the kinkiest. Plus, have you seen her lips?"

Before I register, I'm moving. His back crashes against the lockers opposite and a shocked grunt spills from him as I press my forearm against his throat. "What the fuck are you doing looking at any girl's lips but my sister's?" I growl, getting right in his face.

"Someone's touchy," he teases, an irritating smirk playing on his lips.

My shoulders tense up once more, my need to wipe it clean off his face almost too much to deny.

"Oak, stand the fuck down," Elliot breathes, sounding utterly exasperated.

"I'm serious," I growl, still glaring death at my best friend.

When all he does is roll his eyes, my fist curls tighter, and I'm just about to pull my arm back to make the hit when he speaks. "I love your sister, Oak. But my eyes still fucking work."

I suck in a breath. "If I ever find out that—"

Elliot grabs me from behind and drags me back. "You'll end him. We all know. You're going to be a good boy, aren't you, Reese?" Elliot says, trying to diffuse the situation.

"I guess I gotta start someday. Might as well be now."

A growl rips from my throat, but before I get to go at him again, Elliot throws me into the bench and demands I get dressed.

I do as I'm told—not because I want to follow orders like a little bitch, but because I want to be out of here before the rest of the team joins us. The last thing I need is more gossip about the previously-goody-two-shoes Tally Darlington.

Hearing it stirs something inside me. Something I really don't fucking like. But no matter what, I'm unable to ignore it.

I've watched her in school for days as the gossip around

her rolled off her shoulders. It's like nothing they do or say can touch her.

It's impressive. But surely, it's just an act.

No one, not even a prude with a stick shoved so high up her arse that she's probably forgotten it exists, wouldn't be affected by the kinds of things I've heard on students' lips this week.

The second I'm dressed, I throw my bag over my shoulder and storm toward the door without a word.

"We didn't want you to walk back with us anyway," Theo calls.

Flipping the three of them off over my shoulder, I blow out of the locker room like a storm.

"Of fucking course," I mutter as I get hit with a sheet of torrential rain.

It's been on and off all day, hence the amount of mud we were all caked in only minutes ago.

But despite the downpour, I don't pick up my pace to get back to the Chapel. Instead, I take off in the opposite direction, hoping the quiet alone time, and the soaking, will help to clear my head.

She's up in there, and she doesn't fucking belong.

There are still loads of lights on in the school buildings, but most students have either left for the night or are hauled up in their dorm rooms.

I don't see anyone as I walk the perimeter of the Orwell Building, the rainwater already soaking through my clothes and dripping from my hair that's now stuck to my brow.

I startle as I round the corner and a door opens almost right on me.

"Christ, I'm so sorry," a polite, posh, and familiar voice gasps.

I look over, and the second our eyes lock, he jumps as far away as he can, his eyes wide with fear. "I-I didn't see you there. I—"

"Is it true?" I demand, cutting off his terrified waffle.

Sebastian Howard and I have never been friends.

He's... well, Head Boy.

The perfect, conscientious student.

Although, saying that, he's not quite as perfect as Little Miss Tally. He's been to a party of ours once or twice. I've seen him with a beer in hand and a girl under his arm. So he's not a total bore, at least.

But does that mean he'd let Tally—

"I-is what true?" he asks naïvely.

There's no fucking way he doesn't know what I'm talking about. He's been the subject of this week's gossip just as much as Tally has. Only he's 'the man' who got the good girl on her knees while she's the whore who's been dishing out blowies to get him onside.

I mean, I can't deny that it stands to reason that it was the only way she could get him to agree to go up against us like he did in the beginning. I bet any benefits she previously offered have halted now he's switched sides.

"You and Tally. Is it true?"

His cheeks redden as rainwater begins to trickle down his face. "Of course it's true."

Internally, his words are like a swift kick between the legs, but I show no reaction openly. There's no fucking way I'm showing this motherfucker, or anyone in this school that I care who she's been getting on her knees for.

"Right. Do you have any evidence?" I ask coldly.

His eyes widen in surprise.

"Or have you already handed it over to the girls? Is that coming tomorrow?"

He swallows nervously. It doesn't make me feel any fucking better.

"N-no. I d-don't have any evidence."

I tsk, shaking my head. "Fucking amateur. Next time you're lucky enough to get a girl to suck your little cock, film it.

You'll thank me later." With a wink, I sidestep him and walk away.

There's somewhere else I need to be right now.

The rain doesn't subside at all after I throw myself into my car and floor it off the school grounds. I turn my music up, trying to drown out my thoughts as my wipers fly across my windscreen, trying to clear the way so I can see where I'm going.

The roads are dead, the sensible people of Saints Cross choosing to stay inside instead of battling the elements.

On any other day, I'd do the same, but my quickly growing obsession has me doing the opposite. I don't even know why I need to do this. There is just something inside me that tells me I do.

Watching her at school should be enough.

The chasers will break her eventually, I have no doubt. But to what end?

She might not be reacting, but it's still hard to watch. She's never going to win this war she's started with us. That much is obvious without going to her stupid petition site to see that she's got less than thirty backers.

I should just let it go. The chasers should let it go.

But I won't. And something tells me they won't, either. They're like a dog with a bone when they get an idea in their head.

I should know. Their wicked intentions are usually focused on us. Not that I'm complaining about the benefits that come with that attention.

The storm thankfully subsides a little by the time I turn onto the street I want. The houses lining it are nice. But they're nothing compared to the houses the four of us grew up in. I guess that's what happens when you put your morals before everything else.

Thomas Darlington could have provided a very different life for his wife and only daughter if he had chosen the right side of the law to practice.

But the self-righteous sap chose the wrong one.

Pulling up a little down the street under the cover of an old willow tree, I push my door open and make my way down toward the driveway. Both her parents' cars are missing, but there is one I don't recognise parked up next to hers.

My brows knit as I focus on the windows, trying to find out who it might be. The lights are all on, the curtains open, but there is no movement inside.

The only friends I'm aware she has are Abi, who doesn't drive to my knowledge, and my sister. And that isn't her car.

Slipping around the pristinely trimmed front bush, I stick to the shadows as I close in on the house. My heart pounds, my blood racing past my ears. I've no idea why. She's probably just in there doing her homework. I can't imagine she does anything exciting with her life.

I'm almost at the first window when the movement of shadows in the farthest one catches my eye. I still, sucking in a deep breath before the front door opens and—

Who the fuck is that?

A guy about our age steps out, but he doesn't immediately walk away. Instead, he lingers while the girl I've come to see hovers in the doorway with her hands stuffed into the pocket of her hoodie.

Unlike at school earlier, her hair is now pulled back from her face, but not neatly, more like she's thrown it up in a rush.

He steps closer, kicking my frustration up a notch before he reaches out, tucking a lock of loose hair behind her ear.

He says something to her, something intimate I'd guess from how close they are, before he closes the distance between them and drops a kiss on her cheek.

15

TALLY

Slut.
 Whore.
 Dirty tramp.

The cruel words hit my body like tiny knives, slicing into my skin, as I cut through the school corridor and slip into the student council office. The second I'm inside and close the door, I let out a weary sigh.

This week has been nothing short of a nightmare.

After Misty's prank Monday, the entire sixth form have taken it upon themselves to make my life hell.

It's never overt enough to draw the attention of the school staff—not that anyone would dare go up against the Heirs and their brand of punishment. Even Mr. Porter fears them, and he's the headteacher.

But the more the Heir chasers and their minions attack, the more determined I am to end their reign of terror.

Even if I feel emotionally and mentally drained.

The irony in all of this is I've barely even been touched by a boy. But thanks to Sebastian and his ultimate betrayal, my classmates all think I'm the kind of girl who will get on her knees in exchange for favours.

Anger boils beneath my skin. Red-hot, scorching anger. And before I realise, I'm screaming into the empty room, a shrill, blood-curdling sound that echoes around me.

The second I'm done, my body slumps against the wall, but I feel marginally better. Until my phone vibrates with an incoming message and I open the link.

"Oh God." I clap a hand over my mouth as I watch the video with my heart in my throat.

Whoever has doctored the footage has done a pretty incredible job, because the girl in the school uniform bent over the desk being spanked by whom I can only assume is supposed to be the headteacher looks... Just. Like. Me.

It's my face on another girl's body.

A *porn star's* body.

I quickly exit out of the video and squeeze my eyes shut, forcing myself to breathe. I will not cry.

I will absolutely one hundred percent not—

"Tally?" a quiet voice asks, and I look over to find Abi standing in the doorway. "Are you okay?"

"You saw it?"

"Everyone got it just now."

"I hate them. I HATE THEM," I scream, kicking the sole of my shoe against the wall over and over as I let the anger and embarrassment take over.

Abigail comes into the room and closes the door behind her. "Come here." She pulls me into her arms and holds me tight.

"Anyone who knows you knows it isn't real. They know—"

"It doesn't matter. They won't stop, Abi. They won't stop until I withdraw my petition. And I can't do it." I pull away to look at her. "I won't."

"Why is this so important to you?" she asks. "I know you've always had a bee in your bonnet about the special treatment the Heirs get, but you didn't seem to mind too much when we all hung out those few times. If something happened... you can tell me."

But I can't tell her. I can't say the words.

So I double down on my obstinance.

"Things need to change, Abi."

"Yeah, I know. But is it really worth all... this? Look at you."

I inhale a shuddering breath and force myself to smile. "I'm fine. I can handle Misty and the Heir chasers. They'll lose interest once they realise I'm not going to back down."

At least, I hope they will.

"Tally—"

"I said I'm fine." Abi flinches at my tone and guilt swarms me. "Sorry, I don't mean to take it out on you. You're a good friend, Abi. It's just been a long week."

As if the smear campaign isn't enough, I have the charity gala tonight, and Deacon refused to take no for an answer. So I'm stuck going as his date.

Yay, me.

A muted groan slips from my lips, and Abi quirks a brow.

"You don't have to worry about me, I promise." I smile brighter. Faker. More forcefully.

"I can stay, help you do whatever you're in here doing."

"It's nothing exciting. I've actually got to head home soon. I have a thing. A charity gala dinner."

"Oh, I think my dad is attending. Your mum is on the board, isn't she?"

"That's the one. It's a big deal for her and the organisation. But they're making me go as Deacon Warrick's date."

"I take it you don't like Deacon."

"You would be right."

"Ever since we were little kids, they've tried to push us together. But he's obnoxious and arrogant and cares more about himself than what's going on in the world."

"Sounds like he'd be good company for the Heirs." Abi smiles while something twists in my gut.

Because Deacon is like the Heirs. Except, he's not. At least, not like Oakley. Because Oakley—

Nope. Not going there.

Oakley is no one to me. Except a very painful, very persistent thorn in my side.

And yet, he's been suspiciously absent this week. I mean, I've seen him around school. With his friends and teammates. Surrounded by his usual harem of girls. But he's kept his distance. Which is... unexpected.

And if I'm being completely honest with myself, a little bit disappointing.

"Anyway, I need to finish up here and get home before my mum starts calling to see where I am."

"Oh okay, well if you want to get together over the weekend, you have my number." Abi offers me a weak smile before ducking out the room in a hurry.

She's a better friend than I am lately; I'm so preoccupied with the petition and my flailing campaign. But I have to see it through.

Because if there's one thing Mum and Dad didn't raise, it's a quitter.

I'm a Darlington, and we always see a project through to the end. Because standing up for what you believe in is important.

But at what cost?

"Oh my, Tallulah, sweetheart, you look... oh my." Mum clutches her chest in a rare display of emotion. It's not that my parents are unemotional, we're just not around each other enough to share the warm and fuzzies often.

"It isn't too much?" I ask, smoothing out the skirt of my midnight blue cocktail dress.

The gala is a black-tie event so we're all dressed up to the nines. Dad looks dashing in his charcoal suit and pinstripe tie, the fleck of silver matching the dress adorning Mum's backless, floor-length gown.

"Darling, it's perfect. Doesn't she look perfect, Thomas?"

"You look beautiful, sweetheart." He comes over and kisses my cheek. "All set for your big date?"

"Dad," I groan.

"I know, I know. But humour your old man, will you?"

"Fine. Just for tonight."

"Atta girl." He brushes another kiss over my cheek. "I'll check to see if the car is here."

It's a rare occasion Mum and Dad both get a night off together, but when they do, they enjoy having a drink and letting their hair down.

Not that I blame them. They both work hard. They deserve a break now and again. But it means as the drinks flow, I'll be left with Deacon for company while they enjoy their night.

"He means no harm," Mum says the second he disappears out of the room. "He just worries about you."

"Worries about me?" I frown, a trickle of unease going through me.

"Well, you're so headstrong, sweetheart. It's a quality that most young men find very intimidating." Her smile is at odds with the concern in her expression.

"I'm eighteen, Mum. Hardly past my sell by date."

"Of course you're not." She laughs—a strangled sound that does little to ease the pit in my stomach. "I know we've always encouraged you to focus on your studies, sweetheart. But it wouldn't hurt you to enjoy yourself occasionally, Tallulah."

"I enjoy life," I reply a little too defensively.

Because although I hate hearing it, she's right.

But I don't want to get out there and meet people if it means meeting people like Deacon Warrick.

"Sweetheart, you spend half your life at Dessert Island, and when you're not there, you're most likely in our kitchen baking up a storm. You're lucky you have your father's metabolism." She gives me a pointed look.

"I do other things besides bake, Mum."

"School-related activities don't count, sweetheart." Her lips twist in amusement, but before I can answer, Dad calls to say the car is here.

"Shall we?" Mum flashes me a bright smile as if she didn't just point out that I'm an eighteen-year-old student with no social life.

The car is practical but nothing flashy, a sleek black SUV with tinted windows. Dad doesn't believe in unnecessary displays of wealth and privilege—for example, owning and driving a ridiculously expensive car.

"Now, before you decide to crucify me, just hear me out, okay?" Dad's brows draw together.

"Dad..." I glance toward the SUV and back to him. "What's—"

"Tallulah, you look ravishing." Deacon steps out of the car, taking the air with him.

"But... I thought we were meeting there." I shoot my father an irritated look.

"We were, but I persuaded Thomas to let me tag along."

I want to wipe the smug smile right off Deacon's face. But I rein in my anger, aware of my parents watching my every move.

"Well, I don't appreciate being ambushed." I brush past the two of them and climb into the car, forgoing the offer of help from the driver.

"Tallulah, sweetheart." Mum follows me inside. "We can explain—"

"It's a little too late for that," I snap. "You completely ambushed me."

"You know how Deacon can be. He's a young man who knows what he wants."

"Hmm." I stare out of the tinted windows, refusing to look at her.

I hate this—hate that they're pushing this thing between me and Deacon so much.

The men climb inside, the air thick and heavy. Of course, Deacon takes the seat beside me, sitting too closely, his hand resting precariously next to my thigh. I flash him a warning look, but he only smirks back.

"Here's to a wonderful evening," Dad says, either oblivious or ignorant to the awkward atmosphere enveloping us.

"Here, here," Mum agrees, taking Dad's hand in hers and resting her head on his shoulder.

The familiar ache spreads through me as I watch them, wondering if I'll ever find that.

If I do, it certainly won't be with a boy like Deacon. But I could never have it with a boy like Oakley either.

Not that I want it with him.

But there's no denying he doesn't make my skin crawl the way Deacon does.

God, everything is so confusing.

I shouldn't be so drawn to him. He's everything I despise. Everything that's wrong with society.

Yet, he's managed to burrow his way into my mind, and now, I can't get him out.

And I'm not sure I want to.

16

OAKLEY

This is probably one of the stupidest ideas I've ever had.

But it's too late to back out now.

Standing in front of the full-length mirror in my bedroom at Dad's, I straighten my bow tie. I look and feel like a dick. I always do when I dress up like this. I'm much more at home in a rugby shirt and a pair of jeans.

But desperate times call for desperate measures and all that.

"Fucking moron," I mutter to myself.

After watching that prick brush his lips against Tally's cheek on Wednesday night, I've tried my best to smother my growing obsession with the girl I should never even look twice at. Especially now I know she's been blowing any motherfucker who could help her get a step up.

She likes to make out that she's better than the Heir chasers, but she's just as bad. The only difference is that it's not an Heir's cock she's been sucking.

But telling myself to stay away and actually doing it are two very different things, and I've found myself tailing her, watching her for some kind of reaction to the chasers' bullshit games this week. But still, I'm yet to see if she's affected.

I tried to find her the moment that most recent video landed on my—and everyone else's—phone this afternoon, but I had to head to practice, and by the time that was done it was obvious that she'd left.

So that left me with one option.

Blowing out a breath, I rearrange the products that line my dresser so nothing is out of place and walk toward my door.

I overheard Dad bitching about this event to Fiona last week when I stopped in. I didn't think anything about it then.

But now, it's all I can focus on.

Having a reason to get close to her outside of school and away from the prying eyes of the rest of the All Hallows'.

Something flutters in my stomach as I make it to the stairs. I tell myself that it's excitement, because it can't possibly be nerves.

I don't get nervous. Ever.

I look my enemy in the eyes and obliterate them without a second thought.

This enemy, though... she's proven time and time again that she's different.

Very fucking different.

Dad's deep voice rumbles up as I descend. It's not until I'm halfway down that I feel eyes on me. Looking up, I find both of them dressed to the nines with their eyes narrowed in suspicion.

"Son, I didn't know you were here," Dad says. "Are you... are you coming with us?"

"Yep," I say confidently. "I thought it would be a good opportunity to network."

Following in my father's footsteps to become a defence lawyer has been my fate since before I was born. It's Dad's dream to have me join the firm and build the Beckworth legacy, and thankfully, I want it too.

And I'm hoping that's enough for them to allow me to tag along to this event.

Dad nods and I release a small, relieved breath.

Looking at Fiona, I take in her deep red dress that matches Dad's pocket square perfectly. "You look beautiful," I tell her honestly.

"Aw, thank you, sweetie. You brush up pretty good yourself. Do you have a date for tonight?" she asks with hope shining in her eyes.

Now that my sister has a serious boyfriend, they seem to have turned their expectations on me.

"No. I'm flying solo," I state, marching toward the door in the hope of ending this line of conversation.

"Do we really have to go?" Dad asks behind me like a petulant child. "I can think of so many better things we could do tonight than be forced to network with the likes of Darlington."

Oh, I don't know, Dad. Fraternising with the enemy seems like a great way to spend the evening.

"Oh, stop sulking, Christian." I march out of the house just as she suggests doing something to make it worth his while later.

Gross.

I climb into the front of the black Range Rover, leaving the back for the lovebirds.

"Good evening," the driver greets. When I glance over, his eyes are a little wide in shock. I guess he was only expecting two guests tonight.

"Change of plans. You're okay with an extra one, right?" I ask, buckling my seat belt as if he's already agreed.

Before he gets a chance to answer, Dad and Fiona climb into the back. Dad immediately starts making small talk with the man beside me as if he wasn't on the verge of a temper tantrum about going tonight.

His ability to read his audience and work the crowd is as

inspiring as it is terrifying. Fuck being on the wrong end of him in a courtroom when he can turn it on and off like that.

It really is no wonder that he's so successful.

Dad and Fiona talk the whole way to the hotel hosting tonight's Restorative Justice Gala. I quickly zone them out in favour of thinking about what the night ahead might hold.

When I first overheard Dad and Fiona talking about this event, he was adamant he wasn't going, so I can only hope that's going to work in my favour and that Tally won't be expecting to see me.

That means I'll have the element of surprise, and with her out of her comfort zone, well... anything could happen.

Those flutters in my belly increase. Yeah, definitely excitement.

Reaching down, I tug at my slim-fit trousers, giving my swelling cock a little bit more space. Just the image of her wide, unnerved eyes and her stunned parted lips gets me going.

There is something fucking wrong with me.

The second we pull up at the front of the hotel, I push the door open and jump out, leaving the driver to deal with my dad and Fiona.

I hover, waiting for them while anticipation zaps through my veins.

Is she already here? Will I walk in and find her smiling and playing her part of the perfect Darlington heir?

But what I don't know is if she's coming alone. That thought squashes some of my previous excitement.

The prospect of her in there with someone else's hands on her body, that prick from the other night maybe, has something I'm not used to feeling stirring within me.

Jealousy.

Fuck. I shouldn't be jealous of anyone being near that traitorous bitch.

But I am.

"Oakley," Dad calls, dragging me from my toxic thoughts.

He nods toward the entrance where there are servers standing with trays of champagne, and I diligently fall into step behind him and Fiona, snagging two glasses as I pass.

The first one I down when no one is watching, needing something to take the edge off, discarding the empty as quickly as I selected it before sipping on the other. I can't help but smirk as I follow them down to the main banquet hall where they're going to be serving dinner tonight. It's instantly obvious that no one was expecting him.

Eyes widen and brows are lifted as colleagues and enemies alike greet him and Fiona like they're long-lost friends.

Many turn to me, bringing me into the conversation as if I already work for my father. It's something I'm usually grateful for. I've never really been made to feel like a child, or anything less than a future leader of this town. But tonight, I have something much more important to think about. I just hope that I make the right noises when they ask me questions, because I'm too busy scanning the area, the sea of faces to find the one I came here for.

"Anderson will be pleased to see you," I catch the man who's just grasped my father's hand say. "He's right over there, talking to Darlington."

I don't miss the way Dad's jaw tenses as Tally's father is mentioned.

It's always been the same. From as early as I can remember, the name Darlington was akin to a swear word in our house. Tally and I were always destined to be on opposite sides. I just never thought it would end up like this. With her trying to bring us down in a way no other has tried before.

"Fantastic," Dad grits out, releasing the man's hand. "It's been too long since I've caught up with him. We'll get a drink later, yes?" Dad says before pressing his hand into the small of Fiona's back and gently pushing her forward, toward the exact place I want to be.

The second we round the corner that reveals Thomas

Darlington talking to the man Dad actually wants to speak to, my eyes land on a young woman wrapped in a midnight blue dress. It's cut low enough to give me just a taste of what is usually hiding behind her pristine school uniform, and fuck if it doesn't make my mouth water.

Dad and Fiona surge forward, greeting Richard Anderson, and while Fiona politely smiles at Thomas and Katherine, Dad pointedly ignores their existence.

There's a part of me that wants to witness the standoff between them, but only a small part, because every other inch of me is purely focused on the girl before me.

"Tallulah, I wasn't expecting to see you here tonight. Thought you'd be at home working on your campaign."

"I have everything under control. Thanks for your concern," she says tersely, although the heat that rises on her cheeks gives away that she's not feeling as cool as she would like me to believe. "Excuse me, my date is waiting for me," she says, lifting her chin in defiance, her eyes locked on someone over my shoulder.

She takes off, attempting to sidestep me, but she's not fast enough.

My fingers close around her forearm, bringing her to a stop beside me as I lower my mouth to her ear. "Does he know what a filthy whore you really are, Prim? Or is that why he's here with you? Because you convinced him the best way you know how—by getting on your knees."

Her entire body jolts at my accusation and she sucks in a deep breath. But just like everything else, she lets it roll off her back.

"Excuse me. Enjoy your night."

"Oh, Prim. I fully intend to." I loosen my grip to allow her to think I'm going to release her. And just as she takes a step forward, I tighten it once more. "A little advice," I murmur. "Get rid of the lap dog."

"Or what?" she hisses.

"Defy me and find out." My lip curls. "I dare you."

17

TALLY

Oakley is here.

He isn't supposed to be here.

The second I noticed him swaggering toward me, my heart sank. He had that look. The one where I know I'm in trouble. But instead of dread, a dark thrill raced through me.

The complete opposite feeling to when I saw Deacon climb out of the car.

I still haven't forgiven my dad. But the free champagne is helping a little.

"Tally, come and meet Kieran." Deacon beckons me over, and I internally groan.

For a second, I imagine telling him no. But I know better than to make a scene at such a prestigious event. Everyone who is everyone in Saints Cross and the surrounding towns is here. Including Oakley, his dad, and his stepmum, apparently.

I risk peeking over at them as Christian Beckworth holds court with a group of men and women, including my father.

It's no secret that there's no love lost between the two of them, but tonight is about raising money for children in care, a cause everyone can agree on.

CRUEL DEVIOUS HEIR: PART ONE

"Tallulah," Deacon hisses, demanding my attention.

"Sorry." I force a smile, moving closer to him.

"It's okay, babe." He hooks an arm around my waist and pulls me into his side a little too possessively. Spiders crawl under my skin at his close proximity.

Deacon has been handsy all night, using any excuse to touch me. It hasn't gone unnoticed by Oakley either, his intense stare following me around the room. His warning ringing in my mind.

Defy me... I dare you.

His eyes snap in our direction, homing in on where Deacon's fingers dig into my waist, and pure rage swirls in his eyes.

A burst of heat rolls through me.

Deacon looks at me like I'm a prize to be won, a thing to be conquered. But Oakley...

Oakley looks at me like I'm the most beautiful girl he's ever seen. Like he wants to possess every inch of me.

It's disarming, the way he affects me so much.

I haven't heard a single thing Deacon has said, so when he asks me what I think, I press my lips together and smile, hoping it'll appease him.

"I knew you'd love it," he says brightly. "Oh good, I think they're serving dinner."

Deacon takes my hand and leads me toward the banquet hall, checking the table plan on his way by. "I could eat a fucking horse. I'm ravenous." He leers at me as if he's imagining I'm his meal.

Gross.

"Darling, over here." Mom signals us to a table near the edge of the room.

At least we're not directly in front of the stage.

"How are you enjoying the gala, sweetheart?" she asks, tight-lipped as I slip out of Deacon's hold.

"It's—"

"I had to switch the table plan. I'm sorry, but I needed to keep your father away from Christian."

"What are you talking about?"

"Just play nice, okay? For your father's sake."

I'm about to ask her what she means when Oakley and his father approach our table.

No.

No. No. No. No.

"Looks like we're table mates." Oakley grins at me like the cat who got the cream.

"Actually, Beckworth, she's with me." Deacon slides his arm around my waist in a disgusting display of ownership.

"Sorry, do I know you?"

"No, but I know you."

"Okay, boys," Mum lets out a strangled laugh, "let's all play nice."

Deacon guides me away from Oakley, but Oakley follows, beating Deacon to my chair. "Tallulah," he purrs, motioning for me to sit.

Deacon scoffs, taking his own seat. I didn't miss the way he tried to loosen his collar, and I suppress a smile.

"Something funny, Prim?" Oakley leans in, his words a secretive whisper meant only for my ears.

"Back. Off," I hiss, hitching my chair away a little. Deacon notices though, flashing me a wolfish grin.

Dear Lord.

This is going to be torture.

I try to catch my parents' attention across the big round table, but they're too busy talking to the couple next to them, completely ignoring Christian Beckworth and Fiona Brown's presence. I've watched her tonight, working the room. Everyone loves her. It's hard to imagine her as Reese's mum. Unless his attention is focused on Liv, he's all thunder and storm clouds whereas Fiona is sunshine and smiles.

Thankfully, the host for the evening—my mum's good

friend Rachel—formally welcomes everyone to the gala and introduces dinner. An army of servers descends on the room, and before I know it, a plate of salad is placed in front of me.

I poke at the roasted figs and goat's cheese.

"Don't play with it." Deacon has the nerve to squeeze my knee. "Eat it."

"Please don't touch me." I grab his hand under the table and shove it away, giving him a forced smile.

"We need to give them what they want." He nods toward our parents, who are laughing at something Mr. Warrick just said.

"Not sure you know how to give a girl like Tallulah what she wants." Oakley cranes around me to wink at Deacon.

"Nobody asked you, Beckworth. Why don't you go find some sad, lonely widow to entertain? You know, I've heard the stories about the infamous All Hallows' Heirs. Apparently, you'll fuck anything if the price is right."

"Deacon!" I whisper-shriek.

"Relax, Prim." Oakley slides his hand under the table and grips my other knee. But instead of making my skin crawl, his touch makes my breath catch in my throat.

My eyes flash to his and he simply smirks before one-handedly eating his salad.

"Mmm, this is good." He expertly finds the slit in my dress and closes his hand around my leg, letting his pinky brush the inside of my thigh. A shiver rolls through me, but I try my best to focus on the food in front of me, the conversation going on around us.

"So, Declan, was it?"

"Deacon." My date shifts uncomfortably beside me. His hand drops to my thigh, but I glare right at him, and he gets the message, pulling at his tie again instead.

"Son, everything okay with your salad?" Mr. Warrick asks.

"Sure, Dad," he mumbles.

"And Tallulah, dear, is everything to your satisfaction?"

"Yes, thank—"

Oakley's hand slips higher, my legs falling open to grant him access of their own volition.

God, he has such a hold on me—my body.

"Tallulah?"

"Everything's perfect, thank you." I smile, almost choking on air when Oakley's finger brushes the edge of my knickers.

All while he eats his food like he doesn't have his hand up my dress.

But I don't stop him.

The truth is, I don't want to. And part of me knows, if I try to, he'll only find a way to make this oh so much worse. So I sit here, letting him touch me and tease, his fingers drawing lazy circles on my underwear, making my stomach tense and tighten.

Deacon tries to engage me in conversation, but I can barely think let alone talk, my fingers curled around the edge of my seat as desire and lust flood every cell in my body.

I want more.

So much more.

But this can't happen. Not here, and certainly not now.

"Oak—"

"Your plate, madam." A server appears out of nowhere, leaning over my shoulder to get access to my barely touched salad.

"What a waste." Deacon tsks. "I could have eaten that if you'd have told me."

"Your date is an arsehole," Oakley murmurs out the side of his mouth.

"Your hand is in places it shouldn't be."

"You love it, don't pretend otherwise. I bet if I dipped my fingers inside, you'd be wet for me."

His crass words make me gasp and everyone looks over at me. "I thought I saw a spider." I grab my napkin and waft it across the table as if I'm searching for an uninvited guest.

"Tallulah, please," Mum warns, and I mouth an apology, lowering my head.

The man sitting on Deacon's left asks him a question and Oakley uses it to his advantage, leaning in closer.

"You really should be more careful, Prim. Unless you want everyone around the table to know what a dirty little whore you really are."

"I'm not—"

"Ah, ah, ah. You shouldn't lie to me, baby. Liars always get caught, and then they get punished." He presses his thumb down hard on my clit and I almost buck off the chair, pleasure shooting through the very core of me.

"Excuse me," I blurt, pushing his hand away. "I need to use the bathroom."

I get up without looking at anyone and hurry out of the room, toward the women's bathroom.

What the hell was I thinking, letting Oakley touch me like that in the middle of dinner? With my parents and Deacon right there?

Except, I wasn't thinking. Because the moment he sat down beside me, all other thoughts drifted out of my mind.

I am so screwed.

The hallway outside the main room is empty, so I slow my pace, trying to catch my breath. But I'm too wired, too confused by the wild thoughts running through my head. The anger that he believes the rumours about me circulating All Hallows'.

I'm not that girl.

I'm not—

"Running away so soon?"

"Oakley." I whirl around on him, frowning when I see the state of his shirt. "What happened to you?"

He stalks toward me. Slow, purposeful strides like a hunter stalking its prey. Only, part of me wants to be caught, to keep playing this game of cat and mouse.

"Some silly little waitress spilled champagne all down me." His eyes glint with mischief as he reaches me. "You should probably come and help me clean up."

Grabbing my wrists, he all but yanks me down the hall and pulls me into a room at the end.

"This... this isn't the bathroom," I say.

"No shit." He drags a hand through his hair, eyes wild with something I can't quite decipher.

"Oakley?" I whisper. Because he's scaring me.

I'm scaring me.

"Did you let him touch you?" He wraps his hand around my throat and pins me against the wall. But he isn't rough. If anything, his touch is reverent as he stares down at me.

"What do you think?" The words tumble out.

"Honestly, after some of the shit I've heard this week, I wouldn't be surprised."

His words are like shrapnel, slicing me open, and I thrash against his hold. "Let me go. Let me go right now."

"Easy, Prim. Easy." He flattens his body against mine, caging me in. "Feisty little thing when you want to be, aren't you?"

"You haven't seen anything," I say through gritted teeth, but he only laughs.

"He wants you."

"Too bad I don't want him."

"No?" Oakley's brow arches at that tidbit.

"He's not my type."

"And who is your type? That drip Sebastian Howard?"

"Why do you care?"

"I don't. At least, I shouldn't. But..." He trails off, leaving me desperate to know what he was going to say.

"Remember what I said earlier?"

"When?"

"Don't push me, Prim. You won't like the consequences."

I narrow my eyes, my heart a wild beating thing in my

chest. "They'll come looking for me," I breathe, the air taut between us.

One of his hands leaves the wall and slides down my spine to squeeze my bottom. A burst of heat explodes inside me, and Oakley smirks.

"Then we'd better make it quick."

18

OAKLEY

My heart is pounding like a bass drum as I stare down at Tally.

She's totally at my mercy with my hand wrapped around her throat. Her large blue eyes stare up at me, giving me the image of pure innocence. An innocence I still can't decide is real or not.

Is it all lies to rile her up? Or has she really been sucking Seb off any chance she gets?

I guess there really is only one way to tell.

But not yet.

Despite how painfully fucking hard I've been since the moment she accepted my touch at the table, my cock isn't my main focus right now.

It's her.

It's always fucking her.

I need to know just how wet she is for me.

Her wanton moan rips through the air as I squeeze her arse, dragging her into my body and allowing her to feel what she does to me.

I hate her. I always have. Yet she gets me harder than anyone else I've ever met.

It's a head fuck.

But it's just sex.

I've never really cared for anyone I've stuck it in in the past, so why should Tallulah Darlington be any different?

Take what I need, rip that stick from her arse, and then walk away.

It should be easy enough. I've done it time and time again. Okay, so maybe not the stick thing. The girls who usually get this close to me don't have many morals.

"You feel that?" I groan, tucking my face into her exposed neck and sucking in a deep breath of her. I grind my hips, ensuring my length presses against her stomach.

"Oakley."

Fuck. The way she moans my name makes it weep for more.

Why her?

Why fucking Tallulah?

And now?

This is the worst possible time for me to want this.

Or is it...

It could be the best.

This could be the best fucking thing that's happened to us since she stood up on that stage and announced her campaign.

I'm making her weak. That much is more than obvious.

I wonder what else I can get her to do.

Releasing her insane arse, I run my hand down the soft fabric of her dress covering her thigh until I find the split that so helpfully allowed me entry at the table.

"Oh God," she whimpers when my fingers collide with the soft, tempting skin of her inner thigh. "We can't, Oakley. You can't—"

A deep chuckle falls from my lips. The vibrations of it makes her shudder against me.

"It's funny that you think being told I shouldn't do something will stop me. When I want something, I have it."

"Arrogant mo—"

"Careful, Tallulah. You wouldn't want to ruin your good girl image by swearing," I tease, remembering the last time we had a similar conversation. "What were you about to say? Moron? Come on, you can do better than that."

"I hate you," she hisses right before my fingers find the edge of her knickers.

"I've got to say, I'm surprised," I confess, finally pulling my face from her neck in favour of studying her.

Her eyes narrow in contempt, but at no point does she stop me as I tease her.

"From everything I've heard this week. I didn't think you'd be wearing any of these. It's much easier access without," I taunt.

"Prick," she breathes.

"Better, I guess," I praise, watching her eyes dilate and her chest heave.

Her dress is strapless, and I can't help but wonder just how easy it would be to tug the fabric down and reveal what's hiding beneath.

But before I get lost in thoughts of her tits, I push the damp fabric to the side and finally discover the truth behind what I haven't been able to stop thinking about.

"Fuck, Prim. You're soaked for me."

"I-it's... it's a natural bodily reaction to touch," she tries to argue.

"Sure, it is," I drawl. "I think it's me. You like to claim that you're better than all the girls who follow us around at school, desperate to get the chance to bounce around on our dicks. But really, you want exactly the same. Don't you, Prim?"

"No," she cries, shaking her head violently from side to side in her pathetic attempt to defy me.

Leaning forward, I let my lips brush against her ear. "Lying little whore."

On the final word, I spear one finger inside her tight

cunt. She cries out at the invasion at the same time a deep rumble erupts from my throat.

Fuck me, she's tight.

"Oakley," she gasps as I curl the digit that's now knuckle deep inside her.

Pulling back so I can watch her, I begin to finger fuck her harder. "Baby," I breathe, studying her darkening blue eyes, "you're running down my hand. Is that how badly you really want me?"

She whimpers, and it makes me damn near desperate to bend her over the table on the other side of this office I dragged her into and fuck her until I've got her out of my system.

With any other girl, I would. But there's something different with Tally.

The chase.

It's addictive.

The high is almost as good as I'm sure it will be when I finally slide inside her, ruining both her body and her plans to destroy the Heirs' reign over All Hallows'.

"Oh my God," she cries, her pussy clamping down so hard on my finger it makes my eyes want to cross.

She's going to feel phenomenal.

Her eyes widen as her release approaches. She looks... shocked, almost.

Well, I guess I am pretty good.

"Are you going to come for me, Prim? The goody-two-shoes Head Girl of All Hallows', handing herself over to an Heir? Who'd have thought it?"

She's too far gone to respond; instead, her eyes flutter closed as she prepares to fall.

"No," I bark. "Look at me. I want you to know exactly who's doing this to you."

Reluctantly, her heavy lids open.

"Good girl," I praise before reality comes crashing down.

"Tallulah?" a deep, familiarly cuntish voice says from outside the door.

I'm sure that Tally's eyes widen almost to the point of pain as Deacon's voice registers in her head.

"Oh my God. Stop," she demands, clawing at my arm to try and drag me from inside her.

I can't help but chuckle at her panic. "What do you think he'd do if he walked in and found me knuckle deep in your pussy?"

"Oakley, this isn't funny," she snaps.

"Oh, but it is."

I wait a beat, watching as her chest heaves and her increased breaths rush over my face. But then I give in and pull my finger from her.

"How do you think you taste?" I ask, holding my hand up between us.

If I thought her cheeks were red before, then it's nothing compared to the colour they turn when I ask that question.

"You want to—" I offer my finger up to her and she rears back.

"Fine. I guess it's all mine. But one day, Tally, one day very soon, you'll be tasting yourself as you clean my dick up after you come all over it."

Pushing my finger into my mouth, I lap at it as her taste explodes on my tongue.

Fuck. This was a mistake.

She watches me with confused yet hungry eyes as I savour her.

Pulling it free, I make a show of licking my lips as Deacon calls out again. "Delicious. I'll look forward to my next taste. Enjoy the rest of your night, Tallulah. You might want to take a few moments before walking back out there."

As I study her reddened cheeks and chest, and look into her dark, desire-filled eyes, I realise my biggest mistake.

I didn't kiss her.

I could have sent her back out there with swollen lips and ruined make-up.

Next time, I promise myself as I take a step back, allowing her to see me rearranging myself.

She gasps, my hard-on more than obvious behind the fabric of my trousers.

"See you soon, Tallulah. Be a good girl now. You won't like what happens if I find out you've got on your knees for that prick as well as Seb."

Her erratic breathing fills my ears until I slip out of the room and close the door behind me.

Deacon is at the other end of the hallway, opening each door and looking inside for his missing date. A wicked chuckle tumbles from my lips as I push into the men's toilets without him ever seeing me.

Thankfully, it's empty.

I make my way to the final cubicle that lines the wall and lock myself inside.

Tally isn't the only one who needs to take a minute after that. Fuck, I'm pretty sure I was gonna come just from watching her fall. It was like I was a pre-teen again and unable to control myself.

She was beautiful. So fucking beautiful.

And such a fucking traitor.

I give myself a few minutes to let my body calm down before I exit the small space, reluctantly wash her scent from my fingers, and rejoin the evening.

Thankfully, my shirt is now dry of the champagne the server didn't have a choice but to spill on me when I knocked her hand.

I needed an excuse to follow Tally, and that was all I could come up with at short notice.

Poor bitch looked horrified, and she's probably already been sacked. But fuck it. I'm sure she's got better things to be doing with her Friday night than serving all these rich, pretentious fuckers.

Dessert is being served as I walk around the perimeter of the room, my eyes locked on the table I was previously sitting at.

I don't return. Instead, I tell a server that I'll take my dessert at the bar before finding myself a seat in the shadows that allows me full view of the room before me.

I throw back a glass of whisky the second the bartender places it in front of me. The moment the glass touches the polished wood before me, a shiver of awareness runs down my spine.

Twisting around, I find exactly what I was expecting. Deacon is leading Tally across the room with his hand on the small of her back. She doesn't look up; instead, her eyes are locked on the luxury carpet at her feet.

A smirk widens across my face as I think about what she might have said to him if he found her hiding in that office.

I can guarantee that it wasn't the fucking truth.

They re-take their seats and are immediately dragged into some bullshit conversation. The second she realises that everyone's distracted, she discreetly glances over her shoulder. Well, I can only assume she thinks she's being discreet. Truth is, I see it all.

Her shoulders are pulled tight, her back ramrod straight as she ignores another plate of food in front of her.

She never finds me, and it only irritates her more.

Can she feel me watching her?

I sure fucking hope so.

I don't move from my hiding place in the shadows all night, and by some small miracle, no one comes to talk to me. It's perfect. I'm a ghost watching as Tally spends the rest of the evening pushing all of Deacon's advances away.

Oakley: one.

Deacon: nil.

Everything is playing out perfectly until the lights lower, the music gets louder, and couples begin descending on the dance floor.

The second he wraps his arm around her waist and guides her in the same direction, my grip on the glass in my hand tightens until I'm sure it's about to shatter.

She doesn't even fight him as he pulls her into his body and begins moving with her.

Anger and jealousy bubble up inside me to the point that I know I'm going to do something stupid if I stay here watching.

Throwing back my drink, I slip out of one of the side doors and leave the gala behind.

I can think of better ways of ending my night than watching that prick man handle what's mine.

19

TALLY

I feel Oakley watching me.

Watching us.

Deacon's touch makes my stomach dance with disgust, but I don't resist. Because the truth is, I need a minute.

After Oakley touched me in that empty office, I need a minute to sort through the confusing thoughts spinning in my head.

He touched me.

And I liked it.

God, I really liked it. And then he stopped and left me feeling restless and needy.

What is wrong with me?

I bury my face in Deacon's shoulder, hiding from Oakley's intense stare. But I realise my mistake the second Deacon wraps his arm around my waist and pulls me closer, whispering in my ear. "I knew you'd come around eventually," he drawls, sending a shudder through me.

"It's just one dance," I remind him, lifting my head to meet his hungry gaze.

"We'll see," he replies smugly, a wicked glint in his eye. As if this—us—is a foregone conclusion.

CRUEL DEVIOUS HEIR: PART ONE

I glance away, refusing to verbally spar with him. Being around Deacon only makes my blood boil, unlike Oakley, who makes my blood sing.

God, I'm a mess. And all the champagne hasn't helped my thought processes any.

"I-I want to go home," I blurt out, much to Deacon's confusion.

"It's still early," he says.

"So? I'm leaving." Pulling away from him, I'm hardly surprised when he grabs my hands and leads me over to where our parents are drinking and talking.

"Oh, Tallulah, there you are." Mum smiles, a glassy look in her eyes as she nestles into my father's side. "Isn't the party fun?"

"Fun, sure, Mum."

"Actually, Mrs. Darlington, Tally isn't feeling so good, so I offered to make sure she gets home okay."

"Such a gentleman," his mother coos, looking proud as punch.

"Of course you should accompany her, Son," Mr. Warrick adds.

"Oh, no, I'll be—"

"Tallulah." Mum smiles again, her silent message clear. *Let him do this.*

Unbelievable.

"Whatever, I'm leaving."

"Don't wait up, sweetheart. The Warricks have invited us back for drinks later."

With gritted teeth, I murmur goodbye and hurry away from them before I do or say something unbecoming for their precious, perfect, amenable daughter.

My gaze drifts over to the bar, but Oakley is long gone.

My stomach sinks.

But what did I really expect?

For him to claim me in front of our families and all their friends.

Our fathers are courtroom enemies. Pitted against each other in their professional and personal lives.

Which makes Oakley my enemy.

My nemesis.

The boy I want to knock off his All Hallows' Heir pedestal.

The boy that infuriates me.

But he's also the boy who ignites a wildfire inside me.

Deacon catches up to me in the foyer, phone in hand. "The car is just coming around."

"You don't have to come with me."

"I want to." He takes a step toward me. "I know you think we're not compatible, Tally..." His fingers glide along my cheekbone. "But just imagine it. The two of us, taking on the world. We'd make the perfect power couple."

"Don't." I shove his hand away and march toward the door, his amused chuckle following me.

It's cold out, goosebumps skittering over my skin as I hurry down the steps to the waiting car. The driver nods, opening the back door. For a second, I think Deacon has given up, but he emerges from the building looking every bit the pretentious idiot he is.

Maybe I should have let him discover me and Oakley earlier. I can only imagine the look on his face, but it would have given him too much leverage over me. Because knowledge is power to boys like Deacon. Especially ones used to getting their own way.

I wouldn't put it past him to play dirty to get what he wants—me.

Before I can climb into the car, he snags my hand and draws me into his chest, staring down at me. "This play-hard-to-get act you've got going on only makes the chase that much sweeter."

"It's not a game, Deacon. I'm not interested in you like that."

"You know, I've heard some rumours coming out of All Hallows' this week." He plucks a loose strand of hair off my face and toys with it. "Rumours about you, Tallulah. About how you're not the prim and proper girl you claim to be."

"It's a smear campaign," I reply, trying to keep my cool despite the quickening of my heart. "Are you... keeping tabs on me?" I tack on, concerned that he knows.

The students of All Hallows' enjoy their fair share of scandal, but the majority of incidents remain off the record, kept within the walls of the old buildings. So the fact that Deacon has heard a bunch of school hall gossip is concerning to say the least.

"I wouldn't exactly call it keeping tabs on you, but I called in a few favours with some friends at AH."

"That's..." I resist the urge to snap at him, rolling back my shoulders. "I would prefer it if you didn't spy on me, Deacon. It's a gross invasion of my privacy and something I'm sure my parents wouldn't take too kindly to."

"Oh, I don't know. Maybe they'd appreciate me looking out for you. Especially if you've taken to making some bad decisions."

"Deacon..."

"Tallulah." He smirks, and I want to throw something at him. He's so infuriating.

I refuse to look at him for the rest of the journey, staring out of the window as the town rolls by. It isn't until the driver pulls up outside my house that I finally address him.

"Thank you for escorting me home, Deacon. I can see myself in."

"Don't be ridiculous. I can make sure you get in okay."

"I am quite capable of letting myself into my house. Driver," I call, "please take Mr. Warrick wherever he wishes to go."

"Tallulah," Deacon warns, grabbing my arm hard enough to make me wince.

"Take your hand off me," I hiss.

"You're playing a dangerous game," he drawls, removing his hand the second the door swings open to reveal the driver.

"Goodnight, Deacon." I climb out and walk away from him with my head held high, refusing to let him see how shaken up I am.

And I don't look back until I'm inside the house with the door locked.

It's been an hour since I got home, and I can't settle. Deacon's threat lingers in the back of my mind. He could have easily pushed the subject tonight, made me buy his silence. He didn't, and part of me is relieved, but the other part can't help but wonder what his motives are.

After changing into some fresh pyjama shorts and a camisole, I go downstairs to make myself a hot chocolate. I'm too restless to sleep, that lingering needy ache still deep inside me, all thanks to Oakley's touch.

"Ugh," I groan as I sprinkle a handful of mini marshmallows onto my hot chocolate, watching them melt slowly.

It's a Saturday night, I'm eighteen years old, and I'm home alone in my pyjamas, drinking hot chocolate by eleven p.m.

Maybe everyone has a point. Maybe I really do need to get out more. But it's not like I have anywhere to go or anyone to call. I've dedicated my entire life to being the good girl. The girl more interested in social justice and doing the right thing than living her own life. And I'm proud of everything I've accomplished, I am. But I'm also—

A noise beyond the back door catches my attention, and my heart catapults into my throat.

CRUEL DEVIOUS HEIR: PART ONE

Grabbing my phone off the worktop, I move over to the window and peer out into the darkness. The security light hasn't come on, so it's probably nothing, but it doesn't stop the pit of dread growing in my stomach.

I check the lock, relief blasting through me when I find it engaged. I'm safe. I have my phone and a whole heap of kitchen knives at my disposal. Not to mention we live on a street with some of the nosiest neighbours in Saints Cross.

Shrugging off the eerie sensation, I turn around to head back to my hot chocolate. But a louder noise stops me dead in my tracks, my heart lurching. I should dial 999 and run and hide somewhere. But something inside me forces me to turn around.

"I'm calling the police," I yell into the empty house, my fingers hovering over the illuminated screen. "Unless you want to end up in the back of a police car, I suggest you run." I press the numbers, blood roaring in my ears.

Run, stupid girl. Run.

I don't know if it's being trapped in that office with Oakley or being trapped with Deacon in the car, but something in me refuses to back down. This is my house. The one place I should feel safe.

The one place I am safe.

"Last chance. I'm—"

A palm slams against the glass panel, scaring the life out of me. A startled shriek spills from my lips as a face comes into view.

"Oakley?" I cry.

He glares at me through the door like a psychopath, his eyes burning with contempt.

"What the hell are you doing?" Without thinking, I rush over to the door, unlock it, and yank it open. "What the—"

He steps forward, forcing me backward.

"Oakley," I breathe, "what are you doing here? You can't—"

"Did you fuck him?"

"E-excuse me?"

"Deacon. Did you let him come back here and fuck you? Did you use him to get back at me?" He closes the distance between us, crowding me against the breakfast island. My back hits the edge of the worktop and I yelp.

"Have you lost your mind? What the hell are you doing lurking about in my garden?"

"Did. You. Fuck. Him?" He wraps his hand around my throat.

"So what if I did, huh? What are you"—I jab his chest despite his vicious grip on me—"going"—jab—"to do"—jab—"about it?"

"Fuck," he grits out. "*Fuck!*"

Oakley releases me and steps back, dragging a hand through his hair. He looks wild and unpredictable, his pupils blown wide with anger and... jealousy?

"This wasn't supposed to happen." He practically growls the words. "You weren't supposed to worm your way inside, Prim."

"What are you talking about?"

"You're fucking in here." He taps his head. "Seeing that fucker with his hands all over you drove me crazy. Hearing the shit people have been saying all week about you and Howard..."

"I'm just a whore, remember?" I spit at him. "Why would you care about someone like me?"

He stares at me, the air crackling between us. He steps toward me, but my hand flies out. "Wait. Why are you here, Oakley?"

I need him to say it.

I need him to say that he feels this strange thing between us.

"Why?" He smirks. A cruel, wicked tilt of his mouth that

makes my stomach tighten. "I'm here to finish what we started."

Oh God.

Heat envelops me, burning me from the inside out.

"Oakley..." I don't know whether I'm warning him to stop or begging him to continue. All I know is whatever he sees in my expression delights him as his eyes sparkle with mischief.

"Now, Prim. Are you going to be a good girl and show me where your bedroom is?" He steps closer still, taking the air with him. "Or do I have to beg?"

20

OAKLEY

My heart races as I stand there still staring at Tally as she tries to decipher the ultimatum I've just given her.

I have no idea if she's figured it out yet, but neither option involves me walking back out the way I came.

I know her parents are still out—I heard them making plans. Almost in as much detail as I heard Deacon's friends discussing what his plans were for the night.

My fists curl as I replay the bet they all made about that prick ending up inside Tally's knickers.

A couple refused to take the wager, but it soon became obvious that was only because they hadn't heard the gossip coming out of All Hallows' this week. The ones who had been fully backing Deacon to finally get a taste of the girl who teases him relentlessly were fully aware of her quickly diminishing reputation as the good girl.

There was one thing they weren't aware of while shaking hands over that bullshit bet.

Me.

There was no fucking way on this Earth was I ever letting that motherfucker finish off what we started earlier.

CRUEL DEVIOUS HEIR: PART ONE

Hell fucking no.

The only person who gets to watch as she falls over the edge is me.

I'll be the one tasting her, making her cry out my name as I show her exactly the reason I have the reputation I do.

Her arms cross across her chest. If she's trying to hide the fact her cami is almost see-through then she does a really shitty job, because her arms make her tits lift, tempting me even more than just seeing her rosy nipples behind the satin.

She pops her hip, giving me all the sass that she usually hides behind her uniform and good-girl persona.

I fucking love that I get to see it.

I just fucking hate that Howard, and whoever else, might have also seen this side of her.

The level of jealousy that stirs in my stomach makes me almost violent.

Howard boards. I know exactly where his dorm is, and the temptation to go and visit in the middle of the night and make him forget that Tally even exists is fucking strong.

Not strong enough to walk away from her right now, though.

"Make a decision, Prim," I tease, forcing a smile onto my lips as I close the space between us.

She's pinned against the counter, stopping her from running.

Dipping my head, I run my nose along the edge of her jaw until my lips are at her ear. "I have no problem getting on my knees and begging, Tallulah. Just say the word and I'll lay you out on this counter, drag these sinful little shorts down your legs, and eat you until you're screaming my name."

Her breath catches before a whimper rumbles deep in her throat.

"You like that, don't you, Prim? You like listening to me tell you what I'm going to do."

"Oakley." If it was meant to be a warning, it falls flat.

"Did the guys who have come before me tell you how badly they needed to eat your cunt, Tally? Or were you too busy choking on their cocks to care?"

I predict her reaction long before her palm gets anywhere near close to my cheek and I catch her wrist, pinning her arm behind her back, quickly snatching up the other one so she can't try again.

"So feisty for a good girl. I'm starting to think you're more of a brat, Prim."

Her chest heaves, her hard nipples pressing against the soft satin of her cami in the most teasing way.

My mouth waters to let the fabric fall away and suck one into my mouth. Just from the small whimpers I've heard from her tonight, I know she's going to be mesmerising as she falls.

"Y-you need to—"

"Take me to your bedroom?" I interrupt, pulling my face from the crook of her neck where I was inhaling her scent. "Let me strip you naked and bury my face between your thighs?"

She gasps once more, her cheek burning brighter than the fucking sun from my filthy words.

"Make a decision, Prim. Lead me upstairs so we can do this in private, or right here, where anyone could see."

Her eyes leave mine in favour of the wall of glass behind me that allows full view of the garden during the day.

A smirk kicks up at the corner of my mouth. She'd be willing to let me take her here, I'm fucking sure of it.

Dirty, dirty girl.

"Three... Two..."

"My room," she whispers.

"Good answer."

She shrieks in fright when I wrap my hands around her waist and throw her over my shoulder.

"Fuck, these shorts," I groan, palming her arse. They're

barely more than a pair of knickers and I am fucking here for them.

"Oakley," she cries when I squeeze her as I hit the stairs.

"Glad you haven't forgotten already."

Without any instruction from her, I walk us straight to her bedroom. And she either doesn't care or doesn't notice that she doesn't direct me.

Kicking her door closed behind us, I stand in the middle of her space and scan everything.

It's... well, exactly as I expected.

A good girl's bedroom.

"Have you ever had a boy in here, Prim?"

"What do you think?" she hisses. "Put me down."

"With pleasure."

Lifting her from my shoulder, I throw her into the middle of her bed before wrapping my hands around her ankles and dragging her closer.

"W-what are you doing?" she pants.

Dragging my palms up her smooth legs, I stop when I get to her knees and spread her legs wide. I can't see anything, but fuck if I don't want to.

"Oh sorry," I tease, ripping my eyes away from her cunt in favour of finding hers. "Wasn't I descriptive enough downstairs?"

She holds my eyes and squares her shoulders.

"You need to leave."

I can't help but chuckle. "After I made all this effort to get up here? I don't think so."

"Oakley, you... you can't be here. If my dad—"

"They won't be back for hours." I step closer and let my hands skim down her thighs. "So you can scream as loud as you like."

"N-no, that's not—"

"Tell me that I was the only one to touch you tonight," I demand. "Tell me he didn't—"

"He wanted me to invite him in," she explains, her voice all raspy and sexy as my fingers massage her thighs. "I-I think he wanted to—"

My body vibrates with anger at just the thought of him thinking about her like this. "What did you say?"

She studies me for a beat, probably seeing every bit of jealousy and desperation in my eyes. "That I'm not interested in him."

"Good girl." At my words, she practically melts into the bed. "Always trying to show everyone that you're such a good girl."

"Oak, I didn't—"

"Shush."

I drop to my knees at the end of her bed and stare up the length of her body.

"Tell me the truth, Tallulah." Her muscles bunch as I drag my hands down her inner thighs before resting two fingers against her pussy. "Has anyone been here before?"

Her cheeks blaze once more, and I'm about to chastise her for ignoring me when she subtly shakes her head.

"N-no, no one has—OAKLEY," she screams when I curl my fingers around the waistband of her shorts and drag them over her legs, discarding them on the floor somewhere behind me.

"Fuck," I bark the second my eyes lock on her pussy.

It's... it's... fuck me, it's so fucking perfect.

"Look at you," I purr, moving my finger to gently tease her. "You're so wet for me, Tally. So ready for me."

I look up just in time to see her slam her lips shut, trapping a pained whimper behind them.

"Don't," I bark fiercely, making her eyes widen in shock. "Don't hide any single reaction from me."

Her lips fall open, and as a reward, I add a little more pressure.

Collecting up some of her juices, I lift my finger, parting her lips and teasing her clit.

"Oh God," she moans.

"Good girl." Her entire body shudders at my praise. "Tell me what you want."

Silence.

Looking up, I find her biting down on her bottom lip. Hesitation and fear fill her eyes while her body burns up for me.

"Nothing wrong with telling me what you need, Prim."

Her lips open and close, but no words escape.

"You want me to finish what we started in that office, right?"

I up the pressure on her clit, reminding her of how good it felt.

"You were so close. You were about to come all over my fingers like a dirty little whore. You want that, don't you, Prim? You want to know how hard I can make you come."

I press harder still, adding my other hand to gently tease her entrance.

She confessed to never being touched before, so as much as I might want to punish her for everything she's done, I also know that I need to be gentle. As gentle as I'm capable of, at least.

"I-I don't know. I've never..."

My movements stop at her confession, and she sits up on her elbows, staring down at me in fright. Silence falls between us as the reality of what we're about to do settles around us.

"You've... you've never... even yourself?" I stutter like a moron.

Until this moment, the dirty talk has come as easy as breathing, but that confession, fuck, it rocks my entire foundations.

She shakes her head, and a wide smile forms on my lips.

"Well, I think it's safe to say that you're never going to forget me."

Holding her open with two fingers, I dip my head and lick up the length of her cunt.

Her taste, that sweetness that I got a tease of earlier, explodes in my mouth as she screams above me.

"Oh God, Oakley."

"Fuck yes," I groan against her cunt, lapping at her as if I'm starving.

I lick, suck, nip, everything I know that's going to drive her crazy as I continue to tease her entrance.

She's dripping for me. Soaking the comforter beneath her. And I can't get enough.

Her fingers twist in my hair, alternating between dragging me closer and trying to pull me away. Like I'm fucking going anywhere.

When I finally push two fingers inside her, she screams so loud it bounces off the walls around us.

I find her G-spot without too much effort and her body begins trembling as I play her toward her climax.

"Oakley, please, God."

I nip her clit with my teeth, and she does something that only fuels my hunger for her even more.

"Shit," she gasps.

My eyes lift to hers, shocked that she swore, but she's too far gone to notice.

Her eyes are closed, her head is thrown back, and she's rolling her hips in time with me, desperate for that little bit more that will send her flying.

I need more. So much fucking more.

Upping the ante, I destroy her pussy with my attention, giving her everything I've got as she continues to cry out.

And then it happens. Her entire body locks up, her cunt squeezes my fingers so hard I almost come in my pants right alongside her, and she screams so fucking loud I'd never believe it was her if my head wasn't currently pinned in place by her thighs.

"Holy fucking shit. Yes, Oakley. Yes. Fuck. Fuck, fuck."

Wave after wave of pleasure rolls through her body as she continues chanting expletives.

I work her through it, not stopping until she's fully come down, and then I pull back with the widest fucking grin on my face.

"Tallulah Darlington, you are a filthy, filthy whore."

21

TALLY

Oh. My. God.

Little tremors roll through me as I try to catch my breath.

Oakley grins down at me, his mouth and chin glistening with my release.

He went down on me.

The first boy ever to touch me there, let alone taste me.

I shouldn't feel as smug and as satisfied as I do because this is bad—this is really bad. But I'm too blissed out to care.

"Look at you," he whispers, leaning over me to press a kiss to my lips. I can taste myself, but it isn't wholly unpleasant, and without overthinking it, I anchor my hands around the back of his neck to pull him closer.

Oakley falls down on top of me, his very obvious, very big erection pressing up against my core. Heat spreads inside of me, an uncontrollable wildfire as Oakley slides his tongue into my mouth, tangling it with my own. He kisses me like he can't get enough. Like he wants to crawl inside me and live there.

It's a lot.

He's a lot.

But part of me loves it.

"Fuck, you're perfect," he rasps. "I can't wait to feel your pretty mouth wrapped around my cock. In fact, you owe me, Prim." His eyes glitter down at me.

"I..." I gulp, so many sensations streaking through me that I can't think straight.

Oakley skates one hand down my body and anchors me beneath him, flipping us so that I'm on top of him and he's smirking up at me. "I'm all yours, baby."

"Oakley, I..."

"Shh." He grabs my face, pushing his thumb into my mouth. "Suck."

Bolts of lust fire off around my body. He's right—I like it when he orders me around.

My entire life has been so built on order, on structure, and doing the right thing, that it feels good to finally let go.

My lips close around his thumb, my tongue swirling around the tip as I suck and lick, putting on the best show I can.

I have no idea what I'm doing, but he seems to like it.

"Fuck, that mouth. Turn around," he orders, and I frown, wondering where he's going with this.

"W-what?"

"You heard me, Prim. I'm not done with you yet." He shuffles down the bed a little, encouraging me to turn away from him. It's a bit clumsy as I reposition myself, but Oakley doesn't stop touching me, running his hands up and down my thighs, my hips, mapping my curves as I tremble above him.

"On your hands and knees," he adds, giving me a little nudge. "You're going to suck my cock, and I'm going to reward you."

"Oakley." Panic rises inside me as I realise what he wants to do. But it's laced with heat. The kind of heat that burns me from the inside out.

He grabs my bottom and spreads me open, swiping his tongue over my sensitive folds.

"Oh my God," I breathe, barely able to get air into my lungs.

"Take out my cock, Prim. Or you don't get to finish, and I'll leave you hot and needy." He laps at my clit, teasing me, making me cry out as my body melts above him.

With a shaky hand, I manage to work his waistband open and pull out his erection. He's thick and long and hard, and... Oh. My. God. There's no way in hell he'll fit in my mouth.

"Don't just look at it," he taunts. "Show me how good you can suck dick."

His words hurt. The fact he ever believed the rumours hurts. But what did I really expect? This is Oakley Beckworth we're talking about. He isn't a good person. He's arrogant and entitled and walks around All Hallows' as if he's better than everyone else.

And when he's done playing this game with me, he'll cast me aside like I'm nothing.

I know this.

And yet, I can't stop.

I want his approval.

I want to show him I'm not the meek, innocent girl he thinks I am.

I want him to want me the way I wanted him that night.

God, I'm in so much trouble.

I close my fingers around the base of his shaft and lean forward. My tongue darts out, licking the tip.

"Fuck," he hisses. "More... suck me down."

Oakley slides two fingers deep inside me, making me cry out. But he doesn't move them, just holds them there. Taunting me. Reminding me what I can have if I do what he wants.

And I both hate him and love him for it.

"Don't keep me waiting, Prim. You won't like the consequences." He crooks his fingers, rubbing that magical spot inside me. The one that makes me see stars.

Testing the waters, I take him into my mouth.

"Come on, baby. You can do better than that." He twists his fingers, making me cry out right as he thrusts into my mouth, and I practically choke on the length of him.

"Oh my God, Oak," I breathe, pulling away. His dark laughter sends shivers down my spine.

"You seem awfully hesitant for someone who loves sucking cock."

"Oakley," I twist around to look at him, our eyes clashing in a violent storm. "You know I've never..."

Embarrassment wells inside me. Shame that I'm giving him all my firsts and he doesn't even care.

He doesn't deserve them. I know that. But I'm too far gone to care. Maybe it's better this way. And then one day, when I finally meet the man who will treat me with respect and love and affection, I won't be inexperienced and clueless.

His brows furrow for a second and then his eyes widen with delight. "Make me come, Tallulah. And maybe one day, I'll give you what you really want." He slaps my bottom, making me yelp. "Face down, arse up, baby."

With a little huff of annoyance, I turn back around, crying Oakley's name when his tongue circles my clit again.

God, he's so good at that. No wonder girls line up at his feet for the Oakley Beckworth experience.

And now, I'm one of them.

I push that thought aside. The fallout from tonight can wait until tomorrow.

Right now, I can blame the champagne, my parents' betrayal, Deacon's wandering hands, and Oakley's dirty words for all the bad decisions I'm making.

Wrapping my tongue around the tip of his length, I slide my mouth down, fisting the base tighter.

"Fuck, yeah. Just like that," Oakley purrs before spearing his tongue inside me. Pure pleasure crashes over me, but I manage to keep myself together, focusing on making this good for him too.

I'm clumsy at first, gagging a couple of times as I take him deeper. But eventually, I find my flow, revelling in the power that trickles through my veins as his groans of approval fill the room.

"Deeper," he begs.

Begs.

Me.

I smirk to myself, breathing through my nose as I sink lower, fighting my gag reflex.

"More…" His voice cracks, his fingers moving lazily inside me as he loses himself to the pleasure I'm bestowing on him.

I can't breathe.

I can't freaking think.

But I do it. Eyes watering, heart crashing wildly in my chest, I swallow him down until he touches the back of my throat. Because Tallulah Darlington isn't a quitter, and when she sets her mind to something, she sees it through until the bitter end.

"Yes, fuck, yes." His fingers dig into my skin, pulling me back onto his mouth as he rewards me with greedy licks of his tongue.

"Oakley, God," I murmur, giving myself a second to breathe.

"Make me come, Prim. And I'll make you come so hard you forget your own name."

His challenge seeps into me, unlocking some dark, repressed part of me.

I want that.

I want him to wreak havoc on my body.

I don't overthink it or analyse it or question it. I just let go and give over to him and the feelings he evokes in me.

"Your mouth is fucking perfect," he praises as I suck him down again, alternating between my mouth and my hand.

"I'm close," he groans. "I'm going to come in your mouth, and you're going to swallow it all like the filthy whore you are."

Oh God.

But there isn't time to think about it. Oakley's legs tense beneath me and then he's coming, hot jets of cum coating the back of my throat. I swallow, forcing myself not to gag.

"Good girl," he drawls, running a hand down my spine and anchoring me on his face as he unleashes himself on me until I'm crying his name over and over.

"God, it's too much. It's too—" Pleasure rocks through me and I lose the ability to hold my body weight, falling down on Oakley's legs in a boneless heap.

He slaps my bottom again, chuckling. "Mmm, my new favourite meal. Come here." The brute practically manhandles me until I'm tucked into his side. "You've never done that before, have you?"

His intense stare unnerves me.

"You know, not everything you hear in the halls of All Hallows' is true."

Something flashes in his eyes. Annoyance? Disappointment? I'm not sure, but before I can ask him what's wrong, he says, "Don't worry, Prim. Something tells me we'll be getting lots and lots of practice."

"What—"

The shrill of my phone startles me and the bubble around us bursts as I blurt, "It's my dad's ringtone."

"Way to kill the moment." Oakley shifts me off his body and clambers off the bed.

It's only then I realise he's still fully dressed and I'm practically naked.

"You're leaving?"

I shouldn't be surprised. I've heard the stories. Oakley Beckworth doesn't stick around long enough to cuddle.

But it doesn't stop the disappointment from springing up inside me.

He straightens out his shirt, buttons his trousers, and runs a hand through his hair. "Wouldn't want Mr. Darlington to realise his daughter is in bed with the enemy." He winks, but the joke isn't lost on me, dread curdling in my stomach.

He's right.

What are we doing?

What am I doing?

"I'll let myself out."

My phone starts ringing again, and I can't think straight. I can't—

"You should probably answer that. Wouldn't want daddy dearest to worry."

Oakley slips into the hall without so much as a goodbye and I sit there, clutching my phone, wondering how things spiralled out of control so quickly.

But the answer is simple.

I'm powerless when it comes to Oakley.

I know he's trouble.

I know he'll use me to his ends without any regard for my feelings.

My head knows it too, it does. But my foolish heart—my traitorous, wanton body—doesn't care.

Because Oakley makes me come alive.

He makes me soar.

I only hope I can survive the inevitable fall.

22

OAKLEY

Tallulah Darlington has never sucked dick before.

That fact was as clear as fucking day as she hesitantly bobbed her head, refusing to properly swallow me down like a good little whore would.

And fuck if that knowledge didn't make my chest swell with pride.

I stole things from her tonight that I didn't deserve.

Am I going to feel bad about it?

Hell fucking no.

Was it the best head of my life? Honestly, no. Or at least, it wasn't to start with. The thought of it being Miss Prim and Proper who was licking at my dick like it was a fucking lollipop sure made up for her. Having her cunt right in my face also helped.

Fuck. That thing is fucking mind-blowing.

So neat, perfect, tight. Un-fucking-touched.

Hell to the fucking yes.

There was a point when she started gagging around my length that I thought she would have a moment of realisation and send me away with an aching dick and unsatisfied balls.

I really should have given her more credit, because after a

little practice, she started to suck me like the pro the chasers have made her out to be.

It was lies. All of it.

Honestly, it's what I expect from Misty and her band of merry bitches.

But Seb?

He's meant to be an honest, stand-up student.

He's fucking Head Boy, and he's running around All Hallows' lying through his fucking teeth about his partner in crime.

I shake my head as the Uber I called after letting myself out of Tally's house pulls up in front of my father's place.

I almost put the Chapel as my destination, but thoughts of walking in to find the guys hanging out and having to field questions about my night seriously fucking put me off. At least here, the only person I'll have to answer to, assuming she's not preoccupied by my best friend, is my sister. And I can handle her inquisition. I've honed my skills over the years.

With nothing more than a grunt of thanks to the driver, I push the door open and trudge down the driveway toward the front door.

All the lights are off, and hope fills my veins that Liv will be tucked up in bed alone and fast asleep.

I'm as quiet as I can be as I place my keys in the bowl in the hallway before toeing my shoes off, sweeping them off the floor and taking them up to my room with me. Thankfully, only silence greets me, and when I get to her room, there isn't a slither of light beneath it.

Feeling like I've won for the second time in an hour, I shut myself in my room and begin stripping out of my clothes. Folding them neatly, I then place them in the laundry basket and walk naked into the bathroom.

Memories from tonight mean my semi bobs as I move.

I'd hoped that maybe getting on her knees might have been what I needed to draw a line under this weird obsession I seem to have developed over Prim. I wanted to find out for good if the rumours were true and tarnish her good girl rep.

I achieved both. And while the latter is a fact that only I'll ever know, it's not something I'm likely to forget anytime soon. Just like how sweet her cunt is.

Fuck.

My tongue sweeps across my bottom lip as I step under the torrent of water in the Jack and Jill bathroom I share with my sister. But much to my disappointment, nothing is lingering, and I realise I used it all up on the way home. I probably looked like a right freak in the back of that Uber, licking my lips, trying to savour her taste.

Feeling desperate, I lift my fingers to my mouth at the same time my other hand wraps around my now fully erect cock.

A groan rumbles at the back of my throat and I close my eyes, putting myself right back there with her taste in my mouth and her lapping at my cock.

"Fuck," I growl, wondering if she's lying in her pretty pink bed, still able to taste me.

I come faster than I've ever known, spilling my seed into the water at my feet.

You've got a fucking problem.

Ignoring the irritating voice in my head, I clean up, hating that I'm washing Tally's scent down the drain but also aware that I can't torture myself with it all night.

I towel off before crawling into bed with my phone in my hand. I fully intend on just checking my socials to find out what the guys have been up to tonight, but really, it should come as no surprise to me that I end up on Tally's Instagram page. She hasn't added anything since I last looked... this afternoon. But she has been tagged in a couple of photos from this evening.

My teeth grind when I find an image of her with Deacon draped all over her like a rash. How I managed not to take the motherfucker to the floor after I heard his dickhead friends talking about the bet they all had, fuck only knows.

I have a plan, though. And Deacon Warrick can rest assured that he'll get his comeuppance after that little stunt.

Tally has enough shit going on around her right now; she doesn't need that tosser making it even worse.

I'm so lost staring at her in that sinful blue dress and the way the slit goes almost all the way to her hip that I don't hear the bathroom door open or my sister step into my room.

"Hey," she says, scaring me to the point that I fumble with my phone.

It tumbles to my sheets, screen side up, and I fucking panic. I'm like a supercharged fucking lunatic as I scramble for it before she catches sight of who I'm staring at like a creep. If I'm really unlucky, she'll also clock that I'm once again hard as nails beneath the sheets.

Suck a fucking pussy, Oakley Beckworth.

"Is everything okay?" Liv asks suspiciously.

Finally, I manage to right my phone and put it to sleep, *I think,* before she's spotted anything. "Yeah, of course. You good?" I ask, my voice weird as fuck.

Narrowing her eyes, she moves closer. "Yeah, just couldn't sleep. Do you mind?" she asks, nodding to my bed.

"Uh... I'm naked," I confess.

"Aw, you worried I'll finally realise how much smaller yours is than your bestie's?"

"No," I spit, irritation rolling through me. "That is not what I'm worried about."

As she pulls the covers back and slips in, clearly unfazed by my lack of clothing, I throw the duvet back and pad across the room to pull on a pair of boxers, grateful as fuck that my sister's mention of her getting up close and personal with Reese has killed my boner.

"You're a pain in my arse," I mutter as I return and slip back under the covers.

Liv shrugs, not in the least bit bothered.

"So what was tonight about? You didn't tell me that you were going to that gala with Dad and Fiona."

"And you didn't tell me that you were fucking my best friend. Problem?"

"Jesus, Oak. You need to let this go. I love him. He loves me. We're not just fucking for the fun of it."

I scrub my hand down my face, trying to get any thoughts of them going at it out of my mind.

"You know, I wouldn't be this much of a dick to you if you fell in love with one of my friends."

"I'm not interested in Charli, Liv."

"One," she starts, lifting a finger, "I should think not. She would eat you alive and you know it. And two," she adds a finger, "I have more friends than Charli."

One of my brows quirks in question.

"What? I hang out with Abigail and Ta—"

Sadness covers her face as she thinks about the girl who's taken up rent-free residence in my head for too long now.

"Abigail, really? Charli wouldn't eat me alive; I've had girls wilder than her before now."

"Man-whore," she coughs.

"Whatever. I like sex, so fucking what? From what I've heard recently, so do you." I make a show of gagging.

"So, who did you go for tonight?" she asks, sinking lower in my bed.

"What makes you think it had something to do with a girl? I might have just gone to network. Uni next year, Liv. One step closer to our future."

"Don't remind me," she mumbles.

"You still haven't applied to SCU, have you?" I glare at her, but she refuses to meet my stare.

The thought of her not coming with us to Saints Cross U doesn't sit right with me. Liv and I have always done everything together. Okay, so being twins, we didn't really have a choice most of the time. But I'm not sure how I feel about embarking on the next chapter of our lives separately.

"What about Reese? You know he doesn't have a choice, right?"

"We all have a choice, Oak," she snaps, reminding me just how much she hates the society we've been born into.

"You do. Reese and I don't. Our fates were sealed the day we came out with a penis."

"Lovely."

"You're not really considering going somewhere else and leaving us, are you?"

She lets the question linger between us, and just when I think she's going to give me an answer, one I possibly won't like, she backpedals.

"You know I'll find my answer on Instagram if you don't tell me."

My brows pinch in confusion.

"The girl. Tonight," she reminds me.

"There wasn't a girl. I really went to network." I hold her eyes steady, hoping like hell she can't see the lie.

Recently, it's something I've been doing all too often. I hate it. But something changed over the summer. Reese leaving broke more than just our friendship; it put cracks in the foundations the five of us had built over the years.

Liv might like to try and distance herself from us, but the truth is, she's a part of us. Just like Elliot is. Just like Theo is. And now she's with Reese, she's only getting deeper.

If he keeps his promises, then one day, she'll be married to an Heir.

She can tell me how much she hates all of this as much as she wants, but she's never going to leave it behind.

"You're a shitty liar, Oakley Beckworth."

"And I think you're a hypocrite," I mutter, hating that we're back to fighting again. It never used to be like this as kids.

Silence falls between us before she shifts onto her side and studies me.

"What?" I bark, hating how my skin prickles with her judgement. "Do you want me to tell you that I went after a girl I shouldn't want tonight, stalked her and refused to leave until she let me between her thighs?"

"No, not really," she confesses. "I'm just... I'm worried about you, Oak. You haven't been... well, you since Reese left. You're angry all the time and... I want you to smile like you used to."

"I'm fine," I lie, finally turning my face to look at her.

Okay, so it's not a total lie. Twice tonight, everything was more than fine. Those short few moments in the office at the hotel, and then in Tally's bedroom. In those minutes, everything was fucking right in my world. Hell, better than right. Fucking perfect.

It's just a shame it won't last.

23

TALLY

Saturday, I'm a mess.

All day, I walk around the house in a daze.

I can't eat, I can't focus, I can't sit still.

"Tallulah, for goodness' sake," Mum chides. "What on earth has gotten into you?"

I'm not sure she'd like the answer to that question, so I force a smile and reply, "I have a test tomorrow."

"Oh, sweetheart, I'm sure it'll be fine. You've never gotten this worked up about a test before."

"It's second year, Mum. If I want to get into university, I can't afford to mess anything up."

She makes her way over to me and drops a kiss on my head. "Don't be so hard on yourself. I'm sure you're more than prepared."

"Prepared for what?" Dad breezes into the kitchen with a smile on his face. As if he didn't ambush me last night.

"I'm still mad at you," I point out.

"Sweetheart, it was just one date. Is Deacon really that bad?"

"Yes, yes he is. He's obnoxious and arrogant and he thinks

it's his God-given right to..." I stop myself, surprised by my outburst.

"Sweetheart"—Mum frowns—"did something happen with Deacon?"

"I can handle the likes of Deacon, Mum. Just promise me you'll both drop this weird obsession you have with him and me ever being anything more than family friends."

"But—"

"No, Dad. I mean it. I don't like Deacon that way, and I never will."

Because another boy holds my heart in the palm of his hands. Or, at least, pulls my strings.

Memories of Oakley last night flood my mind and heat curls in my stomach. The way he took control and bent me to his will... it shouldn't be as thrilling as it is. But I liked it. I liked being at his beck and call.

I press my thighs together, trying to ignore the ache inside me.

If he doubted me before, there's no way he can doubt my innocence now.

But I'm not sure it changes anything.

Because he's Christian Beckworth's son, and I'm Thomas Darlington's daughter.

We're on opposites of the line, enemies in every sense of the word. He's everything my father has spent years trying to warn me to stay away from.

Yet, I let Oakley into my life. My bed. And, I fear, my heart.

Stupid, stupid girl.

But sometimes I see glimpses of the boy behind a mask. I'm my father's daughter. Driven with a strong sense of moral and social justice. I've always believed in fighting for what is right, because I've watched my father do it.

Maybe Oakley is his father's son, too.

We're both products of our upbringings. Puppets to the masters who pull our strings.

Except, I'm not sure that's true. Oakley enjoys being an Heir. I've seen it. Seen how he flaunts his status and popularity, wielding his power over the rest of the students at AH.

He'll never change.

And neither will I.

I'm not sure I can stay away from him, though.

Because the truth is, I don't want to.

By the time Monday morning rolls around, a swarm of butterflies is going crazy in my stomach. My hands won't stop trembling as I approach the main All Hallows' sixth form building.

A group of girls all cut me with an icy glare, but there's no sign of Misty or her friends.

Oh God.

Misty.

If she ever finds out about me and Oakley, she'll be out for blood.

Strangely, a sick sense of satisfaction goes through me at that thought.

My phone buzzes in my pocket and I dig it out, confused at the unknown number.

> Unknown: What I wouldn't give to bend you over the wall, lift up your school skirt, and bury my face in your pretty pussy.

> Tally: Who is this?

> Unknown: Who do you want it to be, Prim?

Relief trickles through me. I wanted it to be Oakley, but it could have been any one of the Heir chasers' puppets.

> Tally: How did you get my number?

> Unknown: Wasn't difficult... You used to be friends with my sister, remember?

A pang of guilt goes through me, but I shove it down. Olivia would hate me even more if she knew I was fooling around with her brother after my declaration of war against the Heirs.

> Unknown: Meet me in the old bike shed behind the gym in an hour.

> Tally: Uh, no. I have class

> Unknown: So? Skip it.

> Tally: Oakley, I can't just skip class. Besides, we're at school. Anyone could see us.

> Unknown: That's half the fun, Prim. Live a little. You know you want to.

> Unknown: I'll make it worth your while.

I glance around, half-expecting to see the Heir chasers pointing and laughing at me. Because Oakley can't be serious. He can't really want me to meet him, at school no less.

Furious with myself—and at him for even suggesting such a thing—I text him back.

> Tally: Friday night was a one-off. It won't happen again.

I scan the grounds, trying to locate him. But wherever he is, he's out of sight. Watching me.

> Unknown: It's cute you think that you get any say in the matter.

> Tally: Oakley!!!

> Unknown: See you around, Prim.

Ugh.

He's infuriating.

But I can't deny his suggestive words make my stomach tighten and twist.

I am in so much trouble.

Everything comes crumbling down around me, though, as I step into the building and make my way toward the second-year lockers.

Everyone is staring at me, snickering and pointing. I hurry down the corridor, holding my head high, refusing to let them see what their whispers do to me.

But the second my eyes land on my locker, I gasp. Pinned to the door is a series of photos. But not just any photos—stills from that stupid doctored porn video circulating.

"Oh my God." I rush up to my locker and start tearing them down, tears pricking the corners of my eyes.

The photos are even worse than the video.

"Tally, what—" Abigail rushes over to me and helps me remove the scarily realistic photoshopped images.

"You need to tell someone about this," she whispers.

"No. It'll only cause more trouble. I can handle it, I promise." I flash her what I hope is a convincing smile.

But of course, the universe isn't done screwing me over, because Elliot Eaton and Theo Ashworth choose that exact moment to enter the building.

"Tut tut, Tallulah. Would have thought you'd gotten the hint by now," Theo smirks, snatching one of the photos out of my hand.

"Give that back," I snap, blushing profusely at the way his eyes dance with hunger as he studies the photo. His gaze flicks between me and the photo, lingering on my chest.

"The editing skills are good enough, but the tits are dead giveaway. Sorry, Darlington, but her rack is ten times better than yours." He flings the photo back at me as everyone watching our little exchange bursts out laughing.

Elliot studies me, his dark gaze cold and assessing, giving nothing away.

"What?" I hiss.

"You should drop the campaign," he says quietly. Quiet enough that no one else can hear him. "It'll only get worse."

"Like you care," I scoff.

"Can't you do something?" Abigail steps up to him. "Call off the witch hunt?"

"I don't control the Heir chasers." He shrugs with that dismissive air of his.

"That's bullshit and you know it."

Me and Theo both suck in a sharp breath at Abi's little outburst. She's usually so meek and quiet, but here she is defending me, pleading my case to the very boy I'm trying to bring down.

"Abi, it's okay." I gently grab her shoulder as the two of them remain locked in a stare-off, neither willing to budge. "Abigail," I try again, and this time her eyes snap to mine.

"Fine. But just for the record, I think you're all being pig-headed." She stomps off down the hall, leaving the three of us staring after her.

"Did that really just happen?" Theo asks, scratching his jaw.

"Come on," Elliot says. "I've got better things to be doing than dealing with this shit." He flashes me another cold look before taking off.

"See you around, Darlington. Who knows, maybe before the term's out, you'll get on your knees for me." Theo cups his crotch and thrusts his hips in a vulgar display that leaves everyone laughing at me.

Again.

With a small, defeated sigh, I stuff the photos in my bag and head for my first class of the morning.

Telling myself it can't get any worse.

By lunch, I'm ready to scream.

In every class, there's someone brave enough to cough an insult or push a note on my desk asking me if I charge by the hour.

Misty was in my last class, and she only encouraged it, smirking in my direction, mouthing things like, 'cum slut' and 'whore' at me.

On the way out of class, she handed me a box of condoms and a card for the sexual health clinic and told me to make sure I was being safe, given my new career choice.

God, I hate her.

I hate her so much, I sat in class plotting all the ways I could end her reign as head Heir chaser.

But most of my ideas involved Oakley, and that isn't an option. Ever. So here I am, hiding out in the library because I can't bear to face my classmates in the cafeteria.

No one else is in here except Miss Sanders, the librarian, and she's busy reshelving books on the other side of the room.

I nibble on my wrap, but I'm not really hungry. Seeing my face plastered all over my locker killed my appetite.

My phone vibrates on the table, and I let out a soft sigh.

> Oakley: Where are you hiding?

> Tally: If I tell you, I'll have to kill you.

> Oakley: I can think of worse ways to go, Prim.

> Oakley: I heard you had a run-in with the chasers this morning…

> Tally: Like you care.

> Oakley: I didn't have you down as the type of girl to quit so easily.

> Tally: Sorry to be such a disappointment.

The little thrill I usually get verbally sparring with Oakley doesn't come. I'm all out of sass and confidence today. Misty and her puppets are winning, and I hate it.

> Oakley: Tell me where you are.

I ignore him.

Oakley doesn't want me, not really. He's just drawn to this push and pull between us, the prospect of ruining Thomas Darlington's daughter.

If he cared at all—and I'm not naïve enough to think he does—he'd call off Misty and her army.

My phone vibrates again, but I don't look at it. Instead, I flick the page of the book I'm reading and try to lose myself in the story.

It works for a little while, transporting me to a fantasyland far away from Saints Cross and All Hallows'.

Until I have the vague sensation of being watched.

I glance around, searching the library. Miss Sanders is still across the room in the stacks. But it isn't her watching me.

Because standing at the door is Oakley.

I gulp, my mouth drier than the desert.

He doesn't look smug that he found me or even happy about it.

He looks furious.

And his anger is all directed at me.

24

OAKLEY

My chest is heaving by the time the library appears before me.

There are so many places that Tally can hide. And this one is pretty high up on my list.

It's where everyone hides, isn't it?

In the very back row of the silent library where no one dares go unless they're trying to forget the world around them exists.

Fury has been bubbling up in me all morning. It started when she refused to skip in favour of spending time with me behind the old bike shed. I've had the image of her on her knees for me in that secluded little spot since almost the minute I left her house on Friday night. And then every time some fucking twat muttered her name, it only made it worse.

If I thought hearing the lies being spilled about her infuriated me last week, then I really underestimated how fucking mad this bunch of popularity-seeking fucktards could make me once I knew just how fucking fake their bullshit is.

Tally isn't a whore. She's nowhere fucking close.

I was desperate to put them right. But what fucking good would that do?

Plus, I can hardly tell anyone the reason I know she hasn't been blowing anyone who so much as glances at her.

Fuck. This is a fucking mess.

The only thing that has made sense since all this blew up was those few minutes I was in her bedroom with my hands on her.

That should not be the case.

She's the enemy. She's always been the enemy.

It's the way it should be.

I should not be spending any time with a Darlington, let alone fantasising over just how fucking fantastic it felt with her lips wrapped around me.

I march toward the library door as if the thing offended me the last time I was here and rip it open with way more force than necessary. It crashes back against the wall, making Miss Sanders, the librarian, look like she's about to piss her pants where she's making herself busy rearranging books that were no doubt in the perfect order already.

But I don't focus on her. I'm too intent on finding the girl who's been driving me crazy for the past week.

Pulling my phone out again, I tap out another message.

> Oakley: You can run, but you can't hide. I will always find you.

The quiet buzz of a phone on a table fills the silence around me and tingles erupt in my stomach.

Bingo.

I take a step forward. It's all it takes for me to see her at the other side of the room. For someone who's meant to be hiding, she's doing a really shitty job.

Her eyes widen and her lips pop open in shock.

Surely, she didn't think I was just messing about? I thought she'd have realised on Friday night that when I want something, I go after it no matter what stands in my way.

With a nod to Miss Sanders, a silent instruction to leave us the fuck alone no matter what, I take off toward my target.

When I'm almost at her table, she slides her chair back as if she's going to run.

It only makes my excitement grow.

"Go on. I dare you," I taunt. "But I should warn you. You won't get far, Prim."

Pushing to her feet, she sidesteps her chair, slowly backing away from me.

Sure, she's making all the right moves to allow me to think she doesn't want me near her. But I see more. I see the desire in her eyes. The memories of our short time together playing out in her head like a movie. She's remembering just how good it felt with my tongue on her clit and my fingers curled deep in her pussy. She's remembering how I stretched her pretty, pouty lips wide around my cock as I hit the back of her throat.

"What do you want?" she demands.

"Me? What do I want?" I ask, pointing at myself as I prowl toward her.

My heart is racing and my cock is aching behind the confines of my trousers. It has been since I taunted her with meeting me earlier.

I was desperate then and I'm fucking dying for it now.

"I thought I made it obvious this morning, Prim. I wanted to make all those rumours everyone is spreading about you true by getting you on your knees in the mud behind the bike shed."

"I'm not just some Heir chaser you can order around, Oakley," she barks, anger darkening her hypnotising blue eyes.

My cock jumps as my name rolls off her lips.

"Say it again. Just make it a little more of a moan this time."

Her eyes narrow and her lips purse. She wants to swear at me, curse me out, I can see it, but Little Miss Prim holds it all back like the good girl that she is. Or at least, she does right now. If Friday night taught me anything, it's that Tally was a dick-sucking virgin and that she forgets all about her manner and politeness when she falls into a blissful orgasm. And fuck if I don't want to hear her cursing up a storm as I push her over the edge again.

I continue to move forward as she backs up.

If she thinks she's escaping me, then she really needs to think again, or at least look anywhere but at me, because she's about to fall straight into my trap.

"Screw you, Oakley Beckworth," she seethes.

"Not quite, but better. Give it to me, Tally. Let it all out. I know they're getting to you more than you're letting on." They sure fucking are me.

"They're nothing I can't handle. And I don't care what they, or anyone else here, thinks of me."

"Even if it's lies."

"I know the truth. Everyone else can swivel."

"The truth," I sneer. "The truth is that the only man's dick you've sucked is mine. Isn't that right, Prim?"

Her chest heaves, her usually light blue eyes darkening with my words.

"Do you remember it as well as I do?" I ask, dragging my bottom lip into my mouth and capturing it with my teeth as I remember. "Do you remember how I tasted? How hard I was between your lips? How it felt when I hit the back of your throat?"

"Stop, please."

A smile twitches at my lips.

"Closer. Just add an *Oakley* on the end."

Her small fists curl at her side and her shoulders tense. "This isn't funny, Oakley."

"Do you see me laughing?"

"Not right now, no. But I'm sure you will be when the footage of this leaks, or when—"

"You really don't trust me, huh?"

"Why would I? What have you ever done to earn my loyalty? You can't even own up to your own actions."

I rear back a little, my brows lifting.

"What are you talking about? I always own my shit."

She scoffs, but her amusement only lasts so long, because finally, she bumps into the bookshelves behind her, alerting her to the fact that I've cornered her.

No one can see us, and if she's quiet enough, no one will have any clue what happens down here.

"Prim? Tell me what you're talking about." I crowd her against the shelves, getting so close that her breasts brush against my chest, sending sparks shooting around my body, all of them ending at my dick.

She sucks in a sharp breath, letting me know that she felt it too.

This... whatever this is between us... it's not just me who feels it.

"You can't bully information out of me. I'm not that girl," she says, holding my eyes firmly and refusing to back down.

"No, but you are the girl who let me eat her out on Friday night before she swallowed my spunk."

Her arm moves fast, but I'm faster, wrapping my fingers around her slim wrist and pinning it back against the books. "Nice try. Now, tell me what you're talking about."

I don't give her an inch of space as I wait for her to confess.

"Go to hell," she seethes. "I'm not telling you anything."

Pressing my knee between her thighs, I give her little choice to part her legs for me. "Wanna bet?"

"Oakley," she gasps as I press my thigh against her pussy.

"Much better."

Wrapping my fingers around her hip, I drag her closer to my body, allowing her to feel just how hard I am.

"Oak, what—"

"This is what you do to me, Prim. You drive me fucking

crazy," I growl, grinding my length into her hip at the same time I up the pressure on her clit.

"The feeling is mutual," she snaps, "but not in a good way."

"So you're telling me that you're not wet for me?"

"I hate you."

"I'm not debating that. I want to know if you're craving a repeat of Friday night as much as I am."

"I'm not," she states, but her voice is far from confident as I continue to grind against her.

"Liar."

"Better than being a whore," she counters. "I bet you can't even name the girls you've been with. I've no idea why I even thought you'd remember."

"Remember? Baby, there is no way I'm forgetting you." Releasing her hip, I trace the fullness of her lips with my finger. "I'm never going to forget how these felt wrapped around my cock, Prim. Ever."

"You're so full of yourself."

"I'd rather you were full of me."

"Never going to happen."

"We'll see."

"Oakley," she gasps a little too loudly when my hand drops from her mouth and disappears beneath her skirt.

"Oh, Prim. These knickers. They're ruined."

And just to prove a point, I twist my fingers around the sides and rip them from her body.

"Oakley," she cries as the flimsy lace falls from her body.

"Fucking love it when you scream my name, Prim." Lifting her underwear, I bring it to my nose, inhaling her sweet scent. "But do you know what I prefer?"

I stare at her. Her pupils are blown with lust, her lips parted as her breath races past, tickling over my face.

"You screaming it as you come for me."

This time, I muffle her cries with my lips as I find her soaked pussy and thrust two fingers inside her.

Just like Friday night, she's so fucking tight it makes my head spin and my cock leak. She's going to feel like heaven when I finally slide inside her and steal what I have no right to claim.

I've never claimed to be a fucking gentleman, though, so I'm not going to think twice about taking her V card as mine.

Despite her arguments, her insistence that she doesn't want me, the second we collide, her tongue meets mine and our kiss turns feral. Our teeth clash as we fight for dominance. I give her just enough to make her think she might stand a chance of being in charge here, but really, she's nothing more than a puppet, and I am pulling every string.

Or at least, that's what I tell myself. The truth is, she could probably ask me to do just about anything right now and I would. Anything to feel those lips a little lower on my body.

Her fingers claw at my shoulders, making me want to shed my shirt to allow her the opportunity to mark me, to ensure that when I stand in front of the mirror later, I have a reminder of what we did.

But we're already risking being caught. It'll be bad enough if we do, let alone being naked at the same time.

"Come for me, Prim. Let me hear that filthy fucking mouth you like to hide behind your pretty façade."

"Oakley," she whimpers as her pussy clamps down on my fingers.

"That's it. Good girl, Prim. Come all over my fingers."

"Fuck, Oakley. Fuuuck."

"Oh shit," I grunt as she follows orders, the sight of her alone getting me way too close to coming in my pants like a fucking pre-teen.

25

TALLY

My body slumps against the stacks, books rattling on their shelves.

"Oh my God, I can't believe you did that." I gawk at Oakley, a bolt of lust going straight through me as he slowly sucks his fingers clean.

"Fuck, you taste good."

"Get out," I choke, still trembling from his touch.

"You mean you're not going to get on your knees and repay the favour?"

"Oakley!"

"Fine." He steps into me, pushing his hard, strong body against the length of mine. His fingers wrap around my throat, holding me. I shouldn't like it.

I shouldn't like it at all.

But his dominant touch does things to me. Unfamiliar, unnerving things.

"You owe me, Prim. And I will collect."

"I—"

His mouth crashes down on mine, stealing my breath and sending every rational thought flying out of my head.

The kiss isn't the kind of kiss you read about in fairy tales.

It's complete annihilation. His tongue plunges into my mouth, curling around my own as his fingers flex around my throat, reminding me that in this moment, I belong to him.

Before I know it, we're clawing at each other, our hips rocking and searching for more... more... more.

"Jesus, Prim. I can feel the heat from your pussy. She wants me to fill her up, doesn't she?" He pulls back to look me in the eye. "Tonight, Prim. Tonight"—he slides one hand down my body and under my skirt, cupping me—"this is mine."

I refuse to answer, pressing my lips—and my thighs—together. His dark chuckle makes my heart stutter in my chest.

"It's cute that you think you get any choice in the matter. You're mine, Tallulah." His eyes flash with hunger. "Mine."

Voices fill the library and panic floods me. "Get off me." I shove him and Oakley staggers back. "You need to go before anyone sees you."

He hesitates, his eyes bouncing between my mouth and my gaze. For a second, I think he might kiss me again, but he thinks better of it and takes off down the aisle, disappearing into the shadows.

My heart races in my chest as I try to fix my uniform, straightening my shirt and smoothing down my skirt. My knickers are long gone, which means I can't stay at school, but I still have to find a way out of here without being seen.

Thankfully, the group of students doesn't linger for long, and ten minutes later, I slip out of the library and head straight for my car.

As I climb inside, my phone vibrates.

> Oakley: Don't hide from me again, Prim.

My fingers hover on the screen to text back 'or what?' but I don't reply, because I know first-hand the crazy lengths Oakley will go to.

God, what have I done?

Things weren't supposed to be this messy. I wasn't supposed to end up here—fooling around with Oakley in secret.

But the real kicker is, now we've started something...

I'm not sure I can stop.

The house is quiet when I get home, not that I expect any different. Mum and Dad both have a lot of work this week. I've grown up in solitude, used to my own company. I order Alexa to play one of my favourite playlists, run upstairs to change—and replace the underwear that Oakley ruined and then stole—and wash my hands. I need to do something. Something that will expend all the restless, confusing energy coursing through my veins. And there's only one thing that will work.

Baking.

I don't reach for a recipe book. Instead, I go rogue, adding ingredients to taste, letting my senses guide me. I've been baking cupcakes and muffins and brownies so much that I can recall the steps in my sleep. But it's the finer details that can completely transform a recipe. A dash of vanilla or a splash of honey, even a sprinkle of salt. I've been inventing new flavours and textures for as long as I can remember.

But nothing gives me more comfort than a good old-fashioned sticky, gooey, chocolate brownie.

I smile as I beat the batter, blowing the hair out of my eyes as I whip it into the perfect consistency. It doesn't bring me the burst of satisfaction it usually does, though. I feel restless still, a potent mix of shame and lust coursing through my veins.

When I stood on that stage and declared war on the Heirs, I didn't anticipate that Oakley would react quite so badly.

Or maybe I did.

Maybe subconsciously, I hoped it would rock his arrogant,

cocky exterior and hurt him the way he hurt me that night at the party at the Chapel.

Ugh.

I pour the batter into the greased tray and sling it in the oven, done with it. It was supposed to help my stress levels, but now, I feel tenser than I did when I arrived home.

At least I'm not still at school, dealing with the constant whispers and stares. I don't care what anyone thinks about me, I don't. But it's not easy being public enemy number one.

Frustrated, I make quick work of cleaning up the kitchen then head upstairs for a shower. I've barely stripped out of my clothes when my phone vibrates.

For a second, I think—secretly hope—it might be Oakley making good on his threat from earlier. But it isn't. It's a notification from Instagram. I open the app and my stomach sinks.

Misty posted a photograph of her and Oakley less than a minute ago, and tagged him in it. She's wrapped around him while he stands there all muddy and dirty from the Saints rugby game.

The caption reads 'someone's going to get lucky tonight after scoring the winning try'.

It already has forty-one replies congratulating the Saints on their win and wishing Misty a good ride.

A shudder rolls through me.

I thought—

Who am I kidding?

Of course Oakley is still hooking up with Misty. Why wouldn't he? She's gorgeous and experienced and in his circle. His dad would probably love him to bring home someone like her.

Jealousy churns in my stomach as I study the photo closer. He doesn't look like he's hugging her back; in fact, he doesn't look like he's paying her that much attention at all.

I throw my phone down with a little huff and push all

thoughts of Oakley Beckworth out of my head. Misty can enjoy her night with him and the Heirs.

I have a date with re-runs of *Friends* and eating my body weight in brownies and ice cream.

It's late and I feel sick.

I guess eating a whole tray of double chocolate brownies will do that to a girl.

My parents never made it home, so I've been home alone for hours with nothing but my own thoughts for company.

Which was fine, until I saw another photo of Misty and Oak. In this one, he looked more interested, his hands resting on her hips as she leaned back into him.

God, I'm such an idiot.

He's probably with her right now, touching her the way he touched me earlier.

I hate him.

But I hate her more. Hate that she gets all of him whereas I only get the scraps he'll allow me.

I'm about to turn off my light and try to get some sleep when my phone buzzes.

> Oakley: What are you up to?

My heart flutters in my chest.

> Tally: None of your business.

> Oakley: Is that code for you're home alone knitting?

> Tally: Goodbye, Oakley.

> Oakley: Wait, come on. Talk to me. I'm bored.

> Tally: Already kicked Misty out? I am surprised.

> Oakley: What are you talking about?

I gnaw my lip, trying to decide on my reply. But he beats me to it.

> Oakley: Prim... have you been spying on me?

> Tally: It was kind of hard to miss all Misty's posts on Insta.

I let out a surprised shriek when my phone blares to life, Oakley's name flashing across the screen.

I should ignore him. Or better yet, hit decline.

But I don't, because it's Oakley. And apparently, I'm a glutton for punishment.

"I told her not to post that shit," he says.

"Why?"

"Because it's not like that between us."

"So you didn't sleep with her tonight?"

"Fuck no! I haven't been with—" He hesitates and, much to my disappointment, changes the subject. "What are you doing?"

"I'm in bed."

"Naked?"

"Oakley!"

"I've been thinking about you all day."

"Liar," I breathe, aware of how dangerous this conversation is. He threatened me earlier, threatened to claim me as his. But it was nothing more than empty words said in the heat of the moment.

Wasn't it?

"You're probably drunk."

"Try high. I dropped some Molly earlier."

"W-why?" I know he dabbles; Olivia has mentioned it before.

"Why not?" I hear the shrug in his voice.

"Are you at the Chapel?"

"Why?" He chuckles. "Want to sneak in and give me my reward?"

"I'll never step foot in that place again."

"So righteous, Prim. But you and me, we're the same."

I snort. "I highly doubt that, Oakley."

"So quick to write me off. But I know what it's like to carry the weight of expectation. To be unsure of where you fit in the world. To want something so much and be afraid that you might never be good enough for it."

"Oakley, what are—"

"Push two fingers into your cunt."

"W-what?" Heat streaks through me at his sudden change of topic.

"You heard me, Prim. I want you to slip your hand inside your pyjamas and finger yourself."

"W-why?"

"Because I'm horny and you're not here, so we'll have to make do. Turn your camera on."

"I can't."

"Don't overthink it, Prim. Just listen to the sound of my voice. Now be a good girl and turn on your camera."

I press the video icon and Oakley's face fills the screen. He's shirtless, his tanned skin glistening under the dim lights. He flexes a pec and grins. "Like what you see?"

I roll my eyes, shifting into a more comfortable position.

"You really didn't sleep with Misty tonight?"

"The only person I want to fuck, Prim, is you. I can't wait to get inside you, feel your tight pussy choking my dick."

"God, Oak..." I cry out, my body coiled tight with desire.

"Now, be a good girl and put two fingers inside yourself. I

want to watch you come, Prim. Want to hear those sexy little moans and that dirty mouth of yours."

"Will you... touch yourself too?"

A roguish grin spreads over his face and he tilts the camera down so I can see his lean body in all its glory. But it's the hand wrapped around his thick erection that steals my breath.

Oakley pumps himself in slow strokes, twisting his hand a little on the upstroke. "I've been thinking about you all day," he rasps. "Thinking about how hot you looked coming all over my hand in the library. Are you touching yourself, Prim?"

"Yes." I slide my hand down my stomach, pushing my fingers into my sleep shorts. I'm already wet, a needy ache growing between my legs as Oakley whispers dirty words to me over the phone.

"Tell me what it feels like," he says, and I whimper. Because it feels good.

Strange but oh-so good.

"Tallulah," he snaps, and my eyes flutter back on the screen. He's watching me now, his eyes boring into me through the phone.

And then he says seven little words that make my insides turn molten.

"Eyes on me while you fuck yourself."

26

OAKLEY

The second her eyes collide with mine, my entire body jolts.

Even through the screen, something crackles between us.

Something forbidden and addictive.

Something I'm unable to ignore.

Hence why I'm alone in my room while the others enjoy themselves downstairs, and I got high like a loser in the hope of forgetting about her for one fucking minute.

Yeah... look how well that turned out.

Earlier, I promised her I'd see her tonight. But sneaking out will invite too many questions, and I can't risk it.

"That's it, Prim," I groan, my hand working my cock, although not as furiously as it wants. I'm too lost in her to focus on myself.

Her blue eyes are dark, her pupils blown as she works herself.

"Has anyone ever watched you get off before?"

I already know the answer, but it doesn't mean that I don't want to hear the words tumble from her lips.

"N-no," she gasps. "I-I've never..."

Her words trail off as my own moan of appreciation bounces off the walls of my room.

"Show me. I want to see your fingers working your clit."

She hesitates, and I'm about to snap at her when the camera finally pans away from her face. Although, her eyes don't leave mine.

But then, her face has gone from the screen, and it's filled with the flawless, toned skin of her stomach, and then her hand disappears into her sleep shorts.

"Prim, that wasn't what I had in mind," I hiss, my grip on my cock tightening, my body begging for release.

"Oak, I-I can't—"

"You can," I encourage her, desperate to see more.

"Oak—"

"Be a good girl, Tallulah, and push those shorts down. Let me see that pretty little pussy."

She pauses. I don't need to see her face to know she's arguing with herself. Doing this... it's totally out of character for good little Tally.

Honestly, I'm surprised she's allowed it to go this far.

For some reason, she seems to trust me.

Fucking stupid, if you ask me. She's currently got a hate campaign running rampant at school, and here she is, getting naked on a video call with me.

Not that I'm going to point that out. There's nothing that could force me to stop this right now.

"That's it, baby," I groan when she begins to shimmy her shorts down, revealing the curve of her hips and the tuft of blonde hair hiding between her legs.

Usually, I'm not a fan. Hell, I've been known to refuse to go down on one of the chasers if they're not fully shaved. But with Tally, I really don't fucking care. It's just another reminder that she's different. That she's not bending over backward to snag one of us. She's just... unashamedly her.

CRUEL DEVIOUS HEIR: PART ONE

It's fucking captivating.

All my life, I've been fighting to be something, fighting to be seen. Trying to prove myself in any way I could.

But Tally, despite knowing that practically everyone in school hates her, still isn't complying with what's deemed normal. She's not bowing down in any way.

It's fucking mind-blowing.

I'm not sure I know anyone else who could handle what she's going through right now like she is.

It's so refreshing to spend time with someone who is that self-aware and literally gives no shit other than about doing the right thing.

Not that she's doing the right thing, of course. And she'll figure out that no matter how hard she pushes this campaign to remove us from this very building, she won't succeed. I mean, she's probably already figuring that out.

She will have to give in at some point. But that doesn't mean I don't want to break her in my own way.

"Oh fuck," I grunt when she finally kicks the fabric away and lets her legs fall open, showing me everything.

My cock jerks in my hand, my orgasm threatening, but I refuse to let go. Not yet.

Loosening my grip, I suck in a couple of deep, calming breaths. "You have no idea how badly I want to crawl between your legs right now and spend the rest of the night making you come all over my face."

"Oak," she gasps, her hips lifting from the bed.

"Are you imagining your fingers are mine? That I'm the one making you squirm and moan like that?"

"Yes," she breathes, her fingers rolling over that little bud of nerves between her folds.

"Are you going to make yourself come for me, Prim?"

"Yes. Keep talking."

My chest puffs out at her demand.

Hell fucking yes.

"Can you prop your phone up anywhere so you can use your other hand?" I ask.

"U-umm," she thinks, clearly thrown for a loop with my question. "Y-yes, selfie stick. Don't move."

"Baby, you couldn't pay me enough to go anywhere right now."

I'm left with the view of her bedroom ceiling as she climbs from the bed.

Running my thumb over the tip of my cock, I collect up the precum that's beading at the slit and rub it into myself, my head full of memories of her licking it up, tasting me.

"Hurry," I groan when she doesn't return quickly enough.

Suddenly, I'm moving again, and I'm gifted the sight of her covered tits as she rights the camera into a stand.

"Fuck yeah. Take your top off, Prim."

"Oakley," she warns.

"Oh yeah, and moan my name at the same time. Fuck, I'm so fucking hard for you right now." Just in case she's doubting my words, I pan my own camera down again so she can see.

"I did that," she whispers to herself.

"Hell yeah, you did. Now, top off, and move back a bit."

She hesitates, but after another bit of encouragement, she finally drags it off, leaving her body bare for me.

"You're so fucking beautiful, Prim. So perfect. So..." *Mine.*

I keep that final thought to myself. It's too dangerous to admit out loud.

"Now what?" she asks nervously, her hands resting on her thighs.

"Stay like that. One hand on your clit, the other on your tits. And don't stop until you're screaming out my name as you come."

Hesitation and indecision flicker in her eyes.

This is so out of character for her. I know that.

The stories flying around about her at school are lies.

I am the only one to get this from her. I know that for a fact.

I'm also the last person on Earth who deserves it.

"Good girl," I groan as her hand slips up her thigh, seeking out her pussy.

"I can't believe I'm doing this," she whispers.

"I fucking love that you're doing this. How does it feel to rebel, Prim?"

"Oakley," she moans.

"That's it, baby," I praise as her hips roll, grinding down on her own hand. "Other hand on your tit. I want to watch you pinching your nipple."

"Oh God," she moans, her head falling back as she follows orders.

"You like doing what I say, don't you, Prim? You like letting go of the girl you think you need to be around everyone else and handing over your control. You like being my slut. Following my orders."

"Fuck, Oakley. I'm gonna come," she cries, and fuck if my cock doesn't get harder as she begins to lose control. I love hearing the filth she spews as she falls over the edge.

It's like a secret that only the two of us know.

Good little Tallulah Darlington has a dirty, wicked mouth when she's getting fucked. Even if it's by her own hand.

"Me too, Prim. I'm so fucking close. I'm going to come all over myself while I watch your sexy little body."

"Yes. Yes. Show me, I want to see your cock."

It's awkward as fuck, but I just about manage to get myself in a position where she can see me which allows me to keep my eyes on her.

"Come for me, Tallulah. Let me hear you scream my name like a good little girl."

"Fuck. Yes, Oakley. Yes. Shit. Shit, OAK," she cries as her body folds in on itself, pleasure saturating her body.

"So fucking beautiful," I groan. "Fuck, Tally. Fuck."

My cock jerks in my hand, and I'm consumed with a level of pleasure I'm not sure I've ever managed to achieve alone.

Her eyes zero in on where I cover myself in the evidence of my release, and she licks her lips.

"You want to taste it, don't you?" Her eyes shoot to mine, her lips parting in shock.

"You can tell me, Prim. There's no shame here. And... I'll do whatever you want me to do. I have no limits."

Reaching for her comforter, she wraps it around her shoulders, covering herself up.

I hate it, but I don't complain. What she just gave me... well, it was fucking everything.

She looks away from the screen, her cheeks blazing.

"Talk to me, Tally. I want to hear your words."

Silence fills the line, and I wait with my heart racing and my semi already gearing back up for round two.

Her shoulders square and her spine straightens as she works up the courage.

The second her eyes find mine again, I know what's coming.

"Taste it for me."

"Filthy, filthy girl," I growl, dipping my finger into the cooling, sticky residue on my stomach.

Her eyes follow my hand, her chin dropping in shock as lust fills her eyes when I paint my bottom lip with my jizz.

"Oakley," she whispers a beat before I poke my tongue out, licking over my lip. "Holy—"

"You can swear, you know. It doesn't only have to be reserved for orgasms."

I didn't think it was possible, but her face actually gets redder.

"I... uh... I can't."

Holding the comforter tighter, she drops forward so she's lying against her pillow and reaches for her phone, resting me in front of her. It's almost as if I'm right there with her.

Silence fills the space between us once more as we just stare at each other.

There is so much wrong with this whole situation, and not just the fact I'm lying here naked, covered in my own cum. But also, everything about it feels so fucking right.

"How was the rest of your day?" I ask.

I already know it was shit. I was there; I'd heard the gossip, the abuse.

She looks down for a second. "It was... fine."

"Liar. Look at me, Tally," I demand, and just like during sex, she does exactly as she's told. "Now tell me what it was really like."

"You already know. You were there," she whispers.

My fists curl in frustration. I thought the chasers would have gotten bored of this hate campaign by now. That or Tally would have been backed into such a corner that she would have dropped hers.

I'm not sure if she's brave or just plain stupid for trying to stand by what she believes in.

"I'm going to talk to Misty, get them to stop."

"No, Oak. You can't do that. You can't be seen to be on my side."

"Wish I was on your side of the bed," I confess.

She studies me through the screen, deep in thought.

"What are you thinking about, Prim?"

"What are we doing here? I mean, I don't do this. I don't video call with anyone, let alone do... that."

"That was fucking hot."

She shrugs, her blush returning. "How do I know you're not going to hand that footage over to Misty so she has actual evidence of me being a whore to send around school?"

"Do you really think that of me?"

"Yes," she answers honestly.

"Ouch," I breathe, covering my heart with my hand.

"Why would I think otherwise? You don't care about me,

Oak. If you did, then you'd remember—" She slams her lips shut, cutting off her words.

"Then I'd remember what?" I growl, pushing myself up on my elbow and glaring down at my phone as if she's lying right here beside me.

"Then you'd remember kissing me before all this."

27

TALLY

He stares at me through the screen, his brows pinched with confusion.

"What the fuck are you talking about?"

"It doesn't matter," I rush out, because I shouldn't have said anything.

He doesn't remember.

It meant nothing to him, and it meant everything to me.

"I have to go."

"Prim," there's a warning in his voice. "I swear to God, you'd better tell me what the fuck you're talking about. We've never—"

"Tallulah? Are you home, sweetheart?" Dad's voice rings out through the house.

"I have to go. My dad is home."

"Tallulah, don't you dare fucking hang—"

But I end the call, inhaling a ragged breath.

I can't believe I did that.

And yet, part of me can. Because I'm powerless where Oakley is concerned.

He brings out something inside me that I can't fight— maybe part of me doesn't want to.

I've spent so many years being the good girl that I can't deny it feels good being a little bit bad.

My phone starts ringing again, Oakley's number flashing across the screen. I quickly silence it and slip out of bed and into the bathroom to clean myself up.

I still feel the lingering sensations from touching myself. From watching Oakley touch himself. It felt so good.

Too good.

But we can't continue doing this... can we?

"Tallulah?"

"Coming," I yell, quickly checking my reflection to make sure I look presentable.

When I slip back into my room, Dad is already peeking around the door. "Everything okay, sweetheart?" He frowns.

"Everything's fine, Dad. I was doing some reading for class, but I'm about to call it a night."

"Listen, Tallulah. I owe you an apology about Deacon. I shouldn't have ambushed you like that. He's just such an accomplished young man, and the Warricks are good people. I only want the best for you, sweetheart. And you're always so busy with school and your Head Girl responsibilities that I know you find it hard to make friends."

"Deacon isn't a nice person, Dad."

"If you say he isn't, then I trust you. I won't push the issue again."

"Thanks."

"Okay, get some sleep, sweetheart. I don't need to leave until a bit later in the morning, so maybe we can have breakfast before you leave? I'd love to hear all about how the campaign is coming."

A wave of shame rolls through me.

I'm not sure he'd like the truth. The campaign is dead in the water, and I'm fooling around with Oakley Beckworth behind everyone's back.

Not exactly appropriate breakfast conversation.

"Sure, Dad," I reply, because now he's asked, he'll expect me to be there.

I'll just have to hope I can throw him off the scent that anything is wrong.

I wake with a start, my alarm an unwelcome sound cutting through the silence.

I barely slept. Oakley had texted me a few more times, demanding I answer his calls.

I didn't.

He wouldn't believe me, anyway.

With a pit in my stomach, I drag myself out of bed and pull on my fluffy dressing gown before heading downstairs in search of coffee and some paracetamol.

It's going to be a long day.

The low rumble of voices from the television drifts down the hall. Dad must be up.

"Morning," I say as I enter the room, expecting to find my father making his breakfast. But he's glued to the TV, coffee cup in hand.

"Dad?" I frown, a strange feeling creeping through me. "What's wrong?"

"Oh, nothing for you to worry about, sweetheart." He releases a weary sigh, dragging a hand down his face.

"What happened?" I move closer to support him, glancing at the news report on the screen. "Judd Alveston," I read the name flashing along the bottom of the screen. "Why does that name sound familiar?"

"It was a case I worked on, sweetheart." A shadow passes over his face. "The Alveston crime family. We put their boss away for life five years ago. News just broke that he's been murdered by a rival gang member in prison."

"Gosh, that's—"

"Karma." Dad gives me a weak smile. "I haven't thought about that case in a long time. It was tough." He gets up and makes his way to the coffee pot, pouring himself another coffee. "You want?"

"Yes, please. Do you think there'll be repercussions?"

"It's possible. These things usually play out under the radar, though." He hands me my coffee and drops a kiss on my head. "Now, tell me all about your campaign."

"There's not much to tell." At least, not much I want to tell him. "The Heirs have a lot of support."

"They do. But your idea is sound and would really benefit students at All Hallows'. Look, I know you said you didn't want my help. But I can pull some strings—"

"No, Dad. This is my campaign. I need to see it through without you or Mum coming to my rescue."

"Okay, sweetheart," he chuckles, holding his hands up in defeat. "Whatever you want."

"Thanks. I've got this," I breathe, rolling back my shoulders. Absolutely not thinking about last night, the way Oakley looked when he—

Stop, Tallulah.

Stop it right now.

"Sweetheart?" Dad frowns and panic rises up in my chest. "Are you feeling okay? You've gone awfully flushed."

"I'm fine, Dad. But I need to get ready or I'm going to be late." I drain my coffee despite it being too hot.

"What happened to having breakfast together?"

"Rain check?" I place my coffee mug on the side and peck him on the cheek. "I love you, Dad."

"Love you too, sweetheart." He frowns with suspicion, but I don't give him time to raise his concerns as I bolt from the kitchen and race upstairs to my room.

Where I force myself to take a cold shower.

And try to blast all dirty thoughts of Oakley right out of my head.

I'm nervous heading into school. Oakley hasn't texted me this morning, but then, I did ignore all his messages last night after we...

Don't even go there, Tallulah.

I need to hold my head high and be strong. If I let Oakley in any more than I already have, I risk losing myself.

Besides, I have a busy week preparing for the annual All Hallows' Halloween Fest. Every year, the student committee runs an event on the school grounds to raise funds for the school. This year, they voted to hold a scare maze through the woods.

Not my idea of fun, but I was outvoted, and the quality of any good leader is knowing which battles to pick.

The events subcommittee has handled most of the arrangements, but there's still some last-minute things to take care of.

Thankfully, my attendance isn't mandatory, because I don't plan on going.

A strange pang goes through me, but I brush it off.

I don't care about some stupid school event.

I don't.

"Tally, wait up," Abi waves across the courtyard, hurrying toward me. "How are you?"

"I'm fine, thanks."

"Really?" Her eyes narrow.

"What is that supposed to mean?"

"I just thought... with the chasers—"

"I told you before I can handle the chasers, Abi."

"Sorry, I'm just worried about you."

"No, I'm sorry." I let out a heavy sigh. "I'm not very good at... this."

"This?"

"Yeah, letting people in. Having friends. You're a good

friend, Abi. If you're up for it, we could go to Dessert Island Friday night and catch a film or something?"

Her brows pinch. "Oh, actually I was thinking of going to Halloween Fest."

"You were?"

"Well, yeah. I didn't go last year, and I just thought I should have the experience. Olivia invited me."

"She did? That's nice." I swallow over the lump in my throat.

"You should come. I'm sure Liv would like to spend some time with you. I know she feels awful about everything."

"I'm not sure that's a good idea."

"Why not? You used to be friends, didn't you?"

I thought we were. But then everything changed. All because of a drunken moment with her brother.

Twin brother.

But I can't tell Abigail that, so I purse my lips and shake my head a little.

"Just... think about it. Please, for me. I've spent my entire life hiding, Tally. I figure it's time for me to step out of the shadows. Maybe we can do it together."

With that, she takes off, leaving me alone.

And a little dumbfounded.

Abigail Bancroft sure is an enigma. But more than that, she's a good person.

I can't go to Halloween Fest, though. The Heir chasers will be there. Not to mention Oakley and the Heirs themselves.

After last night, I plan to avoid him as much as possible.

I head straight for the student council office, hardly surprised to find a hive of activity given the event is this weekend. But everyone falls silent when I step inside.

"Don't stop on my account," I snap.

"Uh, sorry," Jenna Crosby, a first-year student croaks. "We we're just—"

"Doing your job?"

I sound like a bitch, but I can't help it. I know they've all heard the rumours. I know not one single person has tried to stand up for me. Why should I extend them any niceties?

"How are ticket sales looking?" I ask. Because the whole point of the event is to raise funds for the school.

"Good. Your war—I mean, the issue with the Heirs—doesn't seem to have affected things."

Of course it hasn't. Teenagers are fickle things. Everyone will be there on Friday night because kids love an excuse to party. And Halloween Fest is always a scream.

Literally.

"I've got some last-minute emails to respond to, so I'll be in the office if anyone needs me."

They won't. Because people treat me like a leper now.

All because I let my pride and principles get in the way. I thought I could hurt Oakley—the way he hurt me—by going after the Heirs.

But the only person with anything to lose here is me.

I realise that now.

I can't beat the Heirs.

I never could.

And no matter how much Oakley affects me, no matter how much he awakens something inside of me, I'll never be able to trust him.

Which is why I have to end things.

Before he takes the one thing I know he'll never want.

My heart.

28

OAKLEY

I toss and turn all fucking night as those final words Tally said to me replay in my mind.

What was she talking about?

What don't I remember?

Irritation is still swirling around inside me like a tornado when I finally give up on sleep and throw the covers off the next morning.

My phone still shows no response to my ignored calls and unread messages.

I'm not sure any girl has ever hung up on me before. Okay, yeah, aside from my sister. They're all usually too keen to hop back on my dick for another ride. They don't ignore me.

Ever.

So the fact she has, that she has the audacity to cast me aside like that we just did together was nothing... well, it fucking pisses me off.

"Look out, angry storm approaching," Liv teases as I stomp toward the kitchen.

I'm dressed—barely. My shirt is hanging open, my tie wrapped around my neck, and my trousers are undone. I didn't even bother looking in the mirror. What's the point? I already know I'm a fucking mess.

Reese's eyes shoot to me before he lowers his lips to run a trail of kisses down the side of Liv's neck, making her squirm on his lap.

"You didn't leave your room all fucking night," Elliot helpfully points out. "Who could possibly have pissed you off?"

"Didn't sleep well," I mutter, turning my back on all of them in favour of the coffee pot.

"Maybe you should lay off the pills then," my sister hisses, shooting daggers into my back.

Briefly, I glance over my shoulder. The disappointment and concern that's darkening her eyes make my stomach knot up.

But fuck that.

Fuck her.

She's sitting there wiggling her arse, getting my best friend's cock hard.

She did the one thing I asked her not to, so why the fuck should she get an opinion on what the fuck I do with my life?

"If I need parental advice, I'll be sure to go see Dad and Fiona," I snap, once again feeling like the world's biggest loser and disappointment.

"Oak, I didn't mean—"

I spin around with my coffee in my hand. The burning liquid spills over the side, singeing my fingers.

Gritting my teeth, I glare at my sister. "Oh no, so what did you mean then? Don't hold back; tell me how you really feel."

"Oak," Reese growls, coming to my sister's rescue like the knight in shining armour he most certainly isn't.

"Fuck off, Reese. This doesn't concern you," I growl.

Lifting Liv to her feet, he steps around her. "When you're shouting at my girlfriend, it has everything to do with me." He closes the space between us, a silent warning in his eyes.

I want to push him, feel the pain he's promising me for taking my bullshit out on Liv, but before I get a chance to taunt him some more, my sister steps between us.

"Leave it, Reese. I can handle Oak."

My brows shoot up. "Handle me? I'm not a fucking toddler who needs looking after. I'm eighteen, for fuck's sake."

"Then start acting like it, and maybe we'll treat you as such."

I glare at her, my fists curled in irritation before I slam my coffee back down on the counter and storm out of the Chapel and away from their judgemental stares as fast as I can.

The air is fresh—too fucking fresh, considering I left barely dressed. The frosty grass crunches beneath my feet, and my breath comes out in white puffs in front of me.

But I don't let it stop me. Instead, I suck deep, bitingly cold breaths and try and calm the fuck down.

I have no idea if I'm just on the comedown, suffering from lack of sleep, or if it's Tally.

Of course it's Tally, you prick.

But why? Why does she have this power over me that no other girl has ever managed to have?

I eventually break through the trees, finding the rock looming in the distance.

It glitters with the frost covering its surface, making it look even more forbidden and tempting than ever.

Fuck the curse and all the myths that surround it. That's for the rest of All Hallows' to fear. We know the truth. The only thing they should be fearing is us. We rule this fucking school, and we're the only ones who can bring the kind of wrath they should be scared of.

I hop up, ignoring the biting cold that stings my arse, and I pull my phone from my pocket.

Still no fucking response.

But instead of focusing on that, I open up my screen recording from last night and hit play.

A massive cloud of white surrounds me as I puff out a large breath when her face fills the screen, but that's nothing compared to when I fast forward to the part she gives me her entire body.

Fuck. This girl's got me in a fucking choke hold, and I've no idea why.

I hate her.

Hate. Her.

So why can't I get her out of my fucking head?

The video keeps playing. My eyes don't move from the screen for a second as my cock gets painfully hard inside my trousers.

The temptation to jerk off to this is strong. But I already know it would be unfulfilling. Without at least her voice, her little sounds of pleasure playing out in real time, I know I'd be almost as frustrated after the release as I am now.

No. When I come again, she's going to be there, in person, following my orders and bending to my wishes.

And I can only hope that when I finally slide deep inside her body that it will shatter whatever this weird little obsession I have with her is and allow me to go on about my life without worrying about my feelings toward my enemy.

By the time I turn up for school, I've missed tutor time and I'm late for my first class.

The second I swing the door open and stomp inside the classroom, all eyes turn on me. All eyes except the pair I'm so desperate to see.

I haven't even taken a step when I discover that it's not only my seat in class that's empty.

Hers is too.

"Mr. Beckworth, how lovely of you to grace us with your presence," Mrs. Waters teases.

"Sorry," I mutter, walking deeper in the room, and reluctantly toward my sister.

Her eyes are narrowed in concern, just like they were earlier, and I know I've got no chance of getting out of her interrogation, no matter how much Mrs. Waters might want us to get on with some work.

"Where the hell have you been?" she hisses the second I lower my arse down beside her.

In front of us, Misty makes no attempt to hide the fact she's staring at me.

Ignoring my sister, I keep my attention on my one-woman fan club. "Hey, Mist. How's it going?"

Her pouty lips curl up into a smile, her tongue sneaking out to run along the bottom one as her eyes drop to my mouth in hunger.

She really is a shameless slut. And suddenly, I'm not seeing the appeal.

Why did I ever think that was a turn-on?

"Ow," I complain when a sharp pain explodes in my thigh.

Looking down, I find Liv has stabbed me with her pen. "I was talking to you," she complains. "Are you capable of holding back the flirting for two minutes?"

"What's got your knickers in a twist, Liv? Reese not putting out?" I ask, immediately wincing and regretting my words.

"No, actually. He's perfect. Gets me off every single time."

"Great," I mutter, scrubbing my hand down my face as Mrs. Waters continues the lesson like I hadn't interrupted.

I have no fucking clue what she's talking about, and something tells me that isn't going to change anytime soon.

"What's going on, Oak? I'm worried about you."

Her words make my spine straighten, but despite her stare burning into the side of my face, I don't turn to look at her.

"Surprised you noticed," I mutter as I get my books out and grab a pen I have no intention of using.

"Don't be a prick. I always notice. Talk to me."

"Like you talked to me?" I snap.

I know it's not fair. I've told her I've forgiven her, but I'm just in that petty kind of mood.

"This is different, and you know it."

"Is it? For all you know, I could be fucking one of your friends behind your back."

Regret floods my veins before I've even finished the sentence, but it's too late to stop.

Thankfully, Liv doesn't read into it in the slightest, and instead of taking me seriously, she throws her head back and laughs.

"My friends have better taste. They're not after man-whores who stick it in anything that moves."

After the way I've spoken to her, I guess that comment is well deserved. But still, it fucking stings.

I guess it's a shame that it's true.

It makes me wonder why Tally has come anywhere near me. Okay, sure. It's not like I've given her much of a choice.

But she could have said no. She could have stopped this at any point. Cut off our video call last night before it went too far.

But she hasn't.

For some reason, she's allowing it to happen.

What's left of the lesson passes me by. The only thing I'm really aware of is Liv's anger and burning stare, neither of which I address as I sit there with my eyes locked on the wall in front of me.

The second the bell rings, I'm out of there, leaving my sister behind to call my name.

But as much as I might have hoped for things to get better, they don't. I might lose my sister as she heads off in the opposite direction for her next class, but it soon becomes obvious that Tally isn't going to be attending this one with me either.

Her seat once again sits empty for an hour while everyone around us forgets she even exists.

I guess I should be grateful they're not all talking about her. Spewing their lies and bullshit. But I'm not.

I'm worried.

And I fucking hate it.

I shouldn't be worried about the girl who's trying to ruin our reign at All Hallows'. I should be happy they've finally got to her. But was it them? Or was it me?

I snag Seb's forearm before he manages to escape another lesson I paid zero attention to and pin him back against the wall as the rest of the class walks past us, too scared to get involved with whatever I'm playing at.

I hate that I'm about to even ask this, but I'm losing my fucking mind here.

"Where's Tally?" I growl, low enough that no one else will hear.

"She was here this morning," he confesses. "But I don't think she made it out of our committee meeting."

Something I don't like passes through his eyes.

But before I do something stupid like throw my fist into his face and demand he tells me everything, I take a step back and nod.

That bit of information will have to do for now. If I have to, I'll beat the shit out of him later for being such a disloyal piece of crap.

Leaving him pinned against the wall with wide, terrified eyes, I take off through the building to where the goody two-shoes hang out in the hope of finding some answers.

29

TALLY

"Hello?" I yell again.

I've yelled so much in the last few hours that my throat is hoarse.

Someone should have stumbled across the office now; it's been ages. I'm thirsty, hungry, and if someone doesn't let me out soon, there's a good chance I'll pee myself.

Knowing Misty and her friends, that's probably what they're banking on. They're probably waiting right outside, ready to capture my emergence on camera.

I hate her.

I hate her.

I hate her.

It's such a strong, visceral reaction to have about someone, but she is not a good person. And these stunts are getting more and more destructive.

What if no one realises I'm in here and I have to spend the night?

What if—

"Tally?" Someone bangs on the door and relief floods me. "Prim, you in there?"

"Oakley?" I cry. "Yes... I'm in here, I'm—"

The door swings open, and I don't think I've ever been relieved to see someone as I am to see Oakley standing there.

"Those fucking bitches," he growls, but I fling myself at him, wrapping my arms around his neck.

"Thank you."

"Easy, Prim." He holds my hips, gently shoving me away so he can get a good look at me. "Did they hurt you?"

"No." I shake my head. "But if I don't get to a toilet in the next thirty seconds, I'm going to pee my pants."

"Go," he barks, and I take off across the room. Thankfully, there's a bathroom right outside in the hall.

After doing my business, I wash my hands and give myself a second to catch my breath.

Oakley found me.

He came for me.

But it doesn't really change anything. It only makes what I have to do harder.

I'm about to leave when the bathroom door crashes open and Oakley bursts inside.

"What on earth are you doing?"

"You were taking forever, I thought— Fuck." His wild gaze pins me in place as he rubs the back of his neck.

"You were worried about me."

"Maybe. Just a little." His mouth twitches in the most adorable way and for a second, I wonder what it would be like if I wasn't Tallulah Darlington and he wasn't Oakley Beckworth. If our fathers didn't stand on opposite sides of the line and he wasn't an Heir.

"Prim?" His voice is a soft caress.

"I'm fine. I just needed a minute."

"Come on, I'm taking you home."

"I don't think that's a good idea."

"Fine. We can go somewhere else, and you can tell me what happened."

"I think we both know what happened. Misty and the

Heir chasers lured me into the office and locked me in there with no way of calling for help."

Panic rushes in and I dart past him, running back into the room.

"What the fuck?" Oakley follows.

"My bag. If they've taken my— thank God." I spot it on the floor by the desk where I dropped it. A quick glance inside confirms that my phone is in there and untampered with.

"This shit ends now," Oakley grits out. "I'm going to tell her to back the fuck off. Shit's going too far."

"Do you really think she'll listen to you?"

"I'll make her."

Jealousy surges inside me, because I can vividly imagine all the ways Oakley will make her submit to his whim.

"No. I'm going to drop the campaign."

"What?" He gawks at me.

"You heard me. It was never going to get the green light, and it's the only way to get them off my back. I'll tell Mr. Porter tomorrow. I still believe in the cause, and I think students at All Hallows' would benefit from a new student welfare centre, but perhaps there's another way."

"Tally, you don't have to—"

"Yeah, I do." I give him a sad smile.

"Tell me what you meant last night about me not remembering kissing you."

"No."

"Prim," he warns, taking a step toward me.

I dart backwards, trying to keep some distance between us. Because if he gets close enough, if he touches me, I'm not sure I'll be strong enough to stop him.

"It doesn't matter, Oakley. This, us, it's done."

"Done?" He rears back like I've slapped him. "What the fuck do you mean, it's done?"

"We can't keep doing this, Oak. I won't. I'm going to

withdraw my campaign, and we can go back to how things were before."

"Before?" Bitter laughter bubbles in his throat. "You think we can go back..." His hand snaps out, wrapping around my throat. But it doesn't scare me, because his touch is tender, reverent almost. "I don't know what the fuck is happening here, Prim. But we're not over until I say—"

"It doesn't matter what you say. We're done. I won't do this anymore."

Because I won't survive it.

Oakley will only pull me deeper and deeper under his spell until he decides he's done with our little game.

"I'm sorry, did I give you the illusion you hold the power here, Tallulah? Because you fucking don't."

"You don't scare me, Oakley. If you'd have wanted to ruin me by now, you would have."

He blinks as if he can't quite believe what I'm saying.

"You think I want to..."

"Don't tell me you've actually gone and fallen for me? I'm Tallulah Darlington. You hate me, remember? You hate everything I stand for. Everything that I am."

My own words cut deep, but he needs to hear them; Oakley needs to remember that we can never be more than what we are now.

A disaster waiting to happen.

"If Misty finds out about us, or the rest of the Heirs, or your sister, or your dad, what do you think they'll say?"

His expression darkens, the muscle in his jaw working overtime. Slowly, his fingers loosen until his hand slips away.

"You're right," he says, his voice completely devoid of emotion. "This. Us. We're done."

There's something behind his eyes that sends a chill down my spine.

"Oak?"

"See you around, Darlington."

Oakley walks out of the room without a backward glance. Like he didn't just swoop in and save me.

Like he didn't just break my heart.

I didn't go home.

I couldn't. If Mum and Dad were there, there would be no hiding my miserable mood, so I headed to the one place guaranteed to lift my spirits.

Dessert Island.

"Here you go, Tally," Lennon sings as he places down my slice of red velvet and salted caramel hot chocolate. "I made it a big slice."

"You're too good to me." I manage a small smile.

He lingers, and I sense he's about to say something I might not want to hear. So I add, "Thanks. If I need anything else, I'll let you know."

"Sure thing." He takes off, a hint of dejection in his expression.

Lennon is cute enough, but I don't feel that spark with him. Which is a shame, because he seems like a good person with good intentions.

Unlike Oakley.

Frustrated with myself, I fork a big piece of cake into my mouth, groaning at how good it is.

But my temporary good mood is ruined when the doorbell rings and I look over to find Olivia and Abi.

Abi spots me and waves, saying something to Olivia before heading toward me.

"I heard what happened. I am so sorry."

"It's fine. You weren't to know."

"No, but I should have asked more questions when I realised you weren't in class. I just thought—"

"Abi, it's fine."

Her brows furrow. "Are you okay?"

"I'm fine. Didn't feel like going home, so I came here."

"I guessed. I went straight to your house after I heard—"

"You did?"

"Of course. I'm so mad at myself. I should have checked."

"What's she doing here?" I flick my head toward where Olivia is in the queue.

"She was the one who told me what happened."

"How did she—"

"I guess Reese told her."

"Of course."

"Is it okay she's here? She was angry. I thought she was going to hunt Misty down and—"

"Hi."

The air thins with Olivia's arrival at my table.

"Hi," I say.

"Can we sit? Lennon is going to bring over our order when it's ready."

"Sure."

"How are you?" she asks me, pulling up a chair.

"I'm dropping the campaign."

"What? Why?" Abigail gasps.

"Because I can't beat them." My gaze lifts to Olivia, and she gives me a sad smile.

"I'm sorry. I knew the Heir chasers would retaliate, but it's been an impossible situation. For what it's worth, I've asked Reese to intervene more than once. But you know how it is. They can't be seen to lose face."

"It was stupid to think I could ever take them on and win."

"So why did you?" She holds my stare, searching my face for answers I can't give her.

"It doesn't matter now. I'm going to tell Mr. Porter tomorrow."

"It's a good idea," Abi offers. "Maybe there's another way

to make it work? A way that doesn't involve taking the Chapel off the Heirs."

"Yeah, maybe."

"Maybe you'll be more open to coming to Halloween Fest now?" She gives me a hopeful smile. "It'll be the perfect opportunity to show everyone you're not going to cower and hide."

"I don't think that's a good idea."

"Abi's right," Olivia says. "You should go. In fact, we could all go together. I miss hanging out with you."

"Reese won't—"

"Reese respects me enough to not tell me who I can and can't be friends with, Tally. I know there's been some conflict of interest since the campaign, but I made it clear to him and my brother that I wasn't going to take sides. And I'm not. I'm Switzerland." She holds up her hands as if it's that simple.

It isn't.

But I don't have the energy to argue.

"You and the committee have worked so hard to get everything together. You should be there to experience it."

"Please." Abi gives me big, puppy-dog eyes. "I've never been before, and I'm so nervous."

"You really want to go?"

"I'm tired of hiding, Tally. And even if I hate it and want to leave, at least I can say I did it."

"Atta girl." Liv nudges Abi with her shoulder and the two of them share a smile.

It feels weird to be on the periphery of their budding friendship. But maybe it doesn't have to be that way.

Maybe if I drop the campaign, I can hang out with them again. Obviously when Olivia isn't around Oakley.

"It's one night," Olivia adds. "If you're that worried about going, we can all dress up. That way you can go and have fun, but nobody even has to know you're there."

"Oh yes, I want to dress up. We could go to Bojangles and see what costumes they have."

"I'm not sure—"

"Pleeeeease." Abi grins. "It'll be fun."

Fun.

It doesn't sound like fun, but maybe it's exactly what I need.

One night to dress up and be anyone but Tallulah Darlington.

30

OAKLEY

"What the fuck was that?" Elliot booms the second he storms inside the locker room where I was sent after being thrown out of our game.

It's been building in me since the moment Tally looked straight into my eyes and told me that we were done. This inferno began growing from that moment on, and inevitably, it was going to explode at some point.

I guess it just would have been ideal if it didn't happen while the Chargers' scrum half was getting in my face.

His taunts weren't even that bad. Most days, I'd take it as inspiration to wipe the floor with their arses, but today was different. And before I knew what was happening, my fist was flying toward his face.

He was more than happy to get in on the action, too. His left hook was fucking brutal. I'm pretty sure my brain is still rattling around inside my head.

"He was being a dick," I scoff, turning my back on our fearless leader, something that is sure to piss him off even more.

Dropping my towel, I reach for my boxers, but before I

have a chance to pull them on, Elliot's palm collides with my shoulder, shoving me backward.

"What?" I snarl, getting right into his face. "Did you want a fucking pop too?"

I hold my hands out to the side in offering.

"Go on then. Or are you too pussy?"

"Leave it, E," Reese says, trying to pull Elliot away from me.

"You don't have to fight for me, Whitfield. Just because you're fucking my sister, it doesn't mean that—"

"I wasn't fighting for you, knobhead. I'd just like for the four of us to get to the party in one fucking piece."

"I'm not going," I scoff, already knowing it's a lie. Liv let slip the other night while I was sulking back at Dad's place that she's invited Tally to go with her and Abi. I even managed to get their costumes out of her so I know exactly what I'm looking for.

"You fucking are. It's our last Halloween Fest. We're expected to be there," Elliot commands.

"Yeah, well. Maybe I'm fucking fed up of everything that's expected of me."

"Jesus, who cracked your nuts in a vice recently?" Theo jokes.

"Fuck off," I bark, finally stepping away from Elliot and dragging my boxers on. "Just fuck off."

I march out of the locker room barely dressed as the rest of the team finally come stumbling inside, looking miserable after their loss.

That I probably caused.

Oh well, too fucking late to do anything about it now.

I stomp toward the car park with my face and fist aching like a motherfucker, but neither of them has anything on the pain that's taken up residence in my chest over the past few days.

I don't bother going back to the Chapel. I know they'll

only want to continue where we left off in the locker room the second they find me, so instead, I go home.

It's a stupid fucking idea. But as I turn into the driveway and park between my sister's and Tally's car, I realise that I really don't care.

Throwing the door open, I climb out, dragging my bag full of muddy kit along with me.

The second I step inside the house, girly laughter hits my ears.

Dumping my shit, I head straight toward it.

"Oh my God, is that really what he said?" Liv asks through her laughter.

"I swear on my life h-he—"

Abi's words cut off the second I appear in the doorway. Whatever her reaction is other than that, I don't see, because my eyes are locked on Tally's.

"I thought you were going back to the Chapel," Liv says, filling the silence, although her demand does little to dispel the atmosphere that's descended with my arrival.

"Change of plans," I growl, stomping forward and ripping the fridge open.

Not finding what I want, I turn toward the cupboard where Dad keeps his liquor. Reaching up, I grab a new bottle of vodka and twist the top.

Taking a swig, I let the alcohol burn down my throat. Any hope I had about drowning the pain out with it is quickly forgotten when I discover it's still in place.

I scan the three sets of eyes trained on me. Abi is mostly curious. Liv is angry. And Tally is... resigned. That sight of it is like a knife through my chest.

I'd rather see her anger, her fire, her hate.

But that... The way she's looking at me as if I'm nothing. I don't know how to deal with it.

"I thought you were all getting the party started early," I

snap, eyeing the milkshake and cake they've been eating with disgust.

"You know, we don't all need to get drunk and high to enjoy ourselves," Liv snaps. "How was the game?" she asks, knowing full well how it went. "I see someone tried knocking some sense into you."

"Oh, this?" I ask, pointing to my swollen eye. "Nah, the guy just discovered that I fucked his sister last week." My words finally get a reaction out of Tally, although, fair play to her, she covers it long before Liv or Abi notice. "She was a fucking shit lay, too. Proper stuck-up bitch. Couldn't pull the stick out of her arse long enough for me to shov—"

"Okay, that's enough. None of us care where you stick your rotten dick. Now fuck off. We're having girls' night."

"I thought you were going to Halloween Fest?"

"We are. After this." Liv gestures toward the table before turning her back on me, dismissing me.

They pick up their conversation as if I was never there, and feeling like a pussy, I walk away with the vodka clutched to my chest.

As much as I might want to down the lot and let oblivion take me. I have other plans for tonight. Plans that involve one of the girls currently sitting in my kitchen.

All I've got to do is wait.

A door slamming makes my eyes pop open and causes my heart to race.

I didn't mean to fall asleep. I guess that game took more out of me than I thought. That, or the fact I've barely slept since being dumped on Tuesday. It was a first for me, that's for sure.

I'm usually the one turning needy girls away. And I don't think twice about it.

What Tally did broke the mould. But then, I guess she always has.

The rules that I hold other girls to don't seem to apply to her.

"Okay, I'm done. Tally, you're next," my sister barks happily. Her words are a little slurred, making me wonder if those milkshakes I saw them with earlier weren't quite so innocent after all.

My heart rate continues to increase as I think about her getting naked on the other side of the door.

My eyes are locked on the light wood dividing us as I swing my legs over the edge of my bed and place my feet on the plush carpet.

More voices come from the other side of our Jack and Jill bathroom, confirming that Tally is heading inside.

My cock swells in anticipation.

She's been here a couple of times before to visit my sister, but I've no idea if she's aware that I have such easy access to her right now.

I stand with my toes and nose practically pressed against the door, listening as she closes the one on the other side and begins shuffling around.

The shower turns on and my hand lifts to the handle.

If she's sensible, she'll have seen this other door and flicked the lock. But if she's not...

Taking my chances, I twist the handle. My heart jumps into my throat when the door opens as the heat of the steam-filled room washes over my face.

My hand wraps around my cock that's straining behind my sweats, squeezing hard enough to make a growl rumble in my throat.

Since Liv got with Reese, my pre-game ritual has been shot to shit, but add Tally into the mix and I'm also missing my game-day blowie. Something I have every intention of rectifying very soon.

Pushing the door wider, I catch sight of her blurred silhouette in the steamed-up mirror. It might be hazy, but it's enough to have my cock weeping and to know that she's got her back to me. I shed my clothes before stepping up behind her, wrapping one hand around her mouth to stop her from screaming, and my arm around her waist, pinning her body back against mine.

She screams despite it being pointless and thrashes against me. But it has the opposite effect to what I think she's trying to achieve.

"Keep fighting, Prim. It makes me so fucking hard," I growl in her ear. "You feel that?" I ask, grinding against her arse. "Been a long fucking time since I felt you on my dick."

She mumbles something behind my hand.

"What was that? I can't hear you."

Pushing her farther into the shower, I press the length of her body against the cold tiled wall, and she trembles against me.

"You like this, don't you? My little whore likes it when I take control." Releasing her waist, I push my hand down her stomach to find her pussy. A groan rumbles deep in my throat when I find her wet and ready for me. "You're such a good girl, getting all wet for me."

She whimpers again.

"Do you know how easy it would be to take you right now? Your pussy is begging to be filled to the brim with my cock."

Whimper.

"What was that? I can move my hand, but you've got to promise not to scream."

Tally is still for a beat, then she nods and I pull my hand away, dropping it to her breast and teasing her nipple just like she did on that video call with me the other day.

"We're not doing this," she whisper-hisses. "You shouldn't be here."

"I do a lot of things I shouldn't, Prim. Didn't you already know that?"

"We're over. You agreed."

"Yeah, well. You owe me still, remember? I'm cashing in."

"Oh God," she whimpers quietly when I thrust two fingers inside her.

"No, Prim. Not God. Oakley Beckworth."

I can't decide if the noise that rips from her throat at my confession is pure desire or irritation. I also don't really care.

Just as she begins to relax back against me, I remove my touch from her, step back a little, and twist my fingers in her hair.

"I'm cashing in right now," I bark, forcing her to her knees.

Water rains down on both of us as her knees hit the tray and her eyes zero in on my hard dick.

"Be a good girl now, Prim, and open those lips for me." With my hand still in her hair, I paint her lips with the precum that's beading on the tip of my cock, but she refuses to part them.

"Look at you, Prim. Everyone thinks you're such an innocent little goody two-shoes. But really, you spend your nights fantasising about choking on my cock."

Her eyes narrow, but not before her pupils dilate, giving away the truth.

"Be a good girl for me, Prim, and let me in."

It takes a couple of seconds, but her need to follow my commands gets too much and I'm able to slip into her hot and addicting mouth.

"Fuck, yes," I groan quietly as she sucks on me.

But I don't give her time to play. We're against the clock, and there's no fucking way I'm allowing my sister to get suspicious and barge her way in here to see this.

"Hold on," I warn her before thrusting my hips, the head of my cock hitting the back of her throat, making her gag.

"Relax, Prim. Take all of me. Then I'm going to send you back out there with the taste of my cum on your tongue to remind you who you belong to."

31

TALLY

"Fuck, *fuck*," Oakley hisses, coating my tongue with his cum as he promised.

I stare up at him in a daze, hardly able to believe what just happened.

What I let happen.

"Get out. Get the hell out." Panic swarms me as I slam my hands onto his thighs, slipping on the wet tiles and falling hard onto my ass.

"Look at you," he drawls, grabbing a towel off the hook and stepping out of the shower. "So eager to get on your knees for me."

"Get out, Oakley, n—"

"Everything okay in there, Tally?" Liv's voice fills the bathroom and I swear I see a flash of panic in Oakley's eyes.

I don't know whether to be relieved or disappointed when he throws a towel at me.

God, I need therapy.

A twelve-step programme that will help rid me of my addiction to an entitled control freak who looks at me like I'm his favourite toy.

"I'm fine," I call back. "I had a slight mishap with the shower, but I'll be out soon."

"Okay, hurry. I stole a bottle of Fiona's wine. It's the good stuff."

"Go," I hiss at Oakley, who's still standing there. Watching me. A strange expression pinching his brows.

He slips out of the bathroom without another word, and I exhale a long breath, wondering how the hell I'm going to go out there and face Liv and Abigail.

Resigning myself to the fact I'll have to wash my hair now it's half soaked thanks to Oakley, I make quick work of showering, dry myself off, and get changed into my black Catwoman outfit.

By the time I join the girls again, Liv is just finishing curling her Harley Quinn pigtails and Abi is staring at herself in the mirror as if she doesn't recognise herself.

"I-I look..."

"Hot as hell." Liv grins. "The guys are going to freak."

"Oh, I'm not sure I want... that."

"Hush. You deserve a little attention tonight. You don't have to do anything you don't want; just enjoy being a kick-arse villain instead of quiet, shy Abigail for a change." Liv shrugs as if it's that easy. Then, she swings her attention to me.

"What the hell happened to you? I didn't think you were washing your hair."

"I... shower malfunction. Can I borrow your hairdryer?"

"Sure, over there. But hurry, we need to leave soon. Oh, and here"—she grabs a glass of wine and thrusts it at me—"a little pre-party drink for Dutch courage."

"I'm not—"

"Come on, Tally. It's girls' night and we're letting our hair down, remember."

"Fine." I snatch it off her and move over to the dresser with the hairdryer. But a knock at the door startles me.

My heart jumps into my throat, because what if it's Oakley?

"Yeah?" Liv calls, but it's Mr. Beckworth who appears in the doorway.

"Hi girls. Big night—Tallulah Darlington?"

"I... umm, hi, Mr Beckworth."

"Well, this is a surprise. I—"

"Dad," Liv hisses. "Don't be weird. Tally is my friend. You know that."

"Yes, well, I just wanted to say have fun tonight and stay safe. It was... nice to see you, Tallulah."

I nod around a weak smile, because what else is there to do?

Awkward tension lingers in the air, but Liv rushes over to the door and ushers him out of her room.

"God, I'm so sorry about that." She throws me an apologetic glance.

"It's fine. I can see why it would be weird." I finish blowing out my hair and then pull half into a ponytail at the back of my head so I can slide the black eye mask over my face.

"What do you think?"

"Nice!" Liv grins. "No one will ever know it's you."

Her words are supposed to give me some reassurance, but instead, they make my stomach dip. I don't want people to know I'm at the party. For Misty and her friends to find a way to ruin my night. But I can't help but think it's not supposed to be this way.

That I'm not supposed to have to disguise myself in order to attend a school party.

A party I helped organise.

"And if they do," Abi adds, "screw them. You deserve to be there as much as the rest of us."

"Abigail Porter, you kiss your daddy with that mouth?" Liv chuckles and then quickly frowns. "Okay, that sounded all kinds of wrong."

"What do you mean?" Abi asks, and Liv looks at me and we burst out laughing.

"Should you tell her, or should I?"

"It's dirty, isn't it?"

"Let's just say, daddy kink is a real thing."

"Daddy ki— I'm not sure I want to know."

"Drink up, Poison Ivy." Liv grins. "We have a party to crash."

"Oh my God, this is insane," Abi says as we approach the entrance to the scare maze.

The dense woods behind All Hallows' has been transformed into an interactive fright experience thanks to the local theatre group we hired. Somewhere in the maze, there are twenty actors dressed as flesh-eating zombies, ready to scare the crap out of everyone as they make their way through the maze to get to the party beyond it.

"Welcome to Halloween Fest," the voodoo doll I know as Krystal greets us. "Tickets please."

Liv hands her three tickets and we slip through the eerie curtain.

There's a chill in the air, but the wine I drank at Olivia's, and my run-in with Oakley, heat my blood.

Excited screams ring out all around us as people make their way through the maze.

"I've never been to anything like this before," Abi says as we move deeper through the carefully mapped out route.

"It's— AHHHH." Her bone-chilling scream fills the air as a gruesome zombie bursts from behind the trees.

"Quick." Liv grabs her arm and we all but run away, laughing.

"That was so realistic." Abi clutches her throat. "My heart is beating so fast."

"Boo!"

A bunch of boys all dressed in black with LED masks rush at us. For a second, I think it's Oakley and the Heirs. But when one of them says, "Shit, it's Whitfield's girl," I know I'm mistaken.

"What's wrong, wankers? Scared Reese will cut off your balls for scaring the crap out of us?"

"Come on, Grendon, she's not worth it."

They take off like a pack of wild dogs, barking and howling as they disappear in the darkness ahead of us.

"Arseholes," Liv scoffs. "Are you both okay?"

I nod and Abigail bites down on her bottom lip. "Once we reach the party, it'll be better. Come on."

Hand in hand we wander through the maze, avoiding any more run-ins with lurking zombies or amped-up second years.

The music from the party grows louder, reverberating inside my chest, doing nothing to ease the knot in my stomach.

"Yes," Liv says. "I can see the end."

"Thank God. I'm not sure I can take much more." Abi presses close to me as we amble along in our heels.

Thanks to our costumes, we all opted for heeled boots. But when we turn the corner and spill out into the clearing, it's apparent a lot of girls didn't.

"Wow," Liv remarks. "And I thought we looked slutty."

"Hey," I protest. "Speak for yourself."

"Come on, let's get a drink." Liv dances her way through the crowd, ignoring the whispers and stares. My heart hammers in my chest, but if anyone recognises me, they don't say anything.

The events committee did an amazing job. A huge gazebo decorated with fake cobwebs carves out the dance floor, and there's a row of buffet tables covered in black plastic sheets housing all the drinks and snacks.

"Let's dance," Abi suggests as she takes her drink from Olivia.

Since it's a school event, it's officially an alcohol-free zone, but everyone—even me, much to my annoyance—knows that people will sneak all manner of drinks in.

I frown, taking my own drink from Liv. "You want to—"

"Dance? Yes." She grins.

I cast Liv a wary look and she shrugs. "The girl wants to dance; let's dance."

I glance around, half expecting to see Misty or the Heirs glowering in my direction. But no one pays us much attention as we slip into the sea of bodies.

"What are the boys dressing up as?" Abi shouts over the music.

"I have no idea. Apparently, it's a big surprise." Liv grabs Abi's hand and weaves it in the air, encouraging the shy, quiet girl to mimic her moves.

I sway awkwardly to the beat, wishing I could get out of my own head.

Wishing that I wasn't thinking about Oakley every two seconds.

A trickle of awareness goes through me, and I glance over my shoulder, searching the shadows. But I can't see anything or anyone that resembles Oakley or the Heirs.

"Dance with us, Tally." Abi grabs my hand, and I realise then that she's a little drunk.

"We need to watch her," I whisper to Liv.

"Relax, I've got her. No one will think twice about touching her."

Her words, although not malicious, land like bullets.

Abigail is Liv's friend. Which makes her friends of the Heirs by association. The same courtesy doesn't extend to me. Not anymore.

Maybe it never did.

Forcing myself to stop thinking about them, I close my eyes and start moving to the beat, surprised at how easy it comes.

Behind the Catwoman mask, I'm invisible. And although

part of me hates that I can't be myself here, another part relishes that for one night, I can be whoever I want to be.

But my momentary good mood is ruined when a ripple of excitement goes through the air.

"Oh. My. God," Liv freezes on the spot, watching as the Heirs appear out of the shadows as if summoned by the devil himself.

"Oh my," Abi chokes out, watching as Elliot—or a half-naked Michael Myers—steps forward and surveys the crowd like a king looking down on his kingdom.

"Why is that so hot?" Liv asks, fanning herself. "That shouldn't be hot, right?"

I assume she's talking about Reese dressed as a half-naked Jason Voorhees and not her brother who is Freddie Kruger or Theo who is behind the Ghostface mask.

"Speech, speech," some idiot yells as if this is their party and not the hard work of the events committee.

Elliot, to my relief, stays put. But Theo staggers forward and lifts his beer in the air. "Happy Halloween, fuckers. Let's get this party started."

The crowd erupts, only heightening the atmosphere, as a gaggle of girls rushes to their sides. Reese spots Liv and makes a beeline in our direction.

That's my cue.

"I need some air," I whisper to Abi, slipping my hand out of hers.

My name is drowned out by the noise as I stumble through the crowd.

It was a mistake coming tonight.

I realise that as I slink into the shadows, watching the party go on around me. This is their world, not mine.

I don't belong here. I never have, and I never will.

And when Oakley is done playing with me, he'll cast me aside like I'm nothing more than a toy he got bored of.

A rush of emotion clogs my throat and I grab a drink, downing it in one.

Another cheer goes up and I glance back, my heart dropping at the sight of two girls pawing all over Oakley as he stands beside Elliot and Theo while they do shots.

I can't watch him flirt with girls all night. I won't.

Slipping back into the maze, I follow the path back. My eyes burn with unshed tears, clouding my vision a little. I quicken my pace, desperate to get out of here and as far away from Oakley Beckworth as possible.

But as I round the corner, I get an awful sense of being watched.

Stopping, I turn around and—

The air whooshes from my lungs as someone grabs me from behind, clapping their hand over my mouth and dragging me into the shadows. Sheer panic douses every inch of me as I'm dragged like a rag doll away from the party, deeper into the woods.

Part of me wants to believe it's Oakley, that he's trying to scare me.

But this feels too cruel, even for him.

I claw at my captor's gloved hand, trying to get him to stop. But he doesn't, and no matter how much I thrash and fight, it's futile.

Until he rounds the side of the Heirs' cabin and shoves me hard, sending me hurtling to the ground.

"Wha— Deacon?" I blink up at him, hardly able to believe my eyes. "What the hell are you doing?"

"Hi baby." He grins at me, an unhinged glint in his eyes. "Miss me?"

32

OAKLEY

Hands shamelessly run up my chest, but unlike the thrill I'm sure would have gone through me a few weeks ago being the focus of attention of not one, but two chasers, all I feel is disgust.

I don't want either of these whores. I want the girl who thinks she's hiding in plain sight just a few feet away.

To be fair, Liv did a good job. The costume was a fucking fantastic idea for more than one reason. Not only does no one other than us know who is hiding beneath that Catwoman costume—yeah, I fucking eavesdropped on that conversation for my own benefit—but she looks fucking insane in that black all-in-one outfit. And the low cut of the neckline. Fuck me, her tits are mind-blowing.

My cock jerks in my trousers as the wandering hands continue. But if they think even an ounce of my desire right now is for them, they're going to be very much mistaken.

"Dance with us, Oak. Let's get the party started off right," Misty purrs in my ear.

My knee-jerk reaction is to say no, to walk away and find some fun that comes in the form of the baggie of pills in my pocket and the girl who's trying to pretend not to watch my every move.

But knowing I have her attention, I can't stop myself.

"Only if it involves both of you," I growl, allowing them to manhandle me into the middle of the dance floor.

They pin me in the middle of their slutty sandwich, and I make a half-arsed attempt to make them think I'm interested. They might have gone to town making themselves look like the desperate sluts they are in their almost non-existent outfits, but I don't even know what they've actually come as. Prostitutes, maybe.

Music pounds from the huge speakers set up around the clearing. It would be easy to lose myself tonight. Hell knows I fucking need it. But with her here, I can't find it in me to pull those pills out and forget about the world.

If someone realises Catwoman is her... if Misty realises she's here...

"Fuck."

"What's wrong, baby? You're tense. Need me to help you blow off some steam?"

Misty's hand slides down over my abs, and before I know what's happening, she's rubbing my very uninterested, flaccid dick.

"No," I bark, my eyes lifting to scan the crowd for my little kitty.

Liv is already lost in Reese's arms, making my stomach knot up. Theo has some chaser caged against a tree, and Elliot... he's standing, watching the party like the fucking king of the world.

I find Abi at the drinks table getting a refill. It's hard to believe she's the shy girl we know her to be. That outfit seems to have given her a little confidence boost. It's a good look on her.

She spins on her heels and wobbles a little, having to reach out for the table to steady herself. Oh yeah, innocent little Abi is getting the full All Hallows' experience tonight.

But my eyes don't linger on her for long, because the person I'm looking for still hasn't appeared.

"Shit," I hiss, shoving Misty and Lauren's hands from my body before I push through the crowd.

My first instinct is to ask Abi where she is. But I can't. No one knows what's been happening between us, and that's the way it needs to stay.

I shoot my sister a scathing look—not that she'd realise it. She's too busy having her face sucked off by my best friend.

Fuck's sake.

"Oakley," a familiar deep voice says behind me, making me spin around.

My eyes narrow on Seb suspiciously.

We're not friends. Hell, we barely ever exchange any words. Especially now I know he's a lying shit.

"What?" I snap, my need to find Tally and make sure she's okay is more pressing than having a conversation with this prick.

"Oakley," Misty whines, her shrill voice making my top lip peel back.

Seb's eyes rip from mine, probably in favour of Misty's barely contained tits. Can't really fault him for it; she's ensured every motherfucker is going to look tonight.

"There's uh... there's something you need to know," he says, turning his attention back on me.

"Oh yeah?" I ask, folding my arms over my chest and taking a step closer.

The pussy swallows nervously, looking up at me like a scared little child as I loom over him. "I-I... umm..."

"Spit it out, Howard. I don't have all fucking night."

"Yeah, okay." He runs a hand down his face. "I just thought you should know that I overheard Misty talking to some guy about the girl in the Catwoman costume," he says in a rush, his voice lowering as he says the final two words that really catch my attention.

"What about Catwoman?" I ask, desperately trying not to show my concern but fearing that I fail miserably.

"I didn't hear it all, but they were planning to hurt her."

My heart rate picks up and blood rushes past my ears as my fear escalates. "Why are you telling me this?"

"Because. Tally dropped the campaign. And..."

"And?" I snap, quickly losing patience.

"And I see things."

"Motherfucker," I hiss. "Where? Where are they?"

He shakes his head. "I don't know, but I heard them talk about the cabin."

My blood runs cold as I think about our cabin through the trees. It'll be deserted right now with my boys here with me. Anything could happen.

"Thank you," I say, but there's little chance of him hearing it, because I'm already halfway to the tree line.

The shadows swallow me up as the sound of the party behind me begins to reduce—not that I can hear much over the pounding of my heart in my ears. I fly through the woodland that separates us from the cabin. Thankfully, I know this land like the back of my hand, and I dodge the trees easily as I run.

My chest is heaving as I break into the clearing in front of the cabin. The wooden building is in darkness as I approach, but a bang from inside lets me know that someone is there.

My heart jumps into my throat as I approach the open double doors. There's a part of me that wants to go racing in to save the day, but something holds me back.

My fear of showing anyone other than Tally just how fucking addicted I am to her, maybe.

Ignoring that thought, I tell myself I just want to assess the situation before throwing myself into the middle of it. Another bang rips through the air, startling me, quickly followed by a cry. But it's not the cry I was expecting.

It doesn't come from a terrified girl who's been cornered by a predator, but a guy—and he sounds like he's in agony.

Another grunt fills the air before two dark figures move through the room before me.

My chin drops as I watch Tally fight.

Literally fight.

In only a few moves, she sweeps the guy's feet out from beneath him, sending him crashing to his back on the old dusty floor.

What the actual fuck?

All the air rushes from my lungs, my cock aching in my boxers as I watch her loom over the shadowed figure. I wait with bated breath for her to say something, but it never comes. She just... watches him.

When she stands back to full height again and spins toward the door, I jump into action, slipping around the side of the building and out of sight.

More than anything, I might want to go to her. To make sure she's okay, to tell her she's a fucking bad-arse and fuck her right here in the clearing for anyone to see.

But I don't.

Even when her sob hits my ears before she takes off running.

A groan from inside the cabin drags my attention back to the guy she's left behind.

I'll see you real soon, Prim, I silently promise.

Moving back to the doors, I close them behind me before reaching for the switch beside me. Light floods the room and my eyes lock on the figure slumped in the corner, dressed head to toe in black.

My footsteps echo through the silence as I close the space between us and reach down. Dragging his hood back, I rip the mask from his face as anger explodes within me like a wildfire.

"Warrick?" I growl, my voice low and dangerous as I stare down at him.

I can't help but smirk at the bruise that's already darkening his cheek.

Tally is a fighter. Who knew?

"You got more than you bargained for tonight, huh?"

"Fuck you, Beckworth," he hisses, getting his feet beneath him to stand.

"Misty put you up to this." It's not a question, I already know it's the truth. "What has she got over you? Because I already know that her pussy isn't enough to make you sign your death certificate like this."

His eyes darken in anger, letting me know that there is something. "Whatever," he murmurs, a slight edge to his voice. "I'm out."

He tries to step around me, but I'm not having any of it and quickly get in his way. "You think that's it? That you'll get your arse handed to you by a girl and you'll get to just walk away?"

"What the fuck do you care? You hate Tally," he sneers.

"Yeah. But do you know what?" I taunt. "I fucking hate you more."

My fingers curl as I pull my arm back. Pure fucking relief floods my body as my hit lands, making his nose crunch and blood begin pouring.

"You fucked up tonight. And I'm going to make sure you remember that for a while."

Not willing to go down easily, Deacon comes at me, ploughing his fist into my stomach before I manage to get another hit.

I welcome the pain.

I fucking deserve it for everything I've done. But mostly, for not protecting her tonight.

Not that she needed it.

Images of physically fighting with her, feeling her tiny fists slamming into my body and watching her literally taking me to

CRUEL DEVIOUS HEIR: PART ONE

my knees fill my mind as I jump on Deacon, forcing him to the ground once more and fucking up his face until he's groaning in pain.

"Fuck you, cunt. This is my school. My fucking territory. My fucking girl. And you have no right to touch anything that belongs to me," I roar.

The taste of copper fills my mouth from the couple of lucky shots he got in. But honestly, the pussy stood no chance.

"Oakley, stop," that familiar voice roars as Deacon goes limp beneath me.

"Took you fucking long enough, Howard. Anyone would think you're a fucking pussy," I seethe, getting to my feet and wiping the blood that's dripping from my chin.

His eyes dart between me and the bloody mess I've left on the floor. "I, uh... I got held up," he stutters.

"Well, thanks for your help and all that. But I've got somewhere I need to be."

Something beside the door catches my eye, making me stop. Leaning down, I pick up Tally's shoes before looking back at Seb.

"You hear anything else that bitch has planned, and I want to be the first person you talk to. In return, I won't tell them you've switched sides. Again."

I take off before he has a chance to answer. I'm not fucking interested in anything he might have to say. While I'm grateful that he gave me the heads up on this, I'm not likely to fucking thank him.

If he really had Tally's back, then he wouldn't have left her alone in her fight when shit got hard to handle. Fucking pussy only cares about himself.

Ignoring the party that's still raging through the trees, I head straight to where I left my car.

There's only one place I want to spend the rest of my night, and it's not fucking here, getting touched up by Misty and her wandering hands. If I so much as see that bitch before I get what I really need, there's every chance that I'll choke the fucking life out of her right in front of the entire sixth form.

33

TALLY

I'm still shaking by the time I shuffle out of the hot shower and pull a fluffy towel around me. A potent mix of adrenaline and fear courses through my veins every time I think about what happened.

What almost happened.

Part of me still can't believe Deacon tried to...

No, don't go there, Tallulah.

He didn't touch me, not really.

I didn't give him a chance.

When he'd grabbed me from behind, I'd been unable to fight back. Too paralysed with fear. But the second we'd gotten to the cabin and I'd seen the dark glint in his eye as he raked his hungry gaze over my body, I'd leaped into action.

I should have told somebody. The second I ran, I should have called my dad or the police or someone.

But creeps like Deacon Warrick have money and influence on their side. And I don't need any more rumours flying around All Hallows' about me.

I'm fine.

He didn't hurt me.

He didn't—

The shrill of my phone cuts through the silence, making my heart lurch into my throat.

I clutch the towel to my chest as I pad across my room and grab it.

> Abi: Are you sure you're okay?

> Tally: I promise, I'm fine. How's the party?

As soon as I was far enough away from the grounds of All Hallows', I'd texted Abi to let her know I was leaving. I didn't tell her the truth. I didn't want her to worry.

> Abi: I'm drunk, Tally. Not super drunk, but I feel so good.

> Tally: Just be careful, okay? And stick with Liv.

> Abi: I will. Reese and Elliot are watching us like hawks.

> Tally: Elliot, huh?

I've noticed her watching him before now. But Elliot Eaton would eat a girl like Abi alive. I get it, though. The appeal. The allure of the Heirs.

> Abi: Oh no, it's nothing like that. He's... well, you know. A boy like Elliot would never like a girl like me.

> Abi: Oh God, forget I sent that.

> Abi: I mean it. Delete it. Please.

Laughter rolls through me, which feels good after my harrowing night.

> Tally: Relax. Your secret is safe with me. Have fun... but not too much. x

Dropping my phone, I pull on my nightshirt and some knickers and climb into bed, leaving the lamp on.

Mum and Dad should be home soon, but it doesn't stop me from staring at the bedroom door, a trickle of fear racing down my spine.

Deacon wouldn't be stupid enough to follow me home.

He wouldn't.

What if he does, though? What if he calls his parents—or worse, mine?

I force myself to take a deep breath. If he knows what's good for him, Deacon will stay far, far away from me after tonight.

But as my eyes grow heavy and my breathing evens out, I can't help but think what if he doesn't?

What if tonight only makes things ten times worse?

His dark gaze is the last thing I see as I tumble into oblivion.

Silently praying he doesn't find me in my dreams.

I wake with a start, my heart racing in my chest, fingers curled in the sheets as my eyes strain against the darkness.

My eyes flick to the digital clock, and I frown when I realise I've barely been asleep an hour.

Listening, I half-expect to hear my parents. Their drunken laughter filtering upstairs. But the house is silent, save for the wind outside brushing up against the windows.

Turning over, I pull the covers closer, burrowing down until—

"Oakley." His name pierces the silence as fear permeates every inch of me.

He's here.

Sitting in my chair, watching me in the dark. "What are you— oh my God."

"You should see the other guy." He gives me a crooked grin, wincing a little as he clutches his busted hand to his chest.

I sit up, inhaling a shaky breath, "What did you do?"

"Couldn't let you have all the fun, could I, Prim?"

"You… you were there?"

He nods, something akin to fury flashing in his eyes. "He tried to hurt you."

"I didn't give him the chance."

"That's my girl."

My heart stutters in my chest at his words, but I manage to force out, "I'm not your girl."

He stands, moving toward the bed, the shadows dancing off the planes of his face.

He reaches for me, but my hand snaps out, my fingers snagging his wrist.

"You're bleeding."

"I'm fine."

"We should get you cleaned up." I choke over the words, because I can't think straight with him looking at me like that.

He came.

Oakley came here for me.

And if the blood caking his knuckles and the fresh bruise forming around his eye and split lip are any indicator, he made sure Deacon paid for trying to hurt me.

Silently, I take Oakley's arm and steer him toward my bathroom. He doesn't protest, and for a second, I smile to myself. But then I remember he found a way into my house in the middle of the night, and things seem less fairy tale and more nightmare.

"How did you get in?" I ask as I root around in the bathroom cabinet, trying to find a first aid kit.

"I have my ways," he murmurs.

"Are you drunk?" He shakes his head, so I add, "High?"

"Not as high as I'd like to be."

Refusing to acknowledge his words, I gently shove him toward the toilet. "Sit."

He drops down, looking up at me with a faint smile.

"What?" I ask, laying out the supplies on the marble vanity.

"Do you have any idea how hot it was, watching you kick the shit out of Deacon?"

"I wasn't trying to be... I just didn't want him to—"

"Fuck, that was a dumb thing to say. But you know I would have stepped in, right? I would never let him hurt you."

"I..." I trail off, glancing away from him. Oakley shocks me by sliding his hands up my waist and dropping his head to my stomach. He inhales a deep breath, and I feel it roll through him.

"Let me take a look at your hand," I say, gently coaxing him out of himself.

He watches me as I work, cleaning the blood from his split knuckles and then applying some antiseptic cream.

"Do you want me to wrap them?"

"No, I've had worse."

"What happened to Deacon, Oakley?"

"Seb Howard pulled me off him before I could do any real damage."

"So he's—"

"Alive?" Oakley lets out a dark chuckle. "Yeah, Prim, he's alive. I'm not ready to add murder to my university application."

"Haha, very funny."

"I thought so." Oakley smirks, reaching for me again. His fingers fold around my bare thigh and slide higher.

"Oak..." I warn.

"I wanted to do it." The words are a quiet, tortured whisper. "I wanted to kill him for trying to hurt you."

"Don't," I breathe as his fingers slide higher still, grazing the edge of my knickers. If he touches me, I'll crumble.

"Let me in, Prim. I need this. I need you."

"I... oh God." The words get stuck in my throat as he dips his fingers into the cotton material and pushes them inside me.

My hand curls around the back of his neck, my nails scraping his skull as pleasure goes off like a firework inside me.

"Eyes on me, Prim. I want you to know exactly who is about to make you come."

"Oak..." I cry, locking my gaze on his as he curls his fingers deep, rubbing my G-spot. My legs start buckling, an intense sensation sweeping inside me.

"That fucker thinks he can touch what belongs to me. You're mine, Tallulah." There's a dark edge to his words that sends a thrill through me.

"I... yes, yes."

"That's a good girl. Come for me. Come all over my fingers."

"Oakley." His name falls off my lips in a rush of ecstasy as I fall against him, trying to catch my breath. "Fuck. Yes."

He brings his fingers to his mouth and sucks them clean, winking at me. "You taste so fucking sweet."

"Oakley, we can't—"

"Yeah, Prim." He stands, pushing himself against me, into my space. "We can."

When he's like this, there's no escaping him. No escaping what I feel in my heart.

Oakley Beckworth is trouble with a capital T, but I want to walk on the dark side. To relinquish my power and hand him the reins. It feels almost as natural as breathing.

It feels... right.

"He tried to hurt you," the tremble in his voice tells me he's barely hanging on, "and I wanted to fucking kill him."

The air crackles violently as we stare at each other. Reaching for me, Oakley brushes his thumb down my cheek, dragging it over my lips as I gaze up at him.

"Oak—"

"Shh." He leans in and kisses me, cupping my face, sending a delicious shiver rippling through me.

It's wrong—we're wrong. But I want this.

I want him.

And I'm tired of trying to fight it.

Looping my arms around his neck, I anchor us together, kissing him harder. Oakley chuckles, his mouth curving against mine as he threads one of his hands into the back of my damp hair.

"You taste like my fucking salvation, Prim." His eyes search mine for a second; then, he's kissing me again, backing me up onto the counter and looming over me. "Is this okay?" he rasps. "Tell me this is okay."

I nod, yanking him back down to kiss me. He feels so good, heavy and strong above me, his body a work of art. One I want to explore.

"Feel this." Oakley grabs my thigh and lifts it around his waist, grinding into me. "Feel what you do to me."

"Oh God," I whimper.

"When are your parents getting back?"

"I-I don't know. They're... they're at an event."

"You'd better be quiet then." He smirks down at me. "Just in case."

"This doesn't change anything," I whisper. "We can't—"

He presses two fingers against my lips, and the words die on my tongue. "Didn't you know, Prim, I'm an Heir. I can do what I want. Take what I want. When I want. And there isn't a damn thing anyone can do to stop me."

His words sink into me, and I see it in his eyes. His silent promise. His refusal to accept that this thing between us is over.

"You're mine, Tallulah, and I think it's time I show you what that really means."

34

OAKLEY

A deep groan rumbles in my chest as I lick into her mouth again. The taste of copper hits my tongue, and I'm sure hers too, as the split that prick gave me opens up once more.

There was no question about where I was going after walking away from that cunt. The party was nothing but an afterthought as I flew across town with her in my sights.

I had no idea if her parents were home, but seeing the house in complete darkness was a relief. Not that them being here would have stopped me.

I stole something the last time I was here that would give me free and easy access to their house. Exactly what I needed.

The sight of her sleeping peacefully in her bed after being such a bad-arse did things to me. Things it shouldn't. I tried to convince myself that she was okay, that I could leave and she'd be safe in her own house.

But I was a selfish arsehole, and there was no way I was leaving without getting a taste of what's mine.

Hiking her other leg higher, I wrap them both around my waist and grind down harder on her pussy. She gasps, stealing the air right from my lungs.

"You get me so fucking hard, Prim. Do you have any idea how badly I want to push inside you?"

"Oakley," she moans, not making the situation any better.

"You want that too, Prim? You want me to steal the rest of your firsts?"

"Oh God," she whimpers, her nails digging across my shoulders, scratching up my skin in the most perfect way.

"Fuck, yeah. Mark me, Prim. Fuck up my back so I'm bleeding for you."

"Please," she moans.

Pushing up, I stare down at her lying out across the counter. The basin is digging into her back, but she doesn't seem to care as she rolls her hips for me, seeking more friction.

"Dirty little whore, aren't you, Prim? You just got off on my fingers, and now you're begging for my cock."

Her lips are swollen and her chest heaving as I continue to grind against her.

"Gonna need more of you than this," I mutter absently as I grip the bottom of her sleepshirt in my hands and rip it straight up the middle, sending buttons scattering everywhere.

"Oakley," she squeals in disbelief, immediately lifting her hands to cover her tits.

I scoff. "Bit late to hide from me, Prim. I've seen them all before. Fucking addicted to them, if I'm honest."

Wrapping my fingers around her wrists, I pry her hands away, leaving her breasts and hard nipples exposed for my pleasure. "Fucking perfect."

Dipping my head, I lick around one of her peaks before sucking it deep into my mouth, making her cry out for me. "What happened to being quiet?" I tease, not giving a shit.

If I had my way, she'd be screaming my name for the entire fucking town to hear.

Switching sides, I suck on her other nipple before biting down on her sensitive skin. She cries out before slapping her hand over her mouth to muffle the sound as I chuckle against her.

"You like my lips on you, don't you, Prim?" I ask as I graze them down her stomach, dipping my tongue into her belly button.

Her entire body trembles beneath me, her need for what I can give her making my cock even harder.

"You fucking undo me, Prim. You've no idea," I confess as I lick across the skin just above the lace trim of her knickers. "I spend my nights dreaming about this pussy. So fucking perfect."

Dropping to my knees, I run my nose up the length of her, breathing her in. "So wet. So sweet."

"God," she moans, her fingers finding home twisted up in my hair.

"Nah, Prim. Not God. Oakley fucking Beckworth. The only man you should ever be worshipping."

Twisting my fingers in the thin sides of her knickers, I rip them apart and let them flutter to the floor as I dive for what I really want. With my palms spreading her thighs as wide as they'll go in this position, I lean forward and lick up the length of her.

"Shit," she cries, her head hanging back into the basin.

"Fucking love making you swear, Prim. Now, let's see if I can do better."

Holding her open, I attack her clit with my tongue, licking, sucking and nipping at her until a whole string of expletives falls from her mouth.

"Such a good girl," I praise, my mouth barely leaving her swollen flesh as I spear two fingers inside her. "And so fucking tight. I can't wait to feel you strangling my cock."

Her muscles spasm at my words, fucking my digits deeper.

"You want that, don't you? You want me so deep inside your body that you'll never feel the same again."

"Fuck, Oak. Please. Fuck me."

"With fucking pleasure. But first..."

I go back to her clit, and I don't let up until she's coming all over my face and my name is bouncing off the walls around us.

The second she's done, I push to my feet, scoop her limp, sated body into my arms, and carry her from the bathroom.

Laying her out naked on her bed, I take a step back and just study her. Her blonde hair is a mess around her head. Her make-up is trashed and so fucking hot smeared across her cheeks. Her chest is heaving, her nipples still hard, one of them circled with my teeth marks.

My gaze drops down her stomach and to her...

"Open your legs for me, Prim. Let me see that pretty little cunt."

She blinks a couple of times as her post-orgasm brain catches up with my words. It's so fucking cute I can barely stand it.

Hesitantly, she does as she's told, exposing herself to me.

"Fuck," I breathe, dragging my hand down my face as I study her.

Fucking perfect. And all fucking mine.

In record speed, I have my jeans undone and on the floor, along with my shoes and boxers.

Her eyes widen the second I take myself in hand and stalk closer to her.

"Oak," she breathes, studying my length, making it leak in anticipation.

Crawling onto the bed beside her, I hold myself out in offering, desperate to feel the heat of her mouth on me "Lick," I demand. "I want you to taste me like I just did you."

Wrapping my hand around the back of her head, I guide her forward, making it easier. Her kiss-swollen lips part before her tongue sneaks out, teasing me with the lightest touch.

"Fuck," I bark, our connection sparking like a fucking electrical current.

Feeling brazen, she circles the head of my dick, her eyes locked on mine the whole time.

"Fuck me, you look good sucking my cock, Prim." Cupping her cheek, I rub my thumb through the smeared make-up beneath her eyes. A twisted part of me wants to be able to wipe her tears away too. But she's already proved that she's too strong for that tonight. There will be plenty of other opportunities, though.

Despite her gentle touch, my release begins to make itself known way too soon and I regretfully pull my dick from her reach.

She pouts at the loss, and I can't help but smile.

"My dirty little girl," I murmur, brushing my thumb over her bottom lip. "I'll feed you my cock all you want later. Right now, I've got something else in mind."

Shuffling around, I settle myself between her legs and drag her lower down the bed so her thighs are draped over mine.

Wrapping my fingers around my length once more, I brush the head through her wetness.

She tenses the second we touch.

"Oakley," she whispers. "I— I've nev—"

"I know, Prim. But you're mine, and I'm not allowing any other motherfucker to take this from you."

"B-but—"

"Are you on birth control?" I demand, ignoring whatever her argument was about to be.

"Y-yes. I'm on the pill," she confirms, much to my relief.

"Good, because we're not having anything between us. Ever."

Dropping lower, I line myself up with her entrance before falling over her. Resting my forearms on either side of her head, I brush my nose against hers, holding her eyes firm. "Trust me?" I whisper.

Her heated eyes bounce between mine before her lips part to answer.

Suddenly terrified that she'll say no, I thrust forward, filling her in one sharp move, causing her to scream in shock.

My teeth grind as her body squeezes me so goddamn tight, I swear I'm going to blow from just being inside her.

Her nails dig into my shoulders, the sting telling me she's drawing blood. Fucking bring it, Prim. I can take all the pain you can dish out.

"Breathe, baby," I whisper. "Relax."

I hold her eyes, trying to force myself to remain still while she adjusts.

She blinks a couple of times before dragging her teeth over her bottom lip.

"You... we're... You just—"

"Mine," I repeat, brushing her lips with mine before sucking the bottom one into my mouth, stealing it for myself.

I kiss her until she finally relaxes beneath me. Her nails release my skin in favour of running her palms down my back, making goosebumps race across my body.

"You feel so fucking incredible," I grit out, my brow pressing against hers. "But I really need to fucking move, baby."

She swallows nervously.

"I promise to make it good."

She nods subtly, and I breathe a sigh of relief.

Testing the waters, I roll my hips, just about managing to catch the groan that threatens as pleasure shoots through my body.

"You're even better than I imagined," I confess, pulling out of her slowly before sliding right back in. "You were fucking made for me, Prim."

Her eyes squeeze tight. I'm not sure if she's still in pain or if it's my words that are causing her to shut off from me, but I don't fucking like it.

Anger surges forward and I reach out, wrapping my fingers around her throat before processing the thought.

Her eyes pop open and her lips part.

"Don't hide from me, Tallulah. Not while I've got my cock buried deep in your cunt. You're going to watch every fucking second of this, remember every moment of me owning you, fucking ruining you for any other fuck who might want to get his hands on you."

All the air rushes out of her lungs, but I don't give her a chance to say anything. Instead, I pull out and slam straight back inside her.

She shoots up the bed, forcing me to sit up so I can wrap my free hand around her hip and keep her in place.

The second I change position, she gasps in shock.

"You like that?" I ask, grinding into her again.

"Y-yes," she stutters.

"Told you I'd make it good. Now, I'm going to keep going until you're screaming my name again and coming all over my dick. Then and only then will I fill you up, painting your cunt with my cum so you remember who you belong to."

"Oakley."

"Yeah, Prim, just like that. And if we're fast, maybe you'll scream it before your parents are home to hear it."

35

TALLY

Waves of pleasure crash over me as I whimper his name.

Oakley.

Oakley.

Oakley.

He groans, collapsing on top of me and nuzzling my neck, sucking the skin there until I'm sure he's drawn blood.

"Oak." I scratch my fingers through his hair, tugging gently.

When he lifts his face, I'm hit with an intense feeling. He looks...

God, he looks gorgeous. A lazy grin on his face, adoration shining in his eyes.

But it's more than that.

What we just did...

I screw my eyes shut and turn away from him, overwhelmed at the moment.

"Prim, Tallulah." His fingers glide under my chin. "Look at me."

"I..."

"You take my fucking breath away." His thumb skims my jaw, lingering on my bottom lip. "Are you sore?"

"A little."

His eyes flick to the clock, and the muscle in his jaw tenses. "What time will your parents be home?"

"I don't know."

"We'd better hurry, then."

Oakley drops a kiss on my forehead and climbs out of bed. I wince, feeling a slight sting between my legs. His eyes home in on the juncture of my thighs and he practically growls. "I shouldn't find it so hot, but I like seeing your blood, Prim. Knowing that I own your first time."

I gasp at the bloody mess coating my thighs and grab at the sheet, but Oakley stops me. "Come on." He holds out his hand to me and I blink up at him. "I'm going to clean you up, and then, if you're lucky, I'm going to kiss your pretty pussy better."

"Oh God," I breathe, letting him pull me from the bed.

He picks me up like I weigh nothing, forcing my legs around his waist and carrying me like a koala into my bathroom.

Setting me down on the counter, Oakley goes to the shower and turns it on, testing the water. "Okay, let's go." He smirks, those intense eyes of his watching my every move.

This feels too intimate. Too much.

Like he's breaking through the last shreds of my carefully constructed walls.

But my body moves of its own volition, swaying toward him as if I'm under his spell. I slip off the counter and Oakley wraps his arm around me, nudging me toward the shower.

"I'm going to clean you up so good, Prim." He sweeps the hair off my shoulder, kissing me there. Gentle. Tender.

All the things he's not supposed to be.

"What are we doing, Oak?" I whisper, and he frowns. But then his gorgeous smile slides back into place.

"In. Now." He slaps my bum and I yelp.

The water is the perfect temperature, and I groan at how good it feels. Oakley presses himself behind me, reaching around to grab the loofah and soap. He lathers it up and then slides it down my chest, over the peak of my breast. A whimper gets stuck in my throat, my body stirring to life again.

"Feel good?" he asks against the curve of my neck. I nod, letting my body relax into his.

He moves the loofah lower, trailing it down my stomach. My breath catches as he traces it over my mound and down my thighs, careful not to apply too much pressure.

"Watching you take my cock was the hottest thing I've ever seen, Prim. Such a good girl for me."

"Oakley," I murmur, my eyelashes fluttering as need curls in my stomach.

"Still sore?"

I nod.

"Too sore?" He drops the loofah, his fingers dancing along the strip of soft hair.

"I— God," I breathe as he glides his fingers over my clit. It feels sensational, pleasure firing off around my body.

"Tell me if it hurts." He dips two fingers inside of me, curling them deep and stretching me. There's a slight ache, but it's not unpleasant.

"So fucking tight still," he rasps, working me with his fingers and thumb until I'm moaning his name. "Never gonna get enough of this pussy. It's mine now, Prim. Full of my cum, just like it should be." His other hand collars my throat and forces me to look at him. "You're mine."

Oakley kisses me, stealing the air from my lungs and his name from my lips as I shatter around him.

"Oh my God," I pant, the orgasm rolling through me, over and over.

His mouth trails down my jaw and throat as I ride the

waves. My heart is a runaway train in my chest, a million questions zipping through my head as I try to catch my breath.

And it hits me then.

I don't want him to leave.

I want him to stay. I want to wake up beside him. To step out of the shadows and stand under the light with him.

But my parents would never stand for it. They would never accept a boy like Oakley.

An Heir.

A Beckworth.

Just as I suspect his father would never accept me.

God, what are we doing?

I gently untangle myself from his hold and turn off the shower. "We should probably get dry."

"Prim?" he asks, watching me.

Studying me.

"It's late." I give him a weak smile. "My parents could be home any minute."

"Yeah." He swallows, raking a hand through his wet hair.

He goes to step out, but I grab his hand. "Oak?"

"Yeah, Prim?"

"How did you get in the house?"

A flash of guilt passes over his expression. "Don't ask questions you might not like the answer to," he says cryptically before stepping out of the shower and grabbing a towel. He dries himself off, wraps it around his waist and then offers me a big fluffy one.

"Thank you."

Things have cooled between us, leaving an awkward tension in the air.

"Oak—" I start but he cuts me off, crowding me against the wall.

"Can I see you tomorrow?"

"T-tomorrow?"

He nods, dropping his head to mine.

"I... where? How?"

Say no.

I should say no.

But I don't, because he's looking at me like I'm all his dreams come true. The way Reese looks at Olivia.

"Leave the details to me. I'll text you."

"Okay."

"You going to be bad with me, Prim?"

I press my lips together, giving him a little nod.

"Gotta admit, I'm not fucking pleased about having to leave you like this." He feathers his lips over mine.

It's on the tip of my tongue to tell him to stay. To risk everything for a chance to spend the night with him.

But I don't.

I can't.

Because no matter how reckless he makes me feel, I'm still the good girl who likes to follow the rules.

Keep telling yourself that, Tallulah.

Oakley gives me one last kiss before backing away.

"How will you get out?" I ask.

"Don't worry about me, Prim. No one will ever know I was here."

He's joking.

It's a joke. Except, it doesn't feel that way.

"Get some sleep. I have big things planned for you tomorrow night."

I linger in the bathroom doorway, watching as he pulls on his clothes. The bruise along his cheekbone looks sore, but he doesn't seem bothered.

I think he's going to leave, but he stalks over to the bed, pulls back the covers and tips his head toward it. "In you get, princess."

"Never call me that," I seethe, stomping over to the bed.

"I'll text you tomorrow." He curls a hand around the back of my neck and drops a kiss on my head.

"Bye," I say, and it sounds so dumb after what just transpired between us.

"Laters, baby." Oakley winks and the stifling tension cracks open, a soft chuckle spilling out of me.

"Go," I urge. "Before they get back."

He pauses at the door, looking at me as if he wants to say more. But then he opens it and slips into the hall.

Taking the final pieces of my heart with him.

"Good morning, sweetheart," Dad says the second I enter the kitchen. "How was your night?"

"It was fine, Dad." I almost choke on the lie. "What about you and Mum?"

"It's almost ten on a Saturday and your mother is still sleeping." His eyes dance with humour.

"Enough said," I mutter, making a beeline for the coffee machine.

"Did you hear us come home? It was late. We didn't intend on being gone so long."

"I didn't," I lie.

The truth is, I did hear them. I heard my dad trying to carry my mum to bed, their love and laughter filling the house.

I barely slept. I couldn't.

Not after what Oakley and I did.

Sex.

We had sex.

I gave him my virginity.

When I woke up this morning after finally falling to sleep sometime around three, I expected to feel a stab of regret. Of shame. But I didn't.

Because I've fallen for him.

I've fallen for Oakley, and there's not a thing I can do about it.

"Oh, I meant to ask you," Dad says, pulling me from my thoughts. "Have you seen the spare key? It's not on the rack."

I freeze, my heart jolting in my chest.

No.

He wouldn't.

Except, he totally would.

Oakley stole a key to my house. That's how he got in so easily.

"I haven't, Dad." I force out the words. "Sorry."

"Strange. I'll get another one cut and replace it."

"Good plan."

I should text Oakley and demand he return the key. But I don't. Because I need coffee if I'm going to survive the day, and then I need to figure out what the hell I'm going to say to him when we do finally talk.

He said he had plans for me tonight. We can talk then.

If he doesn't bewitch me with his playful smirk and dirty words.

Jesus, I have it bad.

"What are you smiling at, sweetheart?" Dad asks, and I frown.

"Just remembered the dream I had." I shrug, guilt coiling around my heart.

I don't like lying to him, but it's not like I can tell him the truth.

"That good, huh?"

"It was pretty awesome."

I think of how desperate Oakley had been for me. How he'd taken control of my body, giving me exactly what I never knew I needed.

Sex.

We had sex.

I don't feel any different and yet, something has changed.

Or maybe I was already changing.

"Did you hear any more about that case?" I ask, trying to steer the conversation away from me and my secrets.

"The Alveston case?" I nod and he adds, "No, it was a cut and dry case of a revenge murder." He shakes out his newspaper. "What's on your agenda today?"

"I'm not sure. I might have a bake fest."

Baking grounds me. Gives me time and space to think through things.

And I have plenty of things to think about.

Hopefully, it will help me figure out what I'm going to do about Oakley and the fact he seems dead set on keeping me.

36

OAKLEY

Unsurprisingly, the Chapel is silent when I stumble through the front door.

I've no idea what time it is, and I don't care.

My body might be here, but my head is still firmly in Tally's bedroom. My focus is solely on her.

Fuck.

She was incredible. She is incredible.

The slam of the front door echoes through the ancient building. I don't bother stopping as I march through our living room, around toward the stairs and head up to my bedroom.

I might have cleaned her up and done my best to take care of her after hurting her, but I didn't wash myself. I couldn't bring myself to do it.

I want her scent on me.

The second I'm in my room, I empty my pockets and shove my jeans and boxers down my legs, folding them both before placing them in the laundry basket. I lost my mask at some point tonight, probably while I was beating the shit out of that arsewipe, Deacon.

Pulling the sheets back, I fall into the coldness, regretting my choices about how tonight ended.

I should still be there. She should be wrapped in my arms with her head resting on my chest.

Fuck no... no, she shouldn't be doing that.

Scrubbing my hand down my face, I try to get my shit together. But I fear it might be too late. Tallulah Darlington is the last person who should make my heart race and my cock hard.

But she is.

And there's fuck all I can do about it.

Without meaning to, she's wrapped me up in her web of innocence and made me want her like I've never wanted for anything else in my life. Ever.

Reaching over to my bedside table, I pull the top drawer open, looking down at my stash of pills.

Fuck. I want her more than I want them.

Grabbing my phone instead, I fall back on my latest obsession and open up her Insta.

I lose myself in her beautiful smile and innocent eyes to the point that I don't hear anyone return to the Chapel. And it's not until my door flies open, crashing back against the wall, that I discover I have company.

"What the fuck?" I bark, my phone falling from my fingers in favour of pulling the covers over my hard dick.

Fuck my life.

"Tell me you weren't jerking off to porn?" my sister asks, her eyes locked on her feet.

"So what if I was? Free fucking country," I snap, my frustration at being interrupted from my Tally time getting the better of me.

Fucking hell, I'm turning into a right pussy.

"Where the fuck did you go? We've been looking for you for hours," Elliot barks.

"I left. Is that a problem?"

His eyes narrow on mine before dropping to the bruise

that's burning up my cheek and then my split lip, but for some reason, he doesn't say anything.

"A little heads up would have been nice," he complains.

"Sorry, Dad. Didn't realise I'd be put on a fucking lead."

"Leave it, yeah," Reese says, trying to keep the peace.

One look at my best friend and I see the same concern that's hiding beneath Elliot's frustration.

"Come on, sweet cheeks. Let's leave the grumpy motherfucker to his right hand."

"Gross," my sister mutters, disappearing out of sight with my best friend's arm wrapped around her.

"I'm out," Elliot announces in favour of locking himself in his room to do whatever the fuck he does in there.

Theo, though, is not as quick to leave me in peace. Instead, he steps farther into my room and kicks the door closed behind him.

"So, who were you jerking off over?" he asks, his eyes lighting up in amusement as he makes a beeline for my phone that's, thankfully, face down on the sheets.

"No one," I snap, reaching it before him and stuffing it under my arse, much to his annoyance.

"Sure. That's why your cock is trying to punch its way out of the duvet," he teases.

"Did you actually fucking want something, or are you just here to piss me off?"

"Who have you been fighting?" he asks, his eyes dropping to my wounds, recognising that they're more than what I got from tonight's game. Fuck, that feels like a lifetime ago already.

"I needed to blow off a bit of steam," I mutter.

"Funny, because the last time I saw you, you were well up for partying the night away. What changed?"

"Does it matter?"

"Yeah, you're acting all weird and shit. I don't like it. I've already got Millie to look after; I don't need to be worrying about anyone else."

"Who said you need to worry about me? Everything is good," I try to assure him, but he doesn't look like he buys it for a second.

"I'm going to find out what's going on," he warns, hopping up from my bed once more.

"Great," I mutter. "What are you doing here alone, anyway? Thought you'd have found a chaser or two to entertain."

"Been there, done that. Got the—"

"Herpes?" I offer.

"Fuck you, man. Just because they let me fuck them in the woods, doesn't mean they're dirty."

"Suuure it doesn't."

"Fucking rich coming from you. I've caught you balls deep in all sorts of places."

"Yeah. I always wrap it, though." I wince the second the words fall from my lips.

You didn't tonight, you stupid prick.

"Who said I didn't? Laters. I need to go wash the skank off my balls."

"Oh, so now you're admitting they're dirty."

"Too fucking right, they were. Filth, Oak. Pure fucking filth. Shame you bailed; you could have joined in."

He winks before leaving me alone in my room once more.

The second my door closes behind him, I dig my phone back out and continue feeding my obsession.

The guys are up long before me the next morning. It's hardly surprising, knowing how long I spent stalking Prim last night. I've seen all the pictures and posts before, but it didn't stop me from looking at each again.

Then of course I was so fucking hard and desperate for another taste of her that I couldn't sleep.

My body was desperate for me to sneak back over to her place, let myself in, and take her once again. Hell, I'd go over just to crawl into her bed and wrap my arms around her.

Pussy.

By the time I eventually drag my pathetic arse out of bed, they guys are all shouting at each other in a way that tells me they're deep in an Xbox battle.

Pulling my phone from its charger, I find my chat with Tally and tap out a message.

> Oakley: Be ready for seven tonight. Wear something sexy… or nothing at all. Your choice. *smiley face*

I sit there for a few minutes, waiting for my message to be read, for her to respond. But neither happens.

"Fuck," I hiss, hating the fear that races through me that she's woken up this morning, remembered what we did and has immediately regretted it.

I've never questioned anything I've ever done with anyone else. Tally should be no different.

But she is. She's Tally fucking Darlington. The girl who can bring you to your knees with nothing more than an innocent smile.

"Jesus fucking Christ."

Knowing I have another pressing issue to deal with, I regretfully pull up another chat and shoot off another message.

Unfortunately, this one is more than willing to talk to me. Whore.

> Oakley: You busy?

> Misty: I'm never too busy for you. When and where?

I shake my head as I consider the fact that she'd willingly

turn up wherever I told her to be naked. And she would be fucking proud of it, too.

> Oakley: Thirty minutes. Pavilion by the lake.

Pulling on a pair of jeans and a black Henley, I shove my feet into my trainers and pocket my phone after getting confirmation that Misty will be ready and waiting. Great.

Liv's eyes are on me long before I've hit the ground floor. I don't need to look to confirm it; her attention makes my skin prickle.

I hate lying to her or keeping any kind of secret, but it's recently become something of a habit.

"Going somewhere?" she asks before the others have even noticed me.

"Nice fucking shiner," Reese says when he eventually drags his eyes from the TV. "Which chaser did you piss off last night?"

"He wasn't with a chaser. They were all at the party he abandoned," Elliot points out while continuing to play COD.

"Who is she, then?" Reese asks, looking way too excited.

"No one. I'm going out."

I'm hardly surprised when light footsteps follow me as I head to the kitchen to grab an energy drink before leaving them to it.

"Where are you going?"

"What's with the fucking questions?" I bark.

Liv rears back, her eyes wide.

"I-I... uh—"

"Sorry," I mutter, feeling like the shittiest brother in the world. Even if she does deserve it for hooking up with my best friend. "I didn't sleep very well."

"I know. I can tell by the state of your face."

"Thanks, Sis," I hiss.

With a can in hand, I walk around her. But she stops me when her fingers wrap around my wrist.

"Where are you going?"

Blowing out a long breath, I twist back to look at her. Disappointment and concern flood her eyes, and I fucking hate it.

I'm always fucking letting people down despite mostly trying to do the right thing.

"Going to meet Misty," I say honestly.

Her face twists up in disgust at my mention of a chaser.

"What?" I snap. "We can't all go around fucking our twin's best friend."

Her eyes narrow and she takes a warning step forward. As if I would ever be scared of her.

"Go anywhere near Abi and I'll cut it off with a blunt knife."

I hold my hands up in surrender. "I'm going nowhere near Abi, Liv. You can put your threats away."

"Good. And if I find out you're lying to me—"

My phone pings in my pocket, cutting off her words. "Are we done? Misty is waiting."

"On her back with her legs spread ready, I assume?"

"Well, we're meeting at the pavilion, so I really fucking hope not."

"She would," Liv mutters, and I have to fight my smirk, because Misty probably would.

"Be good," I say.

"I'll try. If you promise to come back in a better mood."

"An hour with Misty should do the trick," Reese shouts over, clearly eavesdropping on our conversation.

"So gross."

"Tell me about it," I hiss, looking between the two of them. "Later."

With a nod at my sister, I take off.

The last thing I want to do is meet up with Misty, but after that little stunt last night with Deacon, it's clear that I need to step in to stop this.

Tally has dropped the campaign. It's time for Misty to turn her attention on someone else.

The second I pull up in the car park, the heavens open.

"Brilliant."

Tugging my hood up, I push the door open and run toward the pavilion. There are a few too many others sheltering under here for the conversation we need.

"I didn't think you were coming," an irritatingly familiar voice says, appearing through the small crowd.

"I was the one who asked to meet you," I say calmly.

The second I look up and find her perfectly made up, her hair styled immaculately in the hope of seducing me, my fists clench, my need to wrap my fingers around her fucking throat and choke the life out of her almost too much to ignore.

"Come on, we're going for a walk."

Thinking of Tally, I force myself to throw my arm around Misty's shoulders and lead her around the back of the pavilion and out into the rain.

"Ew, Oak. Really?" she complains, putting her hands above her head as if that will protect her.

"The rain is the least of your worries right now, Misty," I say darkly, shoving her forward the second we step into the darkness under the trees.

She stumbles, her foot catching on a root and sending her crashing to the ground.

Exactly where she belongs.

Stepping up to her, I loom over her as she scrambles to get back up.

"W-what's going on?"

"I think you're the one who needs to be explaining a few things, don't you, Mist?"

37

TALLY

"Are you sure you're okay?" Abi asks me for the third time since I joined her at Dessert Island.

I didn't want to come, but she was worried after my sudden disappearance last night, so I agreed to meet her.

Besides, I couldn't resist the allure of my favourite red velvet cake.

"I'm fine. I promise." The lie barely tastes sour, I've said it that many times today.

I check my phone for the hundredth time, a small thrill going through me. It's almost five-thirty.

Oakley is picking me up at seven.

"Okay, that's like the eighth time you've checked your phone. What's going on?"

"I... nothing."

"You can trust me, Tally. If there's something going on..."

"There's not."

"So Oakley disappearing last night right around the time you did is a coincidence?"

"What are you talking about?" I rush out a little hastily.

Too hastily.

Abigail's brow lifts, accusation glittering in her eyes. "Something's going on with the two of you, isn't it?"

"No. No!"

"Tally, come on. This is me. I see things."

"You..." I let out a heavy sigh. "I don't know what you're talking about."

"Fine. Have it your way. But if you ever want to talk, I'm here."

"You're a good friend, Abi," I say. "What are your plans for tonight?"

"Not a lot. I'll probably watch a film or read. Unless you want to hang out?"

"I can't, I have..."

"Plans?" Her brows waggle.

"Abi."

"Fine. Keep your secrets. Just be careful, okay? The Heirs are... intense."

I frown at her words. "Did something happen with you and Elliot?"

"What? No! Why would you even say that?"

"Geez, relax. I was just—"

"Well, don't," she snaps, and I don't know who's more surprised. Me, or her.

"Sorry, I... I think I made a fool of myself last night."

"Why, what happened?" I ask, and she blushes, lowering her gaze to her coffee mug.

"I hugged Elliot."

"You... hugged Elliot? That doesn't sound so scandalous."

"I didn't just hug him, Tally. I really hugged him. Like wrapped myself around him and clung on for dear life."

I smother another a chuckle, imagining the big broody rugby player tackle-hugged by a girl as meek and delicate as Abigail Bancroft.

"It's not funny. I was a little bit drunk, and I could hardly stand straight, and he was right there."

"What he say?"

"That's the thing... he didn't say anything. He just kind of held me awkwardly and helped me into the back of the taxi. Oh my God, I'm such an idiot." She drops her head to her forearm and groans.

"I'm sure everything is fine. Elliot is a little intimidating, but he doesn't seem like the big bad scary boy everyone makes him out to be."

Her eyes lift to mine. "You can't tell anyone about this. Promise me."

"Who am I going to tell?"

She narrows her eyes with unspoken meaning.

"Oh, hush," I murmur, pushing my chair back and standing. "I need to go. But I'll text you later, okay?"

"Have fun with your plans." There's a hint of amusement in her voice, but I ignore it, giving her a small wave before I duck out of the cake shop and start the short walk to my house to get ready for my date with Oakley.

The second I head up my drive, I realise something is wrong. Two police cars sit outside my house, sending a trickle of unease through me.

Oh God. Did Dad find out about Deacon? Did somebody tell him?

Did Oakley—

"Tallulah." Dad comes ambling out of the house, looking a little shell-shocked. "I wasn't expecting you home yet."

"What's going on?" I glance from him to the plain-clothed police officer behind him.

"This is DI Graham Knights."

"Hello."

"Tallulah." He offers me a tight smile. "Why don't we go inside?"

Dad ushers me into the house and we all file into the living room.

"Can you tell me where you've been this afternoon, Tallulah?"

"Been? Why? What's going on? What's—"

"Sweetheart, the sooner you answer DI Knights questions, the sooner this will be over."

"Dad, you're scaring me."

"I'm sorry, Tallulah. There's no need for immediate concern, but we do need to ask you some questions to help us establish possible motive."

"M-motive? Motive for what? What is going on?" Frustration bleeds from my words.

DI Knights glances to my father. "We should take her up there."

"Graham, with all due res—"

"Dad, this is crazy. Just tell me what's going on. Where's Mum? Is she—"

"Your mother is fine. She's out of town." He drags a hand down his face, and I see the torment in his eyes. "When I got home, I went up to see you... your room..."

My room?

Dread churns in my stomach, and without thinking, I stand and take off toward the stairs.

"Sweetheart, wait—"

I take two stairs at a time, blood roaring in my ears. A couple of forensic officers greet me. "I'm not sure you should be up here," one says, but DI Knights' voice comes from behind me. "Let her through. Just don't touch anything."

The second I step into my room, my world crumbles. "Oh my God," I breathe, my hand snapping out to grab onto something and steady myself, because this is... this is horrifying.

My room is completely trashed, clothes and trinkets strewn everywhere, the contents of my desk swiped onto the floor in a fit of what I can only imagine was rage and destruction.

Tears spring into my eyes as I take in the mess, the utter sense of devastation I feel at the gross invasion of privacy.

Then my eyes snag on my bed, the dark red puddle on my sheets. "What is—"

"Wait, Miss Darlington. You shouldn't—"

Before the officer can stop me, I pull back the sheet and clap a hand over my mouth at the rush of bile up my throat.

"What is that?" I stare at the small, massacred animals—rats, if the long bloody tails are anything to go by—tears streaming down my cheeks.

"Oh. Sweetheart." Dad rushes up behind me and wraps his arms around me. "I didn't want you to see this."

"I don't understand." I twist around to look at him. "Who would do something like this?"

My mind instantly flicks to Misty and Deacon. She called me a rat once. Left a dead rat on my windscreen—at least, I'm pretty sure it was her. But this is a lot, even for someone as cruel as Misty Dalton. And would Deacon go this far just to prove a point?

"Do you have any idea who might have done this, Tallulah?" DI Knights comes up beside me.

"I... no. It's horrible."

"Was anything else tampered with? In the house, I mean?"

He glances at my father again, who nods.

"There is no evidence of a break-in, and your father is certain he locked the door."

"Me too. And I always check it. Twice."

"Shit," my dad murmurs. "The key."

"The key?" DI Knights frowns.

"I only remembered just now, but we're missing a spare key to the house. I've looked everywhere."

"Is it possible someone took it?" He looks between us both.

"A cleaner maybe? Or a handyman? I'll need a list of everyone with recent access to the house."

"Tallulah, sweetheart, you've gone as white as a sheet."

"I... I need some air." I rush out of the room, clutching my throat.

He wouldn't do something like this. He wouldn't.

Things between me and Oakley are real. He wants to take me out on a date, for Christ's sake.

But a little voice of doubt rings in my head.

Someone let themselves into our house and trashed my room. Violated my space.

Someone who had easy access.

Someone who had a key.

The key that Oakley took.

Oh God.

I make a beeline for the back door. I need fresh air; I need to think.

He played me.

Oakley played me, and now the police are involved.

God, I'm such an idiot.

He doesn't care about me. He only cares about destroying me. About putting me in my place and exerting his power as an Heir.

And the worst thing about it all... I knew.

I knew exactly the kind of boy Oakley Beckworth was, and I still let myself fall for him.

I smother a whimper, pain and betrayal lashing my insides. Here I was, falling deeper with every stolen kiss, every touch and whisper, and Oakley was—

No.

I don't believe that. It was real. It is real. I felt it. Every time he looks at me, kisses me, it's there, crackling between us.

Pulling out my phone, I pull up his contact and hit call. But it goes to voicemail.

I try again, murmuring, "Pick up, pick up."

But his voicemail kicks in again.

I fire off a text.

Defeated, I scroll to Olivia's number and hover my thumb over the button. If I do this—if I call her—it's opening myself to all kinds of questions. But I need to speak to him.

She answers on the second ring.

"Tally?"

"Liv, hi." My voice trembles. "This is going to be a strange question, but I need you to answer it, okay?"

"Okay," she replies.

"Do you know where Oakley is?"

"Oakley? You're calling me to ask about Oakley?"

"Just... answer the question, please. It's important."

"I saw him earlier. He was going to meet Misty. I don't know what he sees—"

"Misty? He told you he was going to meet Misty?"

My heart sinks.

"Yeah, why? What's going on?"

"Nothing. I have to go. Bye." I hang up, my body trembling.

He's with her.

Oakley is with Misty, and he has a key to my house.

I didn't want to believe it.

But there's no disputing the facts, and the truth I hadn't wanted to believe falls into place.

All while I've been slowly falling for him, it's been nothing more than a game to him.

A game I've clearly lost.

CRUEL DEVIOUS HEIR: PART TWO

1

TALLY

"Sweetheart?" Dad pokes his head into the guest room. "Can I get you anything?"

"No thanks," I murmur, barely looking at him.

"Tallulah." He comes inside, closing the door behind him. "You're worrying me, sweetheart. If there's something—"

"Somebody broke into our house and trashed my room, Dad. They massacred a rat and left it in my bed..." A shudder rips through but I force myself to take a deep breath. "Sorry if I'm a little quiet but it's a lot to process."

"Of course, sweetheart. I know you told Graham you didn't know anything but if you did, you can tell me. Perhaps the kids at school—"

"God, Dad. They're idiots but they're not sickos. I don't know who would have done something like this." The lie sticks to the roof of my mouth.

"Okay, sweetheart. It's late, I'll let you get some rest. I'm sure we'll get to the bottom of this. I'll be right downstairs if you need me, okay?"

With a small nod, I turn my back to him and clutch a pillow to my chest.

It's been a couple of hours since I got home. Since I realised what my stupid, foolish heart hasn't wanted to believe.

Oakley played me.

He played me so well I let my defences down and told myself that maybe, just maybe the connection between us was real.

That it was more than hatred turned into attraction.

I'm such an idiot.

Of course, when seven thirty rolled around, there was no sign of Oakley. Not that I ever expected him to come. Let alone waltz up to the front door with the police and my father home.

Oakley Beckworth is a liar and a cheat, and I want nothing to do with him.

My phone taunts me from the desk but I refuse to get it and turn it back on. I need to be alone. I need to figure out how to pick myself back up after his betrayal.

I need to figure out what I'm going to do about Misty and the Heir chasers. Because I don't doubt for a second that she and Oakley were behind this.

A fresh wave of tears slide down my cheeks as I replay last night over in my head—the things Oakley said. The things he did to me.

Lies all of it.

Every touch, every kiss, and whispered word.

I squeeze my pillow tighter, breathing through the ache in my heart.

The first boy I gave myself too…

And he ripped out my heart and stomped all over it.

I barely slept. By the time sunrise peeks through the curtains, I feel like I've been hit by a truck. Everything hurts. My bleary eyes. My chest. My lungs.

My heart.

I hate waking up in the guest room.

I hate that I can still feel the slight sting between my legs, I hate that I can still taste him.

Still remember how he felt above me. Inside me.

God, I hate him.

I *hate* him.

But not nearly as much as I hate myself.

Throwing back the covers, I drag myself out of bed and head into the en suite bathroom. It's Sunday. Tomorrow is school. If everyone hasn't already heard, they will by the time classes roll around.

I can picture Misty's face. Her smug smirk as the news works its way around the All Hallows' gossip mill.

Maybe I should tell my parents, in case the truth comes out. But how can I? How can I ever tell them that I got into bed with the enemy—literally—and let him do dirty wicked things to me?

The answer is, I can't. They won't understand.

They won't—

"Tallulah, sweetheart, are you awake?" Mum calls from the hallway.

"In the bathroom," I yell back, hoping she'll leave me alone.

Of course, she doesn't.

I find her waiting in the bedroom when I slip out of the en suite. "Oh sweetheart." She rushes over to me and pulls me into her arms. "It's all going to be okay, Tallulah. Your father is going to get the locks changed and the police are looking into all possibilities. But you know, baby, if you know something that might help—"

"I don't, Mum. I already told Dad, I don't know anything."

"Okay, okay." She strokes my hair, the way she did when I was a child. "I'm sure we'll get to the bottom of it."

An awkward tension falls over us full of unspoken words and secrets.

Secrets I'll never tell.

Because I'm a fool. I'm the girl who played with fire thinking she wouldn't get burned.

"Come on, let's go downstairs and I'll make your favourite breakfast."

"Okay."

I follow her down and curl up on the big chair in the kitchen.

"Tea?" Mum asks, and I nod. "I'm going to get your room cleaned up today. The police said…"

I zone out, staring out of the back door, the garden beyond.

One day.

One more day and then I'll have to face them.

To face him.

I'm not sure I can do it. I was so bold and confident playing Oakley's game. Part of me had truly believed that there was something between us, something more than just rivalry fuelled by hate.

My chest tightens but I breathe through the pain, the panic I feel closing in around me. I've always been the good girl. The apple of my father's eye. If they find out the truth… it will destroy them.

A knock at the front door sends my heart into overdrive and I grip the arm of the chair, my eyes darting toward the hallway.

"I wonder who that could be at this time," Mum murmurs. "Your father isn't due back for a little while. Maybe it's the police with an update." She abandons the kettle to go and open the door.

I don't know what to do.

A part of me wants to run upstairs and hide in the guest room. But that would be silly, and she'd only have more questions.

So instead, I sit there. Waiting. Silently panicking.

"Tallulah," she calls. "It's for you."

Me?

Oh God.

I get up on shaky legs and make my way down the hall, every step like treading quicksand. What if it's Deacon? What if—

"Olivia."

"Hey, I know it's early, but can we talk?" Her eyes flick to my mum before settling back on me. "In private."

"I... sure. Come in."

"I'll be in the kitchen," Mum says, shooting me a look that says she wants answers the second we get done.

"What's the matter?" I ask, trying to keep my expression neutral.

"Have you seen Oakley?" she whispers, glancing down the hall.

"I... what? No. Of course I haven't. Come on, let's go upstairs."

Olivia follows me but we don't speak again until we're inside the guest room. She glances around with an unspoken question in her eyes.

"This isn't my room." I don't expand. "What do you mean, have I seen Oakley?"

"He's missing."

"Missing?"

She nods. "He didn't come home last night or go to the Chapel. Reese called Misty, she hasn't seen him either."

"But I thought you said he went to meet her?"

"He did. She said they hung out for a while then he left."

"And you thought I might have seen him?"

She narrows her eyes a little, studying me. "After your strange phone call last night... yeah. What's going on, Tally?"

"Nothing. I don't know what you're talking about."

"So you randomly called to ask me if I'd seen Oakley for shits and giggles?"

"I... it's complicated."

"Complicated how? What aren't you telling me? Did he do something? Because I swear to God, Tally if he hurt you—"

"He didn't. At least, not in the way you're thinking."

Relief flickers over her expression but morphs into a frown. "What do you mean? What's going—" The shrill of her phone cuts her off and she digs it out, answering it. "Reese? Yeah, what? Oh my God..." The blood drains from her face. "Yeah, okay. No, I'm at Tally's house. Yes. Okay, I'll be there."

"What's wrong?" I ask the second she hangs up.

"It's Oak. He's at the hospital?"

"What?" I shriek, clutching my throat.

"He's in bad shape apparently. I don't know what happened, but it looks like he was attacked."

Attacked?

"I... what? Attacked? I don't understand."

"The boys are there now trying to figure out what happened. I've got to go."

"Of course, I understand. I hope he's okay?" The words fall out before I can stop them.

Because I don't understand what's happening.

I don't—

"Tally?"

"Yeah?" I blink, trying to catch my breath.

"Is something going on with you and my brother?"

"I... no. Of course not." The lie makes me flinch. "You should go. Text me when you know anything."

Her brows crinkle and for a second, I think she might push the issue. But she doesn't. She gives me a small nod. "Yeah, okay. I'll speak to you later." Liv rushes out of the room, concern etched into every crack in her expression.

Oakley is hurt.

He was attacked.

The same night someone broke into my house and trashed my room.

What is going on?

I grab my phone off the desk and power it up. The second it comes to life, I wait.

And wait.

But nothing but a couple of texts from Abi and a few missed calls from Liv appear.

Next, I check social media. Half-expecting to find Misty or the Heir chasers celebrating their victory. But there's nothing. No mention of the party or Deacon or me.

Something about the whole thing doesn't feel right.

It doesn't change the fact Oakley stole the key and had free access to my house. No matter how much I wish it wasn't true, he was complicit in whatever happened last night.

I know he was.

But it still doesn't explain why he was attacked.

Unless it's all part of his ruse. To make sure that he has an airtight alibi should I go to the police.

I let out a weary sigh and drop on the edge of the bed, rubbing my eyes. I should hate him—I do hate him. But hearing he's in the hospital, knowing that he's hurt... I can't stop myself from caring.

Because deep down, I'm a good person.

I am.

Even if Oakley broke me.

Even if he betrayed me.

I still care.

And I hate it.

2

OAKLEY

I grit my teeth as pleasure rushes through my body. The kind of pleasure that makes your eyes roll back in your head and every single nerve ending you possess to sing with delight.

Sex has never been like this.

Never.

Pushing a little deeper, I contain the groan that rips from my lips.

It. Is. Just. That. Damn. Good.

I roll my hips, fighting against her tightness. Desperate to get as deep as physically possible. I need her to remember this for... for forever.

I want to brand myself on her soul just like she branded herself on mine.

There is nothing I do, no minute that passes where I don't think of her, when I'm not obsessing over our time together. Wishing that it could be different. That we could just be us.

I'm over the secrets, the stolen glances and hook-ups in the shadows when no one is looking.

I want this.

And I want the fucking world to know it.

CRUEL DEVIOUS HEIR: PART TWO

Fire burns within me. Each thrust into her body making my balls ache in such a good way.

"That's it, baby. You're such a good girl," I praise, thrusting a little deeper and sliding my hand up her body.

Her skin is perfect. It's like silk, and smells like fucking heaven.

She is heaven.

Everything I don't deserve, but everything I crave.

Squeezing her breast in my hand, I watch as she throws her head back, crying out my name like it's her favourite thing to say.

It's everything.

Every-fucking-thing.

Moving my hand higher, I wrap it around her delicate throat. Her pulse thunders beneath my fingertips, her eyes widening in shock as I cut off her air. "So fucking beautiful, baby. Look at you taking my cock like a champ."

She groans at my words, her pussy flooding my cock as I praise her.

She fucking loves it.

"I need you to come, baby. Need to feel that cunt squeezing me so goddamn tight I forget my own name." She nods eagerly, her eyes locked on mine. "You're nearly there, I can feel it. Put your fingers on your clit. Show me how you do it."

She swallows roughly but her hesitant hand slips down her belly.

The shy, innocent act does things to me, and I have to bite down on my cheeks. I'm forced to stop moving completely to hold off blowing inside her before she falls. Because she always comes first. Always.

"Fuck, baby. Wanna do this for the rest of my life. I'll do anything to keep fucking doing this," I groan, almost sounding in pain as her fingers collide with her clit, her muscles clamping down around me and pushing me that little bit closer to the edge.

"Oakley," she cries, her fingers rubbing circles over her clit, doing exactly what she was told and showing me what she likes. Giving me the best kind of instruction manual to her body.

"That's it. Fuck, you look so hot right now. And all fucking mine."

"Yes, yes," she agrees eagerly as her orgasm races forward. "I'm gonna... I'm gonna... OAKLEY," she screams, not caring about anyone hearing her.

And fuck if I care either.

I want this. Her. Us. Everything.

Fuck what everyone else thinks.

They're not here right now. They can't feel this connection, this intense thing that's been burning between us for weeks now.

I've known her all my life. But I never, ever thought it could turn into something this powerful.

"Fuck, yeah. Baby, your pussy is like nothing else I've ever felt," I groan, fighting to hold off just a little longer, needing her to ride out every second she can before I pump her full.

"Come, Oak. Let me feel you," she demands, relaxing a little as her release subsides, leaving her chest heaving, her skin flushed and her eyes blown with pleasure.

Wrapping her legs around my waist, she digs her heels into my lower back, forcing me deeper.

"Make me yours, Oakley," she orders, and with my eyes locked on hers.

I fall.

And fall.

And fall.

"MISTY," I bellow, losing myself in the pleasure.

My body jolts and I suck in a sharp breath, confusion

warring within me. But not before my stomach swirls with acid, burning up my throat and threatening to escape.

My heart beats faster, and in only a few seconds, something starts beeping beside me.

I have no idea what it is, but it's fucking annoying.

I try to move my arm, to search for... her. But I can't.

I shudder at the memory as something nudges into my brain that something is wrong.

Very fucking wrong.

My body is heavy. Like someone has poured concrete through my veins and left me to deal with the consequences.

The beeping stops, and I swear I hear a voice, but I can't register the sound.

Warmth spreads from my shoulder, all the way down my arm, but it does little to calm me down.

I can't move. I can't...

I was just coming hard. Really fucking hard, but surely it wasn't enough to—

Darkness consumes me, sucking me back under leaving the panic and confusion behind.

I'll fucking take it.

Here, I can breathe.

Here, I'm not drowning. I'm floating.

Almost like being high.

And I fucking love being high.

When the darkness begins to lift once more, soft yet familiar voices fill my ears.

"They have no idea," Reese says. "No evidence yet. They're hoping he'll remember everything when he wakes up and give them some answers."

"It can't have been a random attack. Oak is better than to be overpowered by some chancers."

That's Theo sticking up for me, although, I'm not entirely sure why.

"Depends how many of them there were."

"He was targeted, I'd put my fucking life on it," Reese states, his voice firm with certainty.

"Then they're fucking stupid. If they know who he is then they have to know that we'll come at them harder. No one touches us and gets away with it," Elliot growls fiercely.

Touches us?

I fight to drag memories that I know are lingering in the dark depths of my brain. But I can't get them. Hell, I can't get anywhere near them.

The last thing... the last person I remember is Misty.

I suck in a sharp breath as images of fucking her come back to me again.

"Oakley," Reese gasps before the sound of chairs scraping against the floor of wherever we are making me wince. "Shit, man. You awake?"

The warmth of a hand covers mine before Elliot says, "If you can hear us, squeeze my hand."

It takes everything I have. Every ounce of strength to try and do as he says. Honestly, I have no idea if I even manage it until he announces, "He did. He's awake. He can hear us."

The relief in his tone is palpable. But it does little to explain what the fuck is going on.

"Fuck, Oak. You scared us for a bit there," Reese says with what I'm sure is a crack of emotion in his voice.

Shit. That's not good. Barely anything breaks my best friend.

Silence falls around us, but the tension and desperation doesn't dissipate, making me even more curious about what's happening.

"Are you in pain?" Elliot asks. "Squeeze once for yes, twice for no."

"If you are, we can call a nurse to give you more meds," Theo assures me.

A nurse?

More meds?

Whatever has happened is not fucking good.

But I'm not actually in pain. So that's a good thing, right?

"One," Elliot says when I manage to squeeze his fingers. It's a little easier this time.

I'm sure all four of them hold their breath as they wait to see if I will do another.

"Two."

"You're gonna be okay, Oak. And we're gonna make sure whoever did this pays. They won't be able to tell their side of the story. We won't leave them to be found." Reese's tone is deadly. So much so, it sends a shiver of fear racing through me. Which is fucking weird because I'm not scared of any of these guys. They're my boys. My brothers.

I've no idea how long they all stand around me, presumably staring at me. But seeing as I cannot open my eyes and find out, I can't confirm that.

But Elliot's grip on my hand doesn't leave. Someone's breath continues to race over my face while another hand on my shin sends warmth shooting up my leg.

Eventually, their soothing presence sends me back to sleep.

Sobbing is the first thing I hear the next time reality comes back to me.

Sobbing from a girl I know almost as well as I know myself.

"Tally?" My voice is rough, and just that one word rips my dry throat to shreds. It fucking kills.

"Oakley, it's me, Liv" she breathes before her hands cup

my cheeks. "Oakley, look at me. I need to see you," she says through her sobs. "I need to—"

I force my eyes open because I need to see her. I can't fucking stand my twin being in pain.

. But I don't see anything. The light is too blinding.

"Oh my God," Olivia cries.

"Turn the lights off," Elliot commands, and a second later, the bright lights from overhead are cut and my vision comes back to me.

All the air rushes out of my lungs as I stare at my sister's devastated face. Her eyes are bright red and puffy, tears and dark make-up stain her cheeks and her bottom lip looks like it's been mauled. And for once, I know it hasn't been done by Reese. How long has she been chewing on the damn thing?

"S-sorry," I whisper, sensing that she needs to hear it.

I might have no idea what's happened, but something tells me that at least part of it will be my fault.

"Oh, Oak."

I try to swallow my grunt of pain when her weight lands on my chest but fuck, that hurts.

"Sweet cheeks," Reese says softly before she's pulled off me.

"I'm sorry," Olivia wails. "I just... I thought I'd lost you, Oak. I-I thought—" She takes a shuddering breath but doesn't finish her sentence.

She doesn't need to.

This is really fucking bad.

Ripping my eyes from my sister, I stare at the guy holding her as she cries. While keeping it together, Reese still looks wrecked. And when I glance at the other two, they don't look much better either.

"Wha—"

My question is cut off when the door opens and my father and Fiona join the party with handfuls of take-out coffee.

He moves to hand Liv the first one, but the second he takes

in her state, his eyes dart to me. "Son, you're awake," he breathes, dumping the coffees with Elliot and Theo and rushing to my side.

He holds my hand in two of his and lifts it from the bed, allowing me to see the cannula that's stuck in the back of it.

If I hadn't already figured it out then that's the final clue I needed to tell me where I am.

"We're going to find them, Oak. And they'll regret the day they ever laid a finger on my boy."

They...

"W-who are they?" I force out, each word more painful than the last.

"We were hoping you could tell us that, Son," he says, realisation already setting in.

I have no idea why I'm here, and no idea who they're talking about. I don't think that was what they were hoping for.

As I stare at all of them, only one thought is filling my mind.

One person is missing.

And I fucking need her.

My eyes land on Liv's again, and they soften with relief. But that's not it. There's more in her brown eyes.

Suspicion.

Fuck.

3

TALLY

Monday rolls around but I don't go to school.
I can't.
Nothing makes sense anymore.

Oakley was attacked. According to Olivia, who messaged me last night after she got done visiting him, he can't remember anything. But he's in bad shape and has to stay in hospital a bit longer.

I barely slept, worrying. About Oakley and whether he's okay. About what will happen if my parents find out the truth. About Deacon and Misty. About going back to All Hallows' because I can't hide forever.

I got myself into such a state that Mum and Dad agreed I can take the next couple of days off. I'm not sure how much they told Mr. Porter, but he agreed it was for the best if I stay at home.

It's only eleven and I'm already going out of my mind.

Dad left early to head to court in London for a big case he's been working on, but Mum stayed behind to work from home.

I'm not used to being coddled but I can't deny, I'm glad she's here.

I can't even bring myself to go into my bedroom, despite it being cleaned and the bedding replaced.

The vibration of my phone startles me, my heart rate spiking. I reach over and grab it off the bedside table.

> Liv: How are you?

> Tally: Shouldn't I be asking you that? How is he?

> Liv: Pissed he can't remember anything yet. Giving the nurses hell. But he'll live.

> Tally: Good, that's good.

> Liv: The strangest thing happened though... He woke up and asked for you.

Oh my God.

I clutch the phone trying to calm my racing heart. Another message comes through before I can reply.

> Liv: What's going on Tally?

> Tally: I... I don't know what you want me to say.

> Liv: How about you start with the truth? I'd demand answers from my brother but he's barely making sense.

The truth? Where do I even start?

I could tell her about the party at the Chapel all those weeks ago. The night I gave Oakley my first kiss only for him to forget about it. Only to find him grinding all up on Misty minutes later.

God, it still makes me feel sick just thinking about it. I'd been ready to throw caution to the wind that night. But Oakley had other ideas.

I don't reply quick enough, and Liv calls me. For a second,

I contemplate not answering, but she lets it ring and ring. Until I have no choice just to pick it up.

"Hello."

"Hi," she sounds broken, and it makes my heart ache. Even though it shouldn't.

Even though I shouldn't care Oakley is hurt.

I do.

I can't help it.

"How is he?"

"He must be feeling a bit better because he's being a pain in the arse. Actually, he wants to talk to you."

"H-he does?"

"Yeah." I hear muffled voices in the background, but I blurt out, "No."

"No? But—"

"I... I can't. I have to go."

I hang up like a coward, my body trembling.

I don't understand. He took that key—stole it. He was involved in the break-in, he had to be.

So why does he want to talk to me?

Maybe he regrets it. Betraying me. *Hurting* me.

It doesn't matter.

It's too late for apologies. And even if it wasn't, it's better this way.

I was a fool to ever think that me and Oakley could be something real. No one will ever accept our relationship.

He's a mistake I should never have made.

One I won't make again.

The day drags. I turned off my phone again after Olivia's call. Cowardly, yes. But the only way to stop myself from obsessing over everything. Wondering if he'll eventually message. Or call. To try to explain.

Nothing he can say or do will fix this mess. And even if I forgive him, my parents never will.

No, I need to put Oakley Beckworth in my rear-view mirror and focus on the future. On passing my A Levels and getting into university.

When I finally go back to All Hallows' I'll keep my head down and my nose out of the Heirs' business.

I'll—

"Tallulah," Mum's voice perforates my thoughts, making me flinch. "You have visitors."

Padding to the door, I rip it open and yell back, "Who is it?"

"Olivia Beckworth and Abigail Bancroft."

Just what I don't need.

But before I can come up with a valid excuse to get rid of them, Mum adds, "I'm sending them up, sweetheart."

"We need to talk," Olivia says the second she reaches the top stair.

"Hello to you too," I mumble, pulling the door wider so she can slip past.

"How are you feeling?" Abi asks, sympathy glittering in her eyes.

"I... honestly, I've been better."

I follow them into the room and close the door behind us.

Before I can get a word out, Liv pins me with a hard look. "You and Oakley then..."

"I..."

"All this time I've been trying to call them off your back and the two of you were—"

"It's complicated."

"That's what he said." She tsks with disapproval.

"He talked to you about me?" I ask, aware of Abi watching us.

Me.

"Not really. But he freaked out when you wouldn't talk to

him. If he wasn't drugged up to the eyeballs, I wouldn't have put it past him to flee the hospital and come looking for you."

A chill runs through me. That sounds like something Oakley would do.

Before he betrayed me.

"I..."

"Tally!" Olivia lets out an exasperated sigh. "What the hell is going on? And no more lies and half-truths."

"I don't know how it happened." Tears burn the backs of my eyes and I try desperately to blink them away. "I've always hated the Heirs and everything they stand for but then we made friends and I... God, I feel so stupid for even saying this."

I glance away, wiping my cheeks.

"We're not here to judge," Abi says softly.

When I turn back to them, Abi is sitting on the desk chair and Liv is standing by the window, watching me carefully. Quietly.

For a second, I wonder what she sees. She's been here, after all. In my shoes. Falling for a boy she once claimed to hate.

Only, she got the boy.

I didn't.

"We kissed. That night at the Chapel when you found us stumbling out of the woods. I kissed Oakley. And then—"

"What. Did. He. Do?" she practically growls the words and I hold up my hands.

"N-nothing bad, I swear. It was just a kiss, but it sparked something inside me. Cliché, I know, right?" I let out a small, weak chuckle. "Anyway, turns out the kiss meant nothing to him. I gave my first kiss to your brother, and he didn't even remember."

"Tally, I—"

"Don't do that. Don't try to make me feel better. It's my own fault, really. I was just so sick of always being the good girl. Of playing it safe and putting my future before my present. Eighteen and never even been kissed." I scoff. "How pathetic."

"Uh, hello." Abi raises her hand and guilt floods me.

"God, Abs, I'm sorry—"

"No, it's fine," she says softly. "I'm not exactly a social butterfly either. But there's nothing wrong with saving yourself for the right boy."

Something flashes in her eyes, but Olivia commands my attention with her next question. "I take it there's more to the story?"

I refrain from rolling my eyes. But I understand her irritation. Oakley is her brother, and I'm her friend. At least, I was. Before everything got messy and confusing.

"I was hurt, and I guess part of me was disappointed in myself."

"So you decided to go after him the only way you knew how."

I nod, hardly surprised that she's pieced it together so quickly. "I figured I could kill two birds with one stone. Bring down the Heirs and hit your brother where it hurt most."

"Oh, Tally." Liv walks over to the bed and plops down. "Why didn't you tell me?"

"It wouldn't have changed anything." I shrug. "I was too embarrassed. But my plan backfired."

"You had sex with him."

Another nod. "It became this game of cat and mouse. But I refused to back down and..."

"Oakley liked that. He liked that you stood your ground. I'm not surprised. It takes a certain type of girl to stand up to an Heir."

"It doesn't matter." Pain ripples through me. "I lost sight of the rules. Let myself get too deep because I stupidly thought..." I inhale a shuddering breath. "I thought he felt the same. But he doesn't. It was nothing more than a ploy to remind me who holds all the power."

Liv frowns. "What happened?"

Before I can overthink it, I blurt out, "He stole a key to my house, and I think he gave it to Misty and the Heir chasers. Someone broke in Saturday night and trashed my room."

"What?" She shoots up.

"Yeah, it wasn't pretty. They left a dead rat in my bed."

"Oh my God, that's... horrible." Abi pales.

"My dad called the police and everything."

"The police?" Liv balks. "What did you tell them?"

"Nothing. I don't want my parents to know how bad it's gotten. But I'm glad to know where you stand on the matter."

"Shit, sorry." Her expression softens. "I'm just trying to make sense of everything. You really think Oakley is behind this? Because I know my brother can be—"

"He took that key, Liv. He was supposed to take me out Saturday night, but I never heard from him, and you said he met up with Misty. You said—"

"Whoa, hold on a minute. You could be adding two and two together and making five here. I assumed he was meeting Misty to hook-up, yeah. Because I didn't know you two were sneaking around behind my back. Maybe he went to meet her to tell her to stand down? Or to put a stop to whatever they had planned? Maybe he realised what a tosser he is and went to set her straight?

"He was attacked, Tally. Assaulted. That doesn't exactly fit your narrative."

We stare each other down, the air thick around us.

"I don't know what you want me to say," I concede.

"Oakley is a lot of things, Tally. I get it. Trust me, I get it. But I know my brother and he wouldn't do that. Not to someone he—" She stops herself.

"He what?" I ask, unable to disguise the tremor in my voice.

"Someone he cares about."

A bitter laugh crawls up my throat. "Oakley doesn't care

about me, Olivia. He doesn't care about anyone but himself and the Heirs."

"You didn't see him."

"I... it doesn't matter. We're done. It's over."

"You need to speak to him first. Maybe if you do he'll remember..."

"I can't, Liv." I fold my arms around myself. "Even if he wasn't the one who broke in, he provided them with the means to do it. He—"

"You don't know that for a fact. Maybe whoever attacked him, stole it. Maybe—"

"Liv, come on. That's a stretch and you know it."

"Please, stop fighting." Abi stands, her wild gaze darting between us. "This isn't helping matters. Maybe Liv—"

Her phone starts blaring and she digs it out of her pocket. "It's him. It's Oakley." Olivia fixes her gaze right on me, as if to say it's your decision. But for as much as I want to hear his voice, to hear him say he had nothing to do with the break-in, I know in my heart of hearts that he did.

"I'm sorry," I whisper, turning away so that they don't see the tears rolling down my cheeks. "But I can't."

"Tally—"

"Come on, Liv. We should give her some space," Abi says, and I want desperately to tell her that space is the last thing I want.

That what I need is my friends. The only two friends I've ever had.

But I don't.

Because if I do, my resolve will crumble.

And I can't let that happen.

No matter how much I want to believe she's right.

4

OAKLEY

"This is fucking bullshit," I roar, ripping my still sore throat to shit before pulling my arm back and launching my phone across the room.

It collides with the wall before clattering to the floor. But nothing about it makes me relax at all.

All afternoon I've been calling her. Call after call. Message after message. But she neither answers nor replies. And something tells me that she's not listening to the voicemails I'm leaving either.

But why?

The last time I remember talking to her, I was telling her what time I was going to pick her up for our date. And now, she won't even talk to me.

What happened in the time between me messaging her and ending up in here?

How could I have possibly fucked anything up while unconscious?

"You need to calm down. You'll have Nurse Ceecee back in here attempting to sedate you again," Reese says in warning.

"She can fuck off with her stupid drugs. The second I'm allowed out of bed I'm—"

"Leaving. I know, Oak. You said like a million times since I got here."

Liv and Reese turned up before the sun rose this morning. It was way before visiting hours officially started, and the only reason I knew they were here was because I heard Liv screaming at a nurse—probably Ceecee and that's why she hates me so much—telling her how unfair it was to split twins up in their time of need.

Somehow it worked because after a while the screaming stopped and my door opened, revealing my red-faced sister and my much calmer best friend.

"Just do as you're told and you'll be out of here in no time," he assures me, stretching out his legs under my bed.

"Because you'd be all calm and shit if you were stuck in a hospital bed, drugged up to your eyeballs and unable to see Liv, who for some fucking reason refuses to talk to you? No, Reese. You wouldn't. You'd be like a caged fucking beast, so less of the fucking 'let's all just calm down, kumbaya shit', yeah?"

He blinks at me, his brows raised.

"What, nothing to say all of a sudden?" I snap. "Why are you even here, anyway? Shouldn't you be at school?" But the second I get a look at the stupidly loud ticking clock on the other side of the room, I correct myself. "Practice. You should be at practice."

"Firstly, I thought you liked being drugged up," Reese quips, making my fists curl and my busted knuckles split open once more.

They're fucked up. The only fucking sign that I even attempted to fight off whoever jumped me on Saturday. Obviously, it didn't help my cause. Or maybe it did. Maybe if I didn't throw those few punches then I wouldn't be sitting in a hospital room right now, but a fucking morgue instead.

Uplifting thoughts, great one, Oakley.

"Not the kind of pilled-up I shoot for, but thanks for that," I snarl.

"And since when is Tally your Liv?"

They've all been grilling me about the reason why I asked for Tally when I first woke up. Something else I don't fucking remember, but they keep bringing it up so much that I can't help but think I probably did.

Hell, I can't get her out of my fucking head at the best of times, so it makes sense that she'd be the first person on my mind when I woke.

"She's not," I snap, staring at my phone on the other side of the room.

If she finally does respond, I'm never going to know because it's over there probably with a fucked up screen at best.

"It's just me, Oak. You can tell me." He holds up his hands. "Judgement-free zone," he offers.

"Why?" I bark, hating that I have to question my best friend's motives these days. "So you can go running back to Liv and tell her all my secrets?"

The second hurt flickers through his eyes, regret knots up my stomach. It's not fair. Pretty much everything I've said to him since I found out about them hasn't been fair. I know that. But I also can't help how I feel.

Oakley Beckworth, always the second-best twin loses once again.

Only this time, it was my best fucking friend.

I don't resent Liv for it. I can't. I fucking love her too much. But all our lives, she's been the golden child. The only girl in our parent's group of friends. The special one who was already treated differently because they felt sorry for her always being surrounded by boys.

She was praised for being the smart one, the good one, the precious little angel. And I was just forgotten in the background, only to be noticed when I fucked something up. Again.

It's made me bitter and I fucking hate it.

Dad loves me, I know he does. But he dotes on Liv on a whole new level.

And now... now she's got Reese too. The one person I could always depend on. My ride or die.

It fucking hurts, goddamn it.

"Because I'm your friend, Oak. Your best friend. And you're hurting and I fucking hate it.

"Yes, I'm in love with your sister, and I know I fucked up in a million and one ways with that. But I'm still me. And I'm still here for you no matter what. You want to tell me stuff that I don't tell Liv. You've fucking got it, man. I'd never sell you out like that."

"I sense a but in there," I mutter.

"But if keeping secrets from anyone, not just Liv, will end up getting you hurt then I'll tell the fucking world if it means protecting you. You or anyone I love. You'd do the same for me too, I know it."

I don't even need to agree. I can see his confidence in me in his eyes.

"We've been hooking up," I blurt.

A wide, shit-eating smile spreads across his lips. "At fucking last."

"You knew?" I balk, my eyes wide.

"No. I didn't know. But something was obviously going on with you and it started when she announced her little campaign. It wasn't hard to put two and two together and get suspicious."

"Well, you could have fucking said something," I scoff.

"Because you'd have confessed." He glares at me, not needing me to say anything to know he's right. "So go on then. Spill the beans."

I sigh, sitting back and attempting to get comfortable. But

something tells me that no matter how fancy the private hospital I'm stuck in is, nothing will be comfortable right now.

Every single inch of me hurts even with the drugs they're pumping me full of.

"I don't even know when it happened but..."

"You've fallen for her, haven't you?"

Memories of my time with Tally over the past few weeks flicker through my mind like a movie.

In the basement when I tried to put an end to her campaign before it even started. The woods beside the Chapel the night we threw our party to prove that we held the power, no matter what. The charity gala, kissing her, feeling how wet she was for me. Turning up at her house after when I couldn't control my jealousy after hearing Deacon's dickhead mates making bets about her.

A groan rips from my lips as I think about the first time she wrapped hers around my cock. How hesitant and delicate her touch was despite the rumours that were flying around about her.

Her taste on my tongue, her curves beneath my hands, her soft mewls as I ate her, and the way she screamed my name.

A noise that's somewhere between a laugh and a cough sounds out from beside me, and when I look over, I find that his previous shit-eating grin is only wider.

"Dude, you're so fucking gone for her." His eyes drop from mine in favour of my sheets. I don't need to look down to know why.

I'm hard as fucking nails from just thinking about her.

"I think it started long before I even realised," I confess, remembering Tally confessing that something happened between us that I clearly don't remember. "But yeah, I think I have."

"Oak, your father is going to have a field day with this," Reese says, trying desperately hard to wipe the smile off his face but failing miserably. "Although I fucking love you for taking the heat off Liv and me for a bit. I might be screwing my stepsister, but you're now sticking it to your mortal enemy."

"Am I?" I ask sadly. "She won't even fucking message me back. There might be no need for Dad to even know about it."

We both fall silent for a few minutes as the weight of my confession settles around us.

"She's fallen for you too, right?" Reese finally asks.

I suck in a deep breath which I instantly regret because it makes my ribs hurt like a bitch. "I hoped that maybe she had, yeah. I was meant to take her out on a date Saturday night. I'd planned all this stuff. It was going to be perfect. Romantic. All the shit she deserves but just look... I fucked that up too."

"What happened wasn't your fault," he reasons.

"Wasn't it?" I bark. "I don't fucking remember anything. Why was I even there?"

"To meet—"

"Misty," I finish for him. "I know. Liv keeps fucking telling me that."

His eyes darken with anger as I speak about her like that but thankfully, he doesn't say anything.

I know deep down, she's just trying to help. Trying to jog my memory. But it's not fucking working. Nothing is.

"Has someone spoken to her yet?"

"The police have interviewed her. But she hasn't been at school."

"Has anyone gone to see her?"

I can read the answer on his face.

"Her mum wouldn't let Elliot and Theo anywhere near her."

"I need to talk to her. But not before I talk to Tally."

"Just focus on getting better so you can get out of here. Once you're back on your feet you can go questioning whoever you like."

"How fucking long is that going to be?" I snap.

Reese shrugs at the same time the door to my room opens

and Ceecee walks inside with a hesitant smile on her face. "Afternoon Oakley, how are you feeling?"

"Awful. When can I go home?"

"We're still monitoring your concussion. And we need to lower your meds before—"

"Just take me off them, give me some pills to take with me," I demand.

"It's not that easy."

"Of course it's fucking not."

"Oak," Reese growls.

"I need to do some checks and change some dressings," Ceecee says, staring at my best friend. I can't help but smirk when I see a little fear in her eyes. "Are you okay to give us ten minutes?"

"Sure. I'll go and call Liv and see if she has any updates from Tally."

My teeth grind that he might get the information I need before I do.

I watch him leave, but not before he shoots Ceecee an apologetic look. But the second the door closes behind him, I close my eyes and shut myself off from her.

I have no intention of talking to her. I'm not here for small talk. I'm here to get better so I can get back to my girl.

My girl...

Fuck.

Something tells me that she never was my girl. And it's looking unlikely that she will be after all this.

Maybe it's for the best.

She's always been too good for me anyway.

5

TALLY

Tuesday afternoon, I decided to stop wallowing and do something productive.

Seventy-two cupcakes later, in four different flavours, the kitchen looks like an explosion has gone off. Bowls and pans litter the flour-dusted counters, a faint trace of vanilla, lemon, and chocolate lingering in the air.

The place is a mess but all the weighing and measuring and stirring has lifted my spirits a little.

I can't hide forever, I know that. I need to dust myself off, put the drama with Oakley and the Heirs behind me, and focus on my future.

Even if everything isn't as it seems, and Oakley wasn't scheming with Misty. This whole mess is a sign that I was foolish to ever get tangled up in his world.

A world I clearly don't belong in.

While the last batch of cupcakes are cooling, I start the laborious task of cleaning up, humming along to the radio. I'm so invested in Taylor Swift singing about heartbreak and red scarves and cardigans, the loud knock at the door startles me.

My brows bunch together as I dry my hands and sling the

towel on the side, trying to formulate what I'll say to Olivia and Abigail.

By the time I reach the front door, I still haven't decided whether I'll let them in or send them packing with a half-hearted excuse. It isn't that I don't want to see them, I just don't know what to say.

But when I check the peephole before opening the door, my concerns melt away replaced with utter shock.

"N-no," I murmur as Oakley roars, "Open up, Prim. I know you're in there." He bangs his fists harder, rattling the door in its frame. "Open this fucking door."

My heart catapults into my throat as I watch his face twist and contort with anger.

He's a mess. Swollen and bruised. But it's the wild glint in his eyes that sends a shiver zipping down my spine.

"Tallulah, I swear to God. Just open the door. I need to see you, babe. I need to—"

I yank the door open and fume, "What the hell are you doing here?"

"I... thank fuck." Relief flickers in his expression. "You're okay. You're—"

"Oakley, you shouldn't be here."

"Fuck that, Prim. I needed to see you. I need— fuck." His fist slams against the door, making me flinch.

"Oak!"

"I woke up and everything had gone to shit." Desperation coats his words. "Liv says I went to meet Misty, but I don't remember anything, I don't fucking remember."

"It doesn't matter." I offer him a sad smile. "This. Us. It's done. We're—"

"No." He takes a step closer, but I inch back, throwing up my hand.

"N-no? You don't get to say that Oak," I seethe. "You played me. God, I'm such an idiot. I thought... no, do you know what? Forget it. I'm not doing this with you. Please leave." I try to shut the door in his face, but he rams his big rugby player body forward, forcing it wider.

"Oakley," I hiss. "Just leave."

"Not until you hear me out. You at least owe me that much."

"Oh, that's cute coming from you. I don't owe you a goddamn thing."

Anger flashes in his eyes as he advances on me. A predator stalking its prey. Except I have nowhere to go. Nowhere to run.

"Oakley, please," I choke on the words, my back hitting the wall as he cages me there with his hands either side of my head.

"Prim, come on." He leans in, rubbing his nose along my jaw, inhaling deeply. "I practically broke out of the hospital to come and see you."

"Well, it was a wasted journey," I snap, feeling a lick of satisfaction at the flash of hurt in his eyes.

"Tell me what happened." He collars my throat with his messed-up hand. "What you think happened? Because Liv was spewing all this stuff at me, and it doesn't make any sense. It doesn't—"

"You know what happened," I bellow. "You stole a key to my house and... and gave it to her. That bitch." My chest heaves with the weight of my words as confusion seeps into his expression. "Misty broke into my house, trashed my bedroom, and left a dead rat in my bed all because of you. I hate you, Oakley Beckworth. I. Hate. You."

He staggers back like I've hit him, dragging a hand through his hair. "What the fuck did you say?"

"You heard me."

"You think I... fuck. *Fuck!*" He yanks on the end of his hair, pain and fury contorting his patchwork face. "I took the key, yeah. But I didn't give it to Misty. I've been trying to keep that bitch off your back. Shit, Prim. You really thought..."

Bitter laughter bubbles in his chest as he shakes his head. "Guess you were right along, we are too different."

"W-what do you mean?" A shudder goes through me.

"I know who I am, Prim. I know what I am. But I thought — nah, forget it," he spits. "What's the point? You've made up your mind, haven't you? Stuck up little Tallulah Darlington and her—"

Tires screech from behind him, sending my heart into overdrive.

"My dad," I breathe. "You need to go Oakley. You need—"

"You," Dad bellows, marching toward the house. "Get the hell away from my daughter."

Before I can stop him, Dad grabs—*grabs*—Oakley and yanks him out of the house, shoving him outside.

"Dad!" I shriek, running after them. "Don't—"

"Stay out of this, sweetheart. I knew, I knew there was more to this than you admitted. Oakley Beckworth, why am I not surprised."

Oakley rights himself, glowering at my father. "You've got this all wrong, sir," he says calmly.

Too calmly.

But my mind is still reeling. Because despite everything that's happened, I know Oakley. At least, I know the parts of him he's revealed to me in the dark.

"I don't know what you think I did, but I'm telling you, I didn't." His eyes flick to mine, silent promise there.

A declaration I'm not ready for.

Because Oakley did this.

He was involved.

He had to be.

It's the only conclusion that makes sense.

"Dad, please. Let's just go inside and I'll explain."

"No. I'm calling the police. He's behind this Tallulah. Of course he's—"

"With all due respect, Mr. Darlington you don't know fuck

CRUEL DEVIOUS HEIR: PART TWO

all about me. And this isn't between you and me, it's between me and—" He holds my gaze and I will him not to say it.

Not here.

Not like this.

"Your daughter."

It's Dad's turn to stagger back. His cloudy gaze finds mine, his brows pinched with realisation. "W-what does he mean, sweetheart?"

"I... I'm sorry, Dad." Tears roll down my cheeks. "I'm so sorry."

Oakley snorts with disgust. As if I failed whatever test he laid at my feet.

But what did he really expect?

He's an Heir.

A Beckworth.

And even if he didn't give Misty that key, it doesn't absolve him from everything else.

"Get off my property," Dad seethes, closing the distance between him and Oakley. "Stay away from me, stay away from my house, but most of all, stay the fuck away from my daughter. She's too good for a jumped-up little prick like you."

Oakley's eyes slide to mine, and time stops. Pretty sure my heart stops beating too.

Because he doesn't look cocky or angry or wild anymore, he looks... defeated.

"Yeah, you're right." He holds up his hands and starts backing away. "Don't worry, Mr. D, I hear you loud and clear."

He spins on his heel and stalks off down the driveway, and I should be relieved.

I should be elated that he's gone.

That I can finally put this whole mess behind me and move on.

So why do I want to run after him?

Why do I want to run after him, grab his hand, and beg for forgiveness?

Silence hangs in the air, laced with disappointment and confusion.

I don't know how long we've been sitting here, in thick, uncomfortable silence. But I don't know what to say.

I don't know how to fix this.

And for as much as I don't want to be thinking about him, I can't get Oakley's face out of my mind. The utter devastation streaked across his face as he walked away from the house.

From me.

"I think we need to talk," Dad finally says, glaring at me across the breakfast island.

"I don't know what you want me to say." I barely meet his eyes.

"Oakley Beckworth, Tallulah? Really?" Disapproval drips off every word. "You couldn't have chosen someone—"

"Choose? God, Dad. You make it sound like there's a line of boys queueing up for their chance with me."

"Sweetheart, that's not... I'm just trying to understand. He's a Beckworth... an Heir. The thing you hate more than anything in the world. It doesn't make any sense."

I give a little shrug, my lips curving into a sad smile. "I'm not sure it works like that, Dad."

"Did he... coerce you? Threaten—"

"No, Dad. No. It isn't like that. I didn't... I didn't plan on getting..." I search for the right words. "Involved with him. But it happened. And now nothing makes sense, and I don't know what to do."

"Oh sweetheart." He rushes over to me, pulling me into his arms. "It's okay, Tally. Everything is going to be okay. I'll speak to Graham and—"

"What?" My head snaps up.

"Well, I need to inform him that you—"

"Dad, you can't. Please."

"Tallulah, that boy is dangerous. He and his friends are a menace to society. I knew there was more to this. Things you weren't telling me. But it's okay, sweetheart. Don't you see you—we—can use this for some good. It will help bolster your campaign. Rally support against the Heirs. It—"

"No, Dad." I yank out of his hold. "This isn't some game, it's my life." My heart. "I'm not going to hand over pieces of myself to be used against them. I won't do it."

"Tallulah," he tsks. "Be reasonable. Oakley Beckworth is—"

"Stop, Dad. Just... stop. This has gotten way out of hand."

"Exactly, sweetheart. That boy came into our house, invaded our privacy, and trashed—"

"I don't think it was him," I whisper.

"Excuse me?"

"I... I don't think it was him, Dad. You didn't see how upset he was, you didn't see—"

"Oh, for goodness' sake, Tallulah. Don't tell me you actually went and fell for the boy? An Heir. A bloody Beckworth? He's brainwashed you, hasn't he? Spun you a right tale? But that's what entitled little pricks like him and his father do."

"Dad!" I gasp, surprised at his outburst.

"I raised you better than this, Tallulah. I thought you were better than this..."

Shame curls in my stomach, and I wait for him to apologise. To take back his cruel words.

"God," he lets out a heavy sigh. "My daughter with that... that boy. I can hardly look at you."

I suck in a sharp breath. I always knew he'd be disappointed. But he isn't even prepared to hear me out.

My lips twist into a sad, defeated smile. "Then don't."

I walk away from him with tears running down my cheeks. And my heart in pieces.

6

OAKLEY

"*I hate you, Oakley Beckworth. I. Hate. You.*"

Her words from before continue to repeat in my head as I stumble down the pavement away from her house, my Uber long gone.

Exhaustion slams into me. My hope, everything I used to fuel my journey gone.

Diminished.

Smashed to fucking pieces with those few words from the girl I should be able to stop thinking about.

I didn't do it. I might not know the whole truth about what *it* actually is. But I know I wasn't involved.

I couldn't be.

I care about her too much.

I fucking lo—

I shake my lowered head.

Streetlights line the quiet residential road I'm barely making progress down, stopping me from hiding in the shadows like I crave to do. Thankfully, cars are few and far between ensuring that no one is witness to the pathetic mess I am right now.

I shouldn't have left the hospital. I knew that before I'd even got out of the room. But I wasn't letting a bit—or a lot—of pain stop me.

I needed to look into her eyes and find out once and for all what was going on.

For all the fucking good it's done.

Right now, I'm just as confused as ever.

Tally seriously thinks I allowed someone to break into her house and put a dead rat in her bed. Is she fucking insane?

Even if I did want to hurt her, I'd never send someone else to do something like that. I fight my own battles. I don't let stuck-up rich sluts do my shit for me.

"Fuck," I grunt when my foot barely lifts from the tarmac beneath me, and I stumble forward into a street lamp.

My phone buzzes almost continually in my pocket.

I knew it wouldn't be long until someone discovered I was missing. I've almost had around the clock babysitting. It was a fucking miracle in itself that I even had five minutes to drag on some clothes and shuffle down the hallway unnoticed.

Stuffing my hand into my sweatpants pocket, I wince as my busted, barely scabbed-over knuckles drag across the fabric.

Stop being such a pussy, Beckworth.

I pull my phone free, staring down at Elliot's incoming call.

Silencing it, I pull up the Uber app instead.

If Tally won't talk to me, then there's someone else I need to hear the truth from.

By the time a car pulls to a stop in front of me, I can barely keep my eyes open let alone put one foot in front of the other.

This was a really fucking bad idea.

It was fine when I had the image of Tally opening her arms to me in my head.

Even if it was a naïve fantasy that was never going to play out.

She's been ignoring all my phone calls, messages, and attempts to talk to her through anyone else.

I just thought that if she saw me, if she looked into my eyes then she might just see whatever it was that made her give me a chance. That allowed her to drop her walls and let me see the real her. Not the perfect girl she shows the rest of the world, but the real one hiding beneath.

Clearly, that was wishful thinking though.

"I hate you, Oakley Beckworth. I. Hate. You."

Despite keeping my eyes on my lap, I'm aware of the attention from the driver, his concerned stare burns into the top of my head.

"I think you need an ambulance, mate, not a taxi," he mutters.

"Can you take me where I want to go, or not?" I snap. My patience with the world ran out the second Tally dismissed everything we've discovered together these past few weeks.

Why wouldn't she? She's ashamed of you.

Oakley Beckworth, just never quite good enough.

My fists curl, my knuckles splitting open once more. But I can't stop it. The hate, the anger, the frustration is bubbling up within me faster than I can control.

And it's only fuelled by the pain.

Pain that I don't remember receiving.

No matter what I do, I can't fucking remember.

I was going on a date with Tally. I was picking her up to take her out and treat her like she deserves.

So why did I go and see Misty like Liv says I did?

What could I possibly have wanted with that bitch?

To warn her off. Surely, that's all I was going to do.

I think back to the Halloween party and the way she'd planned with Deacon to take her out. It has to have been because of that.

I was going to rip her a new one, consequences of anyone finding out that I was rooting for the enemy be damned.

They were teaming up and plotting against her. The girl who only wanted to do the right thing and make our school a better place. I might not like what Tally was trying to achieve because she was taking a hit out on us at the same time, but I also can't deny that what she was fighting for was right.

All the students at All Hallows' deserve better support. We're not fucked up enough not to identify that our lives, our thoughts, aren't fucking normal. And I can think of a few students, even in my medicated stupor who could really use that extra support.

The drive to Misty's parent's house is short. Too fucking short for my liking. She could easily get to Tally's and home again unnoticed.

The driver pulls the car to a stop in front of their driveway, and I sit there staring at the house. The lights are on, and Misty's car is sitting out the front.

With thoughts of her hurting someone I care about giving me a fresh burst of energy, I shove the car door open and step out, grunting thanks to the concerned driver.

Thankfully, my legs hold me up and I don't end up flat on my face on the pavement, which was a real concern.

He doesn't drive away the second I close the door like I'm sure he usually would, but while he might be worried, I push thoughts of him to the back of my mind.

As I emerge onto Misty's driveway, I'm relieved to see that her car is the only one here.

The last thing I fucking need is another pissed-off parent right now.

Mr. Darlington was more than enough for one night.

The second I come to a stop on her doorstep, I jab my finger against the ball, covering the little camera with my other palm. There's a good chance she's already seen me, but if she hasn't, I'd like this little visit to be a surprise.

Nothing happens for the longest time, and I start to think that she's not here.

Disappointment sits heavy in my stomach as I prepare to leave. All of this and the only fucking answer I got is that the girl I've gone and bloody fallen for hates me.

Way to fucking go, Beckworth.

I'm just about to spin away from the door when footsteps on the other side hit my ears. My breath catches, making my ribs hurt like a motherfucker as the lock disengages and the door is pulled open a crack.

"Oakley," Misty gasps, her eyes widen in shock as she pulls the door wider. "Oh my God. Are you okay?"

My eyes hold hers for a beat before dropping to her towel-clad body.

"Do you want to come in? You look like you need to sit down, or sleep, or something?"

When I don't respond, she begins shifting awkwardly from foot to foot. Her skin erupts in goosebumps as the cool autumn air washes over her still damp body.

"I haven't actually finished showering, so you could join me if yo—" She yelps like a little bitch as I wrap my fingers around her wrist and tug her out into the cold, letting the heavy front door slam behind her.

I grit my teeth as her body presses against mine, my ribs once again screaming in pain.

Unwilling to let her touch me, let alone hurt me, I lift my hand, wrap it around her throat and slam her back against the door. Or at least, that's what I attempt to do, but what is in my head and what my body is capable of right now are two very different things.

It doesn't stop her from gazing up at me with a mixture of fear and desire in her eyes though.

"What happened on Saturday, Misty?" I demand, holding her eyes firm.

Her lips part but she's not quick enough to spill the answer I'm looking for and my fingers tighten around her throat, letting her know exactly how dangerous I can be, even in this state.

"Don't play me, Misty. Why did I meet you?"

Her tongue sneaks out, licking across her bottom lip as her hand lifts to press gently to my chest. My skin burns from her touch, and not in a fucking good way.

Smacking her arm away, she thankfully lets it drop to her side.

"We hooked up, obviously. Why else would you have met me?" she asks, tilting her head to the side.

"Bullshit," I hiss. "I haven't touched you in weeks. There's a fucking reason."

She shrugs. "What can I say? You were missing me. You always said that no one else sucked your dick like me."

"You're lying," I seethe, praying to fucking God that she is.

No. She is. She fucking has to be.

There is no fucking way I'd have agreed to hook up with her hours before taking Tally out, it just wouldn't have happened.

"Oakley," she whispers. "There's no shame in admitting you miss me."

She bats her eyelashes at me, doing her best to pull me under her spell. But while I might have played along with her in the past, it's not going to work now.

Sensing that she's not going to win, she pulls her Ace card, tugging at the towel that's tucked under her arms and letting it fall to her feet. I grit my teeth so fucking hard, I've no idea how one doesn't crack.

She continues to stare at me, an accomplished smirk growing on her lips.

I have two options, tell her she's a whore and get nothing in the way of answers. Or play her game and hope for the best.

I suck in a deep breath and lean forward, letting my nose brush along the line of her jaw while swallowing down the bile that races up my throat. "I know I didn't meet you to fuck you, Misty. That's why you're so desperate for me now. So why did I meet you?"

"Oakley, I already told you," she lies.

"Okay, let's try this a different way." My fingers tighten enough to cut off her air for a beat. "Where did you go after?"

"Home to shower. We worked up quite a sweat in those woods," she purrs. "I offered for you to come with me but—"

"The woods where I was jumped?" I ask, cutting her off. "Don't happen to know anything about that, do you, Misty?"

"I've already spoken to the police. I have no idea what happened."

"I don't believe you," I seethe, pulling back to look her dead in the eyes.

Lights illuminate the driveway behind us but neither of us reacts.

"That's a real shame, Oak," she says, sweet as fucking sugar.

It sets my teeth on edge and sends a shiver of disgust down my spine.

Car doors slam closed behind me. Four to be exact. And without looking back, I know who it is.

"Oakley, what the hell are you doing with this tramp?" my sister barks.

Releasing Misty, I stumble back, and finally, my legs give out. Thankfully, someone is there to catch me.

"What's wrong, Misty?" Theo taunts. "You look like you need a cock to suck. If you want to get down on your—"

"Theo," Elliot barks. "Go inside, Misty. No one wants to see your overused cunt. Especially not your neighbours."

"I-I can't," she whines, snatching up the towel and wrapping it back around herself. "The door locks itself."

"Then you'd better hope your parents were stupid enough to leave a window open, huh?"

I'm dragged toward the car and pass out long before I hit the seat.

7

TALLY

"Are you sure you're ready to go back?" Dad asks me for the third time since I dragged myself downstairs and into the kitchen.

"Yep." I grip my coffee mug with vigour, inhaling a deep breath.

It would be easy to stay at home and hide. But it isn't a long-term solution. I'll have to go back eventually. And sitting in the guest room all day, going out of my mind wondering if he's okay, isn't helping me.

I still can't believe my dad knows. That he physically dragged Oakley off me.

God, when did life get so complicated?

When you decided to play cat and mouse with Oakley Beckworth.

"I won't lie, sweetheart, I don't like it. I don't want you anywhere near that boy."

"Dad," I sigh, trying to hold it together. Trying not to replay yesterday's disaster show over in my head.

After Oakley left and everything blew up in my face, Dad ignored me for hours. Until Mum got home and demanded we sit and talk as a family. Their 'we're worried about you' speech was some of the most painful minutes of my life. But they promised not to tell the police. To deal with it themselves.

Whatever the heck that means.

"No, Tallulah. Don't *Dad* me," he says, and I flinch at the disapproval in his tone.

The utter disappointment.

"Your mother and I aren't stupid. We understand you're an eighteen-year-old girl with urges and desires—"

"Dad," I shriek, but he keeps going.

"But Oakley Beckworth? An Heir? We taught you better than that, sweetheart. He's... he's everything that's wrong with society. He's the very thing I have spent my life fighting. And you—"

"Okay, Dad, I get it. You're disappointed. You can't look at me. You hate—"

"No, Tallulah. I am many things"—his expression softens—"but I could never hate you. I just... I don't understand."

"And you think I do?" Bitter laughter bubbles inside my chest, spilling out in a rush. "It happened, Dad. And Oakley said he didn't—"

"Jesus, sweetheart. You really like him, don't you? You actually went and fell for the boy and now he's blinded you to the kind of person he truly is."

"I—" I press my lips together, trapping the words there. Because he's right.

I did fall for the boy, and I am letting my feelings for him skew the truth. Even if Oakley wasn't directly involved in the break-in, he took the key.

"You know, Tallulah, I'd feel a hell of a lot better about this if you let me call Graham."

"Dad, you promised."

"I know, I know. But he deserves to have the full force of the law thrown at him. Maybe it will knock Christian down a peg or two, learning what a manipulative, scheming little prick his son really is."

"Dad, Oakley didn't manipulate me."

He tsks, staring at me like he doesn't even know me. "Of course he did, sweetheart. He made you believe that he actually cared about you so that he could... ruin you. Ruin us. I wouldn't be surprised if his father was in on the whole thing."

"Dad!" I gasp. It's no secret there's no love lost between my father and Mr. Beckworth but this is a lot, even for Dad.

"Fine, fine." He releases a long, steady breath. "We won't go to the authorities with this, but your mother is meeting with Mr. Porter this morning, and I intend on paying Christian a visit today. Oakley isn't to go within talking distance of you, Tallulah. You go to school, you keep your head down, and you do not engage him. Understood."

"Dad—"

His hand slams down on the table, making me wince. "Do you understand?"

I nod, swallowing down the tears burning my throat.

"I mean it, Tallulah. If he comes within an inch of you, I want to know."

"Okay, Dad, I got it. You don't have to keep—"

"Keep what? Protecting you? Ensuring you don't make the same reckless mistake twice."

"I have to go." I tip the remainder of my coffee down the sink and rinse my mug, leaving it in the sink.

"Tallulah, sweetheart, I didn't—"

But I'm gone. Hurrying out of the kitchen and down the hall.

Everything is such a mess.

Oakley.

My parents.

The campaign.

As I grab my bag and rush from the house, tears spilling down my cheeks, I can't help but think it's all my fault.

I walk to school. It's a dreary November day but the bite in the air grounds me. Fills my lungs and clears my head.

Whilst part of me understands my father's anguish over finding out about Oakley and me, the other part can't reconcile how he could say so many horrible things. As if I woke up one day and planned to fall for an Heir.

Oakley Beckworth is the last boy on earth I ever dreamed I'd want. But here we are.

I can't get him out of my head.

No matter how messed up everything is, no matter how much he hurt me, I can't stop thinking about him.

So much so, I pull out my phone and torture myself with all his messages.

I haven't heard from him since he walked away last night but then, I didn't expect to. Something changed in that moment. And despite the circumstances, I knew it was my fault.

There had been a moment, a split second where Oakley had looked at me, silently pleading for me to choose him. To stand up for him.

And I didn't.

Instead, I chose the easy route.

The coward's way out.

Burrowing deeper into my coat, I pocket my phone and hitch my bag up my shoulder. Maybe walking wasn't such a good—

A car horn blares behind me, sending my heart into my throat.

"Need a lift?" Abi smiles at me through the cranked window.

"You scared me half to death."

"Come on, get in."

With a resigned sigh, I yank the door open and duck inside. "I could have walked."

"I know but I've been worried about you. You've been avoiding me."

I roll my eyes. "I've been avoiding everyone, Abi."

"You can talk to me, you know. I'm Switzerland."

"Everything is such a mess. Oakley turned up at the house last night."

She nods. "Olivia told me."

"She did?"

"Yeah. She's worried too."

Her texts that I've left unanswered had said as much. But I didn't know what to say to her. To Abi. To anyone, really.

"She said Oakley and your dad got into it?"

"My dad was so angry, Abi. I've never seen him like that before."

"I guess it's to be expected. You're his daughter. His only child. He just wants to protect you."

"Yeah, I know," I sigh, dropping my forehead to the glass. "But I'm a teenager. Sometimes we screw up and make mistakes..."

"Is he?"

"What?" I glance over at her.

"Oakley, is he a mistake?"

"I... I don't know what to believe or think anymore. I was so sure he was behind the break-in."

"And now?"

"I'm not so sure."

"You need to talk to him, Tally. Liv is really worried about him."

"If my dad finds out—"

"You're eighteen, what's he going to do? Ground you?"

"Who are you right now?" I ask, shocked at the frustration in her voice.

"Sorry." She blushes, keeping her eyes on the road. "I've just been thinking about things a lot lately. About life. About the future."

"Abi?" My brows pinch. "Are you okay?"

"I... yeah. Yes." Her smile doesn't reach her eyes and I can't help but think I'm missing something. "Look, I don't know anything about boys or dating or any of that stuff, but you obviously feel something for Oakley, right?" I manage the smallest of nods and she adds, "So you owe it to yourself to hear him out."

"I..." I snap my mouth shut because she's right.

Deep down, I know she is.

But the truth is, I'm scared. When we were sneaking around behind everyone's back, it was different. Because I wasn't being judged. I wasn't disappointing anyone.

"Just think about it," she says, taking the turn for All Hallows'.

The school looms in the distance, making dread churn in my stomach.

"Tally?"

"Maybe this wasn't such a good idea," I murmur.

"You can do this, I promise. The longer you stay away, the harder it will be to come back."

"Y-yeah."

By the time she pulls into a parking spot, my heart is racing, and my palms are slick with sweat.

"Ready?" she asks.

"Yes." No.

We climb out and a few kids glance our way. I don't know how much people do or don't know but I do know that my parents expect Mr. Porter to have a handle on the situation.

"Come on." Abi motions for me to follow her toward the entrance. But I'm rooted to the spot, unable to move. "Tally?"

"You go on ahead," I suggest. "I'm just going to give myself a second."

"I can wait, it's no problem."

"No, you go. I don't want to make you late. I'll be right in, I promise."

Abigail's brows crinkle. "Tally—"

"Abi, please. I just need to be alone for a minute."

"Yeah, okay." With a sad smile she takes off toward the building and I start backing up.

I can't do it.

I can't go in there.

Spinning on my heel, I keep my head down and hurry in the opposite direction. I shouldn't have come here. Not yet.

Panic rises inside me, making it hard to breathe as I cut across the path leading past the car park and toward the main gates.

Nobody calls after me, but then, why would they?

The second I slip out of the gates, a sense of relief moves through me. My phone vibrates and I dig it out of my pocket, hardly surprised to see Abi's name.

> Abi: Are you okay? I can wait outside class.

I type out a reply as I hurry across the road, desperate to get as far away from All Hallows' as possible.

> Tally: You don't need to do that. I'll be fine.

> Abi: You're coming to class though, right?

I glance over my shoulder, relieved to see the school shrinking in the distance. My parents will freak out when they find out I'm skipping class. But I can't do it. I can't be there.

My phone vibrates and I half-expect another concerned text from Abi.

It isn't Abi though.

> Oakley: Can we talk? I know shit got out of control last night, but I really need to talk to you, Prim. Please, I'm begging you...

Begging me.

Another time, those words might have given me a thrill. But now they only make me sad.

I close out his message, and open the one from Abi, contemplating to text back. I am so deep in thought, I don't hear the van screech up beside me until it's too late.

Until a masked man jumps out from the sliding door and grabs me.

"Help!" The word tears from my throat, drowned out by a black glove pressed against my nose and mouth.

Fear turns my blood cold, but I refuse to be a victim again, thrashing and bucking for my life.

"Fucking hell," he grunts when my head snaps back, catching him in the nose as he tries to wrestle me into the van.

"What—"

He shoves a handkerchief over my nose, the cloying scent of chemicals flooding my senses.

"N-no, please, don't." I claw at his hand, trying my hardest to get leverage. But everything inside me turns heavy, the edges of my visions fraying.

"What... do... me..." My tongue feels like cotton in my mouth, my eyes rolling back. "No..." I cry, feeling myself slip deeper and deeper into the abyss.

"Shh," a voice whispers from the darkness. "This will all be over soon."

8

OAKLEY

Shouting rouses me from sleep, but the drugs still pumping through my system mean that I don't recognise them, or register any of the words that are being thrown around downstairs.

I woke up at some point in the middle of the night desperate for a piss and discovered that I was in my bed at Dad's house, dressed in only my boxers. But no one else was here, and when I stuck my head in my sister's room, she was fast asleep in her bed, but she wasn't alone.

There might have been a time in the past when my loneliness would have had me staggering into her room and crashing in her bed, or even in the chair. But those times are long gone.

Since she started hooking up with Reese, there's a distance between us that was never there. She was always my rock. The one person I could always turn to no matter what. But that's no longer the case.

He's her rock now. The one she turns to when shit is going wrong.

Not me.

No one turns to me anymore.

And in turn, I don't know where to go either.

Tally.

Images of our time together play out in my mind as the shouting continues downstairs.

Memories of her are the only things that give me comfort right now. Even after what happened last night with her dad, how she cut me down and refused to acknowledge that there was anything between us. Or believe that I could have had anything to do with that fucking dead rat. After everything, how could she even think that?

I drift off with the sound of shouting continuing in the distance, the drugs are stronger than my curiosity to find out what's going on.

When I come to again, the afternoon winter sun is shining through my open window and my skin tingles, letting me know that I've got eyes on me.

Ripping my eyes open, I glance at the chair in the corner of my room and find my dad sitting there dressed in his standard suit although he doesn't look as put together as he usually does. His jacket is nowhere to be seen, his tie is loose and crooked, and his top few buttons are undone. His hair is a mess, and his eyes are tired.

Guilt tugs at my chest. It's all my fault.

He should be working right now, but he's not. He's sitting here watching over me because I fucked up. Again.

Unfolding his arms, he rests his elbows on his knees and studies me harder. The intensity of his gaze makes me wish the bed would just swallow me whole.

"How are you feeling, Son?"

Gritting my teeth, I push myself up so I'm sitting and rest back against the headboard. "Yeah, you know…"

"You should still be in the hospital."

"Not what my discharge papers say," I mutter.

"Because you signed them despite medical advice," he seethes. "What is going on with you, Oakley?" His eyes narrow, his jaw ticking with irritation. A sign without barely saying a word that he's already on his last nerve.

It's not very often Christian Beckworth loses his shit. But when he does, it's not pretty.

And it's definitely not something I have the energy for right now.

"I didn't want to be there any longer. Felt like a zoo exhibit, everyone sitting and staring at me."

"You're lying," he growls, his eyes not wavering from mine.

"I just wanted to come home," I sigh. "Is that so hard to believe?"

"Wouldn't be if it were the first place you went."

My mouth opens to respond but no words appear so I quickly close it again.

"I had a visitor earlier."

The shouting...

Shit.

"Did you want to explain why the first place you went after discharging yourself was the Darlington's house?"

My stomach knots up and my heart starts to race. I should have known he'd find out. I wasn't exactly discreet.

I should have guessed when I first heard the shouting. Of course, Thomas Darlington came straight here this morning to have it out with my father.

How dare Christian Beckworth's son corrupt his precious daughter?

Memories of the shouting hit me, and I forget about myself for a few seconds in favour of her.

If he's really that angry, what happened after I left last night?

What did he say to her?

My fist curls in my lap as concern bubbles up within me. But what's the point? My concern isn't going to get me anywhere.

She won't talk to me. I need to swallow the bitter pill of rejection and find a way to forget about everything that happened.

"So?" Dad snaps, refusing to let this go.

"Tally and I, we—"

"Oakley," Dad sighs. "Tallulah Darlington, really?"

I shrug as he continues studying me with his see all eyes. "I didn't exactly plan it," I mutter, focusing my attention on the windows instead of him.

"Should have known we were heading for trouble when your sister befriended her. She's an attractive girl, I should have guessed that—"

"Seriously?" I hiss. "You're going there?"

Anger bubbles up within me.

"Oh, calm down, Oakley. I'm not after your girl."

"She's not my girl," I snarl.

"I want the truth, Son. Not the bullshit that Darlington spewed at me about a dead rat and how you corrupted his daughter."

"I had nothing to do with the fucking rat," I spit.

"Exactly what I told him. Sneaking in and leaving dead animals," he scoffs. "Not exactly our style. If we want something we go for it. We have no fear of letting our enemies know when we strike," he says passionately.

"Right," I mutter.

"So you don't have a key and easy access to their house?"

"Um..."

"Oakley, help me out here."

"I have a key for easy access, yeah. But not for trashing her room and depositing dead animals. I had other intentions when I snuck in at night."

A proud smirk twitches at Dad's lips as he hears my unspoken words loud and clear before he remembers the situation.

"Tallulah Darlington, Oak." He shakes his head. "Of all the girls in this town."

"I haven't done anything he's accusing me of. I've been trying to protect her."

"Go on," he encourages.

So I do.

Everything from Tally's campaign announcement to last night on her driveway.

Dad eventually left, happy that I was telling the truth and promising me he'd get Thomas off my case. I believed him because my father is nothing but a professional, although this might be one of his bigger challenges.

Thomas Darlington isn't going to let this go easily.

Not when it involves Tally.

With my stomach growling and my need for more painkillers getting the better of me, he left to get everything I needed and disappeared again when his phone rang.

I've spent the last hour sitting here alone irritating myself with memories that serve no purpose other than to remind me what could have been.

It's over.

Tally made that more than clear last night.

Even if she did believe me over the whole dead rat thing, she made it more than obvious that she would never put me before her father, her family. The rivalry between the Beckworths and the Darlingtons.

A door slamming somewhere in the house barely registers as I drown in my own misery, but the pounding of footsteps up the stairs catches my attention a few seconds before a fist pounds on my door.

"Oak? You in there?" Liv shouts.

"Uh... yeah," I call back, confused as to why she doesn't just storm in, nothing usually stops her.

Something I'm sure she has nightmares about after storming on me jerking off more than once. You'd think she'd have learned before now.

The door opens and she hesitantly peeps inside. "You're alone," she says with a frown, looking around my room as if someone is going to jump out of hiding any second.

"Yeah, why? Who were you expecting to be here?" I ask as my sister, Abi, Reese, Theo and Elliot all pile into my room.

"Tally," Abi says. "Have you seen her?"

"What? No, why?" I ask sitting forward in bed, pain exploding from my ribs.

"She never turned up to class," Liv explains.

"So call her. She's probably eating cake at Dessert Island," I say in the rush.

"She's not. We've been there and her phone just rings out."

"At home?"

Abi shakes her head. "No one is answering the door."

Throwing the covers back, I get to my feet, albeit slowly. "I've got a key. We can go and search. She can't have gone far."

The way they both stare at me makes me think they believe this is bigger than her hiding.

"She wouldn't, Oak, and you know it. Tally isn't weak. She wouldn't run from this, no matter how hard it is."

My sister stares at me, silently begging me to believe her.

"I'm not sure I know her all that well," I confess, remembering the way she dismissed me last night.

"Bullshit," she snaps. "You know her better than anyone. You know her strength better than anyone."

I study her, standing in the middle of my room wearing nothing but my boxers and a shit tonne of bruises while they all stare at me.

Abi included but she looks a hell of a lot more awkward

than the rest of them. I want to dismiss their concerns because they're right. Tally is strong. Stronger than anyone knows. Wherever she is. Whatever she's doing. She'll be fine.

I'm sure of it.

Although, I can't deny the trickle of unease that works its way through me.

There's no harm in heading out to prove that I'm right.

Right?

Liv takes matters into her own hands, marching over to my wardrobe and pulling out a pair of sweats and a hoodie.

"Get dressed," she demands, shoving them into my chest none too gently, seeing as I'm suffering. "Where's her key?"

"Uh..." My eyes dart to the box on my dresser and she gets her answer.

I'm still trying to get my foot into my sweats when she plucks the key from the box and holds it from her finger.

"Come on, let's go."

"A little fucking help here?" I ask, failing miserably.

Abi is the first to rush over, dropping to her knees and holding the waistband of my sweats for me. I step my first foot in before I look up, finding Theo and Elliot watching the two of us. But while Theo looks amused, Elliot's grinding his teeth in irritation.

"What? Did you want to get up close and personal with my cock?"

"What?" Abi gasps in horror, thinking I'm talking to her and releases my sweats.

"I'm not getting it out, don't worry," I assure her.

She swallows nervously but continues to help me dress. All the while, Elliot glares at us.

"Okay, can we go now?"

"You're freaking out for nothing," I tell my sister, hoping it's enough to squash the panic that's rising within me. "Try her phone again."

"On it," Abi says, pulling her phone from her pocket.

Thankfully, Dad isn't anywhere to be seen as we head to the front door. I'm not sure hunting down a missing Darlington was exactly what he had in mind when he warned me to stay away while things cool down.

"She's going to be fine," I say as we pile into cars.

"Let's hope you're right, huh?"

But as we take off and head in the direction of Darlington's house, the dread that's already taken up residence in my stomach only gets heavier.

Liv wouldn't have raised the alarm unless she was really concerned. Especially after knowing what went down last night.

It leaves me with one terrifying thought.

Something bad has happened...

And once again, I wasn't there to protect her.

9

TALLY

"Oakley?"

"Yeah, Prim."

"I'm sorry I didn't choose you."

"It's okay, baby. Everything is going to be okay." He cups my face, leaning down to kiss me. I anchor my arm around the back of his neck, trying to get closer. I can't lose him.

I won't.

"I'm sorry," I murmur between kisses, tears dripping down my cheeks. "I know you had nothing to do with the break-in. I know you wouldn't—"

"Shh." He slides his finger over my lips, easing back to look at me. "You are so fucking beautiful, Tallulah. I won't let anyone take you from me. Not your father or mine. You're mine."

"Yours." A shiver runs through me at the intensity in his eyes.

The love.

No, that isn't right. Oakley doesn't love me.

He can't.

Can he?

"Shh, Prim. Mine." He captures my mouth in another

slow, bruising kiss. Pressing me against the wall, pinning me there with his hips.

The feel of his hard length rocking into me makes me whimper. Moan his name.

"I need you," he breathes. "I need to feel you wrapped around my cock. Squeezing me. Do you want that, baby?" His hand glides up my collarbone and his fingers wrap around my throat, shoving my head back against the wall.

"Oakley," I gasp, and his mouth curves with wicked intent.

"Fuck, I love it when you moan my name all breathless and needy. Are you going to scream for me, Prim? When I slowly fuck the life right out of you, are you going to scream?"

His fingers tighten, closing around my airway, sending a bolt of panic through me.

"Oakley," I gasp, clawing at his hand. "I-I can't... breathe."

"That's the point, isn't it?" His eyes darken, his expression morphing from pure lust to something wild and cruel.

"Oak—"

He squeezes tighter, my eyes bulging, my lungs on fire as I struggle to breathe. "Does it feel good, Prim? Being at my mercy? There's no escaping me now."

The edges of my vision blur as I slowly suffocate at the hands of the boy I love.

The boy who stole my heart and refused to give it back.

"O—"

"Shh, don't fight it, baby. Don't fight me. No one will ever take you from me. You're mine, Tallulah. Mi—"

"Wake up." Pain ricochets through my stomach and my eyelids flutter open but I'm in utter darkness.

"Wh—"

"Wake the fuck up." Another blow to my stomach has me crying out in agony.

"S-stop. Please... stop."

I clutch my body, tears streaming down my cheeks. Everything is hazy, my muscles heavy and stiff.

What the hell happened?

Where am I?

Where—

"Let's go." Someone roughly grabs me off the floor and starts dragging my limp body.

I'm too weak to even try and fight them off. Something isn't right, I feel... drugged.

Drugged.

Oh my God.

The memories slam into me one after another. Arriving at school with Abigail. Deciding I couldn't do it and turning around and leaving.

The van...

The masked man...

The overwhelming scent of chemicals...

Then nothing.

Fear grips me in its chokehold. This isn't happening.

It can't be happening.

"Help," I scream, except my voice is quiet and raspy. Like I'm thirsty and unable to speak.

What the hell did they do to me?

Panic consumes every inch of me, threatening to swallow me whole but I refuse to go willingly.

Stop.

Think.

You're strong.

You can figure this out.

You can—

My body jostles over the uneven ground, pain shooting down my hip bone.

God, that hurt.

"P-please, stop. I need—"

My thigh collides with something sharp, and I cry out but the man doesn't stop dragging me away from wherever we were to wherever we're going.

Think, Tallulah.

Think.

Maybe it's another prank. Another sick attempt from Deacon or Misty to unnerve me. If it is, they've really overstepped the mark.

I don't need Thomas Darlington as my father to know that kidnap and drugging a person is a serious offence in the eyes of the law.

Then another thought washes over me.

The cabin was one thing. Even the break-in could be construed as kids messing around. But kidnap?

Surely Deacon or Misty wouldn't go that far?

Another wave of pain floods me as something sharp catches my side, dragging along my waist.

"W-wait, oh God, please..." I clutch my side, hardly surprised to feel something wet and sticky coating my fingers.

Blood.

The man stops dragging me. "Fuck," he exhales a harsh breath. "Come on. Get up." He hauls me off the ground, and I can just make out the shadow of his silhouette through the blindfold tied around my eyes.

I'm powerless but to slump against him as he hauls me up and throws me over his shoulder like a sack of bricks.

Blood rushes to my head, making everything spin as a wave of darkness creeps in, taking me with it.

This time when I wake, I'm alone, shackled to a small bed. The blindfold is gone and there's a thick bandage around my midriff, a red tinge to one section.

I take in my surroundings. The small mostly bare room, save for the bed and a small bedside table. My mouth instantly waters at the sight of the bottle there. I manage to sit up, groaning in pain as I reach over and snatch the bottle of water up.

It's not easy unscrewing the lid with my wrists bound and then tied to the bedpost with a short length of rope, but I somehow manage to get it undone.

When I've drank my fill, careful not to overdo it in case I pass out again, I try to get my bearings.

Where am I?

What do I know?

How the hell am I going to get out of here?

I don't have many answers but the most obvious is that either Deacon is secretly a psycho kidnapper slash serial killer or this has nothing to do with Misty and Deacon.

A violent shudder goes through me. It doesn't make any sense. Why would somebody take me?

Kidnap and drug me.

My parents are good people. They don't get involved with the shadier going ons in Saints Cross and the surrounding areas.

I sit there, cold and alone, trying to wrack my mind for a plan. A way out of this nightmare.

But the longer I consider my options, the harder it becomes to think.

My body is half-slumped down the bed, my limbs achy and heavy, a strange sort of fog lingering over my thoughts as I watch the door. The only way in and out of the small room.

Whoever has taken me wants me subdued and weak, that much is for sure.

If I didn't know better, I'd say that I was still drugged, still—

My eyes flick to the half-drunk bottle of water, a sick feeling washing over me.

Was the cap seal still intact or did the bottle open without any resistance?

Think, Tallulah. Think.

But everything is murky, like trying to find your way out of a dense forest in the dark.

I fight against the seductive tug of oblivion, pinching my wrists in an effort to stay lucid. But it's futile. I can't fight whatever the water was spiked with and before long my body melts into the mattress.

I don't completely black out like before. I'm aware of my heartbeat pounding in my chest. My tongue stuck to the roof of my mouth.

I'm aware of the door creaking open, the dark silhouette standing there, watching me. His eyes glinting in the shadows.

But I can't speak. I can't move. Or scream or demand to know what's going on.

I can't do anything but lie here.

Weak and powerless.

I thought going up against the Heirs, that playing Oakley's game, was scary... but this makes all that look like child's play.

"W-who... there..." the words barely rise above the sound of my heartbeat.

The man watching me from the door doesn't move. He doesn't speak. He just stands there. Watching. Stalking.

Preying.

And only one thought remains in my mind, a feeling I can't shake.

This time I might not survive.

10

OAKLEY

I can barely breathe with the massive lump that's lodged itself in my throat. The closer we get to Tally's house, the thicker the tension in the car gets.

"She'll be fine," Abi says from beside me. "We're just freaking out because it's so unlike her, but she'll be there. Probably just in the shower and couldn't hear us something," she continues rambling.

I'm not sure who she's trying to help but it's putting me more and more on edge.

And that isn't helped when Reese finally turns into Tally's driveway and only her car sits there.

"She'll have headphones in, drowning out the world and those who hurt her," Abi continues, shooting me a glare.

"I didn't— That wasn't—"

"She doesn't know that. She's in there right now as miserable as you are. We need to fix it."

"Bet she looks better," Reese quips, glancing at the stare of my face in the rear-view mirror.

"Fuck off."

Opening the door, I grit my teeth as pain assaults my body when I try and climb out.

"What if Mr. Darlington is home?" Abi calls after me.

"Fuck him. I'm not scared of him. Tally is the only one that matters."

I don't need to look back to know they're all sharing a look.

Yeah, I just confessed to caring about her. So fucking what?

I do.

And right now, they've got me worried.

Rushing toward the front door, I rain my fists down on the door. Each hit searing through my body. Despite sleeping most of the day, my body seems to get heavier with every second that passes.

Bloody painkillers.

"Tally," I bellow, my fists not faltering as the others approach.

Liv drops to her knees beside me and flips the letter box open, screaming Tally's name through it.

"Just use the key. If she's here, she's clearly ignoring us," Reese demands.

My heart pounds as Liv pushes the key she stole from my room into the lock. The six of us spill into the empty house and immediately split up to begin our search.

I make a beeline for the stairs, my need to check her room myself making my legs move faster than they want to. When I get to her door, I pause with my fingers twisted around the handle. Images of time spent with her inside fill my head, making me miss her that much more.

My desperation to discover she's here and fine has me throwing the door open.

But it's empty.

She's not here.

"She's been staying in the guest room since..."

Abandoning Tally's room, I follow my sister to another but we both come up short when we find that empty as well.

"This isn't Tally, Oak. She doesn't just disappear."

We pad down the stairs with the weight of the situation pressing down on our shoulders.

"Anything?" Abi asks.

"Nope. No sign of her."

A red flashing light in the corner of the entryway catches my eye.

"We need to go," I say nodding toward it. "Darlington probably already has the cops on us for breaking and entering."

"We didn't break anything. We're worried. And he needs to be too," Liv argues.

"I'll let you try and explain that to him," I mutter, stalking out of the house with my shoulders slumped and my head lowered.

"Now what?" Elliot asks once we've all congregated in the driveway.

Everyone looks at me as if I've spent all this time with Tally getting to know her deepest secrets instead of trying to get between her thighs.

You did. She let you in just like you did to her.

Shaking that thought from my head, I say the only thing I can think of.

Other than us, there are only two people who would want to hurt Tally.

"Deacon Warrick," I mutter.

Silence falls as they all stare at me.

"Deacon Warrick?" Elliot asks. "Why?"

"I-I don't know why, but he's out for her."

"Out for her? Tally? Why?" Reese asks, beating Liv to it.

"Friday night, he... he tried to hurt her at Halloween Fest," I confess.

"WHAT?" Liv and Abi both shout.

"That's why she left early. Seb tipped me off that something was happening. I beat the shit out of him, then followed her home to make sure she was okay," I confess, rubbing the back of my neck.

"So it was him? He was the one who jumped you?" Elliot asks.

"Maybe," I confess.

"Well, what the fuck are we waiting for?" Reese barks, ripping his driver's door open and dropping inside.

"Why didn't you tell us?" Liv asks, disappointment dripping from her words. She holds my eyes, making me feel about two feet tall.

"It doesn't matter now, does it?" Abi sighs. "Let's go and talk to him."

"He isn't going to help us," I warn.

"Well, we don't know that until we try," Liv argues, finally ripping her eyes from mine and climbing into Reese's car, leaving Abi and me to take the back again.

"What's his issue with her?" Reese asks after pulling out of Tally's driveway.

"He wants her, and she's not interested. He isn't taking too kindly to her rejection."

"He's a prick," he mutters. "Never fucking liked him."

"Feeling's mutual."

"You should have told us, told Dad when you woke up," Liv seethes.

My fists curl in my lap, but I don't respond. What's the point? It's too fucking late to fix it now.

"I know he's a cunt, but do we really think he's capable of abducting Tally?" Reese asks absently.

"Abducting her?" Abi whimpers.

"Worse case, Abi," he reasons.

"He dragged her out of our Halloween party to—" I cut my words off with a harsh swallow.

"To?" Liv prompts.

"Well, I don't know for sure, but we all have imaginations. When I caught up with them, she was kicking his arse."

"What?" Reese asks with a laugh.

"She used to do tae kwon do or something as a kid. Really good apparently," Abi says.

"Yeah, that makes sense. She was a bad-arse. Fucking floored me."

"You mean it got your cock hard?" Reese smirks before Liv throws her arm out and slaps his shoulder. "What? Trust me, Liv. If I watched you take some cunt down with some fancy moves then I'd be—"

"Do not finish that sentence," I warn.

Silence falls over the car as we head across town.

"How are we going to play this?" Reese asks, forgetting about his previous line of thought. "All of us rocking up at the Warrick's front door will look suspicious as fuck."

"Abi and I will go," Liv offers.

"No, you fucking won't. You heard what he was going to do to Tally. You're not getting anywhere near that sick fuck," Reese growls possessively.

I get it, I don't want my sister anywhere near him either.

"Liv and I will go," I say. "It needs to be me."

"Oakley," Reese warns.

"I won't let her out of my sight," I promise.

He glares at me in the rear-view mirror, clearly unimpressed with my suggestion.

"I'll go," Abi offers.

"No," Liv argues. "I need to. I've already let her down too much."

I want to argue with her, tell her that she's wrong. But honestly, she's right.

Everything got so fucked up after Tally announced her campaign. It might have brought us together, but I'm not sure the rest of what Tally has suffered through makes any of it worth it.

The bullying from the chasers. Deacon and his belief she belongs to him. Losing her friendship with Liv.

I shake my head. All of this is my fault. And I still don't really know why.

I did something which started the domino effect of all this. But she hasn't told me. And something tells me that she never will now.

I guess I deserve that for being such a selfish prick.

Elliot pulls his car up behind us down the street a little from Deacon's house, and Liv and I push our doors open and climb out.

"What's going on?" Elliot asks through his open window.

"Liv and I are going to see if he's here. You can head back to the Chapel if you want, we'll catch up later."

"No," Elliot and Theo say simultaneously.

"Thanks," I mutter, appreciating their support right now more than I can explain.

"Come on then, Bro. Let's go see what this dick has to say."

As we turn into the driveway, hope fills me that at least someone will be home because there are multiple cars parked up and almost every light in the house is on.

"What are you going to say?" Liv asks after I've pressed the doorbell.

I shrug. I'm hoping it'll come to me.

Footsteps get louder on the other side of the door.

There was a very slim chance of the person we really wanted answering the door, but still, my heart sinks when I find Mr. Warrick standing on the other side of the threshold with his arms crossed and a scowl on his face.

Very welcoming.

"Can I help you?"

"We're looking for Deacon. Is he home?" I ask, crossing my arms and mimicking his stance.

His eyes track my injuries, but he doesn't say anything.

"No. He's actually out of town for a few days," he says. "Have you tried calling him?"

"No. We were just in the area and thought we'd stop by on

the off chance. Do you know when he'll be back?" Liv asks while I continue studying him.

He grinds his teeth, making his jaw pop and there's a vein pulsating in his temple. "I'm not sure."

Liar.

"He's visiting family up north."

How convenient.

"Sorry to interrupt your evening," I say, wrapping my hand around Liv's arm and dragging her away.

"What are you doing?" she hisses once the door is slammed behind us. "We don't know anything."

"We do," I assure her.

"Oh? Did you hear something I didn't?" she snaps.

"Yeah. Mr. Warrick is a liar. He's covering for that piece of shit. And if he's as good at hiding his son as he is lying for him, we'll find him in no time."

"What the fuck do we do now?" she asks as we march back toward the car.

Reese is out of the driver's seat, waiting for us anxiously.

"Time to call in the expert. Take us home, Reese. We need Dad."

"What did he say?" Reese asks.

"Enough," I mutter, dropping into the car.

"He said nothing," Liv argues.

"Deacon did this. Wherever he is, Tally is too. I'd put money on it."

"So where is he?"

"Don't know. But we will find out," I say fiercely, picturing Tally continuing to hold her own against him.

She's strong. She won't let him win.

She can't.

It's not a fucking option.

11

TALLY

I come to with a start.

A pained groan slips from my lips as my eyelids open, heavy and sore.

Everything hurts.

My limbs. My muscles. Even my skin feels too tight for my body.

I roll onto my back, my wrists smarting where the restraints rub against my skin.

I have no idea how long I've been out. No concept of time. Except... oh God.

"Hello," I cry out. "I need to use the bathroom. Now," I try to yell but my voice is barely more than a raspy whisper. "Hello, please. Please, I—"

The door creaks open, the stream of light blinding me.

"I-I need to pee."

The man lets out a gruff tsk of disapproval.

"Please. If I don't get to a bathroom, I'm going to wet myself."

He storms toward me, his features concealed by the long straggly hair falling into his face. He leans over me and fiddles with the restraints before hauling me off the bed and over his shoulder. The sudden movement makes my bladder squeeze and I tighten everything inside me, desperately trying to hold it in.

"Quick," I murmur. "Please—"

"Shut the fuck up," he grumbles, walking me down the same hallway I was dragged down earlier.

Yesterday.

Days ago.

I have no concept of how much time has passed except the fact I didn't wake up in a puddle of my own urine suggests it hasn't been that long.

He shoulders a door open at the end of the hallway and lowers me to my feet. "You get one minute. Try anything and next time I'll leave you to piss yourself."

He has a hint of a cockney accent. A thick London lilt that isn't that common around Oxfordshire.

"W-who are you?" I ask.

"One minute," he grunts, grabbing the door handle and pulling it closed.

I hover over the toilet, retching at the stench. Wherever we are, the place is rundown. Dirty and unkempt. Damp patches and mould litter the walls, the toilet seat caked in all kinds of things I'd rather not think about.

Breathing through my mouth, I shove down my ripped school tights and hike up my skirt wincing at the nasty looking cut along my thigh. It's scabbed over, dried blood crusting my skin. I whimper in pain as I peel my tights from the wound, opening it up again.

God, an open wound in a place like this is a recipe for a disaster.

Once I'm done, I shake a little and pull up my knickers. It isn't ideal but it's better than trying to find something clean to wipe myself with.

A violent shudder goes through me as I take in my dire

situation. I can barely stand straight, my limbs still lagging from the drugs working their way out of my system.

"You done?" My captor shouts, banging the door so hard my heart lurches into my throat.

"Just a minute." I quickly scan the room for anything I can use as a weapon. But before I can locate something the door flies open, crashing against the mildew-stained wall.

"We need to go. Now." He grabs me without warning and swings me up and over his shoulder, sending streaks of pain rippling through my side.

"I can walk," I protest, hanging limply down his back.

"Quicker this way."

He's clearly not a man of many words and I don't know if that's a good thing.

I don't know anything except the utter sense of desperation and despair I feel.

Once we're back in the room, he plops me down on the bed again and secures my wrists to the restraint wrapped around the bedpost.

"Please, you don't need to do that. I'm not going anywhere. I'm not—"

"Just following the boss's orders," he murmurs, making sure I can't get free.

"The boss? Who is—"

"Better for you, you don't ask questions." He retreats to the door, his big imposing body blotting out the light.

"W-wait," I cry. "Please, don't—"

The door slams shut, the sound reverberating through me as tears slide down my cheeks.

This can't be happening.

Except, it is.

I've been kidnapped.

Taken, drugged, and dumped in some ramshackle house.

But why?

It doesn't make any sense.

Misty and Deacon can't be behind this. They're twisted but they're not this sick.

Think, Tallulah. Think.

This doesn't feel like a college prank gone badly. It feels... wrong.

My gut is telling me I need to get out of here. That I need to run while I can.

But I'm shackled to the bed, my bloodstream still poisoned with drugs.

Even if I did manage to escape, there's no telling what I might find on the other side of the door.

I need a plan. One better than 'make a run for it'.

I inhale a shuddering breath, refusing to give into the panic closing in around me.

This is bad.

So bad.

But it could be worse.

It could always be worse.

I just need to—

Voices outside the door send a bolt of fear through me and I press my back further against the headboard, making myself as small as possible.

"Couldn't let... piss herself."

"And if she'd escaped? What then?"

"Come on boss... like... happen."

I strain to make sense of their heated conversation, but their voices grow fainter along with their heavy footsteps as they move away from the door.

Surely, someone must know I'm missing by now.

My friends.

My parents.

The police.

Oakley.

God, just thinking about him—thinking about how I left things—makes my heart ache.

What if I never see him again?

What if I never get to explain?

Fear crashes over me. Dark, unrelenting fear, dragging me under until I can't breathe.

Until my lungs burn and my eyes sting.

And my life splutters out of me in cold, harsh breaths.

"Wake up." A voice from the darkness demands. "Wake the fuck up."

The ground beneath me shakes and trembles and I slowly crack an eye open, trying to figure out what's happ—

"Boss wants to see you."

Everything comes rushing back at once.

Deacon trying to hurt me.

The break-in.

My bedsheets smeared with blood.

Oakley and my father arguing.

Oakley's bloody, bruised face.

Hearing the desperation in his voice as he pleaded his innocence.

Watching him walk away, my heart splintering in my chest.

Trying—failing—to go back to class.

The van.

The masked man.

Being dragged into this room and locked up like an animal.

"Why?"

"I don't ask questions, now let's go." He leans his big body over me to release the restraints.

"How long was I out? What day is it? What—"

"Time to go." He lifts me like a rag doll, and I realise I can barely feel my limbs.

The drug should be wearing off now. Shouldn't it?

"What did you give me?" I murmur. "I feel… weird."

"It'll wear off."

"The water—"

"Stop talking." He goes to sling me over his shoulder, but I blurt, "No, please. Don't."

"Fuck's sake." He cradles me in his arms, carrying me toward the door.

I'm weightless but heavy all at the same time.

This can't be the side effects of the spiked water. That was hours ago.

At least, I think it was.

But something isn't right.

Something isn't—

"Ow," I cry out as my head bumps against the wall.

"Shit. Fuck." The man hoists me closer to his chest, the hallway spinning as I try to focus on wherever he's taking me. "Just keep your mouth shut, yeah. Whatever the boss says. Whatever he does… just keep quiet."

"What—"

"Shh," he hisses, and I bite my tongue. Trying to figure out whether he's helping me or just trying to make his life easier.

Maybe he's the answer to getting out of here.

Maybe I can—

"Whatever you're thinking right now, don't waste your energy. The boss owns me and I'm not looking to put my neck on the line for some spoiled little princess," he snarls the words and any hope I had withers and dies.

"They'll come, you know. My parents. They won't stop until whoever's doing this is—"

"Bring her in," a commanding voice says from somewhere beyond the door we've stopped at.

"Please," I whisper, suddenly overcome with paralysing fear.

I don't want to go in there.

I don't want to meet whoever is responsible for this.

I cling to his body tighter, burying my face in his chest, his musky scent flooding my senses. He smells like sweat and cigarettes and whisky.

"Put the girl down, Merrick."

"Down you go." He tries to wrestle me out of his arms, but I dig my nails into his skin, refusing to go without a fight.

"Feisty little thing isn't she?" the voice says but I've only got eyes for the man holding me.

Please, I silently beg. Don't do this. Don't put me down.

For a second, I think he might understand. I think he might help. But then he shoves me off of him and I crumple to the floor in a breathless heap.

"That'll be all."

He moves away. His presence evaporating as he walks out of the room leaving me alone.

"Hello, Tallulah," the voice says, turning my blood to ice as I watch the man in the shadows. He steps forward, revealing a leg, then another, then his arms and torso come into view. And finally his face.

Everything inside me stills as a wicked glint flashes in his eyes as he studies me. "I've been looking forward to meeting you very much."

12

OAKLEY

"**D**AD," I bellow the second I crash through the front door.

He's here, his car is parked outside.

"DAD," I roar again when there's no movement.

"He'll be in his office," Liv says from behind me, forcing me into action.

My heavy footsteps pound on the hardwood floor as I move toward the back of the house. I don't bother knocking like I usually would, instead, I twist the knob and throw the door wide open.

It bounces off the door as Dad jumps from his desk in shock. His eyes widen as they land on me, anger crinkling at the sides, but I stand my ground.

This is more important than whoever is talking to him through his AirPods.

The others come to a stop behind me, and the second he takes them all in, he knows he's lost.

"Annabel, can I call you back?" he asks, mentioning his assistant.

He doesn't say a word, but whatever she says must be an

agreement because not three seconds later he pulls his AirPods from his ears and tosses them onto the tabletop.

"Oakley," he growls. I can already hear his next words. They're ingrained into me.

Never invite yourself into my office without permission, you've no idea what kind of case I might be working on. Confidentiality is—

"Tally's missing," I blurt, silencing my imaginary arse-kicking that was coming.

He scrubs his hand down his face before falling back into his chair. "Oakley, I—"

Seeing the same defeat in his that I can, Liv pushes forward.

"She is, Dad. She never turned up to classes this morning. She's not at home, at any of her favourite places. She's not answering her phone."

"She could be anywhere, she's a pissed-off eighteen-year-old girl. And after everything, I don't blame her for hiding."

His eyes find mine and the honesty I find there is like a punch to the gut.

"She's not hiding, Dad. Something has happened," I agree.

"Oak, I know you're... spending time with her, but I promise you that doesn't make you a psychic where she's concerned."

My teeth grind in irritation.

I get it. He hates the Darlingtons. Always has done.

But that doesn't mean he gets to dismiss this like it's nothing. Like I'm being over the top being concerned for her safety.

"Are you telling us that you'd ignore your gut feeling if Fiona suddenly vanished on you?" I sneer, unwilling to let this go.

"Tally isn't Fiona," Dad reasons.

"Not to you she's not," I roar, walking deeper into the room.

If he wants to let this go and ignore me, then he will have to physically remove me first.

"He's right, Dad," Liv adds. "Something is wrong here. Tally wouldn't hide. She's too strong, too stubborn."

"Typical fucking Darlington," he mutters under his breath.

Silence falls and when no one offers anything up, I blurt. "I think Deacon Warrick has her."

"Deacon Warrick? As in the son of their best friends?" He looks sceptical, to say the least, but I push on, and explain everything that's happened between them in the weeks leading up to this weekend.

"So you're saying it was Deacon who jumped you?" Dad asks, reading between the lines. "You just said that Misty was working with Deacon and that's how he got access to her at the Halloween party. So it stands to reason that Deacon and his mates were waiting for you in the woods behind the pavilion when you met Misty on Sunday."

"That's not the biggest issue right now," I sneer. Yes, I might want vengeance if that is the case, but right now I need my girl back where she belongs and unharmed.

"I think it's very much the issue. He put you in the hospital, Oakley," Dad growls possessively. "I'll rain hell down on—"

"Later," I snap. "If I'm right and he has Tally then a GBH charge for jumping me will be the least of his worries. Abduction, imprisonment, ra—"

My word cuts off as Liv steps up to me and wraps her hand around my upper arm. "We'll find them, Oak. You said it yourself. Tally can handle Deacon."

"That's probably half of what's fuelling this little vendetta. She handed him his arse and left him to be finished off by me."

"Wait, you're involved in all this?" Dad asks, picking up on the nugget of information I left out when telling my previous story.

"He touched her, Dad. Dragged her off to our cabin to—" I swallow thickly, unable to really consider his intentions.

He wants her. That much is more than obvious. I never thought he'd go to those kinds of lengths to get it.

"How long has she been gone?"

"I drove her to school this morning, but she never made it to any classes," Abi explains. "She was... out of sorts. I was worried but I thought she'd figure herself out before the bell went. I never sh-should h-have l-let h-her," she stutters.

My eyes almost pop out of my head when Elliot moves closer to her and wraps his arm around her shoulder when she starts to break.

"All my fault," she sobs.

"No, Abi," Liv assures. "It's not. You never could have known."

"Do we even know she left campus?" Dad asks. "She could be on school grounds."

"You have access to the CCTV, don't you?" I ask.

"Umm..."

But before he gets to give me the answer I already know, pounding comes from the front of the house.

"Tally," I breathe, hopping out of the chair and running faster than my body is willing to go.

A loud grunt rips from my lips as I collide with the front door.

As I scramble to open it, the others are hot on my heels. But instead of finding my girl standing on the doorstep looking perfect as ever like I hoped, I find another Darlington. One who looks ready to rip my head off with his bare hands.

"WHERE IS SHE?" he roars, surging forward and taking me with him.

He slams me against the wall, all the air rushing from my lungs as he glares down at me with dark, terrified, angry eyes. "WHAT HAVE YOU DONE WITH MY DAUGHTER?"

Pain lances through my body, cutting off any argument about having anything to do with this. Thankfully, the others have my back. The fact he's cutting off my air supply doesn't fucking help either.

"This wasn't Oakley," Liv pleads. "We've been out looking for her. We're worried too."

"Thomas," Dad booms. "I always knew your nice guy attitude was an act. Get your hands off my fucking son." Nothing but pure hatred oozes from Dad's eyes.

It's not something I want to see right now. If this is as bad as the knot that's twisting up my stomach, then we need to be on the same team for once. Not opposing ones.

The arm that's pressed up against my throat loosens a little, thank fuck, and I suck in lungfuls of air. "She never made it to school and we can't find her," Thomas says, defeat pushing his anger aside for a beat. "And it's your fault."

Finding some strength, I slam my palms against his chest, sending him stumbling back into Elliot and Theo. Neither of them makes a move to help him. They do the complete opposite, in fact, and step aside.

I'm still smirking when he rights himself and spins back around. "Where is she?" he barks, holding my eyes once more.

"If I fucking knew that, then she wouldn't be missing. Fucking hell."

"Oak," Dad warns.

"She ran because of you."

"No," I counter. "She's been taken."

Thomas shakes his head, barely able to believe the words that just fell from my lips.

"We've been to your house," I confess, making his jaw tick in frustration. "She didn't pack anything. She didn't plan this. She hasn't gone of her own accord."

"Give me my key back," he demands, holding his hand out.

"Because you'll keep her safe?" I snarl. "I don't like the sound of that. Under your watch, someone broke in and trashed her room. Left a dead fucking rat in her bed. I don't trust you with a hair on her head."

"She's my daughter," he argues.

"SO WHERE IS SHE?" I roar, my heart slamming against my ribs. "She's been taken and you have no fucking idea who's done it."

He shakes his head.

"It's all your fault. You were the one pushing the idea of a relationship between them. If you'd just listened to her, you might have realised what a fucking creep he is."

"W-who are you—"

"Deacon Warrick," I spit. "You didn't even know he tried to attack her Friday night, did you? He dragged her out of the Halloween Fest and took her to our cabin to—"

"Stop," he begs, scrubbing his hand down his face. "You're lying. Deacon would never. He's a good man, he—"

"Fucking unbelievable. You don't believe me?"

"So I guess you're going to try to tell me that you showed up all white knight and saved her," he sneers.

"No," I state, pride for my girl flooding through my veins. "I didn't save her. She saved herself. She'd handed him his arse before I got there. I just added a little more pain after she'd done. Then he tried to set me up by making her think I planted that rat."

"No, you're lying. You're fucking lying. All of this is because of you. You corrupted my daughter and now look. She's gone, and—"

"Just leave," I demand, marching forward and taking his arm in a punishing grip. "We don't need your help. You've already proved yourself useless in all this."

We're at the still open door when Dad's booming voice

floods the hallway. "Stop, Oakley. You want to find her fast, then we're going to need all the help we can get." My grip on Thomas relaxes, hating that he's right. "I've got the CCTV. Let's go and—"

"CCTV?" Thomas asks, twisting around to look at my dad.

"Outside the school. Abi said she took her there but then never came to class. We need—"

"Lead the way," Thomas demands, gesturing for Dad to go ahead.

He takes off, leaving us trailing behind.

Dad spins his monitor around so we can all see. The video starts playing and I'm sure everyone in the room stops breathing as Abi's car rolls toward the car park.

Just like she described earlier, they don't get out right away, but when they do, it's obvious from Tally's stance, the way she looks at the building, that she's not happy about being there.

"I tried to convince her to come inside," Abi says as if what we're watching needs explaining. "She promised she would. This is all my fault."

All the air rushes out of my lungs as Tally is left alone in the car park. And then after a few minutes, she turns and walks away, leaving the camera's view.

"Well, how does that help?" Thomas spits. "She could still be anywhere."

Dad quickly and silently pulls up another camera's feed and we catch up to her, watching as she walks out of the school gates and disappears out onto the street.

But then that's it.

"I'll get in touch with a contact to get the feeds from the street cameras."

"Oh no," Thomas spits. "I'm not being involved in anything dirty with you."

Dad rears back. "Do you want to find your daughter, Thomas?"

"Yes," he confirms. "And I will. The right way."

Before anyone can say anything, he marches from Dad's office, and then soon after, the sound of the slamming front door echoes through the house.

"Well... he's kinda ungrateful," Theo quips.

"Now what?" I ask, feeling totally deflated.

Dad looks over, taking the matching looks of desperation on our faces. "We're going to find her by whatever means necessary. It's about time that Thomas learned once and for all that there's only one way to really get a job done."

13

TALLY

"W-who are you?" I croak, trying hard to place the man's rugged face.

But no matter how much I search my hazy mind, I can't place him.

I don't recognise him.

Not even a little bit.

"The who is not important." He slides his hands into his black slacks and looms over me.

Everything about him screams power. The tailored suit. The dark eyes and slightly curled smile. A wolf in sheep's clothing.

"What do you want from me?"

"What do I want?" He drawls, reaching for a strand of my hair and tugging on it. "I want so many things, Tallulah."

He stares at me intensely, making a shudder rip through me. I don't like it, the way he's looking at me.

"I... I want to go home. Please, just let me go."

"You know I can't do that." He lowers his face to mine, inhaling deeply. "I need you to do something for me. Do you think you can do that?"

"W-what?" I gulp.

"Come with me." He grabs my shoulder and leads me across the room to a lonely chair. "Sit." Roughly, he yanks me down and I cry out.

He takes his time, restraining my hands behind my back, tight enough that my arms smart.

"P-please."

"Shh." He brushes my jaw before walking away.

Suddenly, the room is plunged into darkness, sending my heart into overdrive. I thrash against my restraints, blood roaring between my ears. But I still when a spotlight comes on, blazing down right on me.

For the longest time, there is nothing. No sound. No movement. Just me, the darkness surrounding me, and the light providing me some small measure of hope.

Because everything feels better in the light.

Even the bleakest of moments.

"Hello," I call out. "Hello!"

Frustration bleeds from my voice, my throat dry and sore. Everything aches and my stomach is hollow. The giant pit of dread eating me up inside.

"Please... I don't understand, I don't—" My brows pinch as something catches my eye.

A small red light in the shadows.

A camera.

The thought hits me, sending a fresh wave of panic through me.

The sicko is filming me.

But to what ends?

"What do you want?" I shriek, desperately trying to free my hands. But it's futile, my wrists and shoulders burn with agony as I fight against the bindings.

God, why didn't I fight?

Why didn't I try to make a break for it when I had the chance?

Because you're weak and vulnerable and you need to wait for the right moment.

But what if the right moment never comes.

What if—

The lights go out, the air shifting. A new wave of fear crashes over me, my breaths coming in short, sharp bursts as I try not to spiral into the panic clawing its way up my throat.

Something brushes my shoulder and a scream rips from my throat.

The spotlight comes back on, and I blink rapidly, sucking in a sharp breath. "Why are you doing this?" I cry, over and over. The overstimulation too much for my weary body and mind.

I can't do this.

I can't.

You have to.

The voices war inside of me as the room plunges into darkness again.

"P-please. Stop. Stop..."

A hand grabs the back of my neck and I scream again, held captive to the fear saturating every inch of me.

Something pricks the side of my neck. A needle.

"N-no. Please..." The room spins. "No..."

But no matter how much I try to keep my eyes open, my lids are too heavy.

"I..."

I tumble into the darkness.

Down...

Down...

...

...

...

Down.

I wake plastered to the dingy mattress again. Everything aches and my stomach—

Bile rushes up my throat and I manage to lean over the bed just in time to throw up everywhere. The rancid smell burns my eyes as I dry heave, purging my stomach of everything.

The door swings open and a gruff voice demands, "What the fuck are you— Shit. Fuck." The guy with long hair stalks toward me, frowning down at me. "Jesus."

"H-help me." I breathe through the stench. "Please, I think something is wrong."

I can barely see straight, the room is spinning as I try to breathe through my mouth. He doubles back and heads for the door and I cry out, "Please."

But he leaves, slamming the door behind him and I sink onto my back, tears soaking my cheeks, running down my neck and dripping onto the dirty sheets beneath me.

I hate this.

How weak and scared I am.

It isn't me.

I'm a Darlington. I'm strong and capable. I know how to defend myself. I know how to disarm a grown man for Pete's sake.

But my body is no longer my own. As if they knew... Knew to incapacitate me with a cocktail of lethal drugs.

I can't make sense of the pieces of the puzzle though, the chemical haze interfering with my ability to step back and look at things with an objective eye.

I have no idea where I'm being kept. No idea who took me. No idea what day it is.

None of it makes sense.

Not one—

The door swings open again, startling me. The man comes around to the side of the bed and places down a fresh bottle of water and a bowl of water along with a towel.

"It's the best I could do."

"W-why?"

"Don't ask questions. Just clean yourself up. And drink something."

"Is it—"

"It's safe. Look, the seal is intact."

It is. But I still don't trust it.

"For fuck's sake. Here." He unscrews the lid and takes a drink. "Now drink." Thrusting the bottle at me, I take it, my fingers trembling.

"I'll clean this up best I can."

He disappears out of the room again and returns with a bucket of water and a mop that's seen better days.

"Thank you."

He grunts some inaudible reply.

"How long have I been out? What day—"

"Don't do that. I can't help you."

"But you are helping me. You are—"

"Fuck," he hisses. "I said don't."

"Is there somewhere I can shower, maybe? Get cleaned up?"

If I can stand under some cold water maybe it'll help shake off the lingering edge of the drugs.

"A shower? What the fuck you think this is? The Ritz?" He snorts. "Ain't no more bathroom visits unless the boss sanctions them."

"But how will I—"

He drags another bucket from the corner of the room and nods toward it.

"You can't seriously expect me to—"

"I don't expect you to do anything." He lets out an exasperated breath. "But the boss—"

"Who is he? Why is he doing this?"

"You ask too many fucking questions. I gotta go before he realises I'm gone."

"But wait," I rush out as he retreats to the door. "Please don't leave me in here. Please don't—"

His hard gaze lingers for a second but then he slips out of the room.

Taking the last shreds of my hope with him.

I'm in and out of it for what feels like an eternity.

My stomach twists and tightens, gnawing with hunger and fear.

The man in the suit doesn't come back. Neither does the man with the long hair.

I'm alone. Locked in a room that smells like stale vomit, shackled to a bed that has seen better days, with no plan or means of escape.

It's been hours.

Days.

I have no concept of time. Of whether it's the middle of the day or the middle of the night. I can only assume this is all part of his plan to strip me of my awareness, another way to unnerve me.

As the minutes pass, I take my time sipping little mouthfuls of water, trying to counteract the drugs in my system and the unquenchable thirst I have.

But drinking means a full bladder. It means another bathroom trip.

Or worse, none.

I hold it for as long as possible, trying to ignore my body's signals. Taking deep, drudging breaths. Willing myself to sleep. Or at least, zone out from the living nightmare I've found myself in.

My parents must be going out of their minds. Abi and Olivia too.

And Oakley... well, I try hard not to think about him.

About the pain contorted into his features as he walked away from me and my father the other day.

Everything was already a mess. But this... this is a new level of hell.

One I might not escape.

No, don't think like that.

You'll get out of this, Tallulah.

But I'm not a fool. I've watched true crime shows enough to know how these things end.

Both men have let me see their faces.

I know what that means—even if I don't want to accept it.

They aren't worried about me getting free and cooperating with the police.

A chill goes through me as the realisation and what it means spreads through me.

They don't expect me to make it out of this.

But I refuse to accept that.

I refuse to accept that I'll die here. Drugged and alone and covered in my own vomit.

I'm only eighteen.

I haven't lived enough yet.

I haven't—

A fresh wave of tears overtake me, drowning out my thoughts and fears as I succumb to the emotions warring inside my chest.

I have to find a way out of this.

I have to save myself.

Because my life isn't over yet.

It isn't.

It can't be.

14

OAKLEY

After Thomas had blown out of the house, clearly unwilling to do what needed to be done to find Tally, the others slipped away. Abi went to hang out with Liv and Reese while Elliot and Theo went back to the Chapel.

They wanted to help but even without Dad demanding some space to work, they all knew it was time to disperse.

I was like a coiled spring, really to go off at any minute, and none of them wanted to be the reason for it.

Their concerns for both me and Tally were etched into every inch of their faces, but they knew they couldn't compete with Dad when it comes to finding the answers, so they left us to it.

Sadly though, Dad's searching and the promise of extra CCTV footage from his contact didn't turn anything up.

He sent me away as well an hour later. Apparently, I was distracting him or some shit.

As I walked toward the stairs, laughter from above hit me like a rock.

How can they be happy?

How can they laugh at a time like this?

Without thinking, I grabbed my keys from the side and threw myself into my car.

I drove around town for hours, but it was dark and mostly deserted. I barely saw another person let alone the girl I was searching for.

Eventually, I found myself parked up on the edge of campus, my car hiding beneath a heavy cover of trees in the hope no one would spot it, and I let myself into our cabin.

We don't use it as much as some of the previous Heirs have, and the second I pull the door open, a musty scent fills my nose, making me question my decision. But the darkness, the solitude was too much to ignore, and I move deeper into the shadows.

Knowing exactly where everything is hidden, I pull out a bottle of vodka, a baggie of weed, and some pills. Unsure of where I wanted this night to go, I collapse into one of the chairs.

Twisting the top of the bottle, I put it to my lips and chuck down shot after shot. I need it, I need something, anything to take the edge off.

Desperation. Anger. Complete and utter helplessness floods my veins and twists up my chest.

She's gone.

Vanished into thin air.

This shit doesn't happen. Not in real life.

Not even in our fucked-up lives.

We've all been involved in some fucked-up shit. But this...

And to Tally. She doesn't even deserve it.

What has she ever done?

Start a campaign against us that she'd already lost before she even announced it?

That doesn't deserve this.

And what did she ever do to piss Deacon off?

Turn him down, probably.

He comes across like the kind of douchebag who can't take no for an answer.

Stuffing my hand into my sweats, I pull my phone free and reluctantly find Misty's number. Hitting call, I put it on loudspeaker and wait for her irritating voice to fill the cabin.

But it never comes.

Instead, I get her voicemail.

"Hey, this is Misty. I'm busy being fabulous." I can't help but scoff. "Please leave me a message and I'll get back to you if I feel like it."

Rolling my eyes, I cancel the call.

She knows something. She has to.

She set me up, I'm sure of it. Nothing else makes sense.

But I didn't steal your key, a little voice says.

I wash that thought down with another couple of mouthfuls of vodka.

Should I be drinking on my meds? No, probably not. But right now, I figure adding to the cocktail of drugs in my system isn't a bad thing.

Maybe they'll help me forget what a fucking shitshow my life is.

And to think, I thought falling for the enemy was the depths of my problems.

Ignoring the pills, I reach for the weed. Pills make me want to party, and partying leads to fucking and there is no way that is happening.

So I take the other option and hope like fuck it helps mellow me out a little.

Every muscle in my body is pulled so tight I'm sure they're only seconds away from snapping. And the pain, despite the meds and the vodka now flooding my system, is still as bad as ever.

Or at least, I'm pretty sure it's pain from the beating and not whatever is shattering inside my chest.

Before long, the room is spinning around me, and my dark thoughts are threatening to take me down once and for all.

You failed her, Oakley.

You promised to protect her, and now you can't even find her.

All you've done is hurt her.

Hurt everyone.

And now look.

I startle when the door on the other side of the cabin opens.

I may not have turned the lights on or be able to see anyone, but I know it's the guys. Or one of them when only a single set of footsteps move closer.

"Fuck off," I grunt, in no kind of mood for a heart to heart.

"No," replies a very familiar voice.

"You drew the short straw, huh?" I mutter after swallowing another shot.

"Lost a fight," Theo deadpans. "Loser gets to hang out with your jolly soul."

I growl in irritation as he drags one of the other chairs closer and drops his annoying arse into it.

"So," he starts, twisting the cap off his own bottle.

"I don't need a fucking babysitter. Go watch Millie if you're feeling the need to care for someone."

"Millie is fine," he assures me. "Spoke to her earlier and she was tucked up in bed safely."

"Good for her," I mutter.

Theo sighs, forcing me to look over. He's cast in shadow but that doesn't mean I miss the concern etched onto his face.

"You're here now, you might as well fucking spit it out."

It irritates the hell out of me that they've been at the Chapel obviously talking about me. But what the fuck am I meant to do about it?

I brought it all on myself after all.

"You really fell for her, huh?"

I don't respond. Don't think it's really necessary after the way I've lost my fucking mind since I woke up in the hospital.

"I get it, man. Under all that innocence and good girl bullshit, she's banging."

My fist curls so tight the splits in my knuckles begin to break apart again.

"And we all know that it's true what they say about the sweet ones," he teases.

"Enough," I hiss under my breath.

But that's not enough to stop Theo. It never fucking is when he's got a bee in his bonnet.

"They put so much more effort in when they're inexperienced to try and please us. Even if it is a little sloppy."

"Theo," I bark.

"What? You gonna tell me she didn't suck you like a va—"

"Shut the fuck up," I boom, shoving his chair as hard as I can. It's not enough, nowhere near. It doesn't move an inch which only ramps up my anger more.

I'm stronger than this. I should be able to push him from that chair with one arm.

But I'm broken. Utterly fucked up both on the inside and the out.

"Oh, did I hit a nerve?"

"I'm not telling you how good Tally sucks my cock, prick," I scoff.

"That good, huh?" I don't need to look over to know he's got a shit-eating grin on his face.

"Why are you fucking here? Trying to ruin my fucking week more than it already is?"

"You're mean when you're angry," he mutters, tipping his bottle to his lips.

"No one is forcing you to be here."

"Oak," he sighs, his concerned eyes burning into the side of my face. "You're right, no one is forcing me. I'm here because I want to be, numb nuts."

"Theo."

"No, don't Theo me, Oakley Beckworth. We're worried about you. I'm worried about you and I'm going to fucking sit here until you talk to me. Shit's been off with you for ages. I've tried... kinda, in my own way."

"You beat the shit out of me," I point out.

"And did it help?"

"Yeah," I confess.

"Okay good. But I'm not doing that this time, and not just because I'm going easy on you because you're all hurt and shit."

I scoff. "Could still take you."

"You need to talk, Oak. What the fuck has been going on?"

"I've been fucking Tally," I confess, hoping it'll be enough to make him leave me the hell alone.

"Yeah, we got that memo. But it's more than that, isn't it? You've fallen for her? For real?"

A pained sigh slips past my lips, and I slump lower in the chair, wishing the entire thing would just swallow me whole. "Does it matter? I can't have her. I was never meant to go anywhere near her. And anyway, she's not even here now so it's all a moot point."

"You really believe that?"

I shrug.

What does it matter what I believe?

She's gone, we have no idea where she is and even if we did... we've all seen what her father thinks of the whole situation. There's no way in hell that he'd ever allow it to continue.

"No, I guess it doesn't because the facts stand for themselves."

"Yeah, she hates me, and she's gone."

"Not the facts I was referring to but okay." He pauses for a moment, taking a swig of his vodka. "What makes you think she hasn't fallen as hard for you as you have her?"

"Because she hasn't. She ended us. She dismissed me in front of her father. She thought I was the one who—"

"And what if she's scared?" he asks.

"Scared? Why the fuck would she be scared?"

"Because she's fallen for the enemy and is trying to find a reason to convince herself it won't work. Sound familiar?"

I don't respond. What the hell can I even say to that?

"Look," Theo starts, turning to look at me. "I know fuck all about love or relationships. I have way more experience when it comes to how not to do it. But if you want her, if you really have fallen for her, then none of the rest of it matters.

"So what if she's a Darlington and you're a Beckworth? You are not your fathers, or your grandfathers. If she makes you happy, makes you smile like Reese makes Liv smile when you're together, then isn't that worth it?"

I stare at him, wondering when one of my best friends had a lobotomy and started giving out romantic advice. But my thoughts soon turn to Tally and the time we've spent together.

He's right. She does make me smile like Reese does to Liv. I also recognise the lightness in my eyes when we're together. Reese has that too. I fucking hate it, but it's there. Right alongside the fierce possessiveness that surrounds him like a thick cloud whenever someone says something about her.

I think about her gentle touch, her whispered words, her innocence and hesitation in contrast to the way she lets go when I push her to the edge. The way she screams my name alongside all the other curse words that spill from her lips in moments of ecstasy. Those few stolen moments that no one has ever experienced. And fuck if I want to be the only one to ever witness it.

The way she falls for me, it's fucking beautiful. Mesmerising. Breathtaking.

"I'm not good enough for her," I argue.

"And you didn't think Reese was good enough for your sister but look at them.

"It's not your opinion that counts here. It's hers. So how about we stop getting off our arses drunk and get out there and find her?"

15

TALLY

Time has no meaning anymore.

It could be hours or days I've been stuck here, drifting in and out of consciousness.

My stomach gnaws with hunger, my throat dry and scratchy. The lingering smell of vomit permeates every breath I take, making me heave more often than not.

I'm alone… and I hate to admit it, but I'm losing hope.

No matter how many times I've yanked against my restraints, it's pointless. They're secured too tightly. If I can't get free, I have zero chance of making a run for it. Not that I have a clue where I'd run to. But it's the only seed of hope I have—that I'll be able to escape.

Because no one is coming for me.

Isn't that what they say?

That in missing person cases the first seventy-two hours is vital. I remember my father telling me once that seventy-five percent of people who go missing are found within twenty-four hours. I don't know if three days have passed yet, but I've definitely been here longer than twenty-four hours. Which puts me in the twenty-five percent category.

Every minute counts now... and I feel like I'm running out of those.

I reach for the bottle of water and take a sip, rationing it just in case. But the second I swallow, the sudden urge to pee overtakes me.

"No... no, no, no," I cry. Because I don't want to wet myself. I don't want—

Heavy footsteps outside my room steal my attention and I wait with bated breath. The door swings open and it's him, the man with the long, scraggly hair.

Relief floods me as I rush out, "I need to pee."

"Boss says no more bathroom trips."

"Please, I'm begging you. Don't make..." I can't even say the words, my voice trembling. "Please."

"Fuck's sake," he mutters, glancing at me and then the door. "You gotta be quick."

"Y-yes, I promise. I can do that. Thank you."

"Try anything and you won't like—"

"I won't, I swear. I just really need to pee."

He gives me a curt nod, coming over to undo my restraints. Once I'm free, he goes to scoop me up off the bed, but I put out my hand to stop him. "I can do it."

His brows bunch together but he steps back, giving me space to gingerly climb off the bed. My muscles roar with agony but I grit my teeth and force myself to stand. I have to do this.

"You good?" he asks, surprising me.

I nod, motioning for him to lead the way.

"You first," he replies, and reluctantly, I move ahead of him.

I'm slow on my feet, my body sluggish. But with every step, a renewed sense of hope fills me. If I can walk, I can run.

And if I can run, I can escape.

I just need the right opportunity.

I take in every detail of the place. The peeling damp walls

of the long hallway. There's no windows, only a couple of doors. The furthest leading to the bathroom, I think.

There's no sounds, no voices in the distance. It's utter silence except for our footsteps as I walk ahead of him.

Maybe I could make a run for it. Try the other door and hope it leads to freedom. But what if it doesn't? What if it only leads to—

No, don't go there.

All hope isn't lost yet.

It isn't.

A sense of resolve washes over me. I'm not a helpless little girl. If my father made sure I learned anything over the years, it was how to defend myself. Verbally and physically.

When we reach the bathroom, the man moves ahead of me to open the door. "Five minutes. If you're not out—"

"Yeah, I got it. And thank you." I look right at him, forcing him to acknowledge me. To see the young woman behind the weary smile and pale skin and not just some job.

Bile churns in my stomach. I swallow it down, refusing to let the fear circling me take hold.

I'm up on two feet and despite the ache inside me, the weariness, my head feels clearer than it has since I first woke up here.

I feel stronger. Maybe not physically but mentality.

"In you go," he says, and I slip past him, my eyes drinking in the decrepit surroundings.

The door clicks shut behind me, making my heart free fall but I suck it up. Once again searching for anything I can later use as a weapon. As quietly as possible, I sift through the debris on the floor and in the rusted bathtub. But just like last time, there isn't anything.

Knowing I don't have much time, I give up and quickly go to the toilet, wincing at the slight burning sensation when I pee.

I'm a mess. Covered in dirt and bruises. But there's

something oddly comforting about it too. Because despite everything, I'm alive.

I'm still here.

Once I'm done, I shake and pull up my underwear, freezing at the sound of voices outside the door.

"Check on the girl?" I hear someone say.

"She's in her room, passed out."

What?

I tiptoe to the door, straining to hear.

"Maybe I'll go take a look."

"Wouldn't if I were you. The boss is pretty feral over this one."

This one?

"What? She got a golden pussy or something?"

"She's just a kid."

"She's at least sixteen, right? Like the rest of them. Fair game if—"

"If the boss finds you're messing around with his girls, what do you think he's going to do?"

"Is that a threat?"

"Nah, just the truth. I need a smoke. You wanna come get some fresh air? Fucking sick of the stale air in this place."

"Yeah, okay."

Their footsteps grow quieter, but I stand there for at least another minute, rooted to the spot, trying to process what I just heard.

Like the rest of them.

Does that mean there are more girls? Here?

Or somewhere else?

My thoughts spin as I try to piece together what I know. But then something else hits me.

I'm alone.

Alone and unguarded...

And my guard covered for me.

My eyes dart around the room, looking for something, anything that might help.

But there's nothing, there's—

My eyes snag on a small window high up in the corner of the room. I hadn't noticed it before because it's covered up but a streak of light bleeds through the slats today.

Meaning it's daylight.

Adrenaline pumps through my veins as I run through my options. I can't climb the wall. I need something to climb on. Something with enough height to give me a chance of cracking open the window.

I scan the room, landing on a narrow vanity cupboard. It's seen better days, but it might just work. Rushing over to it, I pick it up and carry it over to the side of the bath.

It's not easy, hauling myself onto the small surface and I swear there's a moment when my heart stops when the whole thing creaks beneath me. But to my surprise—and utter relief—it holds, and I can reach up to work off the slates covering the window.

There's a deep ledge but I'm not sure I'll be able to hoist myself up. Not with how weak I am.

But my shot at freedom is right there.

If I don't at least try, I may never get another chance.

Pushing onto my tiptoes, I flatten myself against the wall and reach for the handle, silently praying it isn't locked. Defeat rocks through me when it doesn't budge but I try again. Yanking with all my might, hoping to God that no one is beyond it.

For a second, fear paralyses me, and I stop. What if I escape only to meet a worse fate?

The men could be out there.

The boss.

No.

This is it. This is my shot at escaping.

With renewed determination, I grit my teeth and yank up hard, sheer relief flooding me when the handle moves out of position. Slowly, I push the window open, my heart crashing in my chest.

This is it.

Now or never.

Gripping onto the frame, I start to pull myself up, the muscles in my arms screaming in protest. I bite down on my cheek, desperately trying to trap the scream building inside me.

It hurts.

Everything hurts so much as I try to scramble against the wall. It's a tight fight as I pull myself through the hole and toward the window but I'm almost there, the fresh air a sign at how close I am.

My eyes blink against the sunlight as I peer through the open window. It never occurred to me I might not be on the first floor but on a higher level of a building. So I'm relieved to discover, I'm not. But even being on the ground floor, the fall down to ground level is going to hurt.

Better than staying here.

With one last tug, I pull my arms outside the window and onto the wall pushing with all my might, unable to trap the yelp of pain as my bandage tears against the window frame as I fall.

My body slams into the ground, the air whooshing from my lungs as I lie there winded. Waiting for any signs of serious injury to kick in.

Everything hurts but I can feel my legs and arms, and I can see. I can see the clouds in the sky and the trees lining the perimeter of the house.

I don't think anything is broken.

I feel okay.

As okay as you can be when you've been drugged and kidnapped and kept locked in a dirty room, shackled to a bed.

But none of that matters.
Because I did it.
I'm free.

16

OAKLEY

A knock on my door drags me from my fitful sleep.

I'd hoped the exhaustion mixed with the vodka and weed would help me shut it all out. But it didn't. Knowing she's out there somewhere, possibly with someone hurting her... or worse. It had me tossing and turning. And when I did manage to drift off, it was full of dreams of her. Some incredible, my mind making me believe that she was here with me, in my bed, in my arms. Other nightmares, forcing me to watch some faceless man take what's mine.

I groan when the knock comes again, followed by the door being pushed open and someone whispering my name.

"Go away," I groan, rolling over and dragging the duvet over my head.

Everything hurts. Fucking everything, but it's the ache in my chest that seems to be the most permanent fixture right now.

"But I have coffee and pills. Something tells me that you're going to need it."

"Fuck," I hiss.

He's right.

With a sigh, I drag my sore body up the bed until I'm

sitting back against my headboard, but I don't open my eyes. I can't. I'm pretty sure if I do the light will singe my pupils to nothing but dust.

My head spins, my mouth is dry as fuck and my stomach continues to roll as if I'm going to need to run for the bathroom any minute.

But I refuse to let it beat me.

Sucking in deep lungfuls of air through my mouth, I will my stomach to settle.

"You were pretty wrecked last night," Reese says quietly.

"I'm sensing that," I confess, dropping my head into my hands as the room continues to spin around me.

"Here. Take these, it'll help."

Pulling my hand from my face, he drops two pills into my palm. I hesitate, hating the way the strong painkillers the hospital was giving out like Smarties knocked me out.

I don't want to float through all of this. I need to feel. I need to experience the pain to help keep me going. I don't want the world with grey tones and numbed feelings. I need this anger, this hatred, this pain to fuel me. I need it to help me find her. To bring her back.

"Just paracetamol, man," Reese says as if he can read my mind. "Still strong as shit, mind you. But not that stuff."

Finally, I crack my eyes open and look at him. He still looks the same as I remember. My best friend. Grey eyes, dark hair, high cheekbones. But also, everything is different. There's a spark there that never used to exist, some of his hard edges have been smoothed out. He looks... happy. And it makes me wonder just how unhappy he was before. He never said anything or gave me any clues that he was miserable in his life.

But then I guess I wasn't before Tally either. When it was just the two of us hanging out, hell, even when we were fighting, everything felt easier. Even breathing felt effortless in a way I'd never experienced before. Is that what it's been like for him?

"You can ask, you know, whatever it is that you're thinking," Reese says, still able to read me like when we were kids.

Taking the bottle of water he offers, I throw back the pills and swallow them before replacing the bottle with a mug of coffee.

The scent fills my room but it's not enough and I lift the mug to my nose, inhaling deeply. The rich scent of the beans fills my nose as my best friend watches in amusement.

Swallowing down my unease, I ask the question that's teetering on the tip of my tongue. "How did you know Liv was the one?"

His eyes go all soft at the mention of my sister. In the past, seeing his reactions to her has been like someone pushing a knife through my chest. But since things changed with Tally, I think I'm starting to understand.

It doesn't matter what is right or wrong, who you hurt outside of the two of you. When it's right, when the connection between you is like a magnetic force dragging you together no matter what, nothing else matters.

"How do you know you love rugby more than football?" he asks with a smirk.

"Because rugby is a far superior game and way better than any other."

"Exactly. There are a million reasons why I love your sister, Oak. More than I could ever put into words. But it boils down to that. She's far superior to anyone else out there, and better in every way," he says, mimicking my words.

A heavy sigh falls from my lips. "I think she feels the same about you," I confess.

"Yeah?"

"Pretty sure someone must have dropped her on her head as a baby or something, but yeah."

"Aw, you love me, man, and you know it."

A smile twitches at my lips as I stare at my best friend.

Things have been weird between us for far too long. I know it's been me holding back and putting a wall between us, but fuck. I need him right now.

It's time to get over the fact he fell for Liv. I mean, honestly, it could be worse. It could have been Darcie or Misty. I shudder as I think about having to put up with one of the chasers for an extended period of time.

"You okay?" Reese asks, concern tugging at his brows.

I study him, no longer seeing him as friend who deserted us but as the man who's fucked up and then owned his mistake. A man who loves my sister in a way she totally deserves. I might give him shit, but since they've been together, he's not so much as looked at anyone else. She's it for him, I know she is.

"I'm sorry," I blurt. His frown gets deeper. "For everything I put you through since you came back."

"Oak," he breathes, his hand landing on my shin that's covered by the duvet. "It's okay. You've nothing to apologise for. I fucked up. I betrayed your trust with Liv. I get it."

Our eyes lock as silence and the weight of our words settle around us.

It's so quiet, I startle when Reese talks again. "We'll find her," he states, his voice full of confidence.

I swallow nervously.

"Talulah fucking Darlington, man?" he shakes his head, a laugh tumbling from his lips.

When I just glare back at him, he scrubs his hand over his face to try and cover his smile.

"Do you have to look so fucking smug?"

"I mean, I kinda saw it coming in a way, but also, I really didn't."

"How? I fucking hated her," I quip.

"Yeah, that's pretty much the reason. Thin line, bro. Very thin line."

"Fucking prick," I mutter.

"Dude, she's hot." I rear back and he chuckles. "Oh, pipe down, I have eyes, man. And despite what you've always thought, she's nice. Liv really likes her."

"Yeah," I agree. "Doesn't mean anything happening between us would be accepted."

"Fuck that. You want her, fucking have her."

"Romantic," I deadpan.

"You know what I mean. Fuck your surnames, the stupid rivalry. That has nothing to do with the two of you. And you know what?"

"Enlighten me."

"I think you make a cute couple. And I'd totally be willing to double date."

He says that not a second after I've sipped my coffee and I only just manage not to cover him in it when he says the words double date.

I swallow, just before coughing a little. "You, Reese Whitfield-Brown, want to double date with my sister, me and Tally?"

"Sure, why not. I can finally show you how to really treat a woman," he teases with a wink.

"My sister," I grumble. "I don't want to watch any—"

"It's sex, Oak. You need to pull the stick out of your arse. You never used to be such a prude." He's baiting me, I can see it in the appearance of his dimple as he fights his smile.

"You know, if you had a sister, I'd have fucked her six ways from Sunday somewhere you could hear by now."

"Lucky me I'm flying solo in the sibling department then. Well, aside from my stepsister. She's hot as fuck. And anyway, you wouldn't want my sister 'cos you're in love with Tallulah Darlington," he sings like a prick.

"Shut the fuck up, I'm not—"

A loud bang from downstairs cuts my potential lie before Elliot bellows for us.

"Sure, you are, and when we find her, you can tell her,

yeah?" Reese asks with a grin. "Ready to go and see what our fearless leader needs?"

Placing my mug on the bedside table, I grit my teeth and drag my sorry arse out of bed.

"You look like an old man," Reese helpfully points out. "You need me to help lower your arse to the toilet?"

"Fuck you," I grunt.

"I was only offering to help. I draw the line at holding it for you, though."

"Only because you'll discover how much bigger mine is."

He throws his head back and laughs like it's the funniest thing he's ever heard.

I take a piss and brush my teeth, grateful that the pills are already kicking in, and when I emerge, I find Reese waiting for me with a clean pair of sweats in his hands.

"Thanks," I mutter, taking them from him and refusing to accept any help as I wrestle them up my legs.

My ribs scream but it's not loud enough. The only person I want to touch me right now isn't here.

"Whitfield, Beckworth, get your arses down here," Elliot bellows again the second we pull the door open.

"All-fucking-right, keep your lacy knickers on," Reese shouts back as we head his way.

My knuckles are white with my grip on the bannister as I use it to support me down. But they're white for a whole other reason when I find who is waiting for us.

"What the fuck are you doing here?" I growl the second my eyes land on Misty, standing in the middle of our sanctuary. "You're no longer welcome here."

"She's come to talk, apparently," Elliot says, eyeing her suspiciously. Theo stands on her other side doing the exact same thing with his thick forearms crossed over his chest.

Misty swallows nervously as she looks each of us in the eyes.

As I study her, I realise that she doesn't look like her usual self. Her heavy, flawless make-up is nowhere to be seen, and the circles under her eyes are dark. Her hair hangs limply around her shoulder and she's wringing her hands in front of her, looking utterly terrified of us.

"So are you going to spit it out, or will we have to force it out of you?" I ask, all four of us closing in around her.

She looks like a lamb that's been led to the slaughter.

"I-I-I..." she stutters, her eyes now locked on her feet.

"You fucking what, Misty?"

"I-I lied."

Before I realise I've registered those two words, I have my hand around her throat, and I'm shoving her back against the wall.

Her eyes widen as she stares at me, tears clinging to her lashes. She trembles violently as I glare pure hate at her.

"Start fucking talking, Misty," I seethe, my nose only a breath from hers.

"I-it was Deacon," she whimpers.

"What was Deacon?"

"H-he was the one who jumped you."

"Where is he, Misty?"

She swallows or at least attempts to with how tight my fingers are wrapped around her throat. I have no idea if she's aware of Tally's disappearance, but something tells me that if she can lead us to Deacon, then we might just find her too.

"Where the fuck is he?" I roar, making her cower, a whimper falling from her lips as her tears finally fall.

17

TALLY

I manage to roll onto my knees and push onto all fours. Pain shoots through my side and I smother a yelp, my eyes darting wildly around the place, checking for any signs of life.

There's nothing.

No one.

Just the dense perimeter of trees and the ramshackle house behind me.

Biting back another agonised groan, I manage to clamber to my feet, sucking in a sharp breath as realisation hits me.

I'm free...

But I have no idea where I am or how to get out of here.

God, this could be a bad idea. I could be jumping out of the frying pan into the fire, but what choice do I have? If I don't make a run for it, I'll end up back in that house. In that room. Or worse.

A violent shudder rolls through me as I steel myself, shoving down all the fear and uncertainty. I can do this.

I have to do it.

Something bangs in the distance, making my heart lurch

into my throat and without overthinking it, I take off toward the tree line, stumbling over my feet.

I'm still weak, fuelled by nothing but adrenaline and hope. If I can just get to a main road, I might be able to flag down a car or find an emergency phone. Something—*anything*—to give me a chance at being rescued.

I burst through the trees in a state of panic, glancing around, hoping to see some sign of which direction I should go. There's nothing. No trodden path or natural break in the thicket, only trees upon trees upon more trees.

"Okay." I inhale a deep breath, glancing around again. The house stands proud behind me. Watching. I want to put as much distance between me and it, so I cut a path straight ahead. I have no idea if it's the right call, but distance is good.

Distance feels safe.

At least, that's what I keep telling myself as I move deeper into the woods.

Oxfordshire is littered with National Parks and vast woodland. I could be anywhere. I might not even be in Oxfordshire anymore.

I tamp down that thought and keep moving, pushing through the pain, the burning ache in my lungs.

After a good few minutes, I stop. Dragging greedy mouthfuls of air into my lungs. It's cold out, colder than I was prepared for.

I glance back, relieved to see the house no longer visible. If I can't see it, it can't see me. But I'm still deep in the woods, no sign of life around.

"Think, Tallulah, think," I mutter, frustration and bleeding into my voice.

I can't go back now that I've made a run for it, which means I have to keep going. But what if I don't find a way out?

What if I keep running and it's just trees and more trees?

I'll need water soon, and when the winter sun drops, the temperature will plummet. I'm not equipped to deal with that.

Oh God.

What if I've made a terrible mistake?

"No, no," I snap. "You can do this. You have to do it, Tally. Move. Keep moving."

With another deep breath, I take off again, dragging myself further into the thicket. Branches scratch me like bony fingers clawing at my arms and legs. But I keep pushing. Keep moving. Putting as much distance as possible between me and that house of horrors.

Eventually, I'll find another sign of life.

Picking up my pace, I duck and dodge the trees as best I can, wincing every time another branch scrapes my face. But every step forward is a step further away. And that's all that matters.

So long as I keep moving, I'm safe.

Safer than I was back there, at least.

My burst of energy doesn't last long. Eventually, I have to stop and catch my breath. I feel like I've been running forever but I know in reality it can't be much more than twenty minutes. There isn't a bit of me that doesn't hurt or ache or scream in protest as I slump against a thick tree trunk. My lips are dry, and my throat is scratchy. And I'm desperate for a drink. But there's nothing but trees. Trees and—

A sound catches my attention in the distance. I try to focus, try to ignore the roar of blood in my ears to figure out what it is.

"A car," I murmur, my lips curving.

I must be close to the road.

Hope washes over me, giving me the push I need to keep on. I inhale another deep breath and push off the tree in the direction of where the sound came from. The woods are still thick, boxing me in on all sides. But I trudge on, grateful that it's still daylight and I'm not wandering around out here in the middle of the night.

I try to think about better things. My parents. My friends.

Oakley.

My heart aches at the thought of him—of what he might be doing.

Does he know I'm missing?

Does he care?

So caught up in my thoughts, I don't realise the trees are slowly thinning out until I can see a swathe of road up ahead.

I clap a hand over my mouth, so overwhelmed that I have to hold myself together as I hurry toward the edge of the tree line.

It's a country road, trees on the far side but I can't place the area. It could be on any country road in rural England.

But it's freedom.

I'm so close. All I need is to wait for a car to drive past and I can flag them down and ask for help.

I take cover behind one of the trees, waiting. It's quiet again. Until... there it is in the distance.

The familiar rumble of a car.

Thank God.

I edge out from behind the tree and move closer to the side of the road. The car appears around the winding road, and relief floods me, so much so, I cry out.

It slows its trajectory as I stumble out into the middle of the road, waving my arms wildly in the air.

"Please, help. Please..." It comes to a stop, and I squint against the sunlight bouncing off the windshield, hoping to see a friendly face beyond the tinted glass.

The door opens and I stagger around the side of the car, aware of how I must look. Bloody and broken and bruised...

"Please, I-I was kidnapped. They... they drugged me and—"

"Now, now, Tallulah."

CRUEL DEVIOUS HEIR: PART TWO

Everything inside me stills at that voice.

His voice.

No.

No.

This can't be happening.

"N-no." I start backtracking but I lose my footing and fall onto my bum. "Please," I cry, tears streaking down my cheeks as he approaches me, a victorious glint in his eye.

"You're quite the troublemaker," he tsks, glancing back toward the car. Another man climbs out and for a second, I pray that it's my guard. The one who gave me a chance to escape.

Disappointment swarms my chest when I realise it's not.

"Expecting someone?" There's a taunting lilt to his voice. "You won't be seeing Merrick again anytime soon. Seems he has a soft spot for broken little girls." He leans down, plucking a strand of my hair. "Shame too, he was one of my best men."

Oh God.

Bile washes in my stomach, and I swallow down the acidic taste.

I try and scramble away from his touch but it's futile. Once again, I'm powerless.

Completely at his mercy.

"Please, just let me go," I beg, my voice cracking with raw desperation.

"Surely, you've figured out by now that's not how this game goes. Get her," he orders the other man.

"N-no, please," I scream, trying to fold in on myself. Trying to disappear.

Rough hands grab me from behind and I'm hoisted against a solid chest. But I refuse to go easily this time, kicking and thrashing with all my might.

"She's a livewire, boss," the man grunts, tightening his hold on me as I catch him in the nose with a swift crack of my head.

"Not for long."

I feel something sharp jab in my neck, a warm trickle through my bloodstream.

Everything turns heavy, my vision blurring in and out as I'm carried toward the car.

"P... p... please," I murmur, barely holding on as I'm thrown into the back seat, the air whooshing from my lungs.

My eyes flutter as I cling to consciousness.

But the drugs are already overwhelming my system.

I was so close...

So...

Close.

And I failed.

18

OAKLEY

The second I get the information I needed, I drag Misty, the lying piece of shit, out of the Chapel.

Heavy footsteps follow me as she trembles beneath my firm grip.

The second we're out in the cold, the rain lashing down on us all, I throw her into the middle of a puddle, just off the main path leading to our sanctuary.

The four of us glare down at her with our chests heaving and our fists curled. She whimpers, her eyes wide and terrified. Good.

"I'm sorry," she manages to force out. But none of us were willing to hear any of it.

"You fucked up, Misty," Elliot warns, his voice low and dangerous. "You just made yourself four new enemies that you really don't want."

"I'm sorry," she tries again.

But it's too late.

There have been people over the years that I've wanted to hurt. To punish for tormenting those important to me, or those too weak to defend themselves. But I have never felt the need for vengeance quite like I do as we stare down at her.

"This is your last chance to tell us anything else you know," Theo growls.

Misty shakes her head.

"Nothing else?" Reese confirms.

"Nothing involving a rat?" I add, making her frown.

"Ew, what? N-no. I don't know what you're talking about. I told you everything."

I don't want to believe her, but she looks so scared that I can't help but accept her words.

"Let's go," Elliot demands, taking off toward where our cars are parked.

"What about her?" Reese asks.

"I'm not giving her any chance to give him a heads up." Assuming she hasn't already, that is.

Reaching down, I pull her phone from her pocket and hold it up to her face to unlock it. She doesn't say a word. Clearly, she's not entirely stupid.

Opening her messages, I find her chat with Deacon and scroll through the last few interactions, looking for clues that she might have tipped him off.

"He doesn't know, I swear," she cries.

We're all soaked through by the time I lean down over her. But she's sopping, seeing as she's sitting in a puddle.

My fingers encircle her throat once more, squeezing enough to cut off her air in warning. "If I find out that you're lying to us. I will fucking end you, Misty."

"I'm not. I swear."

"Okay."

She shrieks in surprise when I lift her to her feet and drag her behind me.

"What are you doing?" Theo asks.

"Not taking any chances."

When we get to our cars, Elliot's engine is already running. Instead of walking to the door, I come to a stop at the boot and unlock it.

"He's going to fucking kill you," Reese warns, reading my intentions.

"Yeah, well. I'm not risking anything."

"Oakley, no. Please," Misty begs when I throw her tiny body into Elliot's boot. "I'm claustrophobic."

Her cries continue long after I've shut her in.

"You're fucking paying to get my car valeted," Elliot complains.

Misty's screams echo around the car.

"Worth it."

"Should have gagged her," Theo mutters darkly.

"Yeah, well I wasn't exactly planning on all this when I woke up," I mutter. "Will you fucking hurry up," I snap at Elliot.

Unsurprisingly, Deacon isn't with family up north like his lying cunt of a father said. He's hiding out much closer to home.

I can't say I'm surprised. The twisted fuck probably wants to sit back and watch everything he'd caused unfold.

Well, I hope he's fucking happy because I'm about to wipe that smile off his face.

Elliot pulls the car to a stop down a secluded lane that will hopefully stop anyone from hearing Misty. Although she went quiet a few minutes ago, hopefully, that continues.

The four of us climb out and walk toward the main street we turned off.

"That's the house," Elliot says, pointing to an old-fashioned cottage. "And if that bitch is telling the truth, he's in a cabin in the garden."

We make our way toward the house, covering our faces with our black hoodies. There aren't any cars in the driveway, and my heart sinks that we might have missed him.

Or that Misty tipped him off and he's waiting for us with his merry band of knobheads in the hope of getting a second shot at me.

I'm not worried, though.

I'm not alone this time. I come as a team, and even with me not firing on all cylinders, I've every confidence in my boys.

But as we slip around the main house, everything is quiet and there, right at the end of the garden, is the cabin in question, and even better, Deacon is laid out on the sofa scrolling through his phone, totally oblivious to what's about to happen.

We keep to the perimeter of the garden to remain out of sight. Elliot starts pointing and giving out silent orders, which just piss me off.

He's mid-pointing when I storm forward.

Fuck this. I've waited long enough to get my hands on this prick again.

Adrenaline races through my veins, helping me to forget how much it hurts just to walk and I throw his door open, making it slam back against the wall to announce my arrival.

Elliot grumbles behind me, but I tune him out as Deacon speaks. "About fucking time Mist. Been hard since you sent me that photo."

My stomach turns over because I know exactly what photo he's talking about.

"Sorry, she's a little tied up right now."

I want to roar like a fucking demon when his eyes widen in realisation.

"Ah, just the man we've been looking for," Theo mutters, walking around me and lowering the blinds to give us some privacy.

Deacon scrambles up from the sofa and starts backing away. "What do you want?"

"What do we want?" I echo. "Where is she?"

"Who? Misty? I don't know, you just said—"

I fly across the room, my body taking on a life of its own before I slam him back against the wall.

CRUEL DEVIOUS HEIR: PART TWO

I want to scream in pain as we collide but my need to make him hurt twice as bad is stronger.

The second my fist collides with his nose a loud crack rips through the air before blood gushes over his lips. Fisting his shirt, I get right up in his face. "One more chance. Where is she?"

His eyes hold mine as blood and tears mingle on his face. "I don't know what the fuck you're talking about."

"Big fucking mistake." Pulling my arm back, I throw another punch that by some miracle, is hard enough it knocks him off his feet.

"Get him up, tie him to a chair. Clearly, this is going to take a little more persuasion," I demand, borrowing Elliot's title of leader for a few minutes. This is my fight. Tally's fucking life. I get to call the shots right now.

I stand in the middle of the room with Deacon's blood sprayed across me and watch my boys follow orders.

He tries to fight, kicks and screams, but he's no match for their strength. Just like I wasn't a match for him and his little crew.

"Not nice being outnumbered, is it?" I taunt, grabbing my own chair and spinning it around so the back faces him before I straddle it and glare at him. "Did you really think you'd get away with all this?"

"Fuck you," he snarls.

"Nah, I'm not really into sore losers. Because that's what you are, aren't you? Couldn't get the girl so you thought you'd take matters into your own hands."

An angry growl rumbles deep in his throat.

"That's what all this is about, isn't it? Making that hit on me, taking her."

His brow furrows. "Taking who?"

I can't help but laugh.

"Such a fucking liar. We know you have her. Where is she, huh? Tied to your bed?"

I nod my head to Reese who's standing directly behind Deacon, silently demanding that he search this entire cabin for any sign of her.

If I'm right, and she is tied naked to his bed, then I trust him to be as respectful to her as he would be if it were Liv.

The thought of that being reality makes my stomach turn over. If he's laid a fucking finger on her, I'll kill him. Fuck the consequences.

She's mine.

"Have who? I don't have anyone," he argues, dragging me from my dark thoughts.

I don't respond. I just sit staring at him while Reese gives the place a once over.

"No sign," he says after a few minutes.

Shit. He's not going to make this easy.

"What the hell are you pricks talking about? I don't have anyone."

Climbing off the chair, I prowl closer, cracking my knuckles as I move. "Wrong fucking answer."

Crack.

A red haze descends on me, and I hit him over and over. Images of Tally tied up somewhere hopelessly fill my mind and I utterly lose my fucking shit.

I don't feel anything but the all-consuming despair that's flooded my system since we discovered that she's gone.

"Oakley, Oak. Fucking stop, okay." I'm dragged back from a bloody beaten Deacon and the haze begins to clear.

"Fuck. I-I—"

"It's okay," Reese says, wrapping his arms around me to keep me upright when my knees buckle.

"Where the fuck is Tally?" Elliot spits in his face.

His eyes are closed, the swelling that's already there enough to stop him from seeing much anyway. His nose is gushing, his lips are split. He's a fucking mess. Nothing less than he deserves.

"I-I—" he stutters, making me want to hit him again. "I don't know."

"You've taken her. Where is she?" I roar.

His eyes open, well, kind of, and they find mine.

"I h-haven't." He shakes his head. "Not seen her. I swear."

Elliot looks at me, and unease rocks through me.

"But you have. You have to be the one who's taken her," I argue. "Who else would take her from me?"

Nothing but the sound of Deacon's rattling breaths can be heard as I wait for someone to fucking answer me.

Finally, my phone ringing cuts through the tension, and I pull it from my pocket, wincing when my busted knuckles brush the fabric.

"Dad," I bark.

"You need to get to the house right now. We have something."

All the air rushes from my lungs.

"Okay, we're coming." I pause. "Dad?"

"Yeah, Son."

I hold Deacon's eyes. "You might have just saved Deacon Warrick's life. Good timing." My voice is cool, calm and collected. At complete odds with how I'm feeling.

"That's great. Now get your arses back here right now."

I hang up, letting the strength of Dad's words flow through me.

Reese is still right behind me, he heard every word.

"Untie him. We need to go," he says for me.

"Untie him?" Theo asks, not looking pleased by that idea.

"It wasn't him," I say, twisting out of Reese's arms. "But if you come near me, my friends, or my girl again. We'll be fucking back. And we might just be the last faces you ever see," I warn. "Now we're even. I hope you enjoy your recovery as much as I am. Prick."

I walk out of that cabin with my hood up once more,

leaving the others to sort him out. I know they won't be far behind.

My arse barely hits the seat when I see them coming.

"What's going on?" Elliot asks.

"No idea. We need to get to Dad's house."

"You okay?" Reese asks, leaning over to keep our conversation between us.

"No. I'm really fucking not. Get rid of our little problem. We need to go."

"You want to leave her here?" he asks, and I nod, staring ahead, trying to figure out what I'm missing.

"You sure that's a good—"

"The two of them deserve each other."

He gives me a terse nod before going around to the boot and dragging Misty out, carrying her toward Deacon's place. Misty's screams hit my ears as Reese dumps her in a puddle and makes his way back to us.

"She could rat us out," he says, climbing into the car.

"She won't," I reply.

She has too much to lose—they both do.

"Ready?" Elliot asks and I nod. The sooner we find my dad the better. I need him. I need him to help me figure out what's going on.

Elliot speeds across town; long before we probably should, we pull into Dad's driveway.

"What the fuck is he doing here?" Theo asks as our eyes land on Thomas Darlington's car.

"Fuck knows, but I think we're about to get some answers." I have the door open before we've stopped moving, and with another burst of energy, I run across the driveway and crash through the front door.

I find Dad and Thomas in Dad's office, staring at his monitor. "What is it?" I ask, my legs keeping me moving without instruction from my brain.

"I got sent this. I know who has her. We just don't know where," Thomas says, his voice filled with defeat.

I come to a stop and the second I look at the screen, my world falls from beneath me.

"Tally," I breathe, pain slicing through my heart as I take her in. "What have they done to her?"

19

TALLY

I come to bound and gagged. Panic saturates every cell inside me.

I came so close... so close and it was all for nothing.

Deep down, I think I knew. Knew that if I didn't make a run for it right then, I wouldn't survive this place.

This... this man.

This monster.

The man currently watching me from across the room with such a calm composed expression I can't believe he's human.

Who is he?

And why me?

I guess I'll never know. Just like I'll never get to tell my parents I love them or tell Oakley I—

No, don't do this, Tallulah. Don't go there. If these are going to be my last few minutes, hours, days on Earth, then I want to spend them strong. I want to look my captor in the eye as he does whatever it is he has planned for me so he knows that he didn't break me.

Not truly.

Not where it counts.

In my heart.

"Even now," he steps forward, not caring one bit that I can see his face. His defined features and soulless eyes.

But why would he when he plans to kill me—or worse.

I shut down those thoughts, refusing to drown in the fear swimming in my veins.

I'd rather be dead than be sold and kept drugged and docile.

"You know it's all his fault," he murmurs, drawing closer toward me until I can smell the overwhelming scent of aftershave and cigarettes. It's so potent it turns my stomach and I retch, whimpering when he grips my face and snaps my head up, forcing me to look at him.

"He took something from me. Something important. And now I'll take the most important thing to him. I'll make him feel even half the agony I felt when—"

"Please," I cry as his fingers squeeze my cheeks until tears run down my face. "I-I don't know what you're talking about."

"Of course you don't," he sneers. "Daddy dearest wouldn't want his precious little girl knowing about this fake world he inhabits."

"D-daddy?" I choke out, and his grins turns feral.

"Your father is the reason you're here right now. How is that for poetic justice?"

"Who are you?" My brows furrow.

"Kane Alveston. Ring any bells."

The words echo through my skull, realisation crashing over me.

"Kane... you're Judd Alveston's son."

Oh my God.

This is worse.

Much worse than I ever imagined.

"Finally, she gets it." Victory glints in his eyes.

But something else niggles the back of my mind. "The break-in..."

"Not just a pretty face, after all." He tsks, running a thumb along my jaw, letting it linger at my lips. I try and jerk away but his expression darkens, stilling everything inside me. "I contemplated sending you back to him piece by piece. But it's messy business."

Bile rushes up my throat as I imagine my parents finding a box on their doorstep.

"Please..."

"Shh, beautiful. Not much longer now. We're going to have ourselves a little family reunion—"

"No, no!" I start thrashing against my restraints, refusing to accept what he's saying. I don't want my father to come here. To witness me like this. I don't want him to come here because I know what it means.

And I can't accept that.

I can't.

I won't.

I don't see his hand fly toward my face before it's too late. Pain ricochets through my jaw, my head snapping to the side as I cry out in agony. Everything burns, my heart pounding so hard I can't catch my breath.

Something warm trickles into my mouth and I spit out a mouthful of blood onto the floor.

"We can do this the easy way, bitch, or we can do this the hard way."

"Go to hell you sick bastard." The words fly out of my mouth before I can stop them.

He hits me again, the room spinning as the chair rocks beneath me from the force of his fist. My vision blurs, tears rolling down my cheeks as I whimper, barely conscious.

"All I need you to do is sit there and wait. If you can't do that, I'm sure we can arrange—"

The crackle of a radio comes from somewhere behind him, a muffled voice saying, "We've got company, boss."

Dread floods me, turning my blood to ice.

CRUEL DEVIOUS HEIR: PART TWO

"Looks like daddy is right on time." He grins at me. "Don't go anywhere. The fun is about to start."

He strolls out of the room, leaving me in silence. Nothing but tears and heartache for company.

Everything that's happened—that is still happening—doesn't feel real. It's the things of a TV drama or suspense novel. It isn't my life.

Except it is.

My father has spent his entire career fighting to make the world a better place. To keep criminals like Alveston off the streets, and this is where it's landed him.

I wish I could feel some sense of relief that he's here, but I only feel bleak despair. It isn't supposed to be this way. I'm only eighteen. I have so much life left ahead of me.

I have—

The door bursts open, and a handful of masked men pour inside, all carrying an array of guns and weapons.

"W-what—"

"Shh," one orders. "We need to move out. Now." He gives a silent command for another man to move around me and cut me free.

"Sorry," is all he says before he shoves a hessian sack over my head. I suck in a panicked breath, but the air whooshes from my lungs as I'm picked up and hoisted over somebody's shoulder.

"Stay still and don't scream," is all I hear before the sound of gunfire and shouting fills the air.

"Go, go, go," someone orders and we're on the move, my body jostling against rock hard muscle.

Fear grips me in a chokehold as more gunshots fill the air.

"Shit," a voice says before I'm falling.

I hit the ground hard, my head cracking off the cold floor. Stars fill my vision as I grapple to pull the bag off my head, but another pair of hands grab me, pulling me to my feet. "We've got to move," a softer voice says. "I'm going to pick you up and run, okay, and all I need is you to hold on."

"I..."

"Now."

I'm hoisted into the air again, blood rushing to my head, making me dizzy.

"I don't feel so good." Warm liquid trickles down the back of my head.

"I-I think I'm hurt."

"Almost there," he says. "Almost th—"

Everything turns hazy, air whipping around me as my body soars. I dip in and out of consciousness, aware of the world around me spinning. Moving. Shifting.

"Shit, she's losing a lot of blood."

Voices flit in and out of my head.

"Johnson, we need a medi-pack."

"Beckworth is going to have our asses for this."

"She's alive, that's all that matters. Kirk, how you holding up?"

"Fucker cut me deep, but I'll live."

"Good, let's burn this place to the ground and get the fuck out of here."

I want to ask what they're going to burn but my lips won't move. Nothing will.

So I stop fighting the tug of darkness and let it swallow me whole.

"Tallulah. Thank God, sweetheart. Thank— Tallulah, what's wrong with her? What the fuck did you do to my daughter?"

My father's frantic voice finds me in the dark and I slowly blink my eyes open, pain radiating through my skull.

"Okay, Thomas, why don't we just give them some room."

"Room? Look at her. Look at—"

CRUEL DEVIOUS HEIR: PART TWO

"Back the fuck up, so I can lay her down."

I'm lifted into the air and placed carefully on a gurney.

"You called Doc?"

"He'll be here shortly."

That voice—

I twist my head carefully to find Christian Beckworth physically restraining my father. "D-dad?"

"Tallulah, sweetheart. I'm here. I'm right here." He manages to break free of Christian's hold and rushes to my side.

"I am so sorry, Tallulah. I'm so—"

"Dad"—the door bursts open again—"where is she? Where — Prim?"

Everything stills, and I'm pretty sure my heart stops dead in my chest as my glassy eyes find Oakley across the room.

"Fuck," he breathes. "What—"

"No." Dad steps in front of me, blocking my view of him. "You need to leave. I explicitly said I didn't want you here."

"Thomas..."

"No, Christian, I'm grateful for what you did to get my daughter back. But this is—"

"D-dad?" I reach for him, grabbing his arm.

"Sweetheart, what is it? What's wrong?"

Shadows swim in my visions. "I... I don't feel so good."

"You hit your head, Tallulah. But the doctor—"

"Dad?" Everything goes black, my senses ripped away from me as panic crashes over me. "D-dad? I'm scared."

"Shh, sweetheart." His voice grows quiet. Distant. "I'm right here. I'm right—"

"Dad, please. What's happening to me? Something's wrong. Something is—"

"TALLULAH?" Oak roars. "Prim? What's the matter with her? Wake up. Why isn't she waking up?"

"Oak, I'm here. I'm right here." I try to speak, to say the words. But nothing comes out.

I can't speak.
I can't move or see.
Is this it?
Is this what death feels like?
I succumb to the darkness again.
Only this time I'm not sure I'll ever find my way back.

20

OAKLEY

Ignoring everything I agreed to in order to get myself here —wherever the fuck here is—to some hidden compound in the middle of the Oxfordshire countryside that I'm sure only a handful of people in the entire country know exists, I burst through the door after hearing voices on the other side.

She's in there, I know she is.

I promised that I'd let Thomas be with her, reassure her that despite all this being his fucking fault, that everything is going to be okay.

But I can't do it.

The pull toward her is too strong.

"Where is she? Where— Prim?" My eyes fall on her petite frame lying out on a gurney. She's so small and helpless. All I want to do is sweep her into my arms and take her back to my bedroom at the Chapel to look after.

But I can't. And it fucking kills me.

For the briefest moment, her tired, pain-filled eyes meet mine and just a tiny part of me that's been missing since she disappeared slots back into place. But it's not enough.

Nowhere near enough to fix everything that's broken inside of me.

But then she's gone, and my view of her is blocked off by her raging bull of a father who thinks he has enough power to keep me from her.

He says something, his deep booming, angry voice filling the small room we're all huddled inside, but I don't hear it past the roaring blood in my ears.

Her weak voice cuts through the air, cutting off the arguments that are happening around me, and at hearing it, everything comes to a stop.

"Sweetheart, what is it? What's wrong?" Thomas says softly, his voice at complete odds to what it was a few seconds ago.

"I... I don't feel so good." My stomach knots and my heart clenches painfully at the terror in her voice.

We've no idea what she's been through aside from the footage and evidence that Thomas started receiving.

After getting that first video while we were with Deacon two days ago, more and more came through.

It was obvious that whoever had taken her wanted to brag about it. They wanted Thomas to suffer and to know what was happening.

It seemed that they wanted him as well but by then, Dad had sought out a team of men to extract her and we had a plan in place. Or more so, they had a plan in place.

"You hit your head, Tallulah. But the doctor—"

"Dad?" she whimpers, her voice ripping shreds from me. "D-dad? I'm scared."

"Shh, sweetheart. "I'm right here. I'm right—"

Unable to keep away, I dart around Thomas before Dad has a chance to catch me and stand at the end of her bed.

"Dad, please. What's happening to me? Something's wrong. Something is—"

Her eyes close and her body slumps in the bed, her head lolling to the side.

"TALLULAH?" I roar, fear like I've never known before rushing through my veins. "Prim?" I dart forward, needing to touch her. Needing to do anything. But nothing helps. My hand on her cool, dirty arm doesn't wake her. My voice doesn't cause any kind of reaction. "What's the matter with her?" I ask through a massive lump in my throat. "Wake up," I beg helplessly, my eyes burning with red-hot tears. I won't lose her. Not like this. Not because of some case her father fucked up years ago. "Why isn't she waking up?"

I stare down at her beautiful face. I don't see the dirt or grime, the bruises or the swelling from what she's been through. I just see Tally, my beautiful Prim, the girl who's unknowingly stolen my heart and thrown my world into chaos.

Strong arms wrap around me from behind, giving me little choice but to move away from her. "You need to calm down," a familiar voice says in my ear.

"What's wrong with her? Please, someone, wake her up," I beg. My voice is broken, frantic and desperate. I barely recognise it.

Dad continues to move me back, dragging me further and further from where I need to be, but I can't find the strength to fight him.

People descend around Tally's bed, poking and prodding her.

I hate it.

All of it.

The only thing that brings me some kind of relief is that Thomas has been shoved aside too.

A woman shines a bright light in Tally's eyes while a man cannulates the back of her hand. Another woman hangs up a bag of something on a hook.

"What's happening?"

"They're doctors and nurses. They're looking after her," Dad says, not that it does much to calm me. "Trust them to do their job."

"I can't. I—" I swallow thickly before my stomach bottoms out when one of the nurse's lifts Tally's shirt to expose a deep cut in her stomach.

Bile rushes up my throat at the thought of someone touching her so brutally, and I gag, desperately trying not to vomit on the floor.

"Get him out of here. He promised," Thomas barks.

"This isn't fair. He cares. He—"

"GET OUT," Thomas bellows.

Leaving is the last thing I want to do but when I heave again, I have little choice unless I want to puke on my feet.

Twisting out of Dad's arms, I run from the room and straight through a door marked toilets I spotted while we were waiting for their arrival.

My knees hit the tiled floor and I empty my stomach, all the while images of what they might have done to her to leave her in such a state flicker through my mind.

She's too good for this, too pure, too innocent.

I heave again, but there's nothing left.

Dropping my arm to the toilet, I rest my head on it. Sweat covers every inch of my body as I suck in greedy breaths to calm me down.

"She's going to be okay," that voice says again. Calm, cool, collected.

It's probably what I need right now, but it's not what I want.

Falling back on my arse, I rest against the cold tiled wall, keeping my eyes on the floor. "How do you know that?" I whisper. "You don't know. You're not a doctor."

"No. But the medical staff in there right now are some of the best. You don't get a job working for—" He swallows his words. "For their organisation without being better than everyone else."

"What if it's not enough?"

"And what if it is?" he counters.

"I need her, Dad. I need—" A sob cuts off my words.

"Bloody hell, Oakley," he sighs, not sounding quite as sure of himself as he was only seconds ago.

His shadow falling over me forces my eyes from the floor, and I look up just in time to see him sliding down the wall opposite me.

Christian Beckworth sitting on the floor of a bathroom, who'd have thought it?

He looks at me with a mix of compassion and understanding in his eyes. Any sign of Christian the defence lawyer is gone. My father is fully present.

"Dad," I sigh, barely keeping my shit together.

"She's got a head injury, Oak. Her body is weak. She needs medical attention and rest. But she's young and fit and—"

"You're guessing," I spit.

"Trust them. They know what they're doing."

"But what happens then? Thomas doesn't want me anywhere near her. I thought... I hoped he was just being a stubborn prick and that when we got her back that he'd... I dunno. Maybe it was stupid."

"He's scared, Oak. His only daughter was abducted by the son of a man he put inside years ago."

"So much for all the moral high ground shit," I mutter.

"He wants her safe just as much as you do. And to him, we're the enemy."

"That's fucking rich when we're the ones who found her. If it weren't for you then—" I swallow down the words. "It's not fair. I need her too."

"Give him time, Oak. If it were you or Liv in there, I'd be a selfish prick too."

"You wouldn't stop Reese if it were Liv."

"The situation is entirely different."

"Maybe. But that's not the point."

Silence falls between us, the lingering scent of my vomit and the god-awful pine air freshener that's in here somewhere making my top lip curl in disgust.

"Say that was Fiona in there." He visibly shudders at my suggestion. "Would you be happy being locked out? Letting someone else support her?"

He shakes his head, his lips pressed into a thin line.

"Oakley," Dad says, his voice all business once more.

I look up, meeting eyes that look so much like my own, I wait for what's coming next.

"Do you think she's the one?"

My breath catches, my heart aches. "Yes," I whisper. "I... I've fallen in love with her."

Dad sucks in a deep breath, although he doesn't look entirely shocked by my confession. More resigned.

"Why don't you see if you can go and find us coffee? I'll see if there's an update."

"Don't you mean, you'll sort out a way for me to be with her?"

"One thing at a time, Oak." His lips purse. "Let's just focus on getting her better, yeah?"

Obviously, I can't argue with that. Climbing to my feet, my body aches as I move toward the basin and wash my hands. I hate the version of myself that stares back at me, but there's very little I can do about it. And until I find a way to hold her in my arms again, I'm not sure it'll get any better.

It takes a bit of searching but eventually, I stumble across vending machines, I punch the buttons for two black coffees, praying they're not going to taste like shit, before selecting the biggest chocolate bar I can find inside the one beside it.

The shitty plastic cups do very little to insulate the boiling liquid and by the time I get to the waiting room Dad and I were ushered to when we first go here, my fingers are burning.

Lowering one cup onto an end table, I take a sip of the other. Bitter, cheap coffee floods my mouth. But as disgusting as it is, it's not enough to stop me. I need it. The warmth, the caffeine.

I down the lot despite it being too hot and then I rip into the chocolate. But I barely taste it, and not just because I singed a layer of skin off my tongue.

Everything other than the pain in my chest is muted right now. And it'll remain the same until I get to look into her eyes and confess to her what I did to my dad in that bathroom. Because it's true. Seeing her so small and helpless on that gurney only cemented what I already knew.

I'm in love with Tallulah Darlington.

I have fallen in love with Tallulah goody-two-shoes Darlington.

I'm shaking my head in disbelief at myself when Dad slips from the room she's inside.

"What's wrong?" he asks, his brows dipped low.

"Nothing. Everything. How is she?"

"Stable. She just needs time. She's been through a lot."

I breathe a sigh of relief. "Can I see her?"

"Oak," he sighs.

"This is bullshit, Dad," I hiss.

"I know. But it's going to take time. They're going to monitor her here for a few hours then see if they can move her home. Once she's there, I'll speak to Thomas again, see if we can talk some sense into him."

I scoff. Aware of just how unlikely that is.

"You need to come up with something epic, Oakley."

"What for?" I ask, confused.

"If you want to prove to him how you feel about her. If you want him on side. You're going to need to pull something out of the bag that is going to convince him. I hate to say it, but just standing there and confessing your undying love isn't going to cut it."

"Brilliant," I mutter.

"If you truly love her, it shouldn't be too hard."

"I do," I argue, hating that he's questioning me and my feelings for her.

"Then it's time to step up and really prove it. To Thomas. To Tally. To everyone."

Fantastic.

Time to put my heart on the line and hope she doesn't stomp all over it.

In public.

21

TALLY

After two days hooked up to a drip in the strange room I woke up in, my father finally took me home.

Thankfully, he didn't try to make me stay in my bedroom—a room I'm not sure I'll ever be able to stay in again after learning Kane Alveston was the one who broke in. Instead, he and Mum had moved more of my things into the guest room. They wanted me to be comfortable.

I'm not sure that's something I'll feel again in a hurry. But they were trying.

Every time I close my eyes, I see him. Watching me. That dark glint in his eyes filled with hatred and revenge. He's gone, I know that. My father told me as much. But I still feel him.

Things aren't much better between me and Dad. He's apologised over and over but words won't fix everything that's happened.

I know it's not his fault, I do. Yet there's a small part of me that can't separate what I endured with the fact that it was all some sick and twisted scheme to make him pay.

We haven't talked about it. I can't.

I won't.

I know part of me should feel lucky things didn't go

further than me being drugged and beaten but I'm not there yet. I'm angry and bitter and broken.

And now I'm a prisoner in my own home.

At least, that's what it feels like. My phone is gone. I've had no visitors. And my parents want me to take the rest of the term off to recover—emotionally and physically.

But that isn't even the worst of it.

The worst part is the gnawing guilt I feel over the fact that I blamed Oakley. I put two and two together and made five.

It was easier to point the finger at him for stealing the key and using it to break into the house and trash my room, rather than hear him out and risk disappointing my father.

A knock at the door pulls me from my thoughts and it opens, Mum's weary face appearing. "You're awake." She smiles but it doesn't reach her eyes.

She's aged years since I got home. Since she saw the state I was in.

"Hi, Mum."

"Oh, sweetheart." Rushing to my side, she perches on the edge of the bed and takes my hand in hers. "How are you feeling?"

"I'm okay."

"You know, you don't have to do that, Tallulah. You don't have to try and be brave, not around me. What you went through—"

"Please, don't." A violent shudder rolls through me. "I know you want to talk about it, but I can't, Mum. I can't do it."

"Okay, sweetheart, okay." She brushes the flyaway hairs out of my face and smiles down at me again. "Your father is beside himself. I'm worried about him."

"I don't know what you want me to say."

"Nothing, Tally. You don't need to say anything. I just want you to know that we're here for you, okay."

I nod because what else can I do?

This feels like an impossible situation.

"Did you get me another phone? I'd like to text the girls."

Her expression tightens. "I'm not sure that's a good idea yet. You're still recovering and—"

"Dad doesn't want me talking to Olivia?" I arch a brow, the skin around my eyes pinching, making everything hurt.

"That's not—"

"Mum."

"He's concerned, sweetheart. We both are. Oakley Beckworth—"

"Oakley's dad saved me, Mum. Without their help, things might have ended a lot differently."

Dad and I might not have talked much since I woke up, but I got the CliffsNotes version as I drifted in and out of consciousness.

I remember Christian being there. Remember the torment in Oakley's voice as he called out for me.

He was there.

And my father sent him away.

I get it and yet, my heart—my stupid, fickle heart—won't accept it.

"Do you have any idea how hard it was for your father accepting Christian's help? If there had been another way—"

"I'm tired." I turn away from her, not willing to do this.

"Tallulah, please..."

I stay silent, swallowing the tears burning my throat. I didn't expect her to understand, she always sides with my father. They're a team.

But it doesn't stop it from hurting.

With a gentle sigh, she gives my hand a squeeze before whispering, "Get some rest, I'll check in on you later."

I don't answer.

Sometimes saying nothing is easier than saying all the things you want to say.

Two days later, I'm not sure I can take a second longer of being cooped up in my room. My parents are all but avoiding me and they still haven't replaced my phone. Probably because they're worried I'll reach out to Oakley.

I'm not sure whether they're right or not.

Part of me is desperate to speak to him but the other part isn't sure where I'd even start.

So I keep those thoughts shelved for another day. Locked tightly in a box labelled Oakley.

A box I might never revisit.

I'm not ready to go back to school yet, to face everyone, the rumours that are no doubt circling. But I feel like I'm going out of my mind, lying here everyday, reliving things. Playing every second of that nightmare over and over until—

"Tallulah, sweetheart, are you awake?"

"Yeah, Mum," I call.

"You have a visitor."

I do?

My heart leaps into my throat, my mind instantly going to Oakley. But then I realise that she would never allow him to visit me. Even if Dad isn't here.

"Abigail stopped by to see how you are."

"Hi." She steps out from behind my mum and smiles.

"Tally's been really quite poorly," Mum says, keeping up the ruse that I've been sick. "But she's starting to feel much better. I'll leave you girls in peace. If you need anything just shout."

"Thanks, Mrs. Darlington." Abi takes a seat next to me, her gaze sweeping over my face, taking in my injuries. "Thank God you're okay," she whispers as Mum leaves us alone. "I've been so worried."

"What do you know?" I ask.

"That you were taken. That Liv's dad helped get you back. No one will tell me much else."

"It's probably best you don't know."

"Tally..."

"I'm okay." Tears prick the corners of my eyes. "I'm okay."

"I came before but they wouldn't—"

"I know. They've got me on lockdown. I think they're scared in case..." I trail off, unsure how that sentence ends.

Part of me knows they're scared after what happened with Alveston but I also wonder if they're just trying to delay the inevitable.

"Oakley..." I can't resist asking. "Have you seen him?"

"Only the day you disappeared. He was beside himself, Tally. I don't think I've ever seen him like that before."

"Have you talked to Liv?"

She nods. "She wanted to come with me but thought your parents might not appreciate it."

"I need to see her, Abi."

If I can't see him, I need to talk to the person closest to him.

"Okay. I'll tell her. Do you think your mum and dad—"

"It isn't their decision. I'm eighteen. They can't keep me locked up forever."

Soon I'll be strong enough to leave the house. I'll return to All Hallows' and have to face reality.

I'll see Oakley.

I don't know what I will say to him when I do, but we need closure. I need to apologise. I need to—

"Deacon and his friends jumped him," Abi blurts. "Oakley was convinced he was behind you going missing. Things got... ugly."

"Oh my God," I breathe.

"Things have been crazy, Tally."

"Tell me about it," I murmur.

"I'm sorry." Her expression softens. "I can't even begin to imagine what you've been through. If you want to talk about it, I'm here."

"I don't." I never want to relive it again. "But thanks."

"They're telling everyone you've been sick?" I nod and she adds, "I guess it's safer that way."

"Yeah. They talked to Mr. Porter. I'm not sure what they told him, but he agreed I don't have to return to classes until after the Christmas break."

"That long?"

I nod again. "They're just trying to protect me."

"Or keep you away from him." She gives me a pointed look.

"Abi..."

"Don't tell me you agree with them? You didn't see how worried he was, Tally. I know things are a mess, but he cares about you. Oakley—"

"Don't, please just don't."

"Sorry." Her phone vibrates and she digs it out of her pocket. "Crap. It's my dad, I need to go."

"Is everything okay?"

"He's not feeling so good."

"You should go but thank you for coming."

"Of course." She stands. "I'll tell Liv you want to see her."

"Thank you. I'm hoping my parents will replace my phone soon."

If they don't it's going to be another thing we fall out over. I can't be cut off from the rest of the world forever.

"And if I see Oakley," she says, "what should I tell him?"

"I... tell him I'm fine."

"Tally..."

"Please, Abi."

"Fine." She moves to the door. "But I think you're making a mistake."

"My parents will never accept him."

"But what about you, Tally? What about what *you* want?"

"I..."

I press my lips together, trapping any reply I might have. Because the truth is, I don't know what to say.

She's right.

Of course she's right.

But it isn't that simple.

"It's okay to choose something for you, you know." A faint smile traces her mouth. "You're not their little girl anymore. You don't have to live to make them happy. Just think about it."

She grabs the door handle, pausing at the last second and glancing back at me. "Because Tally, if you don't find a way to talk to Oakley soon, I'm not sure anyone will stop him from trying to see you."

22

OAKLEY

The Darlington's changed the locks.

That's the first thing I discovered when they finally brought Tally home. As soon as darkness fell that night, I was slipping through the shadows and waiting for a sign that her parents had gone to bed. But it was pointless because the second I tried to push the key into the lock, I had confirmation of what I already knew.

I'd been locked out.

I was hardly surprised. After what happened, I'd have changed the locks too. But I needed to cling onto something. Some kind of hope that I'd be able to get to her after being forced to the sidelines by the security. Thomas made it more than clear that I was allowed nowhere near her, and they sure followed orders.

The day after my failed break-in, I grew a pair of balls and boldly walked up to the front door ready to bleed my heart out all over Thomas Darlington's feet for the chance just to see her. Even if she was sleeping. I just needed to lay my eyes on her to reassure myself that she really was okay.

But I got exactly nowhere.

He point blank refused to listen to anything I had to say and eventually I had little choice but to follow his order and get off his property before he had the cops do it for him.

Overkill if you ask me but the prick never did listen to reason. Well, aside from the day he came to Dad for help to get Tally back. And thank fuck he did. Because if it weren't for him sharing the messages he was receiving from Alveston then we might still be scrambling around now trying to find her. And with every day that passed, they had even more chances to hurt her. To take her from me in more ways than she already had been.

So with my tail between my legs, I reluctantly left. I needed alcohol to drown all this shit out more than I needed to spend the night in a fucking cell.

So here I am, four days after she's been released, and I haven't seen or heard anything from her. All I know is that she's okay.

Her parents have had her locked down like she's some kind of criminal and from what the guys have said. And they've fed Mr. Porter some line about her being really ill, and that it's unlikely that she'll be back before Christmas.

There's no way I can wait until next year to see her.

Next fucking year.

The guys have tried everything they can think of to get me to go back to school and practice. I know that Coach is going to have my arse for missing so much but without her, it all feels pointless. Plus, they don't really need me. They won their last game by a fucking mile.

They don't need me. Tally apparently doesn't either.

What's the fucking point?

I fall back in my bed with a groan, the room spinning around me just like it has for the last few days. Being drunk or high makes it easier to forget what a waste of fucking space I am.

I couldn't keep Tally safe from Misty, or Deacon. So I stood no chance against Alveston.

Even if I could get into her house, why would she want to see me?

I've no idea what time it is, but there are voices rumbling downstairs, so it's past four at least. Since I stopped leaving my room, they seem to have stopped coming by to check on me.

Fine by me. All they want to do is talk about what happened and tell me about what I missed at school and why I need to come back.

Even hearing from Reese that he and Theo beat the shit out of Seb as payback for everything he's been involved in with Tally didn't perk me up all that much. I should have been the one to deliver that message. But I couldn't even do that.

Footsteps pound up the stairs but I barely even flinch. They won't be coming here.

I sigh, closing my eyes.

"Wait, you'll probably regret this," Reese says, but whoever he's talking down doesn't seem to heed the warning because not a second later, my door flies open, slamming back against the wall.

"What the fu— Abi?"

Pushing myself so I'm resting back in my palms, Abi stares at me as if I'm some kind of extraterrestrial creature. She swallows nervously, heat blooming on her cheeks.

It's only as I register her embarrassment that I remember I'm only in a small pair of boxers.

"I... um... could you put some clothes on?" she says, her eyes locked on the wall.

Another door opens down the hallway, footsteps heading our way before Reese steps aside to allow Elliot to march in, demanding to know what's going on.

"Oh my God," Abi gasps, but this time she doesn't avert her eyes quite so quickly. Instead, she blatantly ogles our leader's exposed chest and abs.

I mean, I guess I can't really blame her. He is pretty cut.

We all are. Probably explains why she looks like she might combust any second.

"Don't any of you wear any clothes here?" she mutters under her breath.

"Me," Reese announces happily.

"Makes a change. What's going on, Abi?" Elliot asks, holding her eyes, making her cheeks blaze brighter.

"Um..." She wrings her hands in front of her nervously. "I've just seen Tally, and I—"

"OUT," I bellow at two of my best friends. "Get the fuck out."

They both hesitate for a few seconds, but after sharing a loaded look, they finally move, closing the door behind them.

"You saw her?" I ask, shifting to the edge of my bed as Abi continues to stand awkwardly by the door.

"Y-yeah. She said to tell you that she's okay," she whispers, still looking anywhere but at me.

Pushing to my feet, I stumble slightly toward my chest of drawers and pull out a pair of sweats. Lowering down to put them on, I shove my right leg in and then lift the other.

But no sooner has my foot left the floor do I start wobbling.

"Oh fuck," I grunt before toppling to the floor in a heap with my sweats around my ankles.

The whisky I've drunk and the unrelenting pain in my chest makes me delirious and I start laughing. It's either that or crying and I point blank refuse to do that in front of anyone.

"Oakley? Oak?" Abi's concerned voice finally breaks through my hysteria and after blinking away the tears filling my eyes, I find her on her haunches beside me with a deep frown on her brow. "Are you okay?"

"No, Abi. I'm not fucking okay. I need her. I fucking need her and they're keeping her from me."

Abi deflates, her entire body shrinking before my eyes

before she drops to her arse and rests against the wall behind me.

Finally, I pull my sweats up and sit beside her.

"I'm sorry. I tried to talk to her, I swear I did."

"None of this is your fault," I say, resting my elbows on my knees and hanging my head. "She's too good for me anyway. Maybe this is how it should be."

Abi shifts a little beside me, but it's not enough to make me look up. "Look, Oakley," she says timidly. "I won't lie to you, on the face of it, yes, she is too good for you. Your reputation around school precedes you. But Tally is no idiot, and if she decided you were worthy of her time, then I trust her judgement."

"Thanks," I mutter.

"She needs you to fight for her, Oak. Prove to Mr. Darlington that you're worthy of his only daughter."

"You really think there is anything I can do that will be good enough, meaningful enough to convince him?"

"I don't know, Oak. That's for you to figure out."

A soft knock fills the room before the door is pushed open and another girl slips into my room.

Considering that not so long ago, our inner sanctum of the first floor of this building was strictly female-free, I think I'm doing okay.

"Hey," Abi says, finding Liv watching us curiously. "Reese said you were up here. How was Tally?"

"Barring up. Her parents are driving her crazy."

Liv scoffs. "She's not the only one. She's eighteen for fuck's sake. That can't keep her locked up like this. It's not right."

"She knows. And something tells me that as soon as she's strong enough, she'll fight it."

"Good. That's good."

Liv and Abi share a look and have a silent conversation that has Abi climbing from the floor.

"I'll text you later," Liv promises before giving her friend a hug and allowing her out of the room. "Why are we sitting on the floor?" she asks, lowering down beside me.

"It's where I fell," I confess.

The warmth of her hand landing on my shoulder makes me flinch. I want to fight her, but I don't have the strength to do so. And honestly, her touch feels too good.

"Oak," she sighs.

"I don't need your sympathy, Liv."

"Well, what do you need then? Because locking yourself in your room getting wasted isn't really getting you anywhere."

"Isn't it?" I say, shrugging my shoulders. "It makes it all easier."

"No, it doesn't. It smothers it. The pain will still be there when you finally get sober."

"If that's meant to help convince me to stop drinking then I've gotta tell you—"

"Oakley," she snaps, cutting me off. "You need to stop this pity party. It's not going to get you anywhere. Look," she says, shuffling to her knees and staring me down. "This situation fucking sucks. What do you want me to say? But you have the power to fix it. You just need—"

"No, I don't. Thomas is adamant I can't see her, that we can't be together. What am I meant to do with that?"

"Prove him fucking wrong. You're not a bad person, Oak. Show him that everything he thinks about you is fake." Finally, I glance up at her, lifting one brow. "Fine, okay. Maybe not as bad as he thinks."

My laugh is hollow and full of pain. "What's the point? She doesn't want me. She doesn't feel for me what I feel for her."

"Are you kidding?"

I shrug. "I love her, Liv," I say, wincing as the words spill from my lips.

I don't look up again, I can't risk seeing the sympathy on her face.

"I love her, I'm trying here but she's not interested."

"You really are a fucking idiot."

"Jeez, talk about kicking me when I'm down."

"Oakley, you kissed her at the very first Heirs party she attended and then forgot about it the second your lips parted."

My breath catches. Everything falling into place.

I kissed her... I fucking kissed her and I forgot.

Fuck.

"You walked away from her and then immediately kissed someone else—Misty, might I add—in front of her."

"Exactly. I'm a prick." Self-loathing curls in my gut. How could I ever forget her? "Why would she want me?"

"Oak, that affected her so much that she stood in front of the whole sixth form and started a war against you."

"Should have seen it coming really, shouldn't I?" A bitter laugh spills off my lips.

God, I'm such a fuck up.

She tried to tell... Tally tried to tell me over and over and I didn't want to hear it.

"You might have done if you weren't so wasted you forgot kissing her. It was her first kiss, Oak."

"What are you trying to say here, Liv? Because right now, you're giving me even more reasons why she should hate me."

Liv sighs. "Do you think that if she didn't care she'd risk her reputation like she has just to prove a point? Do you think she'd have put herself right in your firing line if she didn't want your attention?"

"She wanted revenge," I mutter.

"She wants you," Liv shrieks. "She loves you Oak, just like you do her. But she's scared, just like you are. There's always a lot to lose when you open up your heart to someone else. You need to trust them and right now, she's got her father in her ear telling her all the reasons she can't trust you. You've got to prove them wrong, Oak. Do you want her? Really want her?

"You know I do."

"Then get up off your arse and do something about it. Tally deserves a guy who's going to fight for her, stand up for her, show her and everyone who's doubting you just how much she means to you."

23

TALLY

Another two days.

I gave my parents another two days before I finally get showered and dressed and go downstairs, ready to state my case for why it is time they allow me to leave the house.

"Tally, sweetheart, what are you doing up?" Mum asks the second I enter the kitchen.

"Good morning to you too," I murmur, helping myself to a glass of orange juice.

"Sorry, baby. I just didn't expect to see you up and about so soon."

"It's been almost a week, Mum. I feel much better."

"That's good, sweetheart." She comes over and cups my face in her soft hands. "You're looking more like yourself."

I nod, offering her a smile. "So I was thinking… maybe I can go venture out today, go meet the—"

"Tally, you know you can't, not yet." Her expression drops. "It's too soon."

"Mum," I sigh. "I'm going out of my mind."

"Abi can stop by whenever you want, but please don't ask—"

"Seriously, Mum," I snap. "I need to get out of the house. I'm going crazy. You still haven't gotten me a new phone. Do you have any idea how isolating that is?"

"We just want to give you time to heal, baby. What you went through—"

"Don't." I jerk away from her touch. Because I'm not ready to do this. I prefer denial. I prefer shoving down all thoughts of my time in that ramshackle house, locking them away where they can't ever hurt me again.

"Tallulah, this isn't healthy."

"No, Mum. What's not healthy is the way you and Dad are keeping me a prisoner here."

Her sharp intake of breath makes me feel like the worst person ever, but I can't do it.

I can't stay locked up here for another minute.

"Your father—"

"You called." He appears in the door, frowning at my appearance. "What's going on?"

"I need to go out, Dad. I need to get some fresh air. Stretch my legs. See—"

"No." His eyes darken. "Absolutely not."

"Dad, come on... I'm better. I feel—"

"No, Tallulah. It's not happening. You went through a huge ordeal, sweetheart. You need time to recover. To process everything."

"Thomas, maybe we should consid—"

"No, Katherine. I will not have her leaving the house and heading straight across town to see... him." He practically spits the words.

"That's not—"

"It's bad enough he refuses to stay away," he mutters, and my head whips up.

"W-what?"

"Nothing." Dad backtracks. "It doesn't matter."

"Dad... what did you do?"

"What's best for you, since you seem so incapable of making good decisions where your future is concerned."

"Thomas!" Mum gasps as I stagger back as if his words are a physical blow.

They may as well have been.

"You think I asked for any of this?" I stare at him with utter disbelief, swallowing down the emotion clogged in my throat.

"That boy is nothing but trouble." Disappointment coats every word. "He will ruin you, Tallulah. Why can't you see that? Why can't you just—"

"Ruin me? *Ruin me?*" I shriek, my voice trembling. "Oakley didn't kidnap me, Dad. He didn't break into my room and leave dead animals in my bed. He didn't drug and beat me. He didn't—"

"Tallulah," Mum snaps, her expression full of pain. "Enough. This isn't helping anything."

"You're right." I stare at them.

My parents.

The people supposed to love me unconditionally.

"I'm going out before one of us says something we can't take back."

"I'm sorry, sweetheart." Dad steps in front of me, apology shining in his eyes. "But that isn't going to happen."

"Y-you can't stop me, Dad. I'm eighteen. I'm—"

"You're my daughter. You live under my roof. You're still recovering. And I refuse to let you leave this house and run off to that... that bad seed."

"Mum?" I search her face for any signs that she'll side with me on this.

"Tallulah..." She implores, and I have my answer.

"I see. So it isn't bad enough that I was taken against my will and kept a prisoner, now I'm a prisoner in my own home too."

"Tally"—Dad runs a hand down his face as he exhales a weary breath—"that's not—"

"I have always followed your rules. I have chased your dreams. Lived the life you wanted for me. But at what expense? I have no friends. No social life. No life experience."

That isn't entirely true anymore, but they don't need to know that.

"My entire life has been about pleasing you. Making you proud. And the first time I veer from your path for me, you act like I'm the disappointment of the century. I'm still me, Dad. I'm still Head Girl. I'm still top of my class. I still do my coursework and meet all of my deadlines. It would be nice to think that I'd earned your trust."

"Sweetheart, we're just worried. Oakley Beckworth is trouble. He isn't good enough for you."

"He's also the reason I'm standing here now." I give them a sad, defeated smile.

They aren't going to budge. Not now. Not tomorrow.

Not ever.

"We'll talk about this later," Dad checks his watch. "I've got an important video call to take."

"Fine." I concede. Because all the fight I felt earlier when I came downstairs has withered away thanks to my rant.

To his cruel words.

"I'll be in my room."

"Sweetheart, you don't have to go back upstairs," Mum says.

I'm already gone though, storming out of the kitchen without another word.

But I don't let the tears fall until I'm safely in my room where they can't hear me break.

That evening when I wake up after a two-hour nap, I find a brand new phone on the end of my bed with a note from my father.

I'm sorry.
Love, Dad xx

It doesn't undo his words from earlier, the pain he inflicted, but it does give me a connection to the outside world.

And for that, I'm grateful.

I unpack the box and switch it on, relieved that the battery is already charged. A fresh wave of irritation rolls through me though when I realise he's registered it to a new number.

I won't be able to text Abigail or Liv, but I can log into my social media accounts and try and contact them that way.

> Tally: I finally have a new phone.

> Liv: Thank God. New number?

> Tally: Yes. Can you text it to Abi too, please?

> Liv: Of course. What about Oakley?

> Tally: I… not yet, Liv. I need some more time.

> Liv: Okay, but you can't avoid him forever.

> Tally: I know.

Unable to stop myself, I search for Oakley's profile and scroll through his latest photos. But there's nothing since the night of the Halloween party.

It's as if his life just stopped.

I shut down those thoughts. Liv is right, I can't avoid him forever. I don't want to. But I also don't know what I'll say to him.

Where I'll even begin.

My phone vibrates and I expect to see Abi's number. Only it isn't.

> Unknown: Tally... Prim...

My heart stops dead in my chest until anger and betrayal slam into me as I aggressively type out a new message to Olivia.

> Tally: You gave him my number.

> Liv: This is Oakley we're talking about. I didn't give him anything. He stole my phone the second he realised I was messaging you.

> Tally: I don't know what to say to him.

> Liv: Maybe try the truth.

The truth.

That sounds easy enough. But I know better. Because things are such a mess.

I am a mess.

Another text comes through. I save Oakley's number and then read his latest message.

> Oakley: Please, Prim. Not being able to see you is killing me. It's killing me, babe.

> Tally: How are you?

I go with something simple. Something safe.

> Oakley: Me? You're asking me how I am?

> Tally: You were hurt...

And there it is. The wreckage—and reality—of our relationship. Deacon and his entitled, elitist friends hurt Oakley... because of me.

Because no matter how much I've tried to fight the patriarchal traditions of this town, to leverage myself above that old-fashioned way of thinking, I'm still viewed as nothing more than a possession. A prize to be coveted. A trophy to be won.

A pawn in a game I can never win.

> Oakley: It doesn't matter. I can take whatever Warrick and his friends dish out. I'd take it ten times over if it meant you were safe. That you'd never gotten hurt... Fuck, Prim. I don't know how to do this. I don't know how to fix this.

The honesty in his words floor me. Oakley is an Heir. He doesn't acknowledge his flaws, he doesn't need to. But something has changed in him. I watched it happen right before my eyes every time we were together.

He cares.

I'm just not sure whether it will ever be enough.

> Tally: Tell your dad thank you. He saved my life.

> Oakley: Tell him yourself.

> Tally: I don't think that's a good idea, do you?

> Oakley: I need to see you. I'm done waiting. Done obeying your father's rules. If you can't come to me, I'm coming to you.

> Tally: Oakley you can't... Not yet.

I need more time. Time to figure out what I want. What I need to say to him.

> Oakley: 24 hours, Prim. You get 24 hours and then I'm coming for you.

A shiver runs through me because I know he means it.

Patience is not one of Oakley's better qualities and I don't doubt if I don't find a way to see him, he would turn up on my

doorstep again.
Consequences be damned.

24

OAKLEY

Liv: You awake?

Oakley: It's six o'clock. I'm not a child.

Liv: You sulk like one.

Oakley: Says the girl who used to cry every time you lost a board game.

I smirk as I think back to that little girl. I've never met such a sore loser in my life. Okay, fine. That's a lie. All I have to do is look in the mirror. It was one of the reasons why I never let her win. She wasn't going to get a chance to see my tears when she beat me.

Liv: I was seven.

Oakley: You mean seventeen?

Liv: I hate you. And to think, I was going to do something nice for you.

Oakley: When has that ever happened?

Liv: You will regret it if I change my mind.

"Fucking doubt it." The reality is that I don't really have time for whatever she's suggesting.

The twenty-four hour warning I gave Tally is almost up and I fully intend on being outside her house, demanding she comes out and faces me no matter what.

Thomas can threaten me all he likes, but Tally is an adult now. I want to hear it from her own lips if she doesn't want to talk to me. Not his.

> Oakley: What do you want?

> Liv: Touchy touchy...

> Oakley: Olivia...

> Liv: Fine. Come meet me down at the rock in ten minutes.

> Oakley: I'm not doing fucking yoga with you. I don't care how relaxing you tell me it is or how much Reese loves it. I am not bending like a pretzel.

> Liv: I bet I can convince you.

> Oakley: No chance. I need a better offer to get me out in the cold tonight.

> Liv: I've already got your guilty pleasure. Just be there.

I lick my lips, thinking of the little lemon meringue pies that Mum used to make for us when we were little. Whenever Liv means business and really wants to cheer me up—or really wants me to agree to something—she cracks out the recipe.

> Oakley: Fine but I want the whole tin.

> Liv: Demanding dick. You'll get what you're given.

> Oakley: I'm sorry. Did you want me there or not?

> Liv: You'll be there.

"Ugh," I grunt. Her confidence in her ability to predict my actions is annoying as fuck.

Swinging my legs off the bed, then I pad through to the bathroom to take a piss and throw myself through the shower.

My hair is still wet when I tug my hood up over my head and head out in the bitterly cold evening.

"This had better be good, Beckworth," I mutter to myself as I make my way through the trees toward where the rock sits.

"Liv?" I call into the darkness when I don't see any sign of another person out here. "I swear to God, if you're fucking with me, I'll—"

"Chill the fuck out, Oak," my sister calls.

I spin around, trying to pinpoint where her voice came from, but I still can't see her.

A twig snaps behind me and I spin around. But I don't find my sister standing there with a tin full of lemony goodness in her hands.

But instead—

"Tally," I breathe, barely able to believe that she's really standing before me.

"Hey," she says, proving that she's not just a figment of my imagination.

"Fuck, Tally. I can't believe you're here."

Before she has a chance to say anything, I close the space between us and pull her into my arms. Her body melts against mine, her arms wrapping around my waist and holding on tight.

Dipping my head, I press my nose into her hair and breathe her in. Sucking in a shaky breath, I fight to swallow down the lump of emotion that blocks my throat.

"You're here," I whisper, still convinced that I might actually be dreaming.

"Oakley," she croaks, making my chest crack open.

"Fuck, Prim. I can't even begin to tell you how much I've fucking missed you."

"Me too," she confesses quietly.

"Look at me," I demand, gently tugging on the end of her ponytail to encourage her out of my chest.

Her blue tear-filled eyes glitter under the bright moonlight we're bathed in.

"Tallulah, I—"

My words are cut off when she reaches up on her tiptoes and presses her lips to mine.

"Oh shit, yeah," I groan, tilting my head to the side and licking across the seam of her lips.

The second she opens for me, I plunge my tongue into her mouth, hungrily seeking out her own, desperate to drown in the kiss.

She hesitates to start with, making my pulse pick up for all the wrong reasons.

If she pulls away now after turning up here to surprise me then I'll break. Everything I've been through in the past few weeks will be nothing compared to watching her walk away after giving me this little bit of hope.

But then with one more slide of my tongue against hers, she jumps off the cliff with me. Her fingers curl in my hoodie at my sides, holding us together as we remember everything we found in each other before all this bullshit.

Needing more, I take a step forward, backing her toward the rock. She gasps the second her back presses against the cold, unforgiving stone behind her.

Her ice-cold hands slip under my hoodie, making a violent shiver rip down my spine. It ends right in my cock, making me even more desperate for her.

"Are you still in pain? Have you healed?" I ask breathlessly, our lips still connected.

She blinks up at me, her breath racing over my face and her hands gripping my sides as if she's scared I'll walk away.

"I'm fine," she whispers into my mouth.

"Will I hurt you if I—"

"If you what?"

Challenge glitters in her eyes and I happily accept.

"This," I grunt, wrapping my hands around the back of her thighs and lifting her, pinning her to the rock with my hips. "You wore a skirt," I groan into her ear before nipping her lobe between my teeth. "It's almost as if you came with this in mind."

"I came to talk," she argues, making me chuckle against the sensitive skin beneath her ear.

"How's that going for you, Prim?"

"You don't follow the rules, Oakley Beckworth."

"Never. Where's the fun in that?"

She cries out as I suck on her skin, marking her as mine as my hand finds its way between us.

"So wet for me, Prim. Have you been thinking about this since Halloween?"

"Maybe," she gasps as I rub her over the lace of her knickers.

"I don't need a verbal answer, Prim. Your body is giving me the truth."

"Oh fuck," she cries, making me smile against her neck.

"Fucking love it when you lose control. Love hearing my prim and proper Head Girl swearing like a trooper because of what I'm doing to her body."

"Yes, yes, more," she begs as I circle her clit.

"Need you, Tally. All I've been able to think about is you. Not having you here, it fucking ripped me apart. I'd have burned the world down to find you, I hope you know that."

"Doesn't matter," she says, trying to push it aside.

"It does matter. I never would have stopped looking. Never."

"Please, Oakley," she whimpers, forcing me to dip my fingers lower.

A growl rips from my throat when I find her dripping for me. I push two fingers deep inside her, curling them in a way that will ensure I find her G-spot.

"Oh fuck. Fuck. Yes, right there."

My heart swells within the confines of my chest as I build her higher and higher. Her head falls back against the rock, her eyes closing as she begins to fall.

"Eyes, Tallulah. I want you to see who is doing this to you."

It takes a few seconds for my demand to register in her lust-filled head. But when it does, her eyes flicker open before locking on mine.

"That's it, baby. I want you looking straight into my eyes as I make you come."

Her lips are parted as she heaves out her breath.

"And you're going to scream my name into the darkness as you fall just to remind yourself of who this pussy belongs to."

"Yes," she whispers.

Pressing my thumb against her clit, I fuck her deeper, harder with my fingers, pushing her over the edge in only a few more seconds.

"OAKLEY," she screams just like I told her to.

"Fuck yeah," I grunt as she squeezes me unbelievably tight.

My cock jerks and my balls ache with the need to find my own release inside her. "Don't get any ideas, Prim. We're not done yet."

A little awkwardly, I manage to shove my sweats and boxers down over my ass, freeing my cock. "Hold my shoulders," I demand so I can release her enough to drag her knickers aside and line myself up with her entrance. "Ready?" I ask, needing to take a second to compose myself.

"I'm not sure I'll ever be ready for you, Oakley," she confesses.

"I can live with that."

Taking her lips in a wet and dirty kiss, I thrust my hips forward, filling her quickly. She's so slick she accepts my size easily, but despite my need to relentlessly pound into her, I force myself to hold still for a beat.

I don't want to hurt her any more than she already has been, even if it practically kills me to do so.

It's her.

It's always been her.

"Please," she whimpers, rolling her hips, showing me that she's ready. That she needs me as fiercely as I need her.

"With pleasure."

Tightening my hold on her hips, I pull almost all of the way out before thrusting back inside. But no matter how deep I get, it's never enough.

And it never will be.

"Missed you, Tally. Missed you so fucking much. I was so scared. When I heard you'd gone... never felt anything like it. Can't live without you. Mine. You're mine." Confessions spill from my lips without instruction from my brain as I take her, reminding both of us that we're here, that she's okay, that despite everything surrounding us, mainly her father, that we can still be the Tally and Oak we found sneaking around in the shadows before all of this.

She still lights me up from the inside out, and from the way she's becoming undone beneath my hands, my thrusts, I think she might just be too.

"Oakley, yes. Please. Fuck... Harder."

Her pleas for more spur me on and I've soon pushed her injuries and everything we've both been through as I rut into her.

I'm probably fucking up her back on the rock, but I can't find it in me to care as we both close in on our releases.

As her pussy clamps me impossibly hard, my dick swells.

"Come with me, baby. I need to feel you squeezing me."

"Yes. Make me come all over your cock, Oakley Beckworth."

"Fuck, I love it when you lose your mind. I love yo—"

"OAKLEY," she screams, cutting off my confession and dragging me under with her.

"Tallulah. Fuck, yes. Tally. My Prim. Fuck. You're everything."

She rests her head on my shoulder, as we both come down from our highs. I kiss her hair over and over, wishing we could go back and do it all over again. And again.

And again.

"Every-fucking-thing, Tally. We're going to find a way through this. I promise you. You're mine. And that isn't changing. Ever."

25

TALLY

My heart crashes in my chest as Oakley lies over me on the rock.

Oh God.

What have we done?

What have I done?

I didn't come here for... for this.

But the second I laid eyes on him, all the emotion and feelings I've tried so hard to keep locked away came hurtling back.

I love him.

I'm in love with Oakley Beckworth.

And the second he pulled me into his arms, I knew I was done for.

I can't walk away.

I don't want to.

I cling onto him tighter, anchoring us together.

"Hey," he pulls back slightly to look at me. "What's wrong?"

"I... God, Oakley, I was so scared. I-I thought..." I suck in a sharp breath, blinking away the tears.

"Shit, shit." He finally pulls out of me, smothering an

agonised groan, as if it physically pains him to leave my body. "Prim, don't cry." He gently brushes his thumb over my cheeks, wiping away the tears. "I can't fucking bear it."

"Sorry, I just... I've been holding this all in."

"Fuck." He breathes. "Come on, let's go somewhere. Just you and me."

"Where?"

"My house."

Everything inside me goes still, fear clawing up my throat. "I-I can't."

"Yes, you fucking can." His expression darkens. "Your old man might not be ready to accept this, but my dad doesn't care. He just wants me to be happy, Prim."

"He does?"

"Yeah, so quit thinking whatever it is you're thinking and come home with me, okay?" He searches my eyes, so much vulnerability in his gaze. "Please, Prim. I need you. I need—"

"Yes, okay. I'll come home with you."

It's impossible to tell him no, and maybe I don't want to. Maybe I want to choose what makes me happy for once.

Oakley helps me clean up the best we can, and we walk hand in hand back through the woods to his house. It's a beautiful place, reminding me of the world they come from.

The world they live in.

"What?" he squeezes my hand as we stand at the front door.

"Nothing." I force a smile.

"It's okay to be nervous."

"I'm not. I just—"

The front door swings open and Liv appears, grinning. "About damn time."

"Hey," I say.

"I'd hug you but I'm not sure I want to after what I heard out there."

"Oh my God," I murmur, burying my face in Oak's shoulder, and he chuckles.

"Relax, I've heard much worse coming from my sister's bedroom. Oh Reese, God Reese, just like that. Right there."

"Wanker," Liv mutters, storming off into the house.

"Come on, we can grab something to eat and drink and go talk in my room."

It's weird, being here as Oakley's... well, whatever we are.

I know what I want to be, I just don't know how to broach it with him. He called me his just now but what does that mean when my father is dead set on keeping us apart?

"Oakley— ah, Miss Darlington." Christian Beckworth appears. "I was wondering how long it would take for Oakley to break the rules." A knowing smile tips his mouth.

"Actually, I came to him, sir."

"I see. Does your father—"

I shake my head. "And I would appreciate it if you didn't tell him. At least, not yet. Not until I've had time to sort through some things."

Oakley squeezes my hand in reassurance, and I glance up at him, a bolt of lightning going through me.

He looks at me with such love and devotion, I'd be lying if I didn't say it's a little overwhelming.

"I'll give you some time. But sneaking around behind his back won't help your cause."

"I know. But I can't stay in that house for a minute longer. Not after..." I inhale another sharp breath. "Thank you, Mr. Beckworth. For everything. For saving me."

"There might be differences between your father and I, but I'm not a bad person, Tallulah. My son loves you very much and he is one of the most important people in my life."

"Dad," Oakley chokes out as my cheeks turn a dark shade of pink.

Did he really just say that?

Oh my God.

"There's a lot we'll need to talk about soon enough. But you look tired." His eyes flick to Oakley and I want the ground to open up and swallow me.

He knows. Mr. Beckworth knows exactly where we've been and what we've been doing.

Dear God.

But he doesn't scold us. Instead, he gives me another warm smile. "You are always welcome here. I'm glad you're feeling better."

"Thank you, sir."

"Christian," he says. "Please call me Christian."

I give him a small nod, watching with disbelief as he walks down the hall and leaves us alone.

"That was a little weird."

"Nah, Prim. That was my old man's way of welcoming you to the family."

"What?" I blink up at him, dumbfounded but Oakley only laughs.

"Come on, babe. Let's go up to my room. Sustenance can wait, I need to be alone with you."

"Say something," I whisper as we lie side by side on Oakley's bed.

It doesn't matter that Liv's around here somewhere or that his dad is downstairs, I only have eyes for the boy next to me.

"I don't know where the fuck to start."

"Is it true?"

"Is what true?" His brow arches but I see the flash of possessiveness in his eyes.

"What your dad said?" My breath hitches.

"You heard that, eh?"

"Yeah. But if you don't—"

"Shit, Prim. Of course I do. I love you so fucking much it

scares the shit out of me. You're so good, baby, you're so fucking good, and I'm rotten to the core. I'm—"

"Don't." I slide a finger over his lips, trapping the words. "None of that matters now."

"No?" His eyes crinkle with emotion.

"No, because I love you too. I'm in love with you Oakley Beckworth. I have been for a little while now."

"You love me, Prim?"

I nod, and his arm slides over my waist, dragging me closer. "Yeah, I do."

"I can't believe I almost lost you." He tucks me into his chest and a shudder rips through me. "Do you want to talk about it?"

"I was so scared," I whisper. "I thought... for a second I thought it was Deacon and Misty or even—" I stop myself but Oakley nudges me backwards, forcing me to look at him.

"Me." Devastation bleeds into his expression. "You thought it was me and the Heirs."

"I didn't know what to think. Everything was so confusing. And I was pretty out of it."

"Fuck, Tally. I know things have been a mess but I would never—"

"I know. Deep down, I knew it wasn't you. But I think it was easier to tell myself that you were the villain in my story than admit that I'd fallen in love with you.

"I'm so used to being the good girl, Oak. The girl my parents expect me to be. I didn't know what to do with all these feelings I had for you. And when I thought you'd betrayed me with Misty—"

"You know I didn't, right? You know I had nothing to do with that?"

"I-I know. It was Alveston. All part of his sick and twisted revenge plan against my father."

"That's so messed up, baby. A high-profile crime family came after your dad, after you..."

"I know." I squeeze my eyes tight breathing through the agony crushing my lungs.

"No one... touched you, right?" They didn't—"

"No," I rush out. "Not in the way you mean."

"Fuck," he breathes, brushing the hair from my eyes. "I'm not sure I could have handled it if—" I flinch and he quickly adds, "Not like that. Nothing will ever change how I feel about you. But if I knew someone had touched you..."

His body trembles violently, pain etched into his expression. "You're here," he whispers, awed.

"I'm here." Taking his hand in mine, I press it against my chest, right over my heart. "Feel that." He nods and I smile. "It's yours now. Promise me you won't break it."

"I swear to you, I would rather die than ever hurt you again." Oakley touches his lips to my forehead, settling the storm raging inside of me.

"You know, my father—"

"Shh. We'll deal with your father when the time is right. Now I just want to lie here with you."

"Do they know?" I ask.

"Who?" A faint smirk traces his mouth.

"Oak..."

"Yeah, they know."

"I bet they're not happy—"

"Prim, listen to me and listen good. No one—not your father or my dad or Deacon fucking Warrick or my best friends—will ever change how I feel about you. I need you to believe me when I say nothing will come between us again. I won't let it."

"Okay."

"Besides, it was Reese and Theo who told me to pull my head out of my arse and go get my girl."

"They did?"

"Yeah"—he smiles—"they did. You're mine now. Which makes you theirs in a way."

My brows pinch at that, and he laughs. "I'm not sure I like the sound of that," I say. "I've spent my entire school life trying to fight against everything the Heirs stand for."

"That was before you got a taste of Heir dick."

"Oakley!" I go to slap him, but he catches my wrist and uses the momentum to roll me beneath him.

"Admit it, you love it."

"I'll never admit it."

"Fine." His expression darkens, making my stomach tighten with lust. "Then I'll just have to make you prove it."

He dives for me, nuzzling my neck with his lips and teeth and tongue. My laughter fills his bedroom, my heart racing in my chest.

He's so charming like this.

Grabbing my wrists, he pins my hands out of the way so I'm completely at his mercy, staring down at me with nothing but love and tenderness. "I love you, Tallulah Darlington."

"I love you too, Oakley Beckworth."

"Do you think you can be quiet?" A wicked glint flashes in his eyes.

"Why?" I frown.

"Because I need you again." His expression softens. "I'll never stop needing you."

26

OAKLEY

"What we had out there on the rock was only a starter, Prim," I groan into her neck as I lick a trail up her skin. Her taste explodes on my tongue and my cock weeps for her.

I need so much more from her after the time we've spent apart, the fear that's practically blinded me the entire time she's been gone. I've never felt so useless, helpless, in my entire life. It's something I never, ever want to experience again.

"Oakley," she moans as I slide my hands up the inside of her hoodie. She shudders at my touch, her skin burning up.

"Tell me you're okay, Tally."

Being outside under only moonlight it was easy to miss the lingering bruises and cuts she sustained under that monster's control. But here, under the bright light of my bedroom, I see them all. The slight darkening of skin under her eyes, the healing split in her lip.

It makes me savage to think of someone, anyone laying a hand on her.

"I'm okay. I want this," she moans when my hands slide around to her breasts. "Oh God."

"I love it when you lose control, when your mouth gets all filthy. And I'm the only one who knows about it."

Pulling the cups of her bra down, I pinch her nipples.

"Shit," she gasps, making me smile down at her.

"Eyes, Prim," I demand, and they immediately flutter open.

Something crackles between us as we still.

Seconds pass as we just stare at each other. My body begs for me to move, to take what I need, but I clearly have better self-control than she does, because she cracks first.

"More," she whispers, and despite it being so quiet I almost can't hear it over the blood rushing past my ears, it shatters my resolve.

Reluctantly, I release her in favour of dragging her hoodie up and over her head, her t-shirt quickly follows but I pause when I find an angry-looking scar on her stomach.

"Oh fuck, Tally." I still, my world crumbling around me once more.

"It's fine. Just waiting for the last few stitches to dissolve."

Lifting my hand, I gently trail one fingertip over the line. "I want to go and kill those motherfuckers all over again for this," I growl darkly.

"You don't have to. They're gone. They paid the ultimate price for what they did."

"No, they didn't. They didn't suffer for long enough. A lifetime of pain and misery wouldn't be enough for them laying a finger on you."

She pushes herself up, sitting so that we're chest to chest. Taking my face in her tiny hands, she looks into my eyes. "They tried to break me but didn't succeed. And if they didn't manage it, then I can promise you that you won't either. Stop treating me like I might shatter any minute. I won't." The strength in her eyes matches that in her words and I'm the one who breaks.

With one hand twisted in her hair and our lips joined, I

unsnap her bra with the other and drag it from her body. "You might regret that," I warn into our kiss.

"Doubt it," she mumbles. "I can handle the likes of Oakley Beckworth."

My chuckle mixes with her shriek of shock as I push her back to the bed.

"This skirt is cute and all. But it's served its purpose." I drag it and her knickers down her legs, throwing them to the floor behind me.

"Beautiful," I breathe, running my eyes over every inch of her.

Pink rises on her cheeks and spreads down onto her chest.

"And mine. All fucking mine."

Pressing my hands to her knees, I spread her legs wider. Her pussy glistens and it makes my mouth water.

"I don't even need to touch you to know how wet you are for me."

She rolls her hips in offering.

"Greedy girl. You remember my warning about being quiet?" I ask.

She nods, her eyes wide, the blue almost black with her hunger.

"Good. That starts now."

In a flash, I'm lying on my stomach and licking up the length of her. Her taste floods my mouth, making me desperate for more. For everything.

"Oakley," she moans loudly as I suck on her clit.

"Quiet," I growl, letting her feel the vibrations of my deep voice.

Clapping her hand over her mouth, she watches me with wide eyes as I continue eating her, alternating between me teasing her clit and plunging my tongue inside her.

She moans and cries out behind her hand, her back arching and her hips rolling in her need for more.

"I want you to come all over my face, Prim. Show me what a dirty, dirty girl you really are."

She cries out again. Even muffled behind her hand, it's loud enough to let anyone who might be outside my door know what's going down in here. I can't help but smirk at the thought. All the times I've been forced to endure Liv and Reese...

Payback really is a bitch.

"Come, Tally," I demand and one more graze of my teeth on her clit makes her fall.

Her hand falls limply onto the bed as she's consumed by pleasure, and she screams out my name.

On the other side of the bathroom, music is turned up and a booming laugh spills from my lips as I bring Tally back to Earth.

Fuck. Right now, life is fucking perfect.

Abandoning her on the bed, I make quick work of stripping naked and crawling back between her legs. "More?" I ask, working myself as I run the head of my cock through the evidence of her release that isn't covering my face.

"Always. Give me everything."

So I do. With her hips gripped tightly in my hands, I thrust forward, filling her to the hilt in one swift move.

She cries out again at the invasion.

"So much for being quiet," I mutter, not really giving a shit if everyone in the entire house hears us.

Her pussy tightens down on my dick and a deep growl rumbles in the back of my throat.

She's here. She's okay. And she's with me.

We might still have a fight on her hands when it comes to her father. But we'll figure that out. Together.

Sweat beads on my brow and runs down my back as I continue fucking her. Addicted to the feeling of her, the sight of her before me, and the noises she makes constantly, as I push her body higher again.

"Touch yourself," I demand, making her eyes widen.

"W-what?"

"Touch. Yourself," I repeat, my eyes locked on hers.

She hesitates, but after a few seconds, her hand slides from where it was gripping my thigh.

"Fuck," I bark the second I drop my eyes, watching her delicate fingers working her clit.

She clamps down on me so tightly I almost blow before she's ready.

Gritting my teeth, I slow my pace, trying to hold off. "Look at you," I groan. "So fucking sexy."

"Oakley," she gasps. "Please."

"I'm all yours, Prim. Put your other hand on your tits, pinch your nipples for me."

This time, she doesn't hesitate, she's too close to the edge to argue with anything.

"Jesus, I don't deserve you," I grit out.

Something I don't like flashes through her eyes as I say those words.

"We'll make it happen, Prim. Me and you, we are going to fucking happen." My release races forward, tingles rushing down my spine and my balls draw up. "Come for me, Tally. Come all over my cock."

I roll my hips, hitting her in exactly the right place and thankfully, she flies over the edge, dragging my own pleasure right out of me.

I roar like a wild beast as I unload in her once again.

"OAKLEY," she cries, her release continuing to roll through her body.

My limbs turn to jelly, and I collapse over her, pressing her tiny body into the mattress, and for a few seconds, I forget about everything and just breathe her in.

So sweet. So perfect. So mine.

"Oak," she whimpers.

"Shit. Sorry," I say in a rush before I roll off. But I don't let her go far. Wrapping my arm around her waist, I drag her into my body. "Did I hurt you?"

"No. I just couldn't breathe," she confesses with a laugh.

"Ah, that's okay then," I joke back.

Rolling onto my back, I pull her closer, bringing her with me and giving her little choice but to lie on my chest. Her ear rests right above my heart, there's no way she can't hear how it races while she traces my abs with one fingertip.

Neither of us speak. We don't need to. Our bodies just did all the talking for us.

It's not until the ding of a phone pierces the silence that either of us moves.

The second Tally's body tenses, my heart sinks.

Without looking at her face, or hearing her words, my subconscious knows that I'm not going to like what's going to happen next.

The foreboding is suffocating as she slowly lifts her head from my chest and twists to sit on the edge of my bed.

"Tally?" I hate how unsure my voice is, how quiet it is.

With slumped shoulders, she hangs her head for a second before she pushes to her feet and walks toward her skirt, pulling her phone from her pocket.

Whatever she reads, it doesn't make her relax.

"Shit," she hisses, shocking the hell out of me.

I've never heard her swear outside of sex before.

"Prim?" I ask, sliding toward the end of the bed, watching her curiously as she begins tugging her clothes back on.

My heart sinks lower into my stomach with every inch she covers.

"I need to go," she says coldly. Her tone is at complete odds to how it has been since I found her out by the rock.

"What's wrong? What's happened?"

"I need to go home. My dad is going to be back soon and if I'm not there..." she trails off. Neither of us needs her to say the actual words.

"Tally?" I say, my voice hard, giving away the fear that's descending around me.

"I need to leave, Oak. If he finds out that I left, he'll—"

"Tally," I bark, getting to my feet and lightly wrapping my fingers around her upper to turn her to face me.

The face that was so full of love only a few minutes ago is now hard. Her jaw ticks with how hard she's gritting her teeth.

"Are we okay?"

Her nostrils flare as she sucks in a deep breath, keeping her lips locked together.

"Tallulah?" I spit, my panic beginning to get the better of me. "What's going on?"

She looks down at her feet.

"I-I don't..."

"Tally," I growl.

"I don't know how we can make this work, Oak," she confesses.

I stumble back, the words making it feel like the rug was just pulled from beneath me.

"No," I bark. "No. That's bullshit. You were with me, Tally." I throw my hand back at the bed. "You were right there with me. You feel this. You said it yourself, you love me. You love me and I love you. We'll figure out the rest."

She looks up at me. Her tear-filled eyes hold mine before she says the words that land like a knife to my chest.

"But is that enough?"

27

TALLY

By the time I get home, I'm a mess.

On the one hand, I wanted to tell Mum the truth. To come clean about being with Oakley and tell her there's nothing she or Dad can do about it.

But the daughter they raised, the good, meek girl who has always put their happiness above her own, wouldn't let me.

Besides, I know my father. And if he finds out that I ran straight to Oakley, he'll throw everything he can at him and Christian Beckworth.

God, what a mess.

But being with Oakley, wrapped in his arms, I felt safe. I felt... loved.

That's all that should matter, isn't it?

That I'm happy and safe and cared for.

My dad won't see it that way though. He'll only see a situation where Oakley has manipulated me.

"Tallulah, sweetheart, is that you?"

Who else would it be Mum? I trap the words, knowing that I need to play this carefully.

"Thank God you're home," she says the second I enter the kitchen. "I was getting worried."

"I told you I was going out with Olivia and Abi for a little while."

"I know but your father—"

"Can't keep me prisoner forever, Mum. I have school, a life... friends."

"I know. Gosh, sweetheart, I know." She rounds the breakfast island and pulls me into her arms. "But he's just beside himself with worry. Especially since Oakley—" She pushes me away and stares at me with concern. "Tallulah, what—"

"Mum. He needs to let that go," I rush out, trying to distract her from whatever's running through her mind. "If it wasn't for Oakley and Mr. Beckworth, I might not be here. I might not—"

"Shh, don't say it, baby. God, don't say it." She squeezes me tighter, anguish rolling off her in waves.

"I'm okay, Mum. I'm okay."

"Tallulah, sweetheart." She holds me at arm's length, her eyes filled with tears. "When I think about what could have happened to you—"

"I don't want to talk about it," I whisper.

"I'm just glad you're okay. And I know things are a mess with your father, but he loves you very much and just wants you to be safe."

"By keeping me prisoner in my own house." I point out.

"That's not fair, Tally. We almost lost you, baby. We almost—"

"Don't." My voice trembles as I pull away from her. "I can't do this, Mum. I'm eighteen. I need to be able to get on with my life."

"Give him time."

"How long, huh? A week? A month? Two?"

She worries her bottom lip, looking at me like she no longer recognises me.

And maybe she doesn't.

I've changed, I feel it in my soul.

What happened will forever shape my life. The person I am. But maybe it started even before then.

Maybe it all started with a drunken kiss in the woods with a boy I was never supposed to love.

"I'll talk to him."

"You will?" My eyes widen, and Mum nods, her expression softening.

"You're right. You're not a child anymore. You'll always be our baby, sweetheart, but you're a young woman now. We have to trust you to make your own decisions."

"Thank you."

I go to walk away but her voice gives me pause.

"But Tallulah?"

"Yeah, Mum?"

"I'll help as much as I can. But there are some things your father won't budge on."

She didn't need to say it.

I knew exactly what she was getting at.

Oakley.

My father would never budge on the idea of me being with Oakley.

"Fine," I snap, storming out of there.

Hating that I gave in so easily.

Hating that I know she's right.

Dad gives me a wide berth when he gets home. I don't know if I have Mum to thank for that or if he's just giving me the cold shoulder after our argument.

Either way, I remain in my room, watching re-runs of Friends while scrolling through my socials.

I'm hardly surprised when Oakley's first text comes through.

> Oakley: We need to talk.

> Tally: We talked earlier...

My chest squeezes at my flippant reply but I don't know what else to say to him. Not yet. Not while everything is such a mess.

> Oakley: If you think for one second you get to walk away from this, you're wrong. You're mine, Prim. Mine.

> Tally: I love you, Oakley, I do. But sometimes love isn't enough.

He doesn't reply and for a second, I worry he might be on his way over.

Until Liv's name flashes up.

> Liv: What did you say to Oakley?

> Tally: Why?

> Liv: Because he just blew through the house like a storm.

> Tally: I only told him what he already knows.

> Liv: Why are you letting them dictate your life, Tally? You love him, don't you?

> Tally: You know I do. But it's not that simple.

> Liv: Seems pretty simple to me. You're eighteen. You don't just have to roll over and accept your dad's word.

She's right but it doesn't change the fact that such things don't come easy to me. He'll never accept Oakley, which means I have to choose.

My father or the boy I love.

When my mum shouts me down for dinner, I decline. Choosing denial instead. Curled up in a ball under my thick duvet, I close my eyes and replay every moment I've shared with Oakley over the last few weeks.

The good, the bad, and everything in between.

It's hard to believe that what started as a game of cat and mouse quickly became so much more. But I think I always knew that he had the power to ruin me.

I want to choose him—to choose my own happiness for once—I do. But there's a little part of me that worries it won't be enough.

That I won't be enough.

That Oakley will realise that I'm not worth it.

For the first time in my life, I no longer feel like something is missing but I know if we can't find a way to make things work, the hole left inside me will be bigger than ever.

And that terrifies me.

I wake with a start, the silvery hue of the moon dancing off the walls as my weary gaze darts around the room.

Something woke me.

The clock on my bedside table indicates that it's the middle of the night. Maybe it was the wind or a cat or—

A tiny crack sounds at my window, sending my heart into free fall. For a second, I contemplate screaming for my parents. But then I remind myself that I'm home. I'm safe, and nothing bad will happen again.

He's gone.

Kane Alveston is gone.

Taking a calming breath, I climb out of bed and pad over to the window, peering out into the darkness. A dark figure stares up at me, his eyes glittering under the moonlight.

Oakley.

He motions for me to open my window and I do. Because it's Oakley and I love him, and he looks... devastated.

I unlock my window and hold the catch to extend it open fully. Oakley expertly climbs the trellis beside my room and grabs a hold of my window ledge and hoists himself inside.

"What are you doing here?" I whisper, wrapping my arms around my chest.

He looks at me, torment etched into his expression, then he stalks towards me and pulls me into his arms, holding me tight.

My heart melts, the terror I felt only seconds ago, washing away.

"I couldn't do it, Prim. I couldn't stay away." He pulls back to look at me. "Don't you get it? I need you. I need—"

I kiss him, wrapping my arms around his neck and erasing every last inch of space between us.

Oakley picks me up and moves to the bed, sitting down with me on his lap.

"Are you drunk?" He shakes his head and I ask, "High?"

"No, I thought about it. Fuck, I was so close... but I couldn't do it. I don't want to be that man for you."

Stroking his cheek, I brush my nose against his, breathing him in. "If my parents catch you in here..."

"I'll be gone by sunrise."

"You're staying?" My brow lifts. "How presumptuous of you."

"I'll go if you want—"

"Stay." I concede because he's here, and he's looking at me like I'm everything he'll ever need. "But you have to behave."

"I just want to lie with you."

"Okay."

"Yeah?" His eyes light up as if he expected me to say no and send him away.

"Yeah. But you have to be gone by seven."

"I promise."

I climb off Oakley's lap and get into bed, waiting while he kicks off his trainers and strips out of his jeans and hoodie.

He slides in beside me, pulling me into his warm body and spooning me from behind. "This is nice," he murmurs into the back of my neck, pressing a kiss there.

I pull him closer, folding my arms over his and letting out a soft sigh.

"I'm sorry I left like that earlier."

"I get it. I fucking hate it... but I get it. Just don't do it again. I'm begging you. I know shit is complicated. I know your dad won't ever accept me. But I'm going to try and win him over, Prim. For you, I'll do it."

I don't reply, I can't.

Because if I do, I might end up making a promise to him I can't keep.

"I need time," I whisper.

"Yeah, I know." The resignation in his voice makes my heart ache. But then Oakley presses a kiss to my shoulder and whispers, "Get some sleep, baby. I'll be right here."

"I love you, Oakley." A ball of emotion lodges in my throat. "I need you to know that."

"I know, Prim. I know. I love you too. So fucking much I can't think straight."

He goes quiet again, but I can hear his thoughts because I'm thinking the same thing.

Loving each other isn't the problem.

The problem is that sometimes love isn't enough.

28

OAKLEY

Tally relaxes in my arms, her breathing deepening almost instantly.

It proves just how much she's still suffering from her ordeal, and it makes me feel like the biggest cunt in the world.

I should have been gentler with her today. I should have just pulled her into my arms and held her tight. But I was a selfish prick that needed more. And even then, it still wasn't enough to calm the all-consuming fear.

She's back. She's okay. She's in my arms right fucking now but still, the fear lingers.

Something tells me that it will for quite some time yet.

It's why her walking out like she did earlier practically killed me.

I naïvely thought that our confessing how we really felt was the beginning of the future, of us figuring a way through all of this together.

But then our bubble burst and reality, Tally's reservations, her own fears, got the better of her and she walked away. She left me standing there begging for her like a pathetic dick. But

I couldn't help it. I'd had a taste of everything I'd been so desperate for and then she ripped it away from me all over again.

I know why. I got it. I really fucking did.

Didn't stop it hurting, though. Really fucking hurting.

And if it weren't for Liv coming to my rescue and trying to make me see sense, then I probably wouldn't be here now.

I'd be back at the Chapel with an empty baggie of pills letting my mind spin out of control in the hope of forgetting.

I shake my head gently, holding Tally a little tighter. I promised her that I'd stop. And I meant it. If it means I get to keep this moment, keep her, then I'll give up everything else. That's how serious I am.

There's just one hurdle left to jump. Or more so, a mountain to scale.

Thomas Darlington.

The stubbornest, most hard-headed man I've ever met.

He's always on the other page, fighting for what he believes is right. Whether it actually is or not is another matter, and a matter of opinion. But whether it's battling with Dad in the courtroom or trying to run his daughter's life for her, once he sets his sight on a goal, there is no stopping him.

I can't knock him. He's good at his job. Really fucking good. Probably one of the reasons Dad's pushed himself to be as good as he is. But that doesn't help my fucking cause right now.

Any normal father, I could probably sit them down and plead my case. But that is never going to work with Thomas.

I've tried talking and only ever received the harsh reality in return.

I am not good enough for his daughter.

A boy like me doesn't deserve a girl like her.

None of it needs saying. I have always been more than aware of the situation.

I am not good enough for Tally. She does deserve better than me.

But here we are. She's stolen my heart and locked it up for safekeeping.

The only thing I can do from here on out is to try and be the guy she does deserve. Try to be worthy of her in his eyes.

It's a big ask.

A really big fucking ask.

But what else am I meant to do?

Walk away?

A silent, pained laugh rumbles up my throat.

Yeah, that will not be happening any time soon.

I don't care if I have to scale the side of his house every night. I'm not letting her go. Not now, not ever.

Thomas is either going to have to let go of his fears and accept me. Accept that I love his daughter more than I ever thought possible. Or we're going to have to do without his permission.

I don't have a problem breaking the rules and defying him. But something tells me that it'll practically break Tally to do it. And I have no intention of causing her any more pain than she's already been through.

I'm just going to need to come up with a killer way to prove to Thomas once and for all how serious I am. That I'm not just some jumped-up Heir with a bad attitude and a questionable drug habit.

I'm not just that. There is so much more to me than that... I think.

I lie there for the longest time with my arms wrapped around my girl, listening to her calming breaths, reminding myself that she's here, that she's mine, all the while my head spinning with ideas.

Honestly, I've no idea what I can do to prove anything to Thomas. But I'll give it my best shot.

"Oak," Tally whispers in my ear. Her hair tickles my chest as she looms over me, the heat of her pussy making me impossibly hard for her.

Sliding my hands up her bare thighs, I find her deliciously naked for me. A deep groan rumbles in my throat as I wrap my fingers around her hips and encourage her to move over me more confidently.

She's so wet for me already. Her juices coat my cock, the perfect invitation to slip inside her.

Best fucking morning ever.

"Oakley," she moans, her breath hot against my ear.

Peppering kisses along the length of her neck and shoulder, I revel in the intensity of this, of us.

I missed it so fucking bad.

Twisting my head to the side, I search out her lips, desperate to have them on mine. But she defies me, instead dropping her mouth to my neck, kissing and nipping my skin.

"Prim," I groan.

"Oakley. Fuck, Oakley," she moans, grinding down over me.

My grip on her tightens, unable to stop myself despite knowing that I'll cause her more bruises.

When it gets too much, I release her in favour of my cock. My need to push inside her, to feel the heat of her body around me is too much to bear. I squeeze the base of my dick, growling with need as I find her entrance.

"Oakley," she moans again before something hard jolts me. "Oakley, wake up."

I gasp, my eyes flying open.

I find her staring down at me, but not quite like she was in my dream.

"Shit."

Dragging her eyes from mine, she rolls them down my

body to where I'm holding my aching dick. "I was dreaming about you," I confess, loving the way her cheeks burn bright red as I begin to stroke myself.

With her eyes locked on my dick, she swallows roughly. Her delicate throat rippling temptingly with the move.

"I'm all yours if you want a taste, Prim," I offer, hoping like fuck she's going to take me up on it.

Her breath catches, and her gaze returns to my face and then to something beside me. "We overslept. You need to go," she says reluctantly.

"You can't send me climbing out of your bedroom window in this state," I plead.

"My parents..." she looks down at her lap. "They'll be awake in ten minutes and—"

"Plenty of time," I confess. "Put your lips around me, and there's every chance I'll blow in two."

"Oakley," she warns, her hungry eyes meeting mine.

She wants to. Oh, does she want to.

I'm seeing more and more of her rebellious side and I fucking love it.

But that doesn't mean I'm going to push too hard.

Her dad finding me here would be really fucking bad for any kind of future between us.

Him walking in to discover his daughter on her knees for me is not the kind of evidence I had in mind to prove I'm worthy.

"Yeah, you're right. I should go," I say reluctantly, swinging my legs off the bed, ignoring my aching dick that taunts me with everything that could be.

"Oak, wait," Tally says softly as I grab my boxers and pull them up my legs.

I don't want to pout like a child who's had his sweets stolen from him, but I can't help it.

"We need to be sensible, Tally. I promised you that I'd be gone by seven and I fucked up."

She scrambles to the edge of the bed and rushes over to me as I drag my hoodie over my head and back toward the window.

"I don't want you to go," she says, ripping my heart in two.

"Prim," I whisper, threading my fingers in the back of her hair and resting my brow against hers.

Her watery blue eyes stare up into mine.

"I love you, Tally. I don't want to fuck this up any more than I already have."

"Did you mean it?" she asks as something mischievous passes through her eyes.

"Mean what, baby? That I love you?"

"No." She bites down on her bottom lip as the heat in her cheeks spreads down to her chest. "That you'll blow in two minutes," she whispers coyly.

"Baby, if you touch me then—" I swallow my words as she reaches for me, rubbing my cock through the fabric of my sweats. "Then I won't last."

"Good because you've got..." She looks over her shoulder. "Four minutes." Wrapping her fingers around my waistband, she drags my sweats and boxers down, freeing my dick again before sinking to her knees.

"Four minutes. Let's see what you can do."

Without wasting any time, she sucks me into her hot, wet mouth until I hit the back of her throat.

My eyes close with pleasure, my fingers twisting in her hair, holding her in place, not that I need to. If I didn't know better, I'd think my girl was as desperate for this as I am.

"Fuck, Prim. Fuck," I bark, trying to keep my voice to a whisper. "So fucking good."

She hums, adding to the sensation of her lips and tongue.

She works me hard and fast.

It's fucking mind-blowing.

And just after the clock has ticked past four minutes, I blow down her throat.

She takes it all, proving to me that there's more to Little Miss Prim and Proper than meets the eye.

Sitting back on her haunches, Tally wipes her mouth with the back of her hand, and smiles up at me with swollen lips.

"Damn, Prim."

A bang from outside her bedroom door bursts our bubble.

"Shit. I promise I'll repay the favour a million times over when I get you alone again," I tell her as I drag my sweats back up.

"A million?" she asks, looking more relaxed than she probably should right now.

"Anything for you."

Footsteps thump down the hallway, getting closer with every second that passes.

"Fuck. I love you, Prim. I'll see you soon, yeah?"

"Yeah," she agrees before I plant a kiss on her lips.

I throw the window open and climb out just as a knock sounds on her bedroom door.

I swear, my heart is still in my throat when I pull up to the Chapel a little over ten minutes later.

The sun has barely risen as I walk through the drizzle to the front door. But even the weather can't bring down my mood.

I feel hope for the first time in what feels like a very long time.

I've got my girl back. She spent the night in my arms, and she told me she loves me.

Just one more thing to figure out, and then I want to shout from All Hallows' rooftops that Tallulah Darlington is mine.

"Oh, lookie who we have here," Theo taunts as I saunter into the kitchen. "Oakley Beckworth is doing the walk of shame with a wide-arse smile on his face. Can you hear that?" he taunts, holding his hand to his ear like a prick. "Heir chasers all over town are sobbing into their pillows."

"Fuck you, Ashworth," I grunt, my smile unfaltering.

"Hey, man. You have a good night?" Reese asks, joining us. Even the sight of the giant hickey on his neck doesn't squash my mood.

"Fucking awesome. Where's your girl and Elliot? I need to talk to you all. I think I've got a plan."

29

TALLY

"I can't believe he did that." A small thrill goes through me as Abi fills me in on Oakley's very public dressing down of Misty.

Apparently, he overheard her and her friends saying some pretty nasty things about me, and he lost it. Got hauled into Mr. Porter's office and everything. Although everyone knows he can't touch the Heirs.

I guess that is one perk of being in love with him.

"What?" I ask with a frown as Abi and Liv watch me.

"You're smiling," Liv says. "It looks good on you."

"Yeah well, despite my four-walled prison and the fact my father isn't talking to me"—I glance around the bedroom I'm now calling mine—"I'm surprisingly happy."

"He'll come around," Abi adds but I catch the uncertainty in her eyes.

She doesn't buy it. And neither do I.

He won't even talk to me about Oakley and his dad. As far as my father is concerned, their help getting me back doesn't negate the years worth of animosity between our families.

Each time Oakley sneaks in through the window—and it's been every night this week so far—he's reassured me with his words and kisses and filthy mouth that nothing will come between us. But as the days go on, and my father makes no concessions on the matter, I can't deny it feels like we're fighting a losing battle.

If only he'd give me and Oakley a chance to sit down and explain our relationship to him. That it isn't some teenage crush. It's real and we love each other. But he can barely look at me, let alone sit opposite the boy he thinks manipulated and defiled me.

I'd be lying if I said I wasn't disappointed. My father has spent his entire life fighting for justice. For the deep sense of social justice he feels. And I love him for it, I do. But he's letting his righteousness get in the way of reality.

Sometimes love doesn't play by the rules, it's messy and hard and unexpected. But it's in those cracks, the dark places that you might find something you never knew you needed.

"I'm not so sure," I murmur, picking lint off my bed covers.

"He's determined to make it right," Liv says with a half-smile that does little to ease the permanent knot in my stomach.

The only time I feel settled anymore is in the dark when Oakley climbs into bed with me and pulls me into his arms.

"I'm not sure it'll work."

"So, you're eighteen now. You don't have to live by your parents' rules anymore. I know it's not ideal, Tally, but you could move out—"

"Come on, Liv. I can't move out. Where would I go?"

"Come and live with us." She shrugs as if it's that simple. "I'm sure my dad and Fiona wouldn't mind. They just want Oakley to be happy. And there's only a few months left until we finish school anyway, and then we'll be off to uni."

The knot in my stomach tightens and twists. Because the future, specifically mine and Oakley's plans for university is another thing we've yet to discuss.

"Oh no, what's that look for?" She frowns.

"I don't know. I'm just confused. I love your brother but there's so many unknowns."

"He won't let you go, you know that, right?" Her brows pull even tighter. "I think deep down, Oakley has always felt second best. I didn't realise how much being a twin, being an Heir, affected him until recently. But you didn't choose him because of those things, Tally. You see what most other people don't. And now he knows what it's like to be the centre of someone's world, he won't give that up without a fight."

"Honestly, I don't want him to." An uncertain smile tugs at my lips. "I want him to fight for me. For us, I do. I guess part of me is just scared about what I might end up losing in the process."

And it wasn't only my father. It was my strength and independence. My dreams and goals.

The ones I'd built my life on.

But part of me knew they were never mine to begin with—they were my parents.

"You deserve to be happy, Tally," Abi says, reaching for my hand. "Even more so after what you went through."

Pressing a smile onto my lips, I squeeze her hand back. "What else did I miss at All Hallows' this week?"

"Not much." The girls share a strange look and I ask, "What?"

"Nothing," Liv smiles. "It isn't the same without you though. We miss you."

"It's weird. I miss it, but I'm also terrified about going back." About what everyone will say.

"Nobody will dare say a word once they realise you're Oak's girl."

Abi almost looks excited about the prospect.

"You know now I'm with Reese and Tally is with Oak, we really need to work on finding you somebody," Liv gives her a pointed look.

"What? No! No, no, no. I'm not good at... that stuff."

"And you never will be unless you start dating."

Abi ducks her head, toying with her hair. Shielding herself.

"Liv is right, Abs." I gently pull her hand away and tuck the strands behind her ear. "You're beautiful and kind and a good friend. Any boy would be lucky to have you."

Something flashes in her eyes, but her expression grows downright terrified.

"Not even with—"

"Tally," she hisses, silently begging me not to say his name.

"I'm going to pretend I have no idea what you're talking about," Liv says. "Because he is not the kind boy you ever need to get tangled up with."

"Come on now, Liv. That's not—"

"Please, don't." Abi rushes out. "Nothing is ever going to happen with me and Elliot. I know it's stupid, but he just makes me feel..." She chews her lip, her gaze wild and nervous. "It doesn't matter. Liv is right. I'm so far out of his league it's not even funny."

"Abi, that's not what I meant. You're too good for a boy like Elliot." I snort at that, and Liv rolls her eyes. "You know what I mean."

I do. But I also know that sometimes there is no stopping these things and I've seen the way she watches him. And I've seen the way Elliot watches her.

There's something there—even if neither of them wants to fess up to it.

I have my own mess to deal with though before I can help Abi come to terms with her crush on the Heirs' vicious leader.

"Maybe we can all do something for Christmas," Abi suggests. "We could go to Oxford for the Christmas market or go ice skating or something."

"That would actually be really nice," I reply.

I've never had this before. Friends who want to actually spend time with me outside of school.

It's just a shame it's all tainted by the unresolved stuff between me, Oakley, and my father.

"I know you think I'm crazy for suggesting you move out," Liv says out of nowhere. "But I think you should at least consider giving your dad an ultimatum. Sometimes we have to push the people we love to get them to bend."

"Yeah, I'll think about it."

Because for as much as I want to avoid that conversation, I can't help but think she's probably right.

After the girls leave, I pluck up the courage to go find my dad.

I know he's home; his car is in the drive and I heard him and Mum talking downstairs.

She gives me a small smile, thumbing to the hall leading to his office as I pass her dicing onion in the kitchen.

My heart races in my chest with every step. I've never feared my father or what he might say or do, not like this. I understand that he can't just abandon his morals and preconceptions all because I've fallen in love with the wrong boy, but he could at least hear me out without making me feel like the worst person in the world.

Reaching his door, I knock gently and wait.

"Come in," he calls but the second I step inside, his expression drops. "Tallulah, I thought—"

"You thought it was Mum."

"No, I just... fine, you got me there." A flicker of a smile ghosts over his mouth. "What can I do for you?"

This doesn't feel like a father/daughter conversation. I feel like an employee visiting their boss, about to be reprimanded for some workplace indiscretion.

"I was hoping we could talk."

"You're ready to talk about what happened?" Hope flashes in his eyes but it quickly dies when I flinch.

"N-no, Dad. I'm not ready... I can't. I—"

"Okay, okay, sweetheart. I'm sorry, that was presumptuous."

"I want to talk about me and Oakley."

The words land like a bomb, thinning the air and making the blood drain from my father's face. "No," he says as if that one word solves everything.

"I am not a child, Dad. You can't tell me who I can be with, who I can love."

"Love," he practically spits the word. "What do you know about the word love? That boy is—"

"That boy saved my life. He and Mr. Beckworth—"

"Don't, Tallulah. Don't push me on this, please. I will forever be indebted to Christian, but I can't, I won't accept his son as ever being good enough for you, sweetheart. That boy is toxic and dangerous, and I don't want you anywhere near him. Do you understand me?"

"I'm eighteen, Dad. I'm not a child. I'm not—"

"Enough!" He slams his palms down on the desk, making the paperweight and photo frames rattle. "This conversation is over."

"You really mean it, don't you?" I stare at him, the man I've always looked up to, the first man I've ever loved and smile sadly. "You'd rather lose me than accept my relationship with Oakley."

"Tallulah," he warns through gritted teeth.

"I will always be your daughter and I will always love you, so much, Dad. But this is my life. My future. And I choose him. I choose Oakley."

I walk out of there with my answer, the one I hadn't wanted to accept.

My father would rather lose me than ever accept my relationship with Oakley.

30

OAKLEY

I sit silently at the table as Liv and Reese tell tales from our week at school.

It's been a long arse week and I've got plenty to say about it, but I can't summon up the energy to find any words.

Coach finally let me return to practice, which helped with my pent-up anger over the whole situation with Tally and her father. Not that bringing me back helped much. We lost our away match the other night by about a mile. It was mortifying. It was my fault, I know it was. My focus was shot, my body barely holding up. Coach made the wrong decision, but it wasn't like I was going to point that out and spend the afternoon on the bench. I wanted to be a part of my team, even if I was the weakest link.

And when I haven't been fucking things up on the rugby pitch, I've been putting my plan into place.

It's brilliant, and Tally, and hopefully Thomas, will love it.

I want to prove I'm serious, that I believe in her, that I will fight for and alongside her in whatever she believes. She's a good person and she wants to help people, and I want Thomas to see that I can be that too, even while being an Heir.

It'll work. It'll be enough, I tell myself as I cut into my steak. It has to be.

"So Oakley, how's work coming on?" Fiona asks, turning the attention on me finally.

"Uh..." I start.

The problem with taking on such a massive project is that I need help. Help and money and Dad and Fiona, thankfully, were happy to offer up both. So was Mr. Easton, thank fuck. Because with their backing, Mr. Porter didn't really stand a chance of disagreeing with my plans.

"Yeah, it's okay. It's a lot more work than I think any of us anticipated."

"And the deadline is tight," Dad adds.

"Yeah, well... I've already waited long enough, don't you think."

"Good things come to those who wait," Fiona says softly, not really helping stretch my patience any.

Silence washes around the table for a few seconds as we eat but it's soon interrupted by the doorbell.

"Who's that?" Dad asks, looking at each of us.

When no one offers up any kind of suggestion or makes an attempt to move, I lower my cutlery.

"I'll go," I offer, pushing my chair back and leaving the room.

Whoever is standing on the other side of the door is small enough that their head doesn't reach the frosted window. Thoughts of who I want it to be there fill my mind and make my heart start to race.

We might have spent every night together since that first time I snuck in, but Tally hasn't come to find me since our night at the rock. And despite not saying anything out loud, I want her to. I want her to leave that house and her father's bullshit opinions behind and come for me instead.

I let out a sigh. It's wishful thinking at best.

Twisting the door handle, I pull it open, expecting

someone for Dad and Fiona, or Abi who's popped over to see Liv. What I'm not expecting, despite my somewhat pointless hope, is my girl.

"Tally," I breathed, my brow wrinkled in confusion.

I stare at her in disbelief, my shock not allowing me to see the reality for a few seconds. But the moment I do, it's like someone stabs a knife straight through my heart.

Her eyes are red, her cheeks wet with tears and her bottom lip is trembling.

"What's wrong? What happened?" I ask, dragging her into the house and immediately into my arms.

She trembles against me, her quiet sobs filling my ears.

"Hey, baby. It's okay. I've got you," I say softly into the top of her head, holding her tighter still, hoping that it'll help keep her together.

We stay locked together for long minutes as she gets herself under control and I silently freak out over all the things that could have her sobbing on our doorstep right now.

"I need you to talk to me, Prim. You're scaring me," I whisper.

She sniffles "I'm sorry," she breathes. "I—" She cuts herself off, pulls her head from my chest and looks up at me with her big, watery blue eyes.

My heart melts looking at her. My need to fix everything that's fucked up in her life to make everything perfect just for her is all-consuming. If only I had that kind of power. But I'm just one person and I—

"I choose you, Oak," she blurts, cutting off my thoughts.

"W-what?" I ask, not believing the words that just fell from her lips.

Her posture straightens, her shoulders squaring before she repeats herself with more strength this time. "I choose you." My lips part as I shake my head in disbelief, but she doesn't allow me to say anything, "I tried talking to my dad. He wouldn't hear any of it. Wouldn't even begin to entertain the idea of us. So I told him that I choose you."

I stare down at her. My mind spinning and my heart pounding in my chest.

"Me?" I ask.

"Yes, Oak."

"Over your parents?" I confirm.

"Over my father's stubborn opinions. I walked out, Oak. I packed a bag and I left."

All the air rushes from my lungs at her confession. "Y-you — fuck, Tally." Dragging her into my body, I crush her against my chest as I try and absorb all this.

She chose me.

He gave her an ultimatum and she chose me.

Emotion burns up the back of my throat making my eyes sting.

"I fucking love you, Tallulah," I blurt, my voice cracked with everything I'm trying to process and keep inside before I slam my lips down on hers.

Before I know what's happening, I have her backed against the wall, her leg wrapped around my hip and I'm grinding into her like my life depends on it. I'm drowning in the best possible way as my heart expands to the point I'm expecting it to explode right in my chest.

And then a throat clears somewhere behind us, effectively throwing a bucket of cold water over our heated moment.

"Shit," I hiss, resting my brow against hers but keeping my eyes shut as I will my body to take it down a notch.

"Good evening, Tallulah," my father says after a few seconds of silence. "What a lovely surprise."

"I'm sorry for interrupting your evening, Mr. Beckworth."

"Christian, please. I think we're long past that, don't you?"

I don't need to look over my shoulder to know the exact expression on Dad's face.

Sucking in one more deep breath, I pull away from her, drag her from the wall and position her in front of me, wrapping my arms around her waist and resting my chin on her head.

"Tally's moving in, Dad," I state.

I have no idea if this was her intention but there is no chance in hell that she's going anywhere else if she's left her parents.

"Oh?" Dad asks with his brows in his hairline.

"I'm sorry, Mr. Beck— Christian. That isn't what I came here for, I just—"

"She chose me, Dad. She told Thomas she wants me," I say, the words sounding foreign on my tongue. "She left. Packed her bags and everything."

Dad takes a few seconds to consider my words before he nods. "I'll go and ensure the guest room is made up."

"What?" I blurt in disbelief. "No, Tally is staying in—" He cuts my argument off with one look.

"Oakley, I understand. Trust me, I do," he says, glancing at where I'm using Tally as a human shield to cover my more than obvious hard on.

"But Thomas and Katherine are still Tallulah's parents, and I will not disrespect them. This is a delicate situation right now, and if you're serious about putting it all right then you need to show Tally, and her parents some respect."

My mouth opens and closes like a damn goldfish as we stare at each other.

"B-but Liv and Reese," I argue as the two of them appear behind him with Fiona hot on her tail.

"Tally?" Liv cries, her eyes narrowing at the sight of her friend clearly distressed—and maybe a little horny.

"I'm okay. Everything is going to be okay." As she said those final words, her hand squeezes mine tight in a silent promise.

"What about us?" Reese asks, having heard his name.

"Reese has his own bedroom which he's been requested to sleep in when he is under this roof.

"Okay, so we'll go to the Chapel then. Elliot won't care and we can—"

"Not yet," Tally says quietly, almost pleadingly.

"Shit," I hiss, aware that she's right.

After everything, it's the last place that she'll want to be.

"Okay," I agree. "I'll do whatever I have to do right now to try and fix all of this."

"Good. You need to prove yourself to be a better man in his eyes, Son. Even if it goes against everything you believe or want. She's worth that, isn't she?"

I glance down at my girl who looks back up at me with so much love in her eyes it makes my knees weak.

"She's worth everything."

Her smile grows slowly, stealing my heart right along with it.

"Go and get her settled, I'll call Thomas to reassure him that she's safe and Fiona will fix what remains of dinner."

"Oh no, it's okay. You all go and finish your dinner, I can—"

"I've finished," I assure her. "And I'll make the call."

Fear flashes in Tally's eyes. "Do you think that's a good idea?"

"I don't need my Dad's help in this, Tally. I'm the one who has to win your father around, not him. Where are your bags?"

"In my car."

"Reese," I demand, "Go get her shit. Liv, can you take her up? I'll only be a few minutes," I say, pulling my phone from my pocket and slipping into the den.

My heart is racing, my hands trembling, but this is the right thing to do.

I find Tally's home phone number as I march across the room and hit call once I'm standing in front of the windows. It rings three times before the line crackles as someone answers.

"Hello?"

Sucking in some strength, I pray that what I say next will be enough. "Mrs. Darlington, it's Oakley Beckworth."

"Oakley," she practically sobs. "Is she with you? Is she okay?"

"Yes," I confirm. "She's here, and she's okay. Upset, but okay. Is it possible to speak to Mr. Darlington?"

Silence greets my question, giving me all the answers I need.

"I don't think that is the best idea right now. He's... he wouldn't be willing to listen," she explains.

"Are you?" I ask, hopefully.

"I, uh..."

"I love you daughter, Mrs. Darlington. I know what your opinion of me is, trust me, I do. But I'm so much more than that. I know I'll never be good enough for her, but I intend on proving that I can be. I want to be everything to her, just like she is me."

"Oakley," she whispers, her voice cracked with emotion.

"Liv is setting up the guest room for her. She's safe and looked after here. You don't need to worry."

"Easier said than done."

"Mrs. Beckworth?" She doesn't say anything so I take that as her listening. "I need you to trust me. I'm going to make this right. I might want Tally to put me before all else, but I do not want her to have to choose between us. She deserves to have everyone she loves in her life.

"When he's ready to hear it, I'll trust that you'll relay everything I've told you to Mr. Darlington. I'm going to go and make sure Tally is settled and has everything she needs. Goodb—"

"Thank you, Oakley. Thank you for taking care of her," she interrupts before I can hang up.

"Always," I promise before I pocket my phone and go and find my girl.

In the fucking guest room.

31

TALLY

I shouldn't be here.

That's all I can think as I stand huddled between Liv and Abi as they scream wildly for the Saints rugby team.

It's Friday afternoon and the team has a home game. It's cold, damp, but no one cares as the boys' run circles around the visiting team.

"Oh my God, ref," Liv bellows as Reese gets taken down by a hulk of a boy.

I don't dare peek around at the rest of the spectators. It had been bad enough turning up with the girls to a sea of curious faces and low rumble of whispers.

My parents would probably have a heart attack if they knew I was here. But I can't keep hiding. Besides, Oakley surprised me last night when he dropped it out that the boys are taking us away for the weekend.

Three nights in a secluded cabin in the Cotswolds.

Just the seven of us, much to Theo's endless disappointment.

"Yes, go... go, babe," Liv roars as Reese gets the ball and throws it to Oakley. A blur of Saints players moves down the pitch, fighting off the opposite.

"Whoooooop," she roars right as the crowd goes wild, celebrating Oakley's winning try of the game.

The referee hasn't even blown the whistle and he jogs off the pitch, scanning the crowd.

"Uh, Liv, what is your brother doing?" My voice quivers as he slows his pace, stalking toward us.

I came here under duress. Because I knew how much it meant for Oakley to have me cheering for him and the team. And because Liv told me how badly he played in his last match.

I didn't come here to make a statement—or a scene. But that's exactly what happens when Oakley pushes through the crowd and pulls me into his arms, crushing me to his chest. His sweaty hair tickles my face as he nuzzles my neck, breathing me in.

"You're here," he whispers, almost reverently.

"I'm here," I reply, sliding my arms around his shoulders and hugging him tight.

The whispers and chatter grow around us.

I guess it's true, they really are together.

She's not the Little Miss Innocent after all.

Stupid slut doesn't know what she's getting herself into.

Oakley tenses at that one, his head snapping up as he tries to pinpoint who was brave enough to say such a thing. But I catch his chin in my fingers, pulling his face back to mine.

"Forget them," I say, smiling. "We always knew this would raise a few eyebrows."

"No one talks about my girl like that and gets away with it." His jaw tics but his expression softens when I lean up and brush my mouth over his.

"Forget them, Oak. They don't matter."

I realise that now.

"I'm so fucking glad you're here, Prim. Seeing you in the crowd lit a fire under my arse. I haven't played such a good game in ages." He presses his head to mine, curving his hand around the back of my neck. Trapping me there. But I wouldn't want to be anywhere else.

In Oakley's arms I feel safe.

"Everyone's watching us," I whisper, gazing up at him.

"Let them watch, Prim. You're mine and there's nothing anyone can do about it."

He kisses me.

Oakley kisses me and my heart almost bursts out of my chest. If there was any remaining doubt about how he truly feels about me, it all melts away like ashes on the wind as he licks his tongue into my mouth, teasing me, claiming me in front of most of the sixth form and a few parents and teachers.

"Oak," someone booms. "Put Miss Darlington down, you're still on my time, son."

Oakley lets out an aggravated sigh before glancing back over his shoulder. "I'll be right there, Coach."

"You should go. I don't want to get you into trouble."

"I'll be done as soon as I can, okay? Wait with the girls and we'll meet you at the cars. I can't wait for this weekend." Lust and love shines in his eyes.

"Go." I nudge his chest, laughing softly when he leans back in, stealing another kiss.

Oakley jogs off back to the rest of the team and Liv and Abi lace their arms through mine.

"What?" I ask Liv as she watches me intently.

"I'm just happy that Oak finally found his happy place."

"Liv, come on. I'm—"

"Yeah." Her lips curve. "You are. His heart is yours now, Tally. Promise me you'll look after it."

The boys take longer than we expected, and the crowd has all but dispersed now, a few girls lingering around no doubt hoping to catch the eye of one of the players. But everyone gives the three of us a wide berth.

Until a figure breaks free from the small huddle gathered outside the changing rooms and heads in our direction.

"What the hell does he want?" Liv sneers as Seb approaches us.

He notices her wrath and his hands shoot up. "I come in peace. I, uh, I was hoping to talk to Tally."

"Didn't my brother tell you to stay the fuck away from her?"

"Liv, come on. I just want to talk."

"It's okay." I gently grab her arm. "I'll be okay."

"Tal—"

But I'm already motioning Seb to follow me over to a quiet spot in the small car park.

"How are you feeling?" he asks, surprising me.

"I'm okay, thanks."

"So you and Beckworth, huh? I figured there was something going on between the two of you."

"What do you want, Seb?" I ask.

"Look, I came to apologise. I was a dick, Tally. I should never have let Misty talk me into helping her get one over on you. I've felt like shit about it ever since. But you know what the Heir chasers are like."

"Relentless comes to mind."

He nods, rubbing a hand over his jaw. "At the Halloween party, I knew she was up to no good. I didn't know... I'm just glad Oakley got to you in time.

"Everyone's saying you've been sick but I didn't know if—"

"I'm okay now," I rush out, not really wanting to get into the specifics with him. Not that I can. No one can ever find out about Alveston.

"Good. That's good. Well, I just wanted—"

"Howard," Oakley growls across the car park "What the fuck are you doing with my girl?"

"Shit, I—"

"He was apologising," I say as Oakley reaches us, sliding his arm around my waist and pulling me into his side.

"He should get on his knees and fucking beg for forgiveness."

"Oak." I lean up, kissing his cheek. "Let's not ruin our weekend before it's even got started."

He relaxes at my words. "Get the fuck out of here."

"Y-yeah, okay." He scurries off, passing Reese, Elliot, and Theo as they join us.

"How long are we going to have to suffer this overprotective boyfriend bullshit?" Theo's brow arches but I see the humour there.

"As long as it takes for everyone to quit giving my girlfriend shit." Oak tightens his hold on me, and I lay my hand on his chest.

"Good game," I say to his friends. Who I guess are now my friends.

There's something I never thought I'd say.

But if I've learned anything about the Heirs in the last few weeks, it's that their bond surpasses obligation or legacy.

They're family.

Not by blood but by choice. And once you're in their circle, they will do anything to protect you.

Oakley claimed me as his and they accepted it... just like that. I'm sure it'll take time for us to find a new way forward, but a white flag has been laid between us. And in a strange way, I'm so relieved.

"Thanks. We're just glad you came," Reese says, pulling Liv into his side. "This one needed to get his head out of his arse."

"Scored the winning try, didn't I?" Oak mutters.

"You girls got everything you need for the trip?" Reese asks.

"Yep. We're ready when you are."

"I still don't know why I couldn't bring someone," Theo grumbles. "Not exactly my idea of a good time being holed up with the six of you."

"What the fuck are you talking about?" Elliot spits. "Me and Abigail have to survive their bullshit too."

Theo gives him a knowing look, but Elliot doesn't take the bait. Either that or he's really that clueless as to the petite girl who spent the entire game holding her breath every time he got the ball.

This weekend should be interesting.

"Me and Liv are driving there together. Alone. So the rest of you can figure out—"

"Babe, we can't do that," Liv protests. "It makes no sense. There's seven of us so we can take two cars."

"I don't mind who I ride with," Abi says meekly. "I'm just really excited to be getting out of Saints Cross for the weekend."

Her gaze flickers to Elliot again but he doesn't notice.

"Why don't I drive Tally and Abi and we'll follow you."

"No. No fucking way," Oak protests. "I need to be with you," he whispers against my ear.

"Jesus, Beckworth, you can manage an hour without her. Come on, lover boy." Theo grabs his jacket and yanks him away from me.

"You got the address for your SatNav?" Reese asks, looking about as pleased as Oakley at the driving arrangements.

"I am quite capable of getting us there, babe."

"You'd better be. Because I have plans for you this weekend, sweet cheeks. Dirty, dirty pl—"

"Seriously, Reese, quit it with that shit," Oakley growls.

"We can get bedrooms next to each other and play who can make their girls scream the loudest."

"Jesus, fuck. There's something very wrong with you. That's my sister, arsehole. My fucking sister."

Reese shrugs, a smirk plastered on his face. "Isn't nothing you haven't seen or heard already."

"Reese," Liv sighs, shaking her head with exasperation. "Can we please just go? We're losing time. And I want to use the hot tub when we get there."

"H-hot tub?" Abi croaks, the blood draining from her face. "I didn't realise—"

"Relax, Red, it isn't anything we haven't all seen before." Theo rolls his eyes. "Now if you lot don't mind, can we go?"

"You sure you'll be okay?" Oakley's brows knit together as he looks at me.

I know what he's thinking because part of me is thinking it too.

But I'm safe.

Alveston is gone. He can't hurt me anymore.

I need to do this. I need to prove to myself—and Oakley—that I can do this.

I rush over to him and throw my arms around his neck. "I'll be fine. Now go. I'll see you when we get there, boyfriend."

"Hmm, say that again, baby." He grins down at me, to a collective round of groans.

"We'll wait in the cars," someone grumbles but we don't break apart.

Not yet.

"I love you, Prim. You know that right?"

"I know." I nod. Giving him a soft kiss. "I love you too, Oakley Beckworth."

So much it terrifies me.

32

OAKLEY

"Will you stop fucking pouting," I say after Theo sighs beside me as I message Tally.

Yeah, I get it. He thinks we're pathetic because we've been parted all of thirty minutes and I already miss her. But there's no need to be such a petulant child about it.

"I'm not," he huffs.

"You are," Elliot says from the driver's seat.

"You all would be too if you were the fucking seventh wheel on this little trip."

"Dude, you get to share a room with me," Elliot says. "What could be better than that?"

"As if you're going to crash with me. Jesus, are you really that fucking blind?"

"What are you talking about?" Elliot asks, making Reese and I snort before he looks back over his shoulder and we share a knowing look.

"Jesus," Theo mutters, tapping at his phone screen.

"Get off Tinder," I tease.

"I thought he'd moved over to Grindr," Reese pipes up. "Used up all the female population of Saints Cross."

"Fuck you, bro. I like anal sure, but I'm not fondling any guy's balls to get it."

"Whatever you say."

"They'd probably come with less drama than the chasers," I say, firing another message off to Tally.

The girls are ahead of us. Fuck knows how, but Elliot doesn't seem too bothered about catching up. If Theo were in the driver's seat, however, we'd have already overtaken them.

"I'll take the drama if it comes with pussy. Take this exit," he suddenly shouts.

"The SatNav says—"

"Fuck the SatNav. I said take this fucking exit."

"Fuck's sake," Elliot mutters before doing as he's told.

"We're not picking up a hooker just so you can get your dick wet this weekend," Reese laughs.

"Oh, so it's okay for you to spend the week inside Liv but—ow," he complains when I slap him around the head.

"You need to stop that shit. We know, she's your fucking sister," Theo moans, rubbing the sore spot.

"And what would you do if one of us started talking about Millie like that?"

"She's still a kid, you sick fuck. I'd kill you."

"Hypothetically, wankstain," Reese mutters.

"Hypothetically, get any thoughts of my sister out of your head."

"Where now?" Elliot asks as he slows toward a roundabout.

"The services on the left."

"What are you playing at?" I ask.

"Getting supplies seeing as you're too busy thinking about Tally's tits to bother these days."

"This isn't that kind of weekend."

"For you lot, maybe not. But I'm going to need something a little more than watching you all hook up to get me through."

Elliot drives into the car park while Theo presses his nose

to the window, searching for whoever the fuck he's agreed to meet here.

"There. Blue Corsa."

"Do you even know who this guy is?" Elliot asks.

"Don't give a shit as long as his gear is good. Two minutes," he says, pushing the door open while the car is still moving and jumping out.

The three of us watch silently as he chats to the obviously dodgy dealer in the blue Corsa.

"Maybe we should have just left him behind," Elliot suggests. "I could just go."

Reese barks out a laugh.

"Lock the doors," I suggest.

By the time Theo walks back over with his purchase safely in his pocket and an accomplished smirk on his face, Elliot is ready.

Just as he reaches for the door, Elliot presses his foot on the accelerator, making the car shoot forward.

"Fucking pricks," Theo shouts as he rushes forward to try the door again. But Elliot is faster.

My stomach aches and I have tears in my eyes by the time Theo finally gets the chance to see that even if the car was stationary that he wouldn't have got in.

"I think I'm going to piss myself," Reese manages to get out between peals of laughter while Theo hammers on the window.

"Let me the fuck in, pussies," he bellows.

Even Elliot's managed to crack his hardened exterior and has cracked a rare genuine smile.

"Do you promise to cheer up?" I shout back, wiping tears from my cheeks.

"I fucking hate you all."

"Was that a yes?" Reese barks.

"Yes, fine. I'll be happy as fucking Larry as you all get your rocks off."

"Aww look, he's pulling his best puppy dog face," Reese laughs as Theo gives each of us the eyes through the window.

"Let the poor fuck back in," I say, feeling sorry for him. We might be teasing him relentlessly, but he's not exactly wrong about the gooseberry thing. Just because Elliot is blind to what's brewing between him and Abi, it doesn't mean the rest of us can't see it.

It may never happen. A part of me hopes it doesn't because I'm not sure Abi could handle the darkness that Elliot harbours. Most don't get to see it. Hell, we hardly ever do these days. As the years have gone on, he's only got better at hiding it. But something tells me that whatever girl he ends up with is going to be subjected to it all. I mean, she'll have to be if she really wants to know what makes our fearless leader tick. And let me tell you, it's not pretty.

"Was that fucking necessary?" Theo barks when he's finally able to pull the door open and climb in. "My balls have shrivelled up, it's so cold out there."

"Good job you don't need them this weekend then," Reese deadpans, earning himself a smack around the head.

"I'm not sharing my goodies with any of you," Theo announces.

"Fine by me," I say happily. "What?" I ask when all eyes turn on me. "I don't need an extra high when I've got my girl."

Reese smiles in understanding. Elliot nods as if he's happy for me, and Theo, well, he just looks confused as fuck.

"Put your fucking foot down, Eaton. Our girls are waiting," I demand, more than ready to get this weekend started right.

And if we're lucky, by the time we get there, the girls will have already unloaded Liv's car of the food, and we can immediately hit the hot tub.

"This place is romantic as fuck," Theo says as we pull up to the log cabin. It's surrounded by down-lighters that make it glow within the forest. "Who the hell decided to allow us to stay?"

"Fuck knows. But let's not give them a reason to regret it, huh?" Elliot says, killing the engine and pushing his door open.

With our bags and the alcohol we had stashed in the back, we make our way inside.

High-pitched laughter hits our ears the second we enter.

"No, Abi. Not like that. Blow it harder," Liv laughs.

My eyes meet Reese's before Elliot surges forward to find out what's going on.

"What the hell?" he barks as we rush in behind her.

Liv and Tally are relaxing on the huge sofa while Abi is on her hands and knees in front of the log-burning stove, trying to get it to start.

"Oh, good. The boys are here. They can start a fire," Abi says, quickly jumping up, trying to hide her embarrassment behind her hair.

"Nah, screw that, Abs. We're more than capable."

"Says the two of you who are sitting with your feet up while I blow—" Abi sucks in a breath, cutting off her words.

"Come on, I'll show you a trick," Elliot offers, gesturing toward the fire.

My eyes collide with Tally's as knowing smirks curl at our lips.

"Missed you," I say, marching toward her and lifting her from the sofa in favour of having her wrapped around me.

"Here we go," Theo mutters as Reese also moves to his girl.

"We've already chosen rooms. Theo, yours is the one with the blow-up doll and tube of K-Y Jelly, you know, in case you get lonely," Liv announces.

"Fuck you all," Theo barks before his heavy footsteps begin to retreat.

"Please tell me that you're not joking," Reese begs.

"Guess you'll just have to find out."

Dipping my head to Tally's ear, I run my nose over the shell. "Show me to our room," I whisper. "Can't fucking wait to have the whole night with you without having to sneak down the hallway."

With my hands on her arse, I carry her in the direction Theo vanished, relying on her to tell me where to go.

"You know your dad knows you sneak in every night, right?"

Of course I fucking do. He caught me sneaking down the hallway in the dark that very first night. He wisely averted his gaze and kept his mouth shut, though.

It wouldn't have mattered what he said anyway. There was nothing that could have kept me away from her seeing as we were under the same roof.

I'll play along so that we're not lying to her parents. She really is staying in the guest room, I just happen to be in there with her.

And while falling asleep and then waking with her in my arms is fucking awesome. This weekend is going to be so much better.

Reese might have joked about seeing who can make our girls scream the loudest earlier, but hell if I'm not taking that challenge seriously while we have a few days without any parents to hear. I can forget about the other girl being my sister in favour of my own pleasure.

"The one on the right," Tally says without looking.

"Fucking need you, Prim," I groan, grinding the heat of her pussy against me as I walk into our room and kick the door shut.

"I won a bet with the girls and got the best room."

"Hmmm," I hum against the soft skin of her neck, not really interested in anything but her right now.

Glancing up, I locate the bed before throwing her back on it.

"Oakley," she squeals as she goes flying through the air. She bounces a few times, while I drag my hoodie off and shove my sweats down my legs.

"Fucking loved having you watch me tonight, Prim. Knowing that you were cheering me on in the crowd made my fucking life."

Prowling toward her naked, her eyes eat up every inch of me. "When I scored that final try all I could think about was having you in my arms. And then I saw you, standing there in the crowd wearing this."

Crawling between her legs, I tease the collar of her Saints rugby shirt and I've been fucking hard for you ever since.

Wrapping my hands around her waist, I flip her onto her stomach, staring down at my number on her back. "You do this?" I ask, tracing my number.

"You like it?" she asks, looking back over her shoulder at me.

Honestly, I hadn't planned to show the entire school tonight that Tally was mine. I wanted to wait until my plan was fully in place and then tell the world, but seeing her there, I couldn't stop myself. And it seems she might just have been on the same page by turning up claiming ownership of me with this shirt.

"I fucking love it. Almost as much as I love you."

"Good. There's more."

Lifting her hips from the bed, she wiggles her arse at me.

"Off?" I ask, not that I need her permission, we both know what's going to happen next.

Wrapping my fingers around the waistband of her leggings, I drag them down, exposing her All Hallows' green underwear.

"Oh fuck, babe," I blurt when the text across her arse is revealed.

Beckworth.

"Just supporting my favourite player," she says with a teasing smile. "I thought you'd love taking them off me."

"You have no fucking idea, Prim."

Dragging her up onto all fours, I palm her arse, making her thighs rub together with need. "I don't think so, Tallulah. The only person who gets you off is me. It's only ever been me, and it will only ever be me. You got that?"

"Yes," she breathes.

Pulling my hand back, I bring my palm down on her arse with a loud crack. She squeals in surprise but unsurprisingly pushes her arse back for more. My good girl loves it when I treat her bad.

"Louder. Who gets you off?"

"You," she cries before I reward her with another slap.

"Fuck yes. You want it?"

"Yes, Oakley. Please."

Crack.

"What do you want?"

"I... I want..."

"Tallulah," I growl, spanking her again. I can't see her arse cheek for the fabric, but I know it's glowing for me.

"I... I want your cock, Oakley. Fuck me. Please. Fuck. Me."

Dragging her soaked knickers aside, I pull her back where I want her and slam inside her with one thrust.

She cries out, ensuring that if everyone in this cabin didn't already know what we were embarking on, they do now. And it's only about to get worse.

"Scream for me, Tallulah. Let the world know you're mine."

33

TALLY

This place is perfect. Secluded enough for us not to have to worry about running into the other guests staying at the nearest cabin over, the décor and furnishings are all amazing, and the hot tub is definitely the icing on the cake.

"Oh my God," I moan as I sink deeper into the water. "That feels sooo good."

"Not as good as Oakley's dick if your screams were any indication." Theo grins and my cheeks flame.

"I..."

"You're only jealous, twatface." Oakley punches his friend's shoulder, grabbing me with his other hand and pulling my body into his side.

Elliot chuckles and it's such a rare sight I gawk at him. "What?" he asks.

"Nothing. Just..."

"She didn't realise you had a setting other than grumpy arsehole," Reese finishes.

"Fuck off, I smile."

"Rarely."

"Where's Abs?" Oakley changes the subject and I love that he includes her in our group. That they all do.

"I'm not sure," I reply. "I gave her a bikini to borrow."

"Maybe Red got cold feet," Theo snorts.

"Red?" Elliot glowers at him.

"Well yeah, all that red hair?" He shrugs. "Red fits. Why, got a problem with that?"

"Why the fuck would I have a problem with—"

"Hey." Abi appears but she isn't wearing the bikini or one of the fluffy robes. She's still fully dressed in her leggings and hoodie from earlier.

"What happened to the bikini I gave you to wear?" I ask.

"It didn't fit. It's no big deal, I can just sit here while you guys do your thing."

"Nah, Red. You gotta come in," Theo says. "Otherwise I might as well be coupled up with Elliot and that's just fucking weird."

"I-I can't." Her nervous gaze darts around us.

"Abi, what's wrong?" Liv asks.

"Nothing, I promise. It's my own fault for forgetting my swimming costume."

"Swimming costume?" Theo asks. "What are you, twelve?"

"Ashworth." Elliot growls, splashing water in his face. "Ignore him, Abs. It's no big deal. You can just come in in your underwear."

"Yes, do that." Theo perks up. "That's totally an idea I can get on board with."

Theo watches Elliot and it's clear he's trying to bait their broody leader into revealing his hand where Abigail is concerned.

A tense beat passes and then Elliot lets out a heavy sigh. "Stop trying to hit on Abigail."

"I'm not—"

"Just quit it. She's not like us," he snaps, and I glance over at Abigail, watching the blood drain from her cheeks. "She's too innocent for the likes of you."

An awkward ripple goes through the air as Elliot settles his intense gaze back on her. "Get in, don't get in. Just don't listen to this wanker."

"I— I…" She turns and bolts back into the cabin, leaving Elliot staring after her with confusion shining in his eyes.

"What the fuck was that?"

Theo bursts out laughing. "That was you being the most clueless idiot to exist. She likes you, dickhead. Little Abigail Bancroft has a crush on the big bad wolf Elliot Eaton."

"Nah… you're wrong," he says, head dipping to the door again. "No way. I'd eat a girl like her alive."

"Don't think you need to worry there, El. You just made it pretty obvious you think Little Miss Innocent can't play with the big boys."

"I'm going to make sure she's okay," I whisper to Oakley, before climbing out.

"Tally?" Elliot calls after me and I glance back. "Tell her I'm sorry if I upset her."

With a small nod, I grab a small towel and wrap it around my body before taking off into the cabin to find Abi.

"Hey." I find Abi in her room, the small double room at the back of the cabin. It's cute though, with a great view of the Cotswolds.

"Hey." She looks up from the book she's reading.

"Want to tell me what's going on?"

"I… I can't get naked, Tally. Not in front of…"

"Abs, you're beautiful. You have nothing to be ashamed of. The boys like to give it the big one, especially Theo. But they're harmless. They like you, babe. You wouldn't be here if they didn't."

"I know." I give her a dubious look and she chuckles. "I do, I swear. But it's just that I... I can't be naked in front of them. Or anyone really."

"I don't understand."

"I'd really rather not talk about it. But thank you for coming to check on me."

"You should have said something before. I feel bad now."

Maybe she couldn't swim or had a fear of water or body issues. I wouldn't have hesitated to stay out of the hot tub with her.

Abi has been nothing but a good friend to me, I want to return the sentiment.

"No, don't. I don't want to ruin anyone's fun. I'm fine in here while you—"

"No, not happening. Let me get changed, you and I can make some cocktails and snacks and hang out while they enjoy the hot tub."

"Really?"

Soft laughter bubbles out of me. "Abi, come on. We didn't bring you to spend the weekend cooped up in your room. We invited you because you're our friend. We want you here."

"Okay." Her smile grows a little.

"You know, Elliot asked me to tell you something."

"H-he did?" Her eyes widen.

"Yeah. He told me to tell you he's sorry if he upset you."

"Oh."

"You know if you like him—"

"Come on, Tally. You heard him and Theo. They think I'm this small, meek girl who isn't strong enough to walk in their world."

"So show them you're not."

Abigail has flourished in the last few weeks. She's brave and stands up for her friends. And I'm glad to have her in my corner. But there's more to the girl with scars on her face and shadows in her eyes.

I don't want to push her too hard though.

"Come on," I add. "We are not going to spend the weekend hiding. You're a beautiful, strong, young woman, Abigail Bancroft. And any boy would be a fool not to see that."

Her mouth curves into a small, uncertain smile. "You're right, I am pretty awesome."

"So awesome."

Our laughter fills her bedroom.

"Okay." She sucks in a sharp breath. "Let's do this." She smooths her hair down, careful to hide her scars. I want to tell her she doesn't have to worry, not around us. But this is Abi's journey. Her path to walk.

And something tells me if she and Elliot ever figure out the strange connection between them, then the world better watch out.

"Prim, get back in here," Oakley whines as I sit around the fire pit with Abi and Liv.

The second we went back out on the deck, Liv got out and joined us for daiquiris and brownies.

Elliot didn't apologise to Abi in person, but he hasn't stopped watching her. If she's noticed, she hasn't let on. But she seems lighter now. Laughing and joking with us, a slight twinkle in her eye as she happily sips her drink.

Things are going to be okay. I realise that now. My parents will come around, and if they really can't, then I guess they're not the people I thought they were.

I love Oakley. And while I may not love the world he inhabits, I know that deep down, he's not a bad person. He's a product of his upbringing, and the privileges and expectations bestowed on him. Without those privileges, I might not be here now to spend the weekend with my friends and boyfriend.

A shiver runs through me, and Liv gently nudges my arm. "You good?"

"Yeah, I am. I really, really am."

"Me too. You're good for him, Tally." She lays her head on my shoulder as we watch the boys goof around in the hot tub.

"Seriously, Ashworth, get your dick away from me," Oak bellows, diving across the tub and trying to wedge himself behind Reese.

"Don't come at me," Reese shoves my boyfriend away. "You started it."

"I did not. I just said that my dick was bigger than Theo's."

"And we both know that isn't true. Maybe we should get the girls to decide."

"No," Reese and Elliot bark at the same time, and a tipsy giggle spills out of me.

"Boys," I roll my eyes, taking another sip of my drink.

"Are they always like this?" Abi asks, looking more than a little flustered to which me and Liv both reply, "Yes."

"They're... a lot," she whispers.

"Try being in a relationship with them," Liv adds. "Reese asked me to measure his—"

"Sweet cheeks," he growls, "we talked about that. No sharing the details of our private time with the girls."

"You asked my sister to measure your dick? What the fuck is wrong with you?"

"Come on, like you haven't asked Tally."

"Like fuck I have."

"Maybe you should," Theo pipes up. "Unless you've got something to hide."

"Oh my God," Abigail smothers her laughter behind her hand.

"Bunch of fucking idiots." Elliot hauls himself out of the hot tub and I'm almost sure Abi has a heart attack.

"Breathe, Abs," I chuckle, unable to deny that she has a point. Elliot's body is cut.

"W-what? I... I don't..." She flusters, and Elliot gives her a crooked smile, high off whatever they've all been smoking as he flips down on the rattan sofa beside her.

"You're all wet," she complains, moving away from him a little.

"You could have been too if you'd come in the hot tub."

"I... I couldn't."

The air ripples between them and I cast Liv a knowing look. But she doesn't look as excited about the obvious moment between them as I do.

And I get it. Elliot is... well, he's Elliot. But maybe they're exactly what the other needs.

'You need to stop,' Oakley mouths from across the deck and I poke my tongue out at him.

So Elliot and Abi are complete opposites. At the beginning of the term, I couldn't ever imagine being here now. With a boy I thought I hated more than anything.

But love has a funny way of creeping up on you like that.

And I wouldn't change it for the world.

34

OAKLEY

"Refills," my sister says, emerging from the cabin with fresh cocktails in her hands for Tally and Abi. How she manages to get them to the table they're sitting around with anything still in the glasses is a fucking miracle.

She's beyond wasted, and from how my best friend watches her, I think he's more than happy about it.

"Will you stop eye-fucking her right in front of me," I hiss, smacking him around the head.

"Can't help it, bro," he says, resting back with his arms across the top of the hot tub. "She's fucking smoking. And she's all mine."

"He's not wrong," Theo adds after releasing a hit of his joint. "She's fit." My teeth grind, and because he's not already rubbing it in enough, he feels the need to add. "Tally too."

"The fuck?"

"What? Just because they belong to you two pussies, it doesn't mean I'm blind. And anyway, it's your fault I'm even looking."

"How the fuck did you figure that?"

Holding his hand out with his spliff pinched between his fingers, he sweepingly gestures around the deck.

"You brought me here and then paraded them around in their bikinis. What the fuck did you think I was looking at?"

"Not my girl's, or my sister's tits," I growl.

"So... sue me. I'm a hot-blooded male, and here I am with no prospects of getting lucky tonight."

Reese snorts. "Ah, you noticed that Abi has zero interest in you as well."

"Fuck off. We all know where her eye is wandering."

All three of us study the unlikely couple sitting around the fire together.

"You think he'd go for it if he ever pulled his head out of his arse and realised?" Reese asks.

"Dunno. You gonna fucking share that or what?" I snap at Theo when he takes another hit without offering it out.

"Fuck you. This is mine. You want more than the hit I've already given you, go and roll up your own."

"You really are a miserable fuck. If you don't cheer up soon, you'll never get laid. Girls don't like miserable motherfuckers."

"Never stopped you getting lucky before Tally cut your balls off and put them into her handbag."

Pushing to my feet, I glare him down. "One day, Ashworth. One day some girl is going to make the catastrophic mistake of stumbling into your life and turning it upside down."

He scoffs. "Un-fucking-likely."

Perching my arse on the edge of the hot tub, I throw one leg over, ready to get out in favour of my girl and a hit.

I might have promised her that I'd reign it in, but I figure it safe to let go when we're all together and celebrating an epic win.

"You're so fucking sure of yourself," I bark, earning the attention of the others.

"What he said," Elliot agrees despite not having a fucking clue what we're talking about.

"I'm never doing this," Theo says, wiggling his finger between me and Reese and Tally and Liv. "It's not happening ever."

"You seriously don't want someone you can spend the rest of your life with?" Tally asks as if it's the most absurd thing in the world.

Just a few weeks ago, I probably would have agreed with Theo. I was fully on team single, fucking anything I could get my hands on.

Cringe.

But then Tally blasted her way into my life. And well... the thought of touching anyone but her makes me want to saw my own hands off.

"Love makes you weak, Tallulah. It's painful and ugly and not worth even a second of my time."

He sucks on his joint as his words continue to echo around us.

I keep my eyes on Tally, hating the wounded puppy look on her face.

"You're wrong," Liv states fiercely. "The right kind of love is the complete opposite."

"Well, excuse me if I don't waste my time with all the wrong kinds of love in order to find the right one. Not worth my energy."

Taking the last drag on his joint, he flicks it over the side before jumping out of the tub and disappearing inside the cabin, leaving a trail of water in his wake.

"Did I touch a sore spot?" Liv asks with a wince.

"He's a big boy, sweet cheeks. He can cope."

Reese and I both leave the water behind in favour of our girls.

"Oakley," Tally squeals as I lift her from the sofa and place her on my lap. "You're wet."

"Sure am, Prim. Question is," I say before leaning into her ear. "Are you?"

"Oak," she warns.

"My brother is such a whore," Liv announces before downing another drink.

"Can't beat 'em, join 'em, babe," Reese says happily before dragging her feet into his lap, massaging them until she lets out a filthy moan.

"Do you have to, Abi doesn't want to watch this shit," Elliot snaps, making Tally instantly freeze.

"But you're okay with it?" Liv asks.

"Fuck no, but I've got somewhat used to it over the past few weeks."

"I think it's sweet," Abi adds quietly, keeping her eyes on her drink.

"You might regret that, Abs," Elliot warns. "But don't say I didn't warn you before the live action porn starts."

Abi's cheeks burn red hot at Elliot's words.

"It's nothing like that, Abi. Don't worry," Tally says in a rush.

"I wouldn't be so sure," Elliot mutters before a loud crash sounds from inside the cabin.

"Is he okay?" Tally asks me.

"Yeah, he'll be fine."

"Did you have to bait him?"

"After he's spent all night giving us shit? Yeah, he deserved it."

"But you know how that shit fucks with his head," Elliot reasons.

"Not my fucking fault," I hiss, making Tally narrow her eyes. "What?" I whisper.

"He's your friend. Be nice."

"I am nice. He just needs to deal with his shit."

"What is his sh— issues?" she asks, not quite drunk enough to unleash her potty mouth.

"Family. His dad's a prick."

She nods in understanding before the man in question returns with a fresh joint.

"Here you go, spunk bubble," he grunts, passing me another.

"See," I say happily, eyeing my prize.

A joint in my hand and my girl on my lap. Does it get any fucking better than that?

"Light me up," I demand once Theo has settled on the other end of the sofa and sparked up.

"Oak," Tally whispers.

"I made you a promise, Prim. I'm not getting wasted, Just... enjoying myself."

She studies me as I take a hit, a lazy smile playing on my lips as the weed begins to take its hold.

"Oh fuck, that's good shit," I breathe. "You ever smoked weed, Prim?"

I don't really need to ask. I already know the answer.

She stares at me, nibbling on her bottom lip innocently.

"Wanna try?"

I offer it up to her, but she just stares at it as if it's about to jump up and bite her.

"Dude, that isn't how you offer your girl a hit, for fuck's sake."

Before I know what's happening, Reese has stolen my joint, taken a hit and has his lips on my sister's. As much as I might hate it, it also doesn't look like a bad idea.

And with the way Tally watches them with intrigue glittering in her eyes, it makes it even more tempting.

Taking it back while he loses himself in Liv, I suck a hit without taking it all the way back, thread my fingers in Tally's hair and drag her in for a kiss.

The second our lips are pressed together, I blow the hit into her mouth.

Her eyes widen in shock, but she doesn't pull away.

"Look at my Prim being a little rebel. What would Daddy think?" I tease.

Twisting around, she straddles me, no longer caring about my wet shorts beneath us.

"I think she liked that," Abi laughs, the cocktails going to her head just as much as the other two. I just hope it helps her relax. I've no idea what all that earlier was about with not getting in the hot tub, but she doesn't need to worry about us judging her for whatever it is.

She has a painful past, that much is obvious. But we're all more than a little familiar with pain and fucked up lives. We also have a little experience with trust issues as well. Honestly, she's in good company.

"Who'd have thought it," Theo muses. "Good little Tallulah loses all her inhibitions around the Heirs just like every other girl at All Hallows'."

"It's different," I breathe as she kisses down my throat. "She's not an Heir chaser. She's my motherfucking queen."

"Fuck yeah, I like the sound of that," Reese agrees while Theo groans. Elliot, he watches the four of us with mild curiosity. Unlike Theo, he's interested in what life might be like with someone standing by his side. After a few seconds, he glances down at the girl next to him while she innocently sips on her drink.

"We should play a game before you all start fucking again," Theo announces.

Abi tenses, sensing she's not going to like what comes next but the rest of us perk up.

"Go on then," Reese encourages. "You clearly already have this planned."

"Truth or dare. Refuse and you have to do a shot of..." He leans over the arm of the sofa and reveals a bottle of tequila from fuck knows where. "This."

"I'm in," Reese says. "I haven't got anything to hide from you motherfuckers."

"I'm not comparing the size of your dick to my brother's. It's just not happening," Liv slurs, predicting where this will end up already.

"It's okay," Tally says around a drunken hiccup. "I will."

"The fuck?"

"It's okay, baby," she soothes, taking my face in her hands. "I already know yours is bigger."

"Don't fucking think so."

"Elliot," Theo announces before the dick-measuring contest can begin.

"You can fuck right off with your tape measure, Ashworth."

"Pfft, I wouldn't waste my time trying to find it." Elliot flips him off. "Truth or dare?"

"Dare."

Theo's face lights up in delight as he rubs his hands together.

Silence falls as we all wait for whatever bullshit he's going to come up with.

"Earlier, you upset Abi."

"Theo," Liv warns.

"It's okay, Liv. Trust me."

She scoffs and continues glaring at him.

"I dare you to make it up to her."

"Oh, it's okay. I know he didn't mean to—"

"How the fuck am I meant to do that. I've already said—"

"No, you didn't," Tally pipes up. "I said it for you."

He nods, tipping his drink back to stall for time.

"Okay," he turns to Abi, his knee brushing her thigh where they're so close. "Abigail, I'm sorry if anything I said earlier hurt you. I don't think you're too weak to handle any of us. In fact, I think you're probably the bravest person here." My eyes widen at his confession. "And if for whatever reason you don't want to put on a bikini and get into the hot tub with us, then that's okay. You don't have to do anything you don't want to do.

But—" He adds when Theo opens his mouth ready to speak. "You need to know that you don't have to hide anything from us. The fact you're here should prove to you that we trust you, so in return, you have our full respect."

"Wow," Tally whispers as Abi quickly lifts her hand to wipe a tear away.

"Thank you," she says quietly.

"Aww, who knew that Elliot could be all cute and shit," Theo says with a shit-eating grin. "Abs, truth or dare?"

She startles like a rabbit in headlights. "Um... d-dare," she stutters.

All of us drill warnings into Theo as he makes a show of thinking about what he's going to ask her to do.

Shoving his hand into the wet pocket of his shorts, he pulls a black Sharpie free and throws it at her. "Give Elliot a tattoo. Anywhere on his body you like."

She swallows nervously.

"It's okay if you refuse. Tequila doesn't taste that bad," Elliot offers, giving her an out.

For a few seconds, I expect her to throw the pen back at Theo's head and accept her drink but then she tucks her hair behind her ear in determination and pulls the cap off the pen.

"Oh shit," Theo laughs as Elliot swallows so thickly that his Adam's apple bobs repeatedly in his throat.

Tonight sure is getting interesting.

35

TALLY

I watch in a mix of surprise and pride as Abi drops to her knees and shuffles over to Elliot. He widens his legs, his dark gaze tracking her every move.

The words predator and prey flash in my mind, only nothing about Abi seems like the unwilling victim right now.

She smiles coyly at him as she places a shaky hand on his leg. But then the hesitation comes, and we all hear her sharp intake of breath.

"I won't bite, Red." He takes Theo's nickname for her and makes it his own in that one sentence. "Not unless you want me too." He gives her a rare smile.

Liv gawks at them, concern glittering in her eyes. I get it. She's protective of Abi and worried that whatever is building between her and Elliot will end badly. But maybe not. Maybe she's the ray of sunshine to temper the storm surrounding him.

When she makes no attempt to move, Elliot arches a dark brow. "I'm all yours."

"Shit," Theo chokes out. "I'm getting hard just watching the two of you."

That's enough to snap Abi out of her daze. Her cheeks

burn as she ducks her head and draws something on Elliot's pec.

I don't miss the way he swallows when she pulls away. "There, a little sunshine to brighten your day."

Reese leans over to get a closer look, exploding with laughter. "Here comes the sun..."

"I don't get it." Theo frowns at her cute handiwork.

"It's the name of a song. My dad's favourite song," Abi whispers. "I dunno"—she shrugs—"it felt right."

"I think it's cute. That would be an amazing tattoo," I say, quickly adding, "on me or you. Not Elliot."

His brows pinch together as he looks down at the little sketch of a sun peeking out of a cloud, her neat lettering going over it in an arch.

"The Beatles, right?" Abi nods and he dips his head. "Cool."

"Okay, fuckers. That was... weird. Elliot, you're up."

"Nah, I've already had my turn. I'm out," he says, pretending not to watch Abi as she moves back to her seat.

"What? No way!" Theo groans. "We're only just getting started. You can't miss a turn."

"I've had a turn," he growls.

"Fucking baby."

"I'll take the dare," Oakley pipes up.

"Oak." I roll my eyes and he nuzzles my neck, making me laugh uncontrollably. His mouth feels nice on my skin. Warm and soft and so freaking tickly.

"Your girl is high," Theo drawls, and I look at him, the laughter subsiding.

"No, I'm not."

"Sure you are. You've got that first-timer glow." He snickers, and I lay my head on Oakley's shoulder.

"I feel great." I stroke my arm, my skin tingling with sensation.

"Oh shit, she's one of those types."

"Huh?"

Oakley grabs my jaw and pulls my face to his. "You feeling good, Prim?" He grins, and I nod some non-sensical noise, still touching myself, running my fingertips along my arm in a feather-light caress.

"So good."

He chuckles, kissing me without warning. I whimper against his mouth, loving how his tongue feels sliding against mine.

"Okay, lovebirds, break it up or I'll find a way to cool you the fuck down."

Oakley mutters something against my lips, slowing the kiss to a pace that has me desperate for him. "You need to behave," he whispers. "Before I drag you to our room and—"

"Seriously, Beckworth. Put your girl the fuck down and get ready to complete the dare of all dares."

"You should know me better than that." Oak pins Theo with a hard look. "I never back down from a challenge."

"Babe, don't," I whine as Oakley moves away from me. "I don't want you to get hurt."

"Might as well save your breath, Tally. My brother and his idiot friends have been doing this kind of shit for years."

"And always lived to tell the tale." Oakley winks at me and my heart is so full of love for him, I'm sure it might burst at any second.

"Okay," Theo cracks his neck, smirking up at my boyfriend. "Your dare, should you choose to accept it, is to run into the middle of that field and shout I'm Oakley Beckworth and I have a tiny dick. But you gotta do it... naked."

"Theo!" I protest but Oakley is already shoving his swim shorts down his legs.

"How many cabins do you think are occupied?" He eyes the other cabins off in the distance.

"I saw people arrive at the next two over. But they're a good ways away."

"You have nothing to prove," I say. "I love your dick, babe. It's so big and thick and I love it when you— What?" I blink at them all as they stare at me with a mix of expressions.

Oakley struts over to me stark naked, cupping said dick, and leans down, brushing his lips over mine. "Try and behave while I'm gone."

"Nooo, we should kiss more. We should—"

"Jesus," Theo murmurs in the background and Oak gives him the finger.

"Right, where were we? Ah, yes. Time to get acquainted with nature."

Laughter fills the night as we watch my boyfriend—my sexy as hell boyfriend—leap over the deck railing and take off across the field, his glorious dick flapping in the wind.

"Hmm, I love him." I smile goofily.

"Do you feel okay?" Abi asks, concerned. "Maybe you should—"

"She'll be fine," Theo barks. "Nothing some munchies and a little loving from her boy won't fix."

"Love you, Abs." I reach over and grab her hand. "And you Liv. I love you both soooo much."

"Fucking lightweight," Theo snorts right as Oakley bellows, "I'm Oakley Beckworth and I have a fucking huge cock."

He's standing in the middle of a field, naked as the day he was born, surrounded by sheep and I couldn't love him more than I do in that moment.

"Yep"—my smile grows so wide my cheeks hurt—"That's my boyfriend."

I wake to a wall of heat. Everything feels a little heavy. My limbs, my muscles, even my tongue as I roll it around my mouth.

"Stop," Oakley murmurs, his hand sliding possessively up my stomach to cup a boob.

A small giggle spills out of me at how ridiculous he is, and how much I love being here with him like this.

"Hangover, baby." His lips brush the back of my neck. "Keep it down."

"Sorry, but you're cupping my boob and—"

"My boob."

"What?"

"You called it your boob. But it's my boob, Prim. This one too." He runs his hand over the neglected one. "Both mine."

"And what do I get in return?"

"Orgasms." He breathes the word in such a sinful way, I have to clamp my thighs together to try and tamp down the ache there. "Lots and lots of orgasms."

"Last night was intense," I say.

"It was the high."

"Pretty sure it was just you." Oakley had kissed and licked and touched every inch of my body. Well, almost.

There is one particular spot that was, and still remains, off-limits. I'm not ready for that. Not yet.

I'm sure Oakley will talk me around eventually, but for now, I'm content in exploring all the other ways he can make me shatter.

"God, I wish we could stay here forever," I whisper.

"We can come back whenever you want to. It can be our thing. Only next time, maybe we can come alone. Just the two of us."

"I'd like that." I entwine our fingers, pulling his arms tighter around my body.

"I love you, Tallulah Darlington. You know that, right?"

"I know." I lean back to kiss him. "I love you too."

"And I need you to know, I'm not going to stop until I win him over, I promise."

"My father is a stubborn man," I point out, hating the

pinch in my chest. But he's my father. The man who raised me. I don't want our relationship to be forever tainted because I chose Oakley.

"I'm sure he is." Oak huffs. "But he doesn't know what I'm capable of either."

"Even if he doesn't come around, I choose you Oakley. I need you to know that."

"I do." He kisses my shoulder. "Now get on up here and ride me woman. I want to see your tits bounce for me this morning."

"Won't everyone be up for breakfast soon?"

"So." He rolls me in his arms, pouting down at me. "I want to fuck my girl. I don't need their permission."

"I'm not sure I can do it. I don't feel so good."

"My girl partied a little too hard, didn't she." His hand slides between our bodies, slipping between my thighs. "Maybe I'll just have to stroke you nice and slow, make you feel all better."

His fingers spread me open so his thumb can circle my clit.

"Oak... oh God," I breathe, my eyelids growing heavy and hooded.

"Feel good?"

"So good."

"You're so fucking wet for me, Prim. It's like your pussy can't get enough."

Because it can't.

He's turning me into a needy, insatiable creature and I love it.

I just love him.

"I never imagined trusting my body with someone the way I trust you," I admit.

"Fuck, baby. You can't say stuff like that to me when I'm trying to be good and not ravage you." He dips two fingers inside me and slowly pumps them in and out, my body stirring to life with every stroke.

"Ah... Oak," I pant. "More, I need more."

He leans in, trailing his tongue along my neck and across my jaw before kissing me hard as he works me faster. Harder. His finger rubbing that spot inside me that makes my body quiver and shake.

"Tell me, Prim. Do you want to come on my fingers or my dick?"

"D-dick. I really need your dick."

"Yeah, you do." He nudges me onto my back, crawling over me. I cry out when his fingers slip away but cry out louder when he slams inside of me, stretching me.

"Fuck, baby, you feel like heaven." Oakley stills above me, gazing down with such intensity, my heart flutters wildly in my chest.

"You and me, Prim. Today. Tomorrow. Always."

"I love you, Oakley."

"I love you too, baby. So fucking much. Think you can be a good girl and stay quiet?"

"What? Why?"

A wicked glint flashes in his eyes. "Because for as much as I love you, I'm going to fuck you like I hate you."

A bolt of lust curls inside me at his heated words.

"Ready?" He smirks.

And I smirk right back.

"Do your worst."

36

OAKLEY

"Do we really have to leave?" Liv whines as we fill the cars with our bags and get ready to head home.

"We'll do it again, sweet cheeks," Reese soothes, pressing a kiss to the top of her head.

She pouts but thankfully shuts up. I don't need to hear how much everyone doesn't want to return to reality. I feel it keenly enough.

Going back means returning to sneaking into the guest room to spend the night with my girl. It means going to school without her. It means taking her back to a place where her parents will still refuse to accept this.

I don't want that for her. I want her to be happy. I want her to have everyone she loves in her corner. But unless her father comes around to the idea of us, then I can't see how that's ever going to happen. And I fear that nothing I do, even everything I've been secretly planning will be enough for him to see the real me.

To him, I'm Christian Beckworth's son. An Heir, a future Scion. Everything he hates about society. Just like Tally used to—okay maybe she still does a bit, like Liv does—but there's little any of us can do about that.

Or is there?

No. I shake my head at my insane thoughts.

I don't want to change who I am to be with the girl I love. I shouldn't have to, just like she shouldn't have to either.

But she also shouldn't have to give up her parents because of it.

"You okay?" she asks, looking up from where she was resting against my chest.

She might have dark circles under her eyes from multiple nights of not a lot of sleep. But the blue of her irises are sparkling with happiness.

This weekend has been everything that we all needed. Even Theo has enjoyed himself, not that he'd ever admit it after all the bellyaching he did.

Liv and Reese have spent some quality time together, so have Elliot and Abi, not that the blind fucking prick has noticed. She's relaxed so much around all of us. It's incredible to see her coming out of her shell and joining in. She's pretty cool, and I can't help wondering if Tally might be right. She could be the perfect ray of sunshine to his darkness. I guess only time will tell.

And me and Tally, well, we're stronger than ever. I love her more than I ever thought possible, and I think she might just feel the same which is why my head is taking me to crazy places like giving everything up for her.

"Shotgun," Theo calls, pulling open Elliot's passenger door and dropping inside.

"Are we going back boys and girls again?" Elliot asks, "Or..."

"Fuck no. I'm staying with my girl," I say, holding her a little tighter.

"Same," Reese says, wrapping his arm around my sister's shoulders.

"Abs, you want to come back with me and Theo or with the pairs of lovebirds?" Elliot asks her.

"Umm..." She screws up her nose. "They're going to spend the whole time touching each other, aren't they?"

"Can't promise anything," Reese says with a laugh, holding his hands up in surrender.

"I'll come with you two," Abi says, shocking the hell out of all of us. "If that's okay with you. You don't have to it—"

"It's cool, Abs," Elliot says. "We can drop you home on the way to the Chapel."

Her cheeks heat as he studies her.

"Are you sure?"

"Wait, that means I have to put up with them touching each other."

"Pfft, as if you'll even notice," Reese jokes. "Ready?" he asks, tugging my sister toward her car.

"Come on, Red." Elliot says before stopping at the passenger side and pulling the door open. "Out," he demands.

"What the fuck? No. I called shotgun."

"I don't care what the fuck you called. Abi is riding with us, so she gets the front seat."

All six of us gawp at him.

"What? I can be a fucking gentleman. And we all know that Theo will be snoring in ten minutes, and I'd rather not have that right next to me."

"Oh yeah, that's the fucking reason," Theo mutters, surprisingly doing as he's told without further argument.

"What the fuck is that meant to mean?"

"Nothing," he grunts. "But I guess you could argue that Abi has better legs than me."

"Too fucking right. Yours look like they belong to a bear they're so fucking hairy."

"He really is clueless, isn't he?" Reese whispers to me as we watch them sort themselves out.

"Yep. Fucking moron."

"Come on, let's move. I've got homework to do when we get back, and something tells me that I'm not the only one." Liv levels us all with a look that gets us moving.

The drive back to Saints Cross is pretty quiet. Liv hooks up a decent playlist and we sit back, reminiscing on the weekend as reality gets closer and closer.

Tally's hand is locked in mine the whole way back, and I hate that as we get closer to home, her body begins to tense up as she remembers everything we left behind.

Leaning into her ear, I whisper. "We'll sort it. All of it."

"I know," she sighs, resting her head on my shoulder wrapping her free arm around me.

"Tallulah Darlington, keep your hands where I can see them at all times," Liv teases from the driver's seat. "I will not have any of my brother's swimmers dying a slow death anywhere in my car."

"Liv," I warn before kissing the top of Tally's head.

"Sorry," she mutters, as Reese chuckles.

I want to laugh but the situation is too fucking depressing to do so.

"I wish things could stay like this weekend," Tally confesses.

"You could come to the Chapel. There where we could—"

"I can't, Oak. Not yet. I'm not ready to—"

"Hey, it's okay. It was just an offer. I'll do whatever you want."

She snuggles closer making my heart swell a little more in my chest.

When Liv pulls into the driveway, a heavy sigh passes Tally's lips.

"Home sweet home," Liv says.

"I'm not sure about homework, sweet cheeks. I could do with a nap and a cuddle."

"Why is it the rest of the school are scared of you lot?" Liv asks with a laugh. "You're nothing but a bunch of teddy bears really."

"Shh, Liv. Keep it down, we've got a rep to keep." I joke.

"You do give good cuddles, though," Tally confesses.

"Cuddles. From what we've heard this weekend, he's good at a lot more than that."

"Bitter isn't a good look on you, bro. Not my fault we won the screaming contest."

"There was not a contest. Not all of us want everyone within fifty feet to know what we're doing at all times."

"Or he's just not good enough," I suggest before pushing the door open and dragging Tally out with me.

"You're a menace, Oakley Beckworth," she warns as I spin her, pushing her back against the car.

"I can live with that."

Slamming my lips down on hers, I take a few minutes to pretend we're still back in that cabin with nothing to worry about.

"Get your horny arse away from my girl," Liv says, smacking me around the back of the head before our bags are dropped at my feet.

"I think you'll find that she's my girl."

"Pfft, if it weren't for me, you'd never have ended up here and you know it. A little appreciation would go a long way," she teases as her and Reese head for the front door.

"I hate it when she's right," I mutter against Tally's lips.

"Do you believe in fate?" she asks, staring up into my eyes.

"I never used to. But now, maybe a little. We were meant to end up here, together. I know that much."

A smile twitches at the corner of her lips before it turns into a wide smile.

"Me too."

After grabbing our bags in one hand, I wrap my other arm

around her shoulders and lead her inside, ready to spend the afternoon working on homework as the prospect of school without her tomorrow looms.

I understand why she doesn't want to come back yet, but fuck, I wish she would. I miss her.

"Oak," Dad booms before we hit the first step. "Can we talk?" he asks, poking his head out of his office.

"Sure. I'll bring these up in a bit," I say to Tally before giving her a kiss and smacking her arse before she continues up the stairs.

"Good weekend?" Dad asks as I close the door behind and stalk across the room to drop into one of the chairs in front of his desk.

"The best. We all needed it."

"I'm glad."

"What's up? Have you spoken to Thomas?"

"Yeah," he says, dragging his hand down his face before rubbing his chin. "He's still refusing to hear a word I have to say."

"Fuck's sake. She's his daughter. Isn't that more important than anything else?"

"He's blinded by anger. He'll come around," Dad says but the confidence in his voice seems to lessen every time he repeats that statement.

"And what if he doesn't? What if all of this is for nothing and he'll never approve? I can't do that to her, Dad. I can't allow her to live her life without her parents."

"There isn't much you can do about it if he decides that's what he wants to do."

"What if I give it all up? The Heirs, being a Scion. Everything.'

His face hardens. "You can't do that, Oakley. It's your birthright."

"So what? It's bullshit and you know it."

"No, it's not. And that won't be necessary. They'll change their minds when they see what you've done and how much good you are capable of."

Slumping in the chair, I rub the back of my neck. I should be all relaxed and shit after a weekend in the hot tub. But ten minutes back in Saints Cross and I'm all het up again.

"Is it all okay? Going to plan?"

"Yes, Son. Everything is all under control. All you need to do now is figure out how you want to unveil it."

"I'll figure it out," I promise. "We done?"

He nods. "For now."

Pushing from the chair, I take off, ready to go and find my girl but I pause the second he says my name. With my fingers wrapped around the door handle, I look back over my shoulder at him.

"No more talk of giving all this up. Everything will work out. You're a Beckworth, Son. It's a part of your DNA."

"Yeah, well. She's a Darlington and that's part of hers. Something has to give here." And if it has to be me then so be it.

Swiping our bags from the base of the stairs, I take them two at a time. The sounds of laughter and happiness comes from the guest room, and I come to a stop in the doorway when I get there.

Scanning the room, I find Tally and Liv sitting cross-legged on the bed, and Reese sprawled out on the too-small chair for his massive frame. All of them with books before them, getting down to work.

We've only got two weeks left before the Christmas break, and while we might have let go this weekend, the fun can only last so long. We've got university applications and A Level exams approaching, shit is starting to get real.

My presence goes unnoticed for a few more seconds before Tally looks up, her eyes brightening and her smile widening when she finds me.

"Come on. You'll know the answer to this," she says, shifting around a little to give me space to join them.

I find that my books are already waiting for me and after a quick kiss from my girl, we all get to work.

Maybe Dad is right.

Maybe it will all work out.

37

TALLY

It's official.

I'm climbing the walls.

All week, I've watched Oakley, Liv, and Reese head off to school while I've stayed behind, studying in my room at the Beckworths.

I asked Christian if he would consider talking to Mr. Porter on my behalf, but he agreed that some time off is a good thing for me. Especially while my dad is refusing to budge. I haven't talked to him still, but Mum did reach out the other day.

The conversation was strained between us. She tried to get me to understand my father's concerns but I'm done listening to his diatribe about Oakley and his family.

I love him and I want to be with him.

Which is exactly what I told my mother.

She told me not to give up on my dad. To give him time to process everything, and I told her that I had no intentions of returning home unless he can at least meet me halfway.

So I'm stuck here, at the Beckworths, in limbo.

Technically, me and Oakley are old enough to get our own

place. But it seems premature. Especially when he has a room at the Chapel.

I'm not sure I'm ready to stay there though. Not after everything with the campaign and my outward disdain for everything the Heirs stand for.

God, how am I ever going to show my face at All Hallows' again? It was bad enough going to the rugby match last Friday.

At least there are only a few days left before everyone finishes for Christmas break. The last day is next Wednesday which means almost three weeks of lazy days with Oakley and our friends.

Something I am more than happy to get onboard with.

Even if I've never spent a Christmas away from my parents before.

Sadness fills my chest, but I shove it down. I refuse to back down on this. All my life I've been the acquiescing daughter, all too willing to follow her parents' rules and principles. But life isn't black and white. There are so many shades of grey in between.

I see that now.

I've lived it.

I don't feel any remorse knowing that Alveston is dead. In fact, the knowledge that he can't hurt me or any other poor, innocent girls again brings me nothing but relief.

"Prim?" Oak calls out and I grab my phone, checking the time.

Lunch already.

With a big smile, I hop off the bed and make my way out into the hall.

"There's my girl." He opens his arms and I rush into them. "I missed you."

"It's only been a few hours."

"A few too many." He nuzzles my neck, breathing me in. "How's your morning been?"

"The same."

"Not too long to wait now."

"Yeah." Panic claws up my throat and Oakley narrows his eyes.

"What's wrong?"

"Nothing, I just... I guess I'm a little nervous about coming back. About what everyone will say."

"You know I won't let anyone hurt you, right?"

"I know."

He takes my hands and puts them around his neck. "You, Tallulah Darlington, are my number one priority, always."

Oakley kisses the end of my nose, but I lift my face, stealing a proper kiss.

"Sneaky," he chuckles, giving me what I want.

What I need.

"There's something I want to talk to you about."

"There is?"

Why do I not like the sound of this?

"Yeah, come on." Oakley takes my hand and tugs me down the hall and into the living room. We sit on the sofa and he pulls me into his side. "There's a thing at school Sunday night."

"A thing?"

"Yeah, it's this silly annual Heir thing. It happens every year but—"

"I've never heard of it."

"Because we keep it under the radar." Oakley smirks. "Mr. Porter lets us use the Grand Hall, there's a fancy dinner and dancing. It's a celebration of tradition and the philanthropy our families are involved in."

"The philanthropy?" I balk. "You did not just say that."

"In case you haven't noticed, Prim, my family, the Eatons, and Ashworths, and Reese's mum, we're all filthy rich. Same goes for the other families. We don't just use that money to buy fast cars and hang out at all the best hotels, you know."

"Could have fooled me." I stick my tongue out but Oakley grabs the back of my neck and dives in, sucking on it.

"Savage," I murmur, pulling away.

"You just get me so fucking hot." He grins. "Back to the dinner. It's a pretty big deal. Black tie. Closed doors. Invite only. I want you to be my date."

"I... Oakley..."

"I know it's scary. I know it's the first time you'll be out in public with me. But this is my world, Prim. I want you to be a part of it."

"I came to your game on Friday."

"Not the same and you know it." Silence echoes between us and I can see the uncertainty flickering in Oakley's eyes. "Do you want me to give it up?"

"W-what?"

"Being an Heir? Do you want—"

"No, Oakley. That is... no. Being an Heir is part of who you are." He's been groomed for this life since the day he was born. I would never ask him to give that up.

But the fact he asked the question tells me all I need to know about the boy I love.

"I told my dad I'd do it. I told him I'd give it all up... for you."

"Oakley." I throw my arms around his neck and hold on tight. "I love you. All of you. Even that part of you."

"You mean that?" He pulls back, searching my eyes for the truth.

"I do. And yes," I breathe, "I'll go to the dinner with you."

"Good, that's good." A huge smile breaks over his face. "I swear you won't regret it."

Nervous laughter peals out of me. "I'll hold you to that, Oakley Beckworth."

Just don't let me down.

"Holy crap," Liv says, poking her head around the door. "My brother is going to die."

"It's not too much?" I smooth my hands down the fitted black cocktail dress.

I've never worn such a delicate expensive dress before, but Fiona and Liv took me and Abi shopping yesterday and they insisted I get it.

Liv has a similar dress in midnight blue and Abi chose a long-sleeved knee length dress in dark green. The contrast with her red hair was stunning. Elliot is going to lose his mind tonight when he sees her.

I didn't realise she would be attending with her dad but apparently Judge Bancroft has a lot of business with Reese's mum, Fiona.

If my dad knew I was going to be rubbing shoulders with some of the town's most wealthy and immoral residents, he'd definitely disown me. But if I'm going to be with Oakley, I have to accept this part of him and his family.

They've been nothing but nice to me. Welcoming and accommodating. I know Christian tried to talk to my dad. I know he's in our corner and supports our relationship.

In fact, he's nothing like I imagined. And more and more I'm realising that the line between good and bad is much thinner than I ever realised.

Good people can do bad things and bad people can still be good.

"Tally, you look beautiful."

"So do you. That colour is amazing on you. God, I'm so nervous."

She comes over to me and fusses with my hair. "You have nothing to be worried about. My brother loves you. Dad and Fiona adore you. And you know I think you're alright."

"Bitch," I gasp, and she chuckles.

"I'm so glad we made friends this year."

"Me too."

"Tonight, I want you to walk in there with your head held high. You're a survivor, Tally. You're brave and beautiful and although I know you never wanted to be part of this world, you belong with my brother."

"Thanks." I hug Olivia tight, so grateful to have not only her friendship but her guidance as I try to navigate my new relationship with Oakley and all that comes with it.

"Girls," Christian calls. "The car is here."

"Ready?" Liv asks me and I take one final look in the mirror. My bruises are gone now, my skin looks healthy, and my eyes glitter with happiness.

And I know the boy waiting downstairs is partly responsible for that.

I follow Liv down, trying to ignore the wild gallop of my heart in my chest as I descend the stairs. The dress hugs every curve of my body, falling down my form like liquid silk. But it isn't until I find Oakley waiting for me that I really acknowledge it.

His eyes widen as he sucks in a sharp breath. Liv joins Reese, kissing his cheek with a smile.

"I think you broke him," he says with a dark chuckle.

"What do you think?" I approach Oakley, a little light-headed from the sheer awe in his expression.

"Fuck, Prim. You look... fuck."

"Might want to find a few more words, Beckworth," Reese teases.

Oakley gives him the middle finger while pulling me into his arms. "You look beautiful, Tallulah." He kisses my cheek.

"Oh my," Fiona appears looking rather lovely herself in a floor-length wine-coloured dress. "Christian don't they all look stunning?"

Mr. Beckworth appears, smiling at the sight of us. "My, my, you kids sure scrub up good. Are you all ready?"

"Ready when you are, Dad." Oak wraps his arm around my waist and guides me down the hall toward the front door.

"Thank you," he whispers. "For doing this."

"Of course."

The driver opens the back door on the immaculate limo waiting for us.

"Thank you, Anthony," Christian says, shaking his hand.

"The champagne is inside."

"Perfect."

We all climb inside, and a zip of excitement goes through me. I've never experienced anything like this, and I can't deny it gives me a little rush.

Fiona offers me a champagne flute. "To celebrate," she says.

"We're celebrating?" I ask, slightly confused.

"Family is always something to celebrate," Christian says, casting Oakley a strange look.

My brows knit as I have a strange feeling that I'm missing something. "What's going on?" I whisper, and Oakley frowns.

"Nothing, why?"

Huh.

"To family." Christian raises his glass as the car whirs to life beneath us. "Reese you were already family so this doesn't really apply to you. But Tallulah, I want you to know that you are a part of this family too. My son loves you very, very much."

"Thank you, Mr. Beckworth."

"I have told you before, please call me Christian."

"Are you looking forward to the night?" Fiona asks me and I nod. "Although I'm not sure I quite understand what it's all in aid of. Oakley explained it but I—"

"Don't worry," Christian says. "It will all make sense soon enough."

He shares another strange look with Oakley and that strange sensation snakes through me again. But before I can ask what's going on, All Hallows' looms up ahead.

"Before we go in there," Oakley whispers, clutching my

hand in his. "I just want you to know that I love you. And there isn't anything I wouldn't do for you."

"Oak?"

The car pulls up outside the Grand Hall and the driver gets out and comes around to open the door.

Sudden panic sweeps through me. This is happening. It's really happening. Once I go in there with Oakley and his family, there will be no going back.

Oakley must sense my hesitation because he strokes his thumb over the curve of my hand and smiles at me. "It's okay, Prim," he says. "After tonight, everything is going to be alright."

38

OAKLEY

Tally's entire body trembles as we make our way toward the hall for tonight's event.

But she's not the only one who's nervous. I might not be lying about the annual event, it's not something Heirs are expected to attend. But this year, things are a little different. It's not just about raising money for a good cause and having a drink with old friends and business partners. Only a handful of people know that we're also here to celebrate something, or should I say, someone.

Dipping my head, I brush my lips against Tally's ear. "I promise you're going to have a good night, Prim."

"I'm sure we will," she whispers back, glancing over at me with those hypnotising eyes of hers.

My fingers twitch on the small of her back, desperate to slide lower and grab her arse. She looks beyond fucking edible right now and I'm having one hell of a job keeping my cock under control when all I can think about is dragging that dress up and pushing my head between—

"Tally," I growl when I lose my fight, my palm moving south. "Are you wearing anything under this dress?"

Her cheeks darken as she studies me closely. "Can't remember. You might have to check later to find out."

My blood runs hot, my chin drops, and I find myself frozen in place just inside the main hall and find Abi and Judge Bancroft waiting to greet us.

"Tally, look at you," Abi breathes, rushing over to hug her friend.

"You too."

Abi giggles. "You should have seen my dad's face. I think it might have been the first time he realised that I'm not a little girl anymore."

"You certainly are not. Just wait until—" Her words are cut off as boisterous laughter approaches from behind. "Talk of the devil," Tally mutters, stepping aside to give Elliot full view of Abi.

He's still busy laughing at whatever Theo said and not really focusing on his surroundings but the moment he looks up, everything changes.

I'm pretty sure he wouldn't have been more shocked if an articulated truck suddenly slammed into him.

With wide eyes and a slack jaw, he takes his time studying the girl in the green dress. Thankfully, Judge Bancroft is distracted by Dad and Fiona to notice, because something tells me that he wouldn't be a fan of his sweet little princess stealing the attention of the big bad wolf.

Tally leans in and whispers something to Abi but it's too quiet for me to hear.

"Looking good, Red," Theo announces, shamelessly checking her out and attempting to bait Elliot but he's still too far gone to notice.

Unfortunately, we're all called through to take our seats before we get a chance to comment on Elliot's reaction.

Our parents all head off in one direction and we go in another.

"No date tonight, Theo?" I ask with a smirk.

"Fuck off. I'm only here because of you."

Tally's brow lifts in question but I silence her by whispering all the naughty things I want to do to her later in her ear.

Fiona got her suspicions up in the car. For a kick-arse lawyer, she sure is shit with bloody secrets.

The seven of us take our seats as servers begin placing starters on the table.

"So what exactly is this then?" Tally asks as Theo scoffs his wood pigeon like he hasn't eaten for a week. Abi pokes at it while Elliot continues to gawp at her, probably way less subtly than he thinks he is.

"It's a silent auction. All the lots are set up in the other room. We're a bit late, but the others will have already been in putting bids on."

"Oh," she says, delicately pushing her fork between her lips.

I shift in my seat, tugging at my tux trousers in the hope of making them stretch a little.

"Problem, bro?" Reese teases from across the table.

'Fuck you,' I mouth, trying to focus on my meal instead of what I really want to eat.

The next two hours pass with little drama but as the time approaches for me to finally confess the reason we're here, nerves start getting the better of me.

"Are you okay?" Tally asks, resting her hand on my thigh to stop it bouncing under the table.

"Yeah, of course."

In the past, I'd have taken something to help get me through it. But that's not who I am now. And I certainly don't want to miss any of tonight. If it goes as well as I hope, then it could be a new start for all of us.

"You're lying," Tally states, her lips pursing in anger.

"Prim," I breathe, not having a clue what to say to get out of this. My heart pounds in my chest as a god-awful screech goes through the room as someone tests the mic.

Oh, holy fuck, I'm going to puke.

Ripping my eyes from Tally's, my gaze snags on my dad's across the room who nods in encouragement.

Behind him, where Tally can't see, a set of doors open, and Mr. and Mrs. Darlington are ushered in and seated at an empty table, especially for them.

Now or never, Oakley.

Sucking in a breath, I close my eyes for a beat in the hope of summoning up some confidence.

"Oak, you're scaring me. What's going on?"

"Good evening, ladies and gentlemen," the emcee says through the speaker system. "I trust that you are enjoying the food and drink on offer tonight enough for you to dig a little deeper into those pockets for our auction. We have some incredible lots on offer, I'm sure you'll agree." He whittles on about breaks on private yachts and alike but it's all a blur as I watch Mrs. Darlington practically inhale a glass of champagne while Mr. Darlington glares right at me, with hard, impenetrable eyes.

"But before we welcome you to have another look and do your bit for our worthy cause tonight, we have a guest speaker who would like to say a few words."

My heart is like a runaway train in my chest as I push my chair back.

Tally's eyes go wide as I stand.

"Oakley, what the hell are you doing?" she whisper-hisses as all eyes turn on me.

"Trust me, Prim. It's for you, all of it."

Leaning down, I steal her lips in a kiss I hope will give me the strength I need to say everything she deserves.

Holding my head up high and squaring my shoulders, I

make my way toward the stage and take the mic. Every single set of eyes in the Grand Hall stare at me. My body heats making me want to tug at my tie and undo a few buttons, but I manage to hold back.

"As you all know, we're here tonight to raise money for an incredible cause. But I must admit that I've gatecrashed a little with something I'm sure you will all agree is also a worthy cause which will help the youth of our community."

My eyes hold Tally's as she stares at me with confusion written all over her face.

"A few weeks ago, someone very important to me stood up in front of a whole room of people, not unlike this, and explained a plan to improve the lives of vulnerable students at All Hallows'.

"The campaign might have run into a few issues and hit more than a couple of bumps along the way, but that was never because it wasn't worthy. The truth is that All Hallows' is crying out for better welfare support for students and I couldn't let this campaign be pushed aside because the intended home for the unit wasn't available.

"So after a lot of discussions and even more hard work, I'm proud to announce that Tallulah Darlington's plan for a new student welfare hub at All Hallows' is now ready to support any students who need its services."

Tally's jaw drops, and even from this distance, I can see tears filling her eyes.

"Two new counsellors have been employed to support our most vulnerable students. They will run group sessions as well as one-on-one support where needed and ensure that all students receive the help they need to reach their potential."

It takes everything I have, but I finally manage to rip my eyes from my girl and focus on her father. His jaw is slack, his glass of whisky paused halfway to his lips.

"Tallulah, would you be so kind as to come up here?" I ask, looking back at her.

Everyone in the room turns to look back as she slowly stands from her chair. She shakes her head as she moves through the tables but like magnets that can't be parted, she closes in on me as if standing next to me up here is exactly where she's meant to be.

The second she reaches me, I hold my hand out and pull her up onto the small platform I'm standing on. "I'm sure many of you know Tallulah. Daughter of the well-respected Thomas Darlington." I nod my head in his direction and Tally gasps.

"Tallulah is Head Girl here at All Hallows', and much like her father, she's passionate about social justice and making the lives of those around her as easy and happy as possible. She saw a gap in the incredible education All Hallows' offers its students and she tried to do something about it despite the backlash she knew she was going to receive.

"But that didn't deter her from doing what was right for those around her."

Turning to her, I lower the mic a little as she wipes a tear from her eye.

"What have you done?" she whispers.

"I love you, Tallulah Darlington. You're kind, selfless, intelligent, funny, beautiful, so many things I need to be more of. You make me a better man, and I want to be worthy of you. I want to prove to you, to everyone, that I can be the kind of man you deserve. I want to support your ideas and bring your dreams to reality. I want to stand by your side and help you fight for injustice and do my bit to make the world we live in a better place.

"Yes, our families might fight on different sides of the line, but ultimately, we all want the same. We all want to live in a world full of goodness, and kindness, and where our children can be educated and supported in the best way possible. And because of you that is going to happen."

A collective sigh ripples around the room.

"Do you want to come and see it?" I ask her, although the rest of the room is also invited.

"What have you done, Oakley Beckworth?" she asks again.

"Come on, Prim. It's time to see what your ideas can achieve."

Passing the mic off, I wrap my arm around her shoulder and push one of the doors open. We're blasted with a rush of ice-cold air and Tally immediately shudders against me.

Slipping my jacket off, I place it around her shoulders and guide her to what used to be the old, run-down building that houses the unused swimming pool and defunct gym.

It needed a lot of work. A *lot* of work. But Dad had the contacts and the deep pockets to make it happen in a ridiculously short time.

"Oh my God," Tally breathes as I bring her to a stop in front of the freshly painted double doors with a red ribbon across the front.

When we turn around her parents are right there with Dad, Fiona and all our friends front and centre.

"Here you go," I say, passing her a huge pair of scissors. "Do your thing, baby."

"This is crazy," she whispers.

"Nah, Prim. The only crazy thing here is how much I love you."

With a wide, beaming smile, she cuts through the ribbon.

"Ladies and gentlemen," I shout. "I declare that the Darlington Centre for Student Welfare at All Hallows' is now open."

With a loud round of applause from everyone who braved the cold to see this, I pull the doors open and gently guide Tally inside to see everything we've done.

But before anyone else can follow, I allow the door to slam behind her and back her up against the wall, and stare down into her eyes.

"I love you, Tallulah. There will never be a dream you have that I won't support you in. Ever."

Her lips part but whatever she was about to say is forgotten when I lean in and steal a kiss, one that solidifies everything I said about her in front of everyone in that hall.

39

TALLY

The centre is incredible. I'm utterly speechless as Oakley gives me the guided tour. The swimming pool has been restored to its former glory. The abandoned rooms have been turned into meeting rooms, and there's a studio perfect for yoga and dance classes. There are also two therapy rooms, a bright and airy reception desk, and a small, enclosed garden at the back of the building that the counsellors and students will be able to use.

I love it.

And I can't believe Oakley and his dad pulled this off. I mean, I can—they're rich. But the fact that he did this... for me, is something I won't get over for a while.

"So what do you think?" He squeezes my hand, peeking over at me as we walk to the front of the building.

"It's amazing. I can't believe it's the same building."

"This is it, Prim." He pulls me around into his arms. "My grand gesture. My shot at getting him on side."

"So you did this for my father?" I arch a brow, my heart fluttering wildly in my chest still.

"I did it for you. For his daughter. For the girl I'm going to marry one day."

"Oakley!"

He shrugs, giving me a roguish smile. "Just talking facts, baby. You're mine. Always. The sooner he gets on board with that. The sooner I can win him over with my amazing personality."

"You're insufferable," I chide, sliding my hands up his chest. "I guess we should go find them?"

We'd left our family and friends for Oakley to give me the private tour. But they can't all be far.

"They'll be in the studio enjoying the free champagne and canapés."

"Of course they will," I chuckle. Because what is this life?

A few weeks ago, something like this would have only fuelled my stance that the Heirs are entitled, attention-seeking idiots. I would have labelled the entire thing as conceited and exorbitant. And whilst I never want to know how much they've spent transforming this place, I can appreciate it for what it is.

Oakley loves me and he wants to make me happy. And this place will benefit the entire student population at All Hallows' for years to come.

I can't be mad at him for that, even if it seems a little excessive.

"I meant what I said up on that stage, Prim. I'll always support your dreams. I know life with me is—"

"Shh." I slide my finger over his lips. "I love you, Oakley. All of you." Replacing my finger with my lips, I kiss him softly. A feather-light brush of my mouth against his.

But a hungry growl rumbles in his chest as he takes control, deepening the kiss and licking his tongue into my mouth.

He feels so good, I press closer. Needing more. Wanting—

Someone clears their throat, and we break apart to find my father at the end of the hall.

"The universe just loves fucking me over," Oakley mutters under his breath and I smother a giggle.

"Dad," I say with a tight expression. "I'm surprised you're here."

"Honestly, so am I."

Taking Oak's hand, I tug him gently toward my father.

Thankfully, he lets me lead. But remains standing strong by my side, his hand on the small of my back in reassurance as we stop in front of the man who is supposed to love me unconditionally.

The man who wants me to choose between him and the boy I love.

"Gosh, sweetheart. You look... you look beautiful."

"Thanks, Dad. How have you been?"

"I'm not going to sugarcoat it, Tallulah. It's been hard. I—" His gaze flicks to Oakley and back to mine. "I'm struggling with this."

"I know, Dad. But my relationship with Oakley is non-negotiable. I love him. He loves me. And we are going to be together."

"I see that now."

He doesn't sound happy about that fact but at least he isn't turning his back on me.

Us.

"This is quite the gesture." He glances around the building. "I had no idea."

"We kept a tight lid on it," Oakley finally speaks up. "I wanted it to be a surprise. For both of you."

"Oh, I'm surprised alright." He runs a hand over his jaw. "Sweetheart, can we talk... privately?"

Oakley stiffens beside me, and I reach for his hand again. My father homes in on it, his expression darkening.

"Anything you want to say to me, Dad, you can say to us both."

"You're serious about this, aren't you? Him? It isn't some rebellious phase or a shot at getting back at me."

"W-what? You think—"

"No, Tallulah. That's not what I meant. Sweetheart, I—"

"Mr. Darlington with all due respect, sir." Oakley steps forward slightly. "I might want your blessing, but the only thing that matters to me is your daughter. I'm not afraid to ruffle feathers and I certainly don't give a shit what you think about me. But for Tally's sake, I'm hoping you can put aside your feelings toward the Heirs and my family and see that I love your daughter, sir. And I will do anything in my power to make her happy. Today. Tomorrow. And for as long as she'll have me."

"Oak," I whisper, tears collecting in my eyes.

My father is quiet. Pensive, even. He studies me and the boy at my side, the air thick with tension. And then he says two little words that give me zero hope of us ever moving past this.

"I see."

My heart sinks. But Oakley brushes his thumb over the back of my hand.

"Just go, Dad." A sigh of resignation rolls through me. "You're never going to—"

"I'm sorry," he blurts. "I am so sorry, sweetheart."

My brows furrow. "I don't understand..."

"I let you down, sweetheart. God, I let you down so much. All I have ever wanted is to protect you. To keep you safe. And I—"

"Dad."

Oakley nudges me forward and I rush toward my father, wrapping my arms around him.

"I almost lost you," he whispers into my hair as we cling onto each other. "I almost lost you and it's all my fault."

Voices fill the hall but Oakley strides toward them and then everything goes quiet again.

"No one will disturb you," he says. "Take as long as you need. I'll go and—"

"Wait, Oakley, son."

My eyes almost pop out of my head as I watch my father extend his hand toward my boyfriend. Oakley frowns but his confusion melts away, replaced with a blinding smile as he takes my father's hand.

"Thank you," Dad says shakily. "Thank you for keeping her safe. For protecting her and loving her. I won't deny it'll take some time to get my head around all this. But my daughter loves you very much. So long as you work to be worthy of that love every single day, then I guess that's all a father can ask for."

Relief floods me. I hadn't realised how much I needed my father to give us his blessing until this moment.

"I will, sir. You have my word."

The two most important men in my life share a look of understanding. And whilst I'm under no illusion that things will be easy between them, it's enough.

More than enough.

"I don't know about the two of you, but I could use a drink," my father says, and soft laughter bubbles in my chest.

"That sounds perfect actually."

"Lead the way then, sweetheart. This is your special night. We should celebrate."

"Your boy did good, Tally," Reese says as we sit in the Chapel, spread out over the various sofas and armchairs.

I haven't been here much but after things wound down at the dinner, Oakley asked if I wanted to come back to the Chapel with them or go home.

But there's nowhere I'd rather be than right here with him and our friends.

Liv is curled up on Reese's lap as he plays with her hair. Theo is busy on his phone while Abi and Elliot ignore the fact that they haven't taken their eyes off each other.

It's perfect.

"He did so good." I loop my arm around Oak's neck and lean up to press a kiss to his cheek.

"Good enough for a reward?" He grins at me.

"Later."

"You could always take her down to the basement," Theo offers. "Show her the— ow, what the fuck was that for?" He rubs his arm, glowering at Elliot.

"Don't be a dick."

"What? I'm just saying we've all heard Little Miss Prude getting freak—"

"I love you, Theo, but I swear to God, if you don't shut the fuck up, I will—"

"Oak." I demand his attention. "It's fine. Theo is just jealous, isn't that, right?"

Everyone laughs except Theo who gives me a curious look. "What's that supposed to mean?"

"Whatever you want it to mean." I shrug, a little tipsy from all the champagne.

But I'd needed it to stand with Oakley and our parents while they awkwardly made introductions. Fiona and Mum had both tried, making small talk about the centre and my dress. But Christian and my father were another thing entirely.

They'd managed it though. Standing in the same room for almost an hour while we celebrated. And when it was time to leave, my parents had pulled me to one side and given me a choice. One free of expectation and ultimatums.

I could stay with the Beckworths or I could go home.

On my terms, in my own time.

It was a lot to process. So I'd thanked them, hugged them,

and watched them leave feeling a whole lot lighter than I had at the start of the night.

"Don't be trying to rub off on me, Darlington," Theo grumbles. "Just because you're happy riding one dick for the rest of your days doesn't mean I'm looking to— ow, the fuck."

"Quit being an arsehole." Liv smirks at him.

"You threw your shoe at my head."

"And I'll throw a whole lot more if you don't quit complaining. We're eighteen, Theo. Time to grow the fuck up."

"You need to put a leash on your girl. Fucking hell, Whitfield, she almost took out my eye." Theo bolts off the sofa. "That's it, I'm out. Enjoy your couple's night. I've got a date with my hand and some high-quality porn." He heads for the staircase.

"What is going on with him?" Liv asks no one in particular.

"Family shit. He'll be okay," Elliot says, his dark gaze flicking to Abi. "You need anything?" he asks her, and she shakes her head.

"I'm fine, thanks."

He nods, and I wonder if anyone else feels like an unwanted spectator to their little moment.

"This is nice," I remark.

"Yeah, all we need now is Theo to meet his match," Reese says, looking right at Elliot. But he doesn't take the bait.

"Nah, Theo isn't the relationship type."

"You can't know that," I say. "All it takes is the right girl."

Oakley hugs me tighter, making those pesky butterflies take flight in my stomach again.

"Right girl. Wrong girl. Doesn't matter much when you're wired wrong," Elliot murmurs, tipping his head back and letting out a cloud of smoke.

Abi watches him with a sad expression, and I know she's reading between the lines. Hearing everything he *isn't* saying.

Elliot Eaton doesn't believe in love.

"I think—"

"Leave it, Prim," Oakley whispers, his fingers slipping along my thigh.

Our eyes lock, heat simmering between us.

"If you're going to make moon eyes at each other all night, take it to your room," Reese chuckles, and Oak gives him the finger.

"Although that doesn't sound like a bad idea. Up you go." He nudges me off his lap and I glower at him. "I'll make it up to you, I promise." He grins, taking my hand and tugging me toward the staircase. "Catch you arseholes in the morning."

"Will you be okay?" I ask Abi, and her gaze darts to Elliot who's still got his eyes closed.

"I think I'll probably just get an Uber and head home."

"Nah, Red," Elliot murmurs. "Stay. You can take my bed."

The collective gasp that goes around the room practically steals all the air.

"I... okay."

"If you need me, text, okay?"

She smiles. "Night."

"Do you think she'll be okay?" I ask Oakley as we climb the stairs.

"Elliot won't hurt her, if that's what you're asking."

"She's so fragile though and he's—"

"No, baby. I didn't mean he won't hurt her as in go too far. I meant, he won't touch her."

"What? Why? It's obvious he's into her."

Oakley leads me into his room, but I only have eyes for him. He pulls me into his arms and pushes me up against the wall, a feral grin on his gorgeous face. And all talk of Abi and Elliot is over. Because the way he's looking at me turns everything inside me molten.

"Do you have any idea how long I've waited to peel this dress off you?"

"I asked you to take me in the bathroom." I sass.

"And as I told you, I like my balls attached to my body. Your old man was right there."

"I didn't have Oakley Beckworth down as a chicken."

"Chicken?" His eyes narrow as he runs his gaze down my body. When he finally locks them back on mine, the air sucks clean from my lungs at the emotion there.

"This is hands down the best night of my life," he admits.

"Oak?"

"I know who I am, Tally. I know what I am. But your father was right. I will spend every day of my life trying to be worthy of you. I need you to know that."

"I do. I love you Oakley. So much."

He lowers his head to mine, breathing me in. "I love you too, Prim."

"Then show me. Show me, Oak."

"You want me to worship you, baby? Get on my knees and pray at your altar?"

I nod, scraping my fingers through the back of his hair.

"Say it, Tallulah. Tell me what you really want."

"I..."

"Say it." He growls.

"Fuck me, Oakley. I want you to fuck me."

"There she is."

"Only for you." I grin, my heart fit to burst out of my chest. Because he makes me happy.

Oakley Beckworth fills the missing piece of my soul.

And I'm never going to let him go.

EPILOGUE

Oakley

"It's going to be okay," I whisper in Tally's ear as we follow Reese and Liv toward Dad's house.

"I know," she lies.

We spent last night, Christmas Eve, together as a group in the Chapel. Mostly for Theo's benefit because the last place he ever wants to be is at home. But unless he wants to abandon Millie—which he'd never do for any long period of time—then he doesn't have much choice over the coming days.

"It could have been worse," I counter.

"I know," she repeats.

"Your parents wouldn't have agreed if they weren't trying."

Since the night I unveiled my trump card where Mr. Darlington is concerned, things have been slowly improving.

Tally hasn't moved home yet, and honestly, I'm hoping she never does.

We've been spending more and more time at the Chapel together. And I want it to stay that way. But I'm also terrified to ask in case she tells me that she has plans to return home for the new year. I don't want a deadline on our time together. I want it to continue for... well, forever.

Liv and Reese disappear inside. He's been complaining he's dying of starvation all morning so he's probably beelining it to the kitchen to steal whatever he can get his hands on.

Tally moves to follow, but I catch her hand and push her up against one of the solid oak beams that make up the porch.

"Oak," she breathes, staring up at me with her huge blue eyes.

"You need to get out of your own head," I whisper, dipping low enough to brush my lips against hers as I speak.

"I'll be okay once they're here and the day has started."

Lifting my hand, I trace the chain around her neck until I get to the entwined hearts charm resting against her sternum. My Christmas present for her.

She has others sitting under the tree in the house beside us, but she doesn't know that.

"I know," I say with a smirk, stealing her words.

Gently, I press the length of my body against hers and finally take what I need, what I know she needs. I expect her to be hesitant seeing as my parents are inside and hers are due here any minute, but the second I push my tongue past her lips, my vixen rears her head. Her licks deeper into my mouth, anchoring us together with her fingers twisted in my hair.

Our surroundings and what waits for us inside the house vanish as I wrap my hand around her thigh and hook her leg up around my waist, grinding into her.

"Anyone would think you've forgotten all about your first gift of the day," she teases as I kiss down her throat.

"Never, Prim. I'll never forget how fucking good it feels waking up to find your lips wrapped around my dick." Fuck, the thought of it alone makes my cock jerk as I grind against her.

She moans and I suck on her neck, and my need to claim every single sound she makes moves my lips back to hers.

I don't hear the crunching of gravel as a car rolls to a stop beside us, and nor does she if the way she clings to me and kisses me back tells me anything.

But then a voice washes over us. It might as well be a bucket of cold water for how quickly it puts an end to what we're both drowning in.

"Oakley Beckworth, put my daughter down right this instant."

"Oh fuck," I breathe, releasing her in a heartbeat before shamelessly shoving her in front of me. Not to put her in the firing line but to hide the raging boner I'm confident my trousers are doing very little to conceal. "My apologies, Mr. Darlington," I say politely.

"Merry Christmas," Tally says happily, okay yeah, and a little breathlessly. I can't help my chest puffing out a little knowing I was the one to make that happen.

"Merry Christmas, Tallulah," Katherine says, moving close to give her daughter a kiss on the cheek. "Ignore him, he's just jealous. He won't have it, but back in the day, he was just as bad as your boy here."

"Mum," Tally warns.

"Boys will be boys, Tallulah. Oakley, looking as handsome as ever," she says, turning to me.

"Thank you." I kiss her a kiss on the cheek in greeting before I'm forced to acknowledge Thomas. "Mr. Darlington, a pleasure as always."

"It's Thomas. And please, stop being such a kiss-arse. It's Christmas, let's just make the best of it."

"We haven't been inside yet, but I can imagine they're waiting," I confess, holding Thomas's eyes.

He rubs his jaw awkwardly but moves toward the front door when I gesture for them to do so.

"Do you have to poke him?" Tally whispers in my ear.

"No. I'd rather be poking you, but they just successfully put an end to that."

"Oakley," she teases. "You need to behave."

Wrapping my fingers around her wrist, I place her palm against my hard cock. "And how do you expect me to do that with this?"

"I don't know. Go... go jerk off in the bathroom or something."

"Without you? And on Christmas Day? I don't think so. We'll just have to be more creative."

"We can't. Both of our parents are—"

"Going to be distracted. Trust me?"

"Oak."

"I'll get Reese and Liv to cover for us. No doubt they'll be up for us doing the same at some point."

She raises a brow at me. "You're willing to cover for your sister so she can go get railed by your best friend?"

"As long as I get to do some railing of my own then I think I can live with it."

"You're impossible."

"I think the word you're looking for is insatiable."

"Yeah, that too."

Voices float through the front door.

"We'd better get in there just in case."

"They're not going to fight. Your dad loves me now."

She glances over at me skeptically.

"Okay fine. He's putting up with me."

"He will love you, he just needs time. Much like I did." Wrapping her arm around my waist, we walk inside the house together.

The scent of Christmas fills my nose as twinkling lights and decorations cover every surface of the hallway.

"Fiona really went all out," I mutter. We were only here yesterday morning but I'm sure there is more.

"It's incredible. I want our house to look like this one day."

"Our house, huh?"

"Yep."

"And will there be kids and dogs running around?"

"You bet."

"How many?"

"At the rate we're going, probably loads."

"Nah, baby. That's what birth control is for. I'm down for sharing you with a couple but not an entire army."

She chuckles as we follow the voices to the kitchen.

Both of us slow to a stop at the sight. My dad and Fiona, Thomas and Katherine all with drinks in their hands and smiles on their faces.

Maybe it's true what they say. Miracles can happen.

> Oakley: Get your sexy arse into the downstairs bathroom right this second Tallulah Celia Darlington.

My smirk widens when she reads it and starts typing immediately.

> Prim: I'm sitting at the table talking to my parents.

> Oakley: So? Make an excuse and get the hell in here. I need you. It's an emergency.

> Prim: What's wrong?

> Oakley: I have a really, really big problem.

I chuckle like a child as I undo my trousers and shove them and my boxers down over my arse. My aching dick springs free. Yeah, a huge fucking problem.

Watching her in that hot as hell dress she chose to wear today has been nothing but punishment. Add trying to be good and not give her father a reason to start hating me again, but I'm just about ready to blow. Pun intended.

> Prim: You're bad.

> Oakley: So are you…

I stroke myself slowly, waiting not so patiently for her to find an excuse and come to me.

Only two minutes later the sound of heels against Dad's wooden floor kicks my heart rate up a notch.

There's a soft knock before the handle twists and the door is pushed open.

A bolt of panic strikes through me that it might be Fiona, or Katherine, catching me with my cock in my hand. But then Tally's blonde hair appears, and I relax.

Without saying a word, she closes the door, flicks the look, and runs her eyes down the length of my body, locking her gaze on my dick.

"I see what you mean, *massive* problem."

"Yeah, what are you going to do about it?"

She moves closer. "I've got a few ideas."

"Yeah," I agree, taking in every inch of her. "So have I."

Lifting her hand, she reaches for me, but I'm faster.

Wrapping my hands around her waist, I lift her onto the counter and spread her legs.

"Oakley," she gasps when I drop to my knees.

"Spent all day thinking about how you taste under this dress."

Sliding my hands up her thighs, I hook my fingers around the edge of her knickers. Lifting her arse from the counter, she helps me out, allowing me to drag them down her legs, exposing her to me.

I lick my lips, staring at her hungrily just like I did my Christmas dinner earlier.

"Oak, we don't have time to—"

Unable to argue with that fact, I dive forward, sucking on her clit and spearing two fingers inside her.

"So wet for me," I murmur against her. "I wasn't the only one sitting out there desperate, huh?"

"Oakley," she moans, her head falling back as I curl my fingers inside her.

With my hair in her grip, I work her until she's right on the edge. Then I pull back, get to my feet before dragging her down and spinning her around.

"Oakley, please."

"Please what?" I ask, flipping her dress up to expose her arse and slick pussy.

"Please fuck me. Hard and fast. I want to go back out there feeling you inside me."

"Jesus, Prim. You get me so fucking hot."

Coating myself in her juices, I push inside her, gritting my teeth as I drown in the heat of her body.

I barely get the tip in when the door rattles as someone tries to use the bathroom.

"Oh shit," Tally gasps.

"You can use the one upstairs, Mr. Darlington," Reese helpfully supplies. "Top of the stairs on the right. I think the excitement has got to Liv. She might be a while."

I can't help but snort. Liv is going to fucking hate that.

"Oh, okay, sure."

His heavy footsteps get farther and farther away before there's another knock on the door.

"You're welcome, arseholes. Now hurry up before I have to give Liv even worse tummy issues and she guts me for it."

I silently laugh as I finally thrust fully into my girl.

"Oakley," Tally screams before I wrap my hand around her mouth.

"Fucking pricks," Reese mutters before he, hopefully, walks away.

I take her exactly as she asked, hard and fast and in only

minutes, she's found her release and her pussy is squeezing me so tight that I've no choice but to fall over the edge with her, filling her up and making her mine like I intend to do for the rest of my life.

She curses up a storm beneath my hand as pleasure floods her body, and I fucking love it.

"You're perfect, Tallulah Darlington. I love you so much," I whisper, kissing her neck.

"I love you too, Oak. Now hurry up, we need to get back out there."

Despite it being the last thing I really want to do, I pull out of her, and allow her to clean up, refusing to leave until we can go together.

Which, in hindsight, is probably a mistake because the second we open the door and step out, we bump straight into her father heading for the kitchen with an armful of empty glasses.

"Oh shit," Tally whispers as we all freeze.

Anger and disbelief rolls off Thomas in waves. He swallows roughly before he pulls on some kind of mask.

"I'm going for refills. Would either of you like anything?" His voice is rough and forced but he's trying and that's all I want for my girl.

"No, thank you. I think we're good." I turn to Tally in question.

"Yes, we're good. We've got everything we need."

He sucks in a sharp breath before continuing on his way to the kitchen. As he passes us, I'm pretty sure he mutters something under his breath about needing strength and I can't help but smirk.

"Thomas," I call before he disappears. He pauses but doesn't look back. "Do you remember when you and Katherine were eighteen?"

He shakes his head, but I'd put everything I own on the fact he's smiling happily as he reminisces on good times.

"Come on, Prim. I think it's time for Pictionary. Reese and I boss this game."

She laughs, focusing back on me again. "I can only imagine. Tell me you don't have the dirty edition."

"Only time will tell."

With my girl tucked under my arm, we walk back into the family room to multiple sets of knowing eyes.

I fucking love it, and I wouldn't have it any other way.

Raine

"What are you studying?" Tally asks me as I fall back into step beside her.

"English, Psychology, and Sociology."

"I'm sure you'll fit right in."

"I think we both know I won't."

"Raine, that's—"

"Save it." I cut her off. "I'm not here to make friends."

She studies me for a second but chooses to swallow whatever bullshit is on the tip of her tongue.

I'm grateful.

Because I meant what I said.

I'm not here to make friends.

I'm here because I have to be. And when I age out...

I'm gone.

After forty minutes of strained conversation and Tally's attempts to get me excited about life at All Hallows', she finally lets me return to the dorm.

I refuse her offer to show me the way. I've got it. The campus might be a vast sprawling place surrounded by perfectly tended lawns and fenced off by an ominous looking forest on three sides, but the majority of the buildings are clustered together, making it easy to remember the route back.

When I reach the entrance, I spot a young girl huddled by

the door, arms wrapped around herself, practically holding herself together. Alarm bells go off in my head as I slow my approach, taking in her skittish appearance.

Don't get involved, I urge myself. *Just keep walking.*

She lifts tear-stained eyes to mine and a life's worth of trauma rises inside me. But I push it down. Force it back into its box.

I'm not that girl anymore.

I'll *never* be that girl again.

But I can't do it, I can't just walk past her without saying something.

"Hey, are you o—"

Her bottom lip quivers and she darts inside the building.

Okay then.

I frown, giving a little shake of my head.

When I finally force myself to go inside, there's no sign of the girl. My stomach growls and I decide to check out the communal kitchen.

I don't expect to walk straight into someone as I enter the room.

"The fuck?" A deep voice growls. "Watch where you're going."

I step back to look at the boy. Man would be a better word for him. He towers over me, his eyes full of fury and fire as he glares down at me.

"Who the fuck are you?"

"Someone who belongs here more than you," I spit, my hackles rising at the violence rolling off him.

He falters, eyes flashing with confusion. But then his icy mask slides back into place. "I don't know you."

"No shit." I fold my arms over my chest, arching a brow. "Stealing from the girls' dorm?" My narrowed gaze drops to the stash of snacks and sweets in his hands. "How original."

"Get the fuck out of my way."

CRUEL DEVIOUS HEIR: PART TWO

"Not until you tell me what you're doing with all that."

I know boys like this.

Arrogant.

Entitled.

Spoiled.

"Move," he barks, literally vibrating with anger. But he doesn't scare me. Not one bit.

Why would he when I've been dealing with guys like him since I grew boobs. Even before then.

"Make me."

The words detonate between us, surprise flickering over his expression.

"You don't know who I am," he muses.

"Should I?"

A slow, wicked smile curls at his mouth, sending a ripple of heat down my spine.

Jesus, this boy is hot.

Hot ... and dangerous.

"Theo Ashworth." He leans into my space, his warm minty breath fanning my face. "It would do you well to learn that name. And remember it."

"Oh my god." Laughter peals out of me. "Does that line actually work?"

"Who the fuck are you?" he asks again.

"Raine Storm." I get all up in his face, smirking with amusement. "It would do you well to learn that name. And remember it."

"What—"

"THEO!" Someone yells, and his entire demeanour changes.

"Fuck," he mutters, grabbing my shoulder and yanking me away from the door.

"Hey," I sneer, spinning around to give him a piece of my mind.

But he's gone.

And for as much as I hate it, all I can think is who the hell was that boy?

Theo and Raine's story is up next!
BUY YOUR COPY OF THE BRUTAL CALLOUS HEIR DUET

BRUTAL CALLOUS HEIR SNEAK PEEK
HEIRS OF ALL HALLOWS' DUET THREE

Chapter One
Raine

"Fancy," I say as my gaze sweeps around the decent sized room.

"You have one of the en suite rooms," Trudy, my social worker says. "Hopefully you'll appreciate your own space." I raise a brow and she lets out a weary sigh. "Raine, come on—"

"Relax, T, I got it." I run a finger over the desk, taking it all in again.

There's a small double bed tucked in the corner of the room, a bedside table, a matching desk and wardrobe, and a small bookshelf with a flatscreen TV mounted on the top.

It isn't much and yet, it's more than I've ever had.

"What do you think?" she asks as I meet her gaze, giving nothing away.

"It's fine."

"Can you try and at least be a little bit excited? It's your last chance to—"

"I know, okay. I know." Everything tightens inside me. I

don't need a reminder of what my arrival at All Hallows' signals.

The posh school on the edge of Saints Cross is the last place I want to be, but Trudy managed to pull some strings with the Deputy Head, her brother, and get me a place.

I don't relish the idea of repeating my first year of sixth form. But it's not like I have much choice in the matter. I'm still seventeen which means I'm still under the care of the Local Authority. And after a string of suspensions and a couple of run-ins with the police, being shipped to All Hallows' is better than being dumped into a young offenders' institute.

"This is your shot at something better," Trudy goes on. "You're a bright girl, Raine. You just need to focus on what's important."

Yeah, like keeping my head down, playing the game, and waiting until I age out of the system.

The second I turn eighteen, I'm gone.

"Your pocket money will be transferred into your account weekly. I'll check in with you every few days at least until you're settled. And Miss Linley expects you at her office first thing Monday morning."

Ah yes, the other requirement of my stay at All Hallows'.

Therapy.

Fuck my life.

"She'll be providing me with regular updates. You're here to attend class. Keep your head down. And pass your A Levels."

In other words, stay out of trouble.

"Got it." I give Trudy a small salute and she rolls her eyes. But after four years together, she is used to me by now.

"I guess this is where we say goodbye then."

"I'd say thanks for everything but we both know it would be a lie," I say, flashing her a wide grin.

"Raine..."

"Yeah, yeah. I got it, T. I can do this."

Not long and then I'll be free.

"All Hallows' is a good school. I really think you can make it work here."

"That's the plan."

"Okay. If you need any—"

"You're hovering," I point out, desperate to wrap things up.

"Good luck, Raine." Trudy makes for the door. "I know that you're not used to this"—she glances around the room—"but it could always be worse. Don't forget that."

As if I can.

With a stiff nod, I watch as she disappears out of the room and leaves me all alone.

Damn.

I'm here.

I'm really here.

At some posh boarding school for Oxfordshire's spoiled rich kids.

What the hell was the board thinking when they agreed to send me here?

I drop onto the end of the bed and take in the room once more, a strange sort of anticipation ripples through me.

The last group home I was in, my room was barely much bigger than a walk-in wardrobe, and I had to share a bathroom with five other kids.

Five.

Having my own bathroom—even if it is only a small toilet and shower—will be worth it.

At least that's what I tell myself as I sit there, in a strange room, in my posh new school, and try not to freak the fuck out.

I'm unpacking the last of my meagre belongings when there's a knock at my door. As I make my way across the room, I half expect to see Trudy standing there, ready to impart more of her words of wisdom.

I don't expect to find a pretty girl with gorgeous eyes and a warm smile.

"Hi, you must be Raine. I'm Tallulah. Mr. Porter asked me to stop by and check in on you."

"Tallu—"

"You can call me Tally." She smiles. "I'm Head Girl of All Hallows'. I—"

"You don't need to do this," I say, trying to spare us both the awkward tension crackling between us.

"Do what?" She frowns.

"This. Pretend to care. I'm not here to make friends so you can run along."

"Good thing for you I'm not here to make friends either then, isn't it?" She stares me down, not missing a beat. "I came to give you the tour. It'll be a whole lot easier doing it now while campus is quiet."

"The tour?"

"That's what I said, didn't I?"

"I'm not sure—"

"Look, I get it. You don't want to be here. I don't particularly want to be here either, but Mr. Porter expects me to give you a tour, so that's what's going to happen." She takes a step back and arches a brow.

"Fine," I find myself saying. Because something tells me she isn't going to run off with her tail between her legs until I've at least stepped foot out of my room. And I guess it would help to get the layout of everything.

"Great." She flashes me a victorious smile that makes me bristle.

"Great," I mutter, pulling my door closed and following her down the hall.

"So this is the girls' dorm. But I'm sure you already know that. There's a common room, a communal kitchen, and a laundry room all at the end of the hall." She points behind us. "Mrs. Danvers is the Dorm Aunt. She's pretty chill. If you have any problems, you can go to her. Just don't try and sneak in any boys after curfew. That's a hard line for her."

"Not going to be a problem," I mutter.

"The dorm is right next to the student welfare building. We're super lucky to have a state-of-the-art facility. Swimming pool, therapy rooms, a studio." She glances at me and smiles. "It's pretty great."

"Great, right."

"Miss Linley is really nice too."

So she knows. It shouldn't really surprise me. The headteacher probably spilled all my secrets while assigning her to babysit me.

"Then in the other direction toward the main building is the boys' dorm."

"What's that building?" I ask, pointing to a church style building in the distance.

"Oh, that's the Chapel."

"The Chapel. So it's a church?"

"Not exactly," she murmurs. Before I can ask her anything else, she says, "Let's check out the sixth form building. I can get you up to speed on where all your classes are and show you the cafeteria."

Tally takes off toward the school and I traipse after her, unable to shake the feeling that all is not what it seems with the Chapel.

But I'm not surprised. All Hallows' is old, steeped in tradition and elitism. It reeks of money. Places like this are always full of corruption and secrets.

"What are you studying?" she asks me as I fall back into step beside her.

"English, psychology, and sociology."

"I'm sure you'll fit right in."

"I think we both know I won't."

"Raine, that's—"

"Save it." I cut her off.

Tally studies me for a second but chooses to swallow whatever bullshit is on the tip of her tongue.

I'm grateful.

Because I meant what I said.

I'm not here to make friends.

I'm here because I have to be. And when I age out…

I'm gone.

After forty minutes of strained conversation and Tally's attempts to get me excited about life at All Hallows', she finally lets me return to the dorm.

I refuse her offer to show me the way back. I've got it. The campus might be a vast sprawling place surrounded by perfectly tended lawns and fenced off by an ominous looking forest on three sides, but most of the buildings are clustered together, making it easy to remember the route back.

When I reach the entrance, I spot a young girl huddled by the door, arms wrapped around herself, practically holding herself together. Alarm bells go off in my head as I slow my approach, taking in her skittish appearance.

Don't get involved, I urge myself. *Just keep walking.*

She lifts tear-stained eyes to mine and a life's worth of trauma rises inside me. But I push it down. Force it back into its box.

I'm not that girl anymore.

I'll *never* be that girl again.

But I can't do it, I can't just walk past her without saying something.

"Hey, are you o—"

Her bottom lip quivers and she darts inside the building.

Okay then.

I frown, giving a little shake of my head.

When I finally force myself to go inside, there's no sign of her. My stomach growls and I decide to check out the communal kitchen.

I don't expect to walk straight into someone as I enter the room.

"The fuck?" A deep voice growls. "Watch where you're going."

I step back to look at the boy. Man would be a better word for him. He towers over me, his eyes full of fury and fire as he glares down at me.

"Who the fuck are you?"

"Someone who belongs here more than you," I spit, my hackles rising at the violence rolling off him.

He falters, eyes flashing with confusion. But then his icy mask slides back into place. "I don't know you."

"No shit." I fold my arms over my chest, arching a brow. "Stealing from the girls' dorm?" My narrowed gaze drops to the stash of snacks and sweets in his hands. "How original."

"Get the fuck out of my way."

"Not until you tell me what you're doing with all that."

I know boys like this.

Arrogant.

Entitled.

Spoiled.

"Move," he barks, literally vibrating with anger. But he doesn't scare me. Not one bit.

Why would he when I've been dealing with guys like him since I grew boobs. Even before then.

"Make me."

The words detonate between us, surprise flickering over his expression.

"You don't know who I am," he muses.

"Should I?"

A slow, wicked smile curls at his mouth, sending a ripple of heat down my spine.

Jesus, this boy is hot.

Hot... and dangerous.

"Theo Ashworth." He leans into my space, his warm minty breath fanning my face. "It would do you well to learn that name. And remember it."

"Oh my God." Laughter peals out of me. "Does that line actually work?"

"Who the fuck are you?" he asks again.

"Raine." I get all up in his face, smirking with amusement. "It would do you well to learn that name. And remember it."

"What—"

"THEO!" Someone yells, and his entire demeanour changes.

"Fuck," he mutters, grabbing my shoulder and yanking me away from the door.

"Hey," I sneer, spinning around to give him a piece of my mind.

But he's gone.

And for as much as I hate it, all I can think is who the hell was that boy?

Download your copy of the BRUTAL CALLOUS HEIR DUET to continue reading.

ABOUT THE AUTHOR

CAITLYN DARE
DELICIOUSLY DARK ROMANCE

Two angsty romance lovers writing dark heroes and the feisty girls who bring them to their knees.

SIGN UP NOW
To receive news of our releases straight to your inbox.

Want to hang out with us?
Come and join CAITLYN'S DAREDEVILS group on Facebook.

ALSO BY CAITLYN DARE

Rebels at Sterling Prep

Taunt Her

Tame Him

Taint Her

Trust Him

Torment Her

Temper Him

Gravestone Elite

Shattered Legacy

Tarnished Crown

Fractured Reign

Savage Falls Sinners MC

Savage

Sacrifice

Sacred

Sever

Red Ridge Sinners MC

Crank

Ruin

Reap

Rule

Defy

Heirs of All Hallows'

Wicked Heinous Heirs

Filthy Jealous Heir: Part One

Filthy Jealous Heir: Part Two

Cruel Devious Heir : Part One

Cruel Devious Heir : Part Two

Brutal Callous Heir : Part One

Brutal Callous Heir : Part Two

Savage Vicious Heir : Part One

Savage Vicious Heir : Part Two

Boxsets

Ace

Cole

Conner

Savage Falls Sinners MC

www.ingramcontent.com/pod-product-compliance
Ingram Content Group UK Ltd.
Pitfield, Milton Keynes, MK11 3LW, UK
UKHW041308180625
6465UKWH00011B/29